A SONG
FOR THE DYING

Stuart MacBride is the No.1 bestselling author of the DS Logan McRae series and *Birthdays for the Dead*.

His novels have won him the CWA Dagger in the Library, the Barry Award for Best Debut Novel, and Best Breakthrough Author at the ITV3 Crime Thriller awards. In 2012 Stuart was inducted into the ITV3 Crime Thriller Hall of Fame.

Stuart's other works include *Halfhead*, a near-future thriller, *Sawbones*, a novella aimed at adult emergent readers, and several short stories.

He lives in the north-east of Scotland with his wife, Fiona, and cat, Grendel.

For more information visit StuartMacBride.com

By Stuart MacBride

The Logan McRae Novels
Cold Granite
Dying Light
Broken Skin
Flesh House
Blind Eye
Dark Blood
Shatter the Bones
Close to the Bone

The Ash Henderson Novels
Birthdays for the Dead
A Song for the Dying

Other Works
Sawbones – a novella
12 Days of Winter (short stories)

Writing as Stuart B. MacBride
Halfhead

Stuart MacBride

A SONG
FOR THE DYING

HarperCollins*Publishers*

This is a work of fiction. Any references to real people, living or dead, real events, businesses, organizations and localities are intended only to give the fiction a sense of reality and authenticity. All names, characters, places and incidents are either the product of the author's imagination or are used fictitiously, and their resemblance, if any, to real-life counterparts is entirely coincidental. The only exception to this are the characters Liz Thornton, Alistair Robertson, Millie Rose Stephen, and Julia G. Nenova, who have given their express permission to be fictionalized in this volume. All behaviour, history, and character traits assigned to these individuals have been designed to serve the needs of the narrative and do not necessarily bear any resemblance to the real people.

HarperCollins*Publishers*
77–85 Fulham Palace Road,
Hammersmith, London W6 8JB

www.harpercollins.co.uk

Published by HarperCollins*Publishers* 2014
2

A catalogue record for this book
is available from the British Library

ISBN: 978-0-00-734431-4

Set in Meridien by Palimpsest Book Production Limited,
Falkirk, Stirlingshire

Printed and bound in Australia by
Griffin Press

For Lorna, Dave and James

Without Whom

As always I've received a lot of help from a lot of people while I was writing this book, so I'd like to take this opportunity to thank: Ishbel Gall, Dr Lorna Dawson, Prof. Dave Barclay, Dr James Grieve, and Prof. Sue Black, for all their forensic cleverness; Deputy Divisional Commander Mark Cooper, Detective Superintendent Martin Dunn, Detective Sergeant William Nimmo, Sergeant Bruce Crawford, Police Dog Handler Colin Hunter, and Constable Claire Pirie, without whom I would've been lost about the change to Police Scotland; Sarah Hodgson, Jane Johnson, Julia Wisdom, Louise Swannell, Oliver Malcolm, Laura Fletcher, Roger Cazalet, Kate Elton, Lucy Upton, Sylvia May, Damon Greeney, Victoria Barnsley, Emad Akhtar, Kate Stephenson, Marie Goldie, the DC Bishopbriggs Wild Brigade, and everyone at HarperCollins, for doing such a stonking job; Phil Patterson, Isabella Floris, Luke Speed, and the team at Marjacq Scripts, for keeping my cat in shoes all these years.

A number of people have helped raise a lot of money for charity by bidding to have a character named after them in this book: Liz Thornton, Alistair Robertson, and Julia G. Nenova.

And saving the best for last – as always – Fiona and Grendel.

the end is nigh

The time has come, the Raven said,
To close your eyes and hang your head,
And walk with me through barren fields,
To stand among the dead.

William Denner

Song for the Dying (1943)

1

'Now I'm no' saying he's *gay* – I'm no' saying he's ho-mo-sexual – I'm saying he's a big Jessie. No' the same thing.'

'Not this *again*...' A crescent moon makes a scar in the clouds, glowering down at them as Kevin picks his way through the frost-crisped grass, breath streaming out behind him. Nipples like little points of fire. Fingers aching where they stick out past the end of his sleeve, wrapped around the torch. The legs of his glasses cold against his temples.

Behind him, the ambulance's blue and white lights make lazy search beams, sending shadows creeping through the trees at the side of the road. The headlights glint back from a bus shelter, the Perspex blistered and blackened where someone's tried to set fire to it.

Nick clunks the ambulance door shut. 'I mean, seriously, look at him: could he be any more of a Jessie?'

'Will you shut up and help me?'

'Don't know what you're so worked up about.' Nick has a scratch at his beard, really going at it, like a dog with fleas. Tiny flakes of white fall from the face-fungus, caught in the glow of his torch like dying fireflies. 'Just going to be another sodding crank call, like all the rest of them. Tell you: ever since they found that woman with her innards all ripped up

1

in Kingsmeath, every time-wasting tosser in the city's been on the phone reporting gutted women. Listen to them, the bloody place should be knee-deep in dead tarts.'

'What if she's lying out there, in the dark, dying? Don't you want—'

'And do you know *why* Spider-Man's a big girl's blouse?'

Kevin doesn't look at him, keeps his eyes on the grass. It's thicker here, the broken-glass stems dotted with rusty spears of docken and dead thistles. Something out there smells musty, fusty, mouldering. 'What if it's real? Might be still alive.'

'Aye, you keep telling yourself that. Fiver says she doesn't even exist.' His fingertips scrabble through the beard again as he kicks through a pile of crackling leaves. 'So, Spider-Man: action is his reward, right? Total Jessie.'

Two more hours till the shift's over. Two more hours of inane drivel and bollocks...

Is something sticking out from underneath that whin bush?

The long dark seedpods clatter like a rattlesnake as Kevin pokes at the branches.

Just a plastic bag, the blue-and-red logo glittering with frost.

'See me? See if *I* save some hot bird from a burning building? I'm expecting cash, or a blowjob at the very least. When did you last see someone going down on Spider-Man? Never, that's when.'

'Nick, I swear to God...'

'Come on, if it was you or me running about in our jammies, squirting random strangers with our sticky emissions, we'd end up on the sex-offenders' register, wouldn't we?'

'Can you not shut up for, like, five seconds?' The tips of Kevin's ears burn, like someone's stubbing a cigarette out on them. Cheeks are going the same way. He sweeps the torch beam back and forth. Maybe Nick's right? This is a waste of time. They're out here, sodding about in the freezing cold, on a Thursday night in November just because some rancid wee sod thought it'd be funny to report a woman's body dumped at the side of the road.

'He's not a superhero: he's a pervert. And a Jessie. *Quod erat demonstrandum.*'

A hundred and fifty thousand people have a stroke every year, why can't Nick be one of them? Right now. Is that really too much to ask?

The hairy git stops rummaging in his beard and points. 'Aye, aye, looks like someone's been getting lucky. Found a right nest of condoms here...' He pokes the toe of his boot into it, rummages. 'French ticklers from the look of it.'

'Shut up.' Kevin chews at the skin on the side of his index finger, breath fogging up his glasses. 'What did they say?'

Nick sniffs. 'Woman, mid-twenties, possible internal bleeding, A-Rhesus negative.'

The tarmac scrunches beneath Kevin's feet as he picks his way around the bus shelter. 'How did they know?'

'That she was here? Suppose—'

'No, you moron, how did they know what her blood type was...?' Kevin stops dead. There's something behind the shelter, something person-sized.

He lurches over, feet slipping on the icy tarmac. But it's only a hunk of carpet, the faded green-and-yellow swirly pattern, spotted with darker stains. Dumped by some dirty scumbag who couldn't be arsed going to the council tip. What the hell was wrong with people these days?

It wasn't like...

There's drag-marks in the grass, leading away from the carpet.

Oh God.

'And don't get me started on Superman!'

Kevin's voice cracks. So he tries again. 'Nick...?'

'I mean, what kind of pervert goes to work wearing blue tights—'

'Nick, get the crash kit.'

3

'—bright red pants over the top? Could he be any more, "look at my crotch, for I am the Man of Steel!" And he's faster—'

'Get the crash kit.'

'—speeding bullet. What woman wants—'

'GET THE BLOODY CRASH KIT!' And Kevin's running, slithering through the grass at the side of the bus shelter. Crashing through the whip-fronds of dying nettles, following the drag-marks.

She's lying on her back, one leg curled under her, the other pale foot smeared with dirt. Her white nightdress has ridden up around her thighs, a yellow cross staining the fabric across her swollen abdomen – distorted by what's been stitched inside. Scarlet blooms through the nightdress: poppies, dark and spreading.

Her face is bone-china pale, freckles standing out like dried bloodstains, coppery hair spread out across frost-sharpened grass. A golden chain glints around her throat.

Her fingers tremble.

She's *alive*...

Six Years Later

2

The wall hit me between the shoulder blades, then did the same to the back of my head. An explosion of yellow light. A dull *thunk* deep inside my skull. A grunt broke from my throat. Then again as ex-Detective Sergeant O'Neil slammed his fist into my stomach.

Glass rippled inside me, tearing, shredding.

Another fist cracked my ringing head to the side, sending fire burning across my cheek. Not O'Neil this time, but his equally huge mate: ex-Constable Taylor. The pair of them must've spent most of their sentences in the prison gym. Certainly would explain how they managed to hit so bloody hard.

Another fist to the guts. Jerking me against the corridor wall.

I lashed out with a right, the knuckles screaming as they tore into O'Neil's nose. Flattened it. Snapped his ugly, wedge-shaped head back. Painted an arc of scarlet in the air as the big bastard staggered away.

Right. One not so much *down* as on hold. A couple of seconds would be enough…

I threw an elbow at Taylor's big round face. But he was fast. A lot faster than someone that size should have been.

My elbow cracked into the wall.

Then his fist smashed into my cheek again.

THUNK – my head battered off the wall. Again.

This time my elbow caught him right in the mouth, an electric shock charging up my funny bone where it mashed through his top lip and teeth. More scarlet in the drab corridor. It dribbled down the front of his prison-issue sweatshirt, spreading out like tiny red flowers on the grey fabric.

He backed off a pace. Spat out a couple of white lumps. Wiped a hand across his mouth, smearing the blood. The words came out all wet and lispy through the gaps where those teeth used to be. 'Oh, you are tho *dead.*'

'You really think two against one is enough?' I flexed my right fist. The joints stabbed and screamed, every movement like someone was digging burning needles through the cartilage and into the bone.

Then O'Neil bellowed. Charged. Face a streaked mess of crimson and black.

CRACK I hit the wall again, all the breath abandoning my body in one tearing groan. A fist in the face. Vision blurred.

I swung, but it went wide.

Again.

O'Neil landed another one, and a choir of vultures screeched in my head.

Blink.

Stay upright. Don't let them get you on the ground.

I wrapped my hand over his face and dug my thumb into what was left of his nose. Gouging into the warm slippery mess.

He *screamed.*

Then it was my turn as Taylor stamped his size elevens down on the bridge of my right foot. Something inside *tore.* Scar tissue and bone parted. Stitches ripped free, wrenching open the bullet hole. And all plans to stay upright disappeared in a wave of raw throat-tearing agony.

Like being shot all over again.

My right leg gave way. The granite-coloured floor rushed up to greet me.

Curl up. Make a ball of arms and legs, protect the vital organs, cover the head...

Feet and fists battered into my thighs, arms, and back. Kicking, punching, stomping.

And then, darkness.

...

'... in't de ... with...?'

'... bloody n ... se, f...'

...

'... n, he's coming roun...'

A sharp jolt to my cheek.

Blink.

Blink.

Cough... It was like someone had taken a sledgehammer to my ribs, and every jagged heave from my lungs just made it worse.

O'Neil stood over me, grinning down with his blood-smeared face, nose skewed off to the left. Voice all bunged up, like he was doing an advert for decongestant. 'Wakey-wakey, princess. Bet you thought you'd never see me again, eh?'

Taylor had a mobile phone to his ear, nodding while he explored the gaps in his teeth with his tongue. 'Yeah, I'll put you on thpeakerphone.'

He pressed something on the screen, then held the thing out towards me.

Fancy new phone. Definitely not allowed in prison.

The screen flickered, going from washed-out brightness to a close-up of someone's face, the features all blurry. Then whoever it was moved back and the whole thing slithered into focus.

Mrs Kerrigan. Her brown hair was piled up in a loose bun on top of her head, the roots showing streaks of grey. A pinched face, with bright red lips and sharp little teeth. A crucifix floating in her cleavage. She pulled on a pair of glasses and smiled. *'Ah, Mr Henderson… Or should I be calling yez,* Prisoner *Henderson now?'*

I opened my mouth, but O'Neil placed his right foot on top of mine and pressed. Shards of burning glass dug into the skin, turning the words into a high-pitched hiss between clenched teeth.

'Here's how this works. Mr Taylor and Mr O'Neil here will be payin' yez a little visit every now and then, and batterin' the livin' shite out of ye. And every time yez are coming up for review – ye know, when they're thinkin' of lettin' yer sorry arse back out on the streets? Every time that *happens they're goin' to give ye another doing and tell everyone ye're the one who started it.'*

O'Neil's grin got wider, a dribble of bloody spittle snaking out from the corner of his ruined mouth. 'Every time.'

'This is what ye get for sticking a gun in my face, ye wee gobshite. Yez're now my pet project, I'm going to screw with ye till I get bored of it, and then I'm goin' to have ye killed.' She leaned forward, out of focus again, till her red mouth filled the screen. *'But don't worry, I don't bore that easy. I plan on screwin' with ye for years.'*

Eighteen Months Later

3

'Sadly, we continue to see a deplorable level of violence perpetrated by Mr Henderson.' Dr Altringham rapped on the table with his knuckles, as if it was a coffin lid. He blew the floppy grey fringe out of his eyes. Adjusted his glasses. 'I really can't recommend release at this date. He represents a clear and continued danger to the general public.'

Twenty minutes of this and I still hadn't climbed out of my seat, limped over to where he was sitting, and battered his brains out with my cane. Which was pretty good going, given how 'dangerous' I was. Perhaps it was Officer Barbara Crawford's calming influence? She stood at my right shoulder, looming over me in my orange plastic chair, her thick knot of keys an inch from my ear.

Babs was built like a fridge freezer, tattoos sticking out from the sleeves of her shirt, wrapping around her wrists and onto the backs of her meaty hands. Barbed wire, flames. 'FAITH' on one set of knuckles, 'HOPE' on the other. Her short hair stood out from her head in tiny grey spikes, dyed blonde at the tips. Very trendy.

They'd done their usual and arranged the furniture so the big table faced a single chair in the middle of the room. Me and Babs on this side, everyone else on the other. Two psychiatrists; one threadbare social worker with big square glasses; and the Deputy Governor, dressed as if she was on her way to a funeral. All talking about me as if I wasn't even there. Could've stayed in my cell and saved myself the aggro.

We all knew where this was going anyway: *release denied.*

I leaned forward in my chair, ribs creaking from yesterday's beating. Every time, regular as clockwork. The only thing that changed was the cast and crew. O'Neil got himself shanked in the showers four months ago. Taylor got released after serving half his term. Then it was two different Neanderthal bastards ambushing me in the corridors and delivering Mrs Kerrigan's 'messages'. And two more after them.

Didn't matter what I did, I always ended up back here, bruised and battered.

Release denied.

Even managed to track down the guy who replaced O'Neil. Caught him on his own in the prison laundry. Broke both his arms, left leg, dislocated every finger he had, *and* his jaw. Mrs Kerrigan just got someone else to take his place. And I got an extra, unscheduled, arse kicking.

The Deputy Governor and the psychologists could hold all the review meetings they liked, the only way I was getting out of this place was in a body-bag.

I closed my eyes. Let it burn.

Never getting out of here.

The walking cane was cold between my fingers.

Should've killed Mrs Kerrigan when I had the chance. Wrapped my hands around her throat and throttled the life right out of her. Eyes popping from the sockets, tongue swollen and black, hands scrabbling against mine while I squeezed and squeezed. Chest heaving on air that wasn't there...

But no. Couldn't do that, could I? Had to play the good guy. The bloody idiot.

And what did *that* get me? Stuck in here till she got bored and had someone slit my throat. Or stab me in the kidneys

14

with a home-made chib, sharpened on a cell wall and smeared with shit for a nice infected wound. Assuming I survived the blood loss.

No more stupid review meetings, just a trip to the infirmary, then on to the mortuary.

At least I wouldn't have to sit here, listening to Altringham's lies. Telling everyone how violent and dangerous I was...

I ran my fingers up the cane till they got to the handle. Tightened my grip. Pulled my shoulders back.

Might as well live down to his expectations and remodel his smug lying face a bit. Could do some serious damage before they dragged me off. Had nothing to lose anyway. And at least I'd get the satisfaction of—

Babs's hand landed on my shoulder, her voice barely loud enough to count as a whisper. 'Don't even think about it.'

Fair enough.

I let my shoulders slump again.

Dr Alice McDonald – psychiatrist number two – held up her hand. 'Now hold on a minute: the murder charge was *dismissed*.' Her curly brown hair made a loose ponytail at the back of her head, a few stray wisps breaking free to glow in the overhead lights. Pale-lilac shirt cuffs poked out of the sleeves of her pinstripe suit. 'Mr Henderson didn't kill his brother, the evidence against him was fabricated. It's a matter of record. The appeal judge—'

'I'm not talking about his brother's murder. I'm talking about this.' Altringham plucked a sheet of paper from the table in front of him and waved it. 'In the last eighteen months, he's assaulted and seriously injured *seventeen* other inmates. Every time he gets anywhere near being released, he attacks someone.'

'We've been over this, it's—'

'Yesterday, he broke a man's nose, and left another with a fractured cheek!' Altringham knocked on the coffin again. 'Does that sound like the actions of someone we should be unleashing on an unsuspecting public?'

Yeah, I got in a couple of good punches, till they forced me into a corner. Grinning and laughing. Letting me swing at them, so it'd look better when they made their formal complaints. But what was I supposed to do, stand there and take it?

Even after all this time…

Alice shook her head. 'It's hardly Mr Henderson's fault that he keeps being attacked. If the prison did a better job of managing inmate interactions, maybe he wouldn't have to defend himself the whole time.'

The Deputy Governor narrowed her eyes. 'I resent *any* implication that this institution isn't doing its duty where custodial safety is concerned.'

Altringham blew out a breath. 'No one's safe where Mr Henderson's concerned. He's pathologically incapable of—'

'That's not the case at all, there's a clear pattern to the attacks *against* Mr Henderson that—'

'Yes, and that pattern is his self-destructive personality! This is nothing more profound than a simple need to punish himself due to survivor's guilt. It's not a conspiracy, it's simple psychology and if you were able to see past your personal bias on this case you'd know that.'

Alice poked Altringham in the shoulder. 'I *beg* your pardon! Are you suggesting that I'm incapable of—'

The Deputy Governor slammed her folder down on the tabletop. 'All right, that's enough!' She glared at Alice, then turned and did the same to Altringham. 'We're here to discuss Mr Henderson's release, or continued incarceration, like professionals. *Not* bicker and quarrel like small children. So, moving on.' The Deputy Governor held out a hand. 'Dr McDonald, you have your report?'

Alice pulled the top sheet from the leather folio in front of her and passed it over.

The Deputy Governor frowned at it for a bit, then turned it over and did the same with the back. Then placed it on the table. 'And Dr Altringham?'

He slid his along to her and she frowned at that for a while too.

Officer Babs leaned in, her voice still an almost-whisper. 'How's the arthritis?'

I flexed my right hand, the knuckles all swollen and bruised from breaking ex-DI Graham Lumley's cheek. 'Worth it.'

'I keep telling you: lead with your elbows, or only punch the soft bits.'

'Yeah, well...'

The Deputy Governor put Altringham's report down on top of Alice's, then sat up straight. 'Mr Henderson, after careful consideration—'

'Don't bother.' I slouched further down in my plastic seat. 'We all know where this is going, so why don't we just cut to the bit where you send me back to my cell?'

'After careful consideration, Mr Henderson, and having reviewed all the evidence and expert analysis, it is my belief that your continuing use of violence necessitates your retention in this facility until a full investigation can be carried out into the events of yesterday.'

So, same as usual then.

Stuck in here until Mrs Kerrigan finally got bored and had me killed.

Now
(Six Months Later)
Sunday

4

'... *more from the scene as we get it. Edinburgh now, and the family of missing six-year-old Stacey Gourdon have issued an appeal, asking her abductors to return her remains...*' The TV in the rec room was mounted in its own tiny cage, high up on the wall, as if the prison thought it was as likely to do a runner as all the other inmates.

Ex-Detective Superintendent Len Murray picked up a plastic chair and stuck it down next to mine. Settled into it, a smile distorting his Robin-Hood-style grey goatee. The strip-lights glinted off his bald head and little round glasses. A big man with a big rumbling voice. 'You're going to have to kill her. You know that, don't you?'

In her private cell, the woman on the television gave a grim nod. '*Stacey Gourdon's bloodstained dress and trainers were found by officers searching woodland in Corstorphine...*'

I stared at him. 'Don't you have something better to do?'

'Ash, the bog-hopping bitch is going to keep you in here till you top yourself, or she sends someone in to do it for her. Time to be proactive.'

'I mean, you've got what, four more years to serve? You should take up a hobby. Woodwork. Or learning Spanish.'

21

The picture changed to a run-down two-up two-down in a manky council estate, a scrum of reporters jostling for position as the front doors opened and a hollow woman stared out with dead eyes and trembling fingers. A fat bloke just visible over her shoulder: bloodshot and sniffing, biting his bottom lip.

The woman cleared her throat. Looked down at her shaking hands. *'We...'* Another go. *'We just want her back. We want to bury her. We want the chance to say goodbye...'*

Len leaned back in his seat and slapped a hand down on my shoulder. Squeezed. 'I know a couple of lads who'll do the job for two grand.'

I raised an eyebrow. 'They'll go up against Andy Inglis for a measly two thousand pounds? Are they mad?'

'They're not local. And they need to get out of the country anyway. Besides: who'd know?'

'... please, she's our little girl ... Stacey was everything to her dad and me...'

'I'd know.'

Palm it off to some pair of idiots? No chance. When Mrs Kerrigan died, it would be with my hands around her throat. Squeezing...

Assuming I ever got out of here.

I turned back to the screen, where Stacey's mother was collapsing, every sob caught in the strobe of camera flashes.

Back to the studio. *'... with any information can call the number at the bottom of the screen.'* The newsreader shuffled her papers. *'Oldcastle Police have confirmed that the woman's body, discovered on waste ground behind the city's Blackwall Hill area in the early hours of yesterday morning, belonged to Claire Young, a paediatric nurse at Castle Hill Infirmary...'*

Len shook his head. 'The trouble with you is you think revenge has to be up-close to be personal. You never did learn to delegate properly.'

'I'm not delegating that bitch's—'

'What does it matter who does it, as long as she's dead?' He shook his head. Sighed. 'You can't kill her yourself if you're still stuck in here. And you can't get out of here till she's dead. Catch twenty-two. And for two grand, you can make it all go away.' Len cocked an imaginary pump-action shotgun and shot the newsreader in the face. 'Think about it.'

'Yeah, because I've got two thousand pounds burning a hole in my pocket.'

'... *appeal to the media's conscience to respect her family's wish for privacy...*'

Good luck with *that*.

'Could always borrow it?'

'That's how I got into this mess in the first place.'

The door to the rec room thumped open and a hard voice cut across the TV. 'Henderson!'

I turned, and there was Officer Babs. She jerked a thumb. 'You got a visitor.'

A man in a brown leather jacket sauntered into the room, hands in his pockets. He was at least a head shorter than Babs, hairy, with thick sideburns.

He wandered over till he was standing between me and the television.

'*Here's the sport now, with Bobby Thompson...*'

Hairy Boy smiled. 'Well, well, well, so you're the ex-DC Henderson I've heard so much about?' His accent was obviously Scottish, but indistinct, as if he didn't really come from anywhere. 'So ... tell me about Graham Lumley and Jamie Smith.'

'No comment.'

Officer Babs appeared at his shoulder, dwarfing him. 'Detective Superintendent Jacobson is having a squint into what happened outside the laundry a fortnight ago. So don't be a dick: cooperate.'

Yeah, right. 'A full Detective Superintendent? Investigating a fight in a prison corridor? Are you not a bit overqualified?'

23

Jacobson tilted his head to one side, staring at me. Eyeing me up and down like he was about to ask me to dance. 'Official report says you attacked the pair of them. Shouting and swearing and crying, like a... Hold on, let me get this right.' He pulled out a small black police-issue notebook. Flipped it open. '"Like a big-Jessie escaped mental patient." That Graham Lumley's got a way with words, doesn't he?'

Len crossed his arms across his big barrel chest. 'Lumley and Smith are lying wankers.'

Jacobson turned a bright, shining smile in Len's direction. 'Lennox Murray, isn't it? Ex head of Oldcastle CID. Eighteen years for the abduction, torture, and murder of one Philip Skinner. Thanks for playing along, but I'd like hear what Mr Henderson has to say. OK? Great.'

I copied Len, arms folded, legs crossed. 'They're lying wankers.'

Jacobson dragged a chair over, then sank into it. Scuffed it forwards a couple of feet till his knees were nearly touching mine. A chemical waft of Old Spice drifted out from him. 'Ash... I can call you Ash, can't I? Ash, the head psychologist here tells me you've got a self-destructive personality. That you sabotage yourself by picking a fight every time you come up for review.'

Give him nothing back but silence.

Jacobson shrugged. 'Of course Dr Altringham strikes me as a bit of a tit, but there you go.' He raised a finger, then pointed it over his shoulder in the general direction of the television. 'Did you see the story about the nurse they found dead behind Blackwall Hill?'

'What about her?'

'Dead nurse. Dumped in the middle of nowhere. Ring any bells?'

I frowned at him. 'You have any idea how many nurses go missing in Oldcastle every year? Poor sods should get danger pay.'

'Smith and Lumley really did a number on you, didn't they?

24

Yeah, there's the bruised cheek and the squint nose, but I'm guessing all the real bruising's confined to the thighs and torso, right? Where it won't show?' Another shrug. 'Unless you strip off, of course.'

'I'm flattered, but you're not my type.'

'Claire Young: twenty-four, brunette, five seven and a half, about eleven stone three. Pretty, in a big-boned kind of way.' He held his hands out, either side of his lap. 'You know, childbearing hips?'

I looked over at Babs. 'Ever fancy a career as a healthcare professional? Bet no one would dare jump you.'

She smiled back at me. 'Might have to – cutbacks. They're talking about voluntary redundancies.'

Jacobson stood. 'I think I'd like to see Mr Henderson's cell now.'

It wasn't exactly a huge room – the set of bunk beds just fit and no more. You could reach out and touch the institution-grey walls on either side with a bit of a stretch. Small desk at the far end, a chair, a sink, and a sectioned off bit for the toilet. Officially large enough for two fully grown men to share for four years to life.

Or one fully grown man who *really* didn't like having a cellmate. Funny how they all turned out to be so accident prone. Falling down and breaking things. Arms, legs, noses, testicles…

Officer Babs filled the doorway, arms folded, legs apart, face like a slab of granite as Jacobson stepped into the middle of the cell, hands out as if he was about to bless it.

'Home sweet home.' Then he turned and squeezed up close to the desk, leaning forward, peering at the single photograph Blu-Tacked to the wall above it: Rebecca and Katie on Aberdeen beach, grinning for the camera, the North Sea glowering in the background behind them. School jumpers on over orange swimsuits. Buckets and spades. Katie four, Rebecca nine.

25

Eleven years and two lifetimes ago.

His head dipped an inch. 'I was sorry to hear about your daughters.'

Yeah, everyone always is.

'Can't have been easy – having to grieve for her while you're stuck in here. Fitted up for your brother's shooting. Getting the crap pounded out of you on a regular basis...'

'There a point to this?'

He reached into his leather jacket and pulled out a copy of the *Castle News and Post*. Dumped it on the bottom bunk. 'From last week.'

A photo filled most of the front page: a close-up of a chunky woman's face, framed with ginger curls, a thick band of freckles across her nose and cheeks like Scottish war paint. A couple of photographers were reflected in her sunglasses, their flashes going. She had one hand up, as if she was trying to shield her face from the cameras, but hadn't quite made it in time.

The headline stretched above the picture in big block capitals: '"CHRISTMAS MIRACLE!" BABY JOY ON THE WAY FOR INSIDE MAN VICTIM'.

Dear God, now *there* was a blast from the past.

I hooked my cane onto the bunk bed's frame and sat on the mattress. Picked up the paper.

EXCLUSIVE

The Inside Man's fifth victim, Laura Strachan (37), has some wonderful news. Eight years after she became the first woman ever to survive being attacked by the twisted sicko who killed four women and mutilated three more, plucky Laura is expecting her first baby.

Doctors thought there was no chance she'd be able to conceive after the injuries she received when the Inside Man cut her open and stitched a toy doll inside her stomach. A source at Castle Hill Infirmary said, 'It is a miracle. There is no way she should have been able to carry a child to term. I am so pleased for her.'

Even better, it looks like the bundle of joy will be an early Christmas present for Laura and her husband Christopher Irvine (32).

Turn to Page 4 for full story ➜

I turned to page four. 'Thought she was all broken inside.'

'You were on the original investigation.'

I skimmed the rest of the article. It was light on fact, padded out with lots of quotes from Laura Strachan's friends and a competition to guess what the baby's name would be. Nothing from Laura or the father-to-be. 'They didn't bother talking to the family?'

Jacobson settled back against the desk. 'Her husband lamped the photographer, then threatened to shove the camera up the reporter's backside.'

I folded the paper and placed it beside me. 'Good for him.'

'It took two years of corrective surgery and a monster lump of fertility treatment, but she's seven and a bit months gone. Should be due last week of December. Some fine upstanding member of the press got hold of her medical records.'

'Other than being a heart-warming story of triumph over adversity, I don't see what this has to do with me.'

'You let him go: the Inside Man.'

My back stiffened, hands curled into fists, knuckles aching. Spat the words out between gritted teeth. 'Say that again.'

Officer Babs shook her head, voice low and warning. 'Easy now...'

'You were the last one to see him. You chased him, and you lost him.'

'I didn't exactly have any choice.'

27

The corners of Jacobson's mouth twitched up. 'It still eats you, doesn't it?'

Laura Strachan grimaced at me from the front page of the paper.

I looked away. 'No more than anyone else we couldn't catch.'

'He killed four women. Then Laura Strachan survives. Then Marie Jordan. And if you'd caught him when you had the chance... Well, you're lucky he only mutilated one more woman before disappearing.'

Yeah, Lucky was my middle name.

Jacobson dug his hands into his armpits, rocked on his heels. 'Ever wonder what the bastard's been up to? Eight years and no one's heard a peep. Where's he been?'

'Abroad, prison, or dead.' I uncurled my fists, held them loose in my lap. The joints burned. 'Look, are we finished? Only I've got things to do.'

'Oh, you have no idea.' Jacobson turned to Officer Babs. 'I'll take him. Get him tagged and his stuff packed up. We've got a car waiting outside.'

'What?'

'We've not made it official yet, but the paediatric nurse found dead yesterday had a My First Baby doll stitched into her innards. He's back.'

My fists curled again.

5

A cold wind grabbed a handful of empty crisp packets and sent them dancing across the darkened car park, pickled onion and prawn cocktail performing an eightsome reel six inches above the tarmac, before disappearing into the night.

Jacobson led the way between rows of vehicles to a big black Range Rover with tinted windows. He opened the back door and gave a little bow. 'Your carriage awaits.'

The radio was playing, a BBC-style received-pronunciation voice drifting out into the cold night air. '... *siege enters its fourth day at Iglesia de la Azohia in La Azohia, Spain. Cartagena Police confirm that one hostage has been killed...*'

I climbed inside and dumped the black-plastic bag containing pretty much everything I owned in the footwell. Paused for a quick scratch at the ankle monitor weighing down my left leg.

'... *by three armed men as worshipers held a candlelit vigil...*'

A uniformed PC sat behind the wheel. His eyes flicked up to the rear-view mirror, checking me out as Jacobson scrambled into the passenger seat.

'... *bringing the death toll to six—*'

Jacobson clicked the radio off. 'Ash, this is Constable Cooper. He's one of your lot. Hamish, say hello to Mr Henderson.'

The PC turned in his seat. Thin with a long hooked nose, hair cut so short it was more like designer stubble. He nodded. 'Sir.'

Been a while since anyone had called me that. Even a sour-faced git like Cooper.

Jacobson pulled on his seatbelt. 'Right, Ash, I'll tell you what I told Hamish when they seconded him to us. I don't care how much history you've got with your Oldcastle Police buddies, you report to *me*, no one else. I get so much as a whiff of you blabbing to any of them, and you're going right back where I found you. This is not a jolly, this is not an opportunity for sabotage or personal glory, this is a team effort and by Christ you will take it seriously.' A smile. 'Welcome to Operation Tigerbalm.' He reached across the gap between the two front seats and thumped Cooper on the shoulder. 'Drive. And if I'm not there for eight, you're screwed.'

The constable eased the Range Rover out of the prison car park and out onto the street. I swivelled around in my seat to watch the place disappear through the tinted rear windscreen. Out. Free. No more review meetings. No more random beatings.

No more bars.

So much for Len's catch twenty-two.

My hands around her throat, squeezing...

I caught the grin: stopped it before it could spread. Settled back into my seat. 'So, what, they're reinstating me?'

Jacobson gave a half-laugh half-snort. 'With your record? No chance – there isn't a police division in Scotland that'd touch you with a stick. You're out because you're useful to me. Do well, help me catch the Inside Man, and I'll make your release permanent. But any screwing up, any dicking about, any sign that you're not giving one hundred and *ten* percent, and I will drop you like a radioactive jobbie.'

Lovely.

He popped open the glove compartment and pulled out a manila folder. Passed it back between the seats as Cooper took us around the roundabout onto a quiet country road with streetlights at the end of it, glittering in the darkness.

'Conditions of release?'

'Case file on Claire Young. Read it. I want you up to speed by the time we hit Oldcastle.'

Might as well. If playing along kept me out of prison for long enough to get my hands on Mrs Kerrigan...

I opened the folder. Inside was a list of statements and some crime-scene photos. 'Where's the post-mortem report? Identification Bureau stuff – physical evidence, fingerprints, DNA, that kind of thing?'

'Ah. That's a bit...' He made a little circling gesture with his hand. 'Complicated. For reasons of potential investigative bias, we're not taking access to those.'

'We're not? Why? Are we thick?'

'Just read the file.' He faced forwards again, shoogled his shoulders from side to side against the seat, then reclined it a couple of notches. 'And do it quietly. I've got a press conference when we get back: one of your idiot mates in Oldcastle blabbed to the *Daily Record*. I need my beauty sleep.'

The A90 rumbled beneath the Range Rover's tyres, while Jacobson rumbled in the passenger seat, mouth hanging open, a little dribble of drool shining in the dashboard lights. PC Cooper kept his eyes front, hands at ten to two on the steering wheel. Mirror, signal, manoeuvre.

Behind us, the bright lights of Dundee faded away into the distance.

The crime-scene photos were all pin-sharp, caught in the flashlight glare: Claire Young lying on her back on a crumpled sheet, the sides folded in around her legs and chest. One arm was curled above her head as if she was just sleeping – but her eyes were open, staring blankly into the camera. Some swelling around the left side of her mouth. A bruise the size of a saucer spread out across her right cheek.

31

The left side of the sheet was crumpled back, exposing the pale nightdress beneath. Two lines of stains marred the fabric, like a lowercase letter 't'. A crucifix without the Jesus. Black, fringed with scarlet and yellow. The nightdress bumped beneath the stain, swollen and distorted by what was stitched inside. A close-up of her palm had what looked like bite marks in the middle of it, an arc of dark purple that curved from the middle finger to the base of the thumb. No blood.

I went back to the statement again.

A woman parks her car at the edge of Hunter's Thicket, lets her Labrador out of the boot, and goes for a walk. She's an insomniac, so it's not that unusual for her to be out walking Franklin at three in the morning. That's why she got the dog. Didn't want some weirdo attacking her. Only Franklin runs off barking into the bushes and won't come back. She wades in after him and finds him tugging at Claire Young's outstretched palm.

She panics for a bit, then calls 999.

Claire Young's mother isn't much more help. Claire was a wonderful girl, everyone loved her, she was their world, lit up every room... Pretty much the same thing every bereaved parent said when their child turned up dead. No one ever complained about what a pain in the arse they were, or how they never did a bloody thing they were told. How they were sleeping with some bastard called Noah even though they weren't even thirteen yet. How you never really knew them at all...

I blinked. Let out a long shuddering breath.

Put the statements down.

Then slid the whole lot back into the folder.

It looked like him. The cruciform scar, the doll stuffed inside, the body dump...

'Cooper, how come there's nothing in here about the abduction site?'

In the rear-view mirror, the constable's eyes widened. 'Shhhhh!'

'Oh, don't be such a big Jessie. Why's there nothing in here about where he grabbed her from?'

Cooper's voice hissed through, as if he was deflating. 'I'm not waking the super up. Now sit still and shut up before you get us both into trouble.'

Oh for God's sake. 'Grow a pair.'

'You think I don't know who you are? Just because you chucked your career down the toilet, doesn't mean—'

'Fine.' I picked up my walking stick, pressed the rubber tip against Jacobson's shoulder and jabbed it a couple of times. 'Wakey, wakey.'

'Gnnnfff...?'

Another poke or two. 'Why's there nothing about the abduction site?'

Cooper found his voice again, only a whole octave higher than normal. 'I tried to stop him, sir, I did, I told him not to disturb you.'

'Nnngh...' Jacobson rubbed his face with his hands. 'Time is it?'

I poked him with the rubber end again and repeated the question.

He peered back between the seats at me, face all puffy and pink. 'They haven't found it yet, that's why, now can I—'

'One more question: who's following us?'

His mouth hung open for a moment. Then he narrowed his bloodshot eyes and tilted his head to the side. 'Following us?'

'Three cars back. BMW – black, four-by-four. Been with us since Perth.'

He looked at Cooper. 'Really?'

'I... Er...'

'Take the next right. That one: Happas.'

Mirror. Signal. Manoeuvre. Cooper pulled the Range Rover into the turning lane and we rolled to a halt. Waited for a gap in the Dundee-bound traffic. Then pulled smoothly across the dual carriageway and onto the country road. Trees hulked on either side of the potholed tarmac, jagged silhouettes in the darkness.

Jacobson peered back towards the rear windscreen. Then smiled. 'That's prison for you. Paranoia is...' The smile faded. He faced front again. 'Keep going.'

Through a patch of forest, the pines sharp and silent, then out into bare fields, cast grey and black in the light of a clouded moon. Stars twinkled in the gaps. Farm windows glowed like cats eyes off to either side.

Cooper cleared his throat. 'They're still there.'

I passed the folder back to Jacobson. 'Of course they're still there. Where else are they going to go? We've not had a turn-off yet.'

A thin band of trees loomed like a wall in front of the car, then past into more fields. We drove through farmland bordered by another line of pines, then Cooper took a left. The headlights behind us did the same. Then a hard right.

Through a tiny village, to the junction. Left at the primary school. And we were heading back towards the A90. Soon as we were through the limit end, Cooper put his foot down, the Range Rover's engine bellowed, smearing the fields past the windows.

The car behind us did the same. Keeping pace as the needle crept up to eighty.

I clipped in my seatbelt. No offence to Cooper, but he looked about twelve years old. 'Either whoever's tailing us is *really* crap at it, or they don't care if we see them or not.'

'Hmm...' Jacobson shoogled his shoulders in the seat again. Settling in. 'In that case, it's either those dicks from the Specialist Crime Division, or your halfwit Oldcastle mates. Keeping an eye on the competition.'

I checked back over my shoulder as we roared through the underpass, then left. The tyres screeched, the back end kicking out for a moment, then we surged up the slip road and onto the dual carriageway north again.

One. Two. Three. Four. Five. Six...

The other vehicle's headlights appeared behind us again, falling into place three cars back.

Specialist Crime Whatsits, Oldcastle CID, or something much, much worse.

Cooper pulled the Range Rover up to the kerb, opposite a boarded-up pub on the eastern fringes of Cowskillin – where it merged into Castle Hill.

No sign of the black BMW.

'Right,' Jacobson turned in his seat and pointed a hairy finger at me, 'you go in there and you wait till I get back from this sodding press briefing. Remember, you're on an investigative team now, not sharing a shower with some hairy-arsed rapist from Dunkeld. Try not to hit anyone.'

I clunked open the rear door and eased out onto the pavement. Bloody right foot ached, like the tip of a red-hot knife was being slowly driven through the bone. That's what I got for sitting in the one position in a warm car for nearly two hours. The walking stick had to take a bit more weight than normal. 'What makes you think I won't just do a runner?'

He buzzed down his window and winked at me. 'Honesty, integrity, and the fact that there's a GPS locator built into your ankle tag.' He popped open the glove compartment again and came out with a little plastic box fitted with an antenna. Pressed a button on the matt black surface. It bleeped. 'There you go: all paired up. Now, if you try to tamper with the thing, or it registers a gap of more than one hundred yards between it and the one your sponsor's wearing, all hell breaks loose.'

'Sponsor?'

He chucked the remote into the glove compartment. 'Go inside and all will be revealed.'

I closed the car door, limped away a couple of paces. Cooper indicated, pulled out from the kerb and drove off into the night. Leaving me all alone with my bin-bag. And my ankle monitor.

One hundred yards.

So what was to stop me going inside, battering my 'sponsor' unconscious, hotwiring a car, chucking him in the boot, and heading off to pay Mrs Kerrigan the kind of late-night visit that would've given Jeffrey Dahmer nightmares? They could send me back to prison for as long as they liked after that. Who'd care?

Not like I'd have anything left out here…

I creaked down and picked up the bin-bag, hoisted it over my shoulder.

The Postman's Head nestled between a closed-down carpet place and a vacant bookshop with 'For Sale Or Let' signs in the window. Behind it, the granite blade of Castle Hill reared up into the dark-orange sky – winding Victorian streets lit by period lanterns, the remains of the castle at the top bathed in harsh white spotlights. From down here the ruins looked like a bottom jaw, ripped from its skull.

An old-fashioned wooden sign hung outside the pub – a severed head wearing a Postman-Pat-style hat. Sheets of plywood covered all of the windows. The paintwork was peeling off the door.

It sat opposite an abandoned building site, the chipboard barrier smeared with graffiti and warning notices. A sign with a faded artist's impression of a block of flats: 'Leafybrook Sheltered Accommodation Opening 2008!' The padlock and chain dripped rust smears down the painted wooden gates. Probably hadn't been opened for years.

A spot of water landed on the back of my hand. Then another one. Not big drops, just tiny flecks. A prelude to drizzle. Can't remember the last time I actually felt the rain on my face… I stared up into the sky. Clouds heavy and dark, reflecting the streetlights' sodium glow, a faint mist of rain growing heavier with every passing second.

The wind got up too, whipping down the street, rattling the corrugated metal fence running down one side of the road, fluttering the 'CONDEMNED ~ WARNING KEEP OUT!' notices stuck to it. Creaking the postman's severed head sign back and forth.

Sod this.

I hobbled across the road, grunting with every step, and tried the pub's door. It opened onto a small airlock. Light came through a pair of frosted glass panels in the inner doors. I pushed through.

God knew when I was last in the Postman's Head. Probably when we had to kick our way in to arrest Stanley-Knife Spencer. Took fifteen of us, six of whom spent the rest of the night in Accident and Emergency, getting their faces stitched back together.

Place was a hovel then and it was even worse now. Two walls were stripped to the bare brick, batons of wood bristling with rusty nail-heads – some of them still clutching little chunks of plasterboard. The scarred bar stretched the length of the room, dotted with stacks of paper, the pump handles sticking up at random angles. A small pile of tools – screwdrivers, spanners, a hammer – lay next to a delicate china mug with the Rangers logo on it.

Someone had heaped up most of the old wooden chairs and tables in the corner by a dead fruit machine, leaving a handful of them behind – arranged in a semicircle around a pair of easels. One held a whiteboard, the other a flipchart, both of which were covered in bullet-points and arrows.

Head-and-shoulder shots of all seven original victims were pinned up by the toilets. Above six of them was a grainy photocopy of a handwritten letter. No white on the sheets, just grey and gritty black. They'd been copied so often that the handwriting was fuzzy, the letters bleeding into each other. A shiny flatscreen TV was mounted above the cigarette machine, little drifts of plaster dust on the floor below.

No sign of anyone.

I dumped my bin-bag on the nearest table. 'SHOP!'

A voice rolled up from somewhere behind the bar, thick and plummy. 'Ah, perfect timing. Be a dear and pass me the adjustable spanner, would you?'

A dear?

I stepped up to the bar and picked the spanner from the pile of tools. Hefted it in my right hand, smacking it against the palm of my left. Good as anything for giving someone a concussion. Have to get to him first though.

I put my good foot on the metal rail and levered myself up. Peered over the edge of the bar into the space behind.

A long man lay on his back on the floor, crisp white shirt rolled up to his elbows, pink tie tucked into the gap between two buttons. Dust smudged the black pinstripe trousers, took some of the shine off the leather brogues. He raised a hairy gunmetal eyebrow at me – it went with the short-back-and-sides and military moustache. 'You must be the ex-Detective Inspector we've heard so much about.' He sat up and brushed his hands together, then held one of them out. 'I believe you're the chap who let the Inside Man get away?'

Cheeky bastard. I didn't shake it, stuck my chin out instead, pulled my shoulders back. 'I've not crippled anyone for days, you volunteering?'

'Interesting…' A smile. 'They never said you were touchy. Tell me, were you always like this, or did losing your daughter to the Birthday Boy do it? Did you get worse every time another card plopped through the letterbox? Seeing him torture her to death, one photo at a time? Is that it?'

I tightened my grip on the spanner. Forced the words out through a clenched jaw, tendons tight in my neck. 'You my sponsor?'

Please say yes. It was going to be a pleasure caving his head in.

6

'Your sponsor?' He laughed, letting it fade into a chuckle. 'Oh, dear me, no. Tell me, ex-Detective Inspector, do you know anything about beer pumps?'

'So who is?'

'You see, I've never really had much to do with them before – more of a gin-and-tonic man myself – but I like to think I can turn my hand to anything. So, did you let him go on purpose, or was it just a bit of incompetence?'

Right, that was it.

And then a voice behind me: 'Ash?'

Alice. She'd ditched the suit for a grey-and-black stripy top and black skinny jeans, a pair of bright red Converse trainers sticking out of the ends. A leather satchel, worn courier style, at her hip. Her curly brown hair, freed from its ponytail, bounced as she charged across the room and jumped at me. Wrapped her arms around my neck. Buried her face against my cheek. And squeezed. 'Oh, God, I've *missed* you!' Tears damp against my skin.

Her hair smelled of mandarins. Just like Katie's used to...

Something clicked deep beneath my ribs. I closed my eyes and hugged her back. And whatever clicked, spread out across my chest, making it swell.

The git in the shirt and tie tutted. 'You know, if you're going to fornicate I'd really rather you didn't do it here. Nip upstairs and I'll get the video camera.'

Alice pulled her head back, grinned at me. 'Ignore him, he's only trying to get a reaction. Best bet is to let him get on with it till he bores himself.' She planted a huge kiss on my cheek. 'You look thinner. Do you want something to eat, I mean I could get something, like a takeaway, or we could go to a restaurant, oh no we can't, Bear wants us to wait here till he gets back from the press conference, I'm so glad you're out!' All done in a single breath.

She gave me one last squeeze, then let go. Pointed at the guy behind the bar. 'Ash, this is Professor Bernard Huntly, he's our physical evidence man.'

Huntly stiffened. 'Physical evidence *guru*, I think you'll find.'

Her hand was warm against my cheek. 'Are you OK?'

I spared Huntly a glare. 'Getting there.'

He leaned on the bar. 'Mr Henderson and I were just enjoying a robust philosophical exchange about his daughters and the Birthday Boy.'

Alice's eyes went wide. Looked from Huntly to the spanner clenched in my fist, and back again. 'Oh... No. That's really *not* a good idea. Trust me, there's—'

'You never answered my question, Mr Henderson.' The creases at the corners of his eyes deepened. 'Why *did* you let the Inside Man get away?'

Alice prised the spanner from my hand and placed it on the bar. 'Professor Huntly thinks being rude to people makes them reveal their true selves, I mean it's nonsense of course, but he refuses to accept that reactions under stress aren't indicative of our inner cognitive—'

'Blah, blah, blah.' Huntly disappeared back down behind the pumps again. 'What's your opinion of psychology, Mr Henderson? Airy fairy nonsense, or load of old bunkum?'

Bunkum?

Alice climbed onto a creaky barstool. Then pulled up the left leg of her jeans a couple of inches. A thick band of grey disappeared into a blocky plastic rectangle, about the same size as a pack of playing cards. My sponsor. 'You'll be staying with me, obviously, I mean it wouldn't really work if you had to live on the other side of the city, what with the hundred-yards thing. I've got us a flat and it's not great, but it's OK and I'm sure we'll be able to make it cosy…'

That complicated things a bit. No way I was going to crack her skull with a spanner. Why couldn't it have been Huntly?

The breath hissed out of me, and my chin dropped an inch.

Probably for the best. Keep a low profile. Be a team player. At least until Mrs Kerrigan was sprawled in a lake of her own blood.

Alice patted the seat next to her. 'Did Bear bring you up to speed on the details?'

'Who the hell is "Bear"?'

A frown. 'Detective Superintendent Jacobson. I thought you knew.'

Bear? Seriously?

Lunatics and idiots.

I sat. 'He showed me the deposition scene photos and a couple of statements. Said we weren't bothering with the post-mortem and forensic results.'

A clunk from behind the bar. 'There we go, that should do it.' Huntly stood, then placed a bucket underneath the middle pump. 'Fingers crossed.' He hauled on the handle and air hissed from the nozzle. 'The press conference should be starting about now: the remote's on the table if you want to do the honours?'

I picked the thing up from the table, pointed it at the TV, and thumbed the power.

41

The screen flickered, glowed blue for a second, then filled with a grim-faced woman in a tight blue suit. '... *just as the school opened, leaving six dead and thirteen injured. Police marksmen fired on the gunman who is believed to be in a critical condition at Parkland Memorial Hospital ...*'

Huntly gave another haul on the pump and water sprayed into the bucket. 'Success. Now all we need to do is clean out the pipes and get a barrel hooked up.'

'... *candlelit vigil on Wednesday. Glasgow now, and the hunt is on for three men who abducted and raped paralympian Colin ...*'

Alice swivelled her seat from side to side. 'I still don't understand why they didn't take you with them?'

He stiffened for a moment. Then untucked his tie. 'Mr Henderson, there's a very good reason why we're not using the operation's forensic and post-mortem results: investigative bias. It's our job to remain objective, independent, and unsullied by operational preconceptions. I would've thought that was obvious.'

I smiled at him. 'Let me guess, you're not allowed in front of the press, in case you come off as a pompous, arrogant, condescending arsebag?'

'... *are appealing for witnesses.*'

'There are three Major Investigation Teams attacking the Inside Man problem. One from Oldcastle Division, one from the Specialist Crime Division. And we,' he swept a hand across the bar, indicating the mothballed pub, 'are the Lateral Investigative and Review Unit.'

'... *in Oldcastle today. Ross Amey is there for us now. Ross?*'

A big man with long hair and a microphone appeared on the TV, the sign outside Oldcastle Force Headquarters just out of focus behind him in the dark. '*Thank you, Jennifer. They call him "the Inside Man"...*'

'Seriously? Three separate investigations?'

'Au contraire, *Mr* Henderson. Things have changed since you went inside to pleasure Her Majesty – there is no

Oldcastle Police Force, there is only Police Scotland. Technically all the MITs are supposed to work together, but in real life Operation Tigerbalm is one big bun-fight between Oldcastle and the Specialist Crime Division to see who has the largest penis. Look on it as the joy of being all one big happy family now.'

'... *discovery of a woman's body last night by ambulance services.*'

'And you lot?'

'No, not "you lot", Mr Henderson, "us", "we". You're part of the team now.'

'Whether I like it or not.'

A lopsided shrug. Then Huntly pointed at the TV. 'Behold: the lies begin.'

The screen filled with a long desk. An array of officers – some in their dress uniforms, the others in suits – sat ramrod-stiff behind it. The only one with all their own hair was a woman, blonde curls raked back from her forehead, what looked like a permanent frown tattooed on her face. A caption flickered beneath her chin: 'DETECTIVE SUPERINTENDENT ELIZABETH NESS, OLDCASTLE CID'.

She cleared her throat. '*First I have to say that our thoughts and prayers are with Claire Young's family at this harrowing time. They've asked me to read you the following statement. "Claire was a sparkling person whose loss will haunt us forever..."*'

Alice wrapped her arm around herself, one hand fiddling with her hair, eyes fixed on the TV. 'Have you worked with Detective Superintendent Ness before, I mean is she going to be someone that's receptive to input from other—'

'No idea. Must be new.'

'"... *ask that you allow us the time and space to grieve for our beautiful Claire..."*'

The pub's inner door clunked open and a thickset woman in a vast padded jacket staggered in, laden down with pizza boxes. She had a woolly hat jammed down over her ears, face half-hidden by a knitted scarf. A plastic carrier-bag hung from one hand, swaying from side to side as she heeled the door shut behind her. 'Did I miss it?'

Huntly pulled a pinstriped jacket from the back of a chair and slipped it on, completing the suit. 'Statement from the family.'

Onscreen, Ness swapped one prepared statement for another. '*Three twenty-three yesterday morning, an ambulance responded to a nine-nine-nine call near Blackwall Hill…*'

The woman in the padded jacket lurched across the room, the contents of her carrier-bag clinking against her leg. 'It's OK, I don't need any help…'

'Sheila, my dearest lady, allow me to assist.' Huntly took the top box off the stack and carried it over to the bar. Popped it open. The heady scent of garlic, onions, and tomato fluttered out, swirling through the air like trapped starlings. His shoulders dipped a notch. 'Oh. This one's vegetarian.' Then he shut the box again.

'*… pronounced dead at the scene. That's all I'm able to say at the moment, other than investigations are ongoing with assistance from our colleagues in the Specialist Crime Division and a team of independent experts.*'

Alice reached across and slid it down the bar towards herself. 'Thank you, Doctor.'

Sheila lowered the remaining pizza boxes onto one of the tables and hauled off her gloves. Slipped her hands in between two of the cartons. 'God, it's perishing out there…' A shiver. The scarf drooped, revealing a pair of round shiny cheeks and a small button nose. Then she stuck a hand out at me. 'Sheila Constantine, pathologist; you must be Henderson. Welcome aboard. You owe me twelve pounds sixty-three.' She turned a scowl in Huntly's direction. '*Everyone* owes me twelve pounds sixty-three.'

'*… will now take questions.*' Ness pointed at someone off camera. '*Yes?*'

A man's voice: '*Are you treating this as a copycat case, or is the Inside Man back again?*'

Huntly opened the next box in the stack. 'Are these *all* vegetarian? Because I specifically asked for a meat feast.'

Sheila struggled her way out of her coat. 'That's enough about your private life, Bernard, we're about to eat. And before you ask: no, I won't take an IOU this time.'

'*... not willing to be drawn into speculation about who's responsible before we've investigated...*'

I stuck my hand in my pocket. Looked at the boxes, then at Alice, then at the boxes again.

A little line appeared between her eyebrows. She nodded. 'I'll pay for Ash, as I'm his sponsor, or maybe we should all chip in as a sort of welcome to the team and—'

'Ah, yes of course.' Huntly slapped a hand against his forehead. 'Mr Henderson is just out of prison. He's financially embarrassed. How very *insensitive* of you, Sheila. We shouldn't be speaking of money at a time like this!'

'*Detective Superintendent, who's running the investigation here, you or Superintendent Knight? Doesn't the Scottish Chief Constable trust Oldcastle to—*'

'*It's standard operating procedure to have multiple Major Investigation Teams working together on a case like this, and I for one welcome any assistance offered when young women's lives are at stake. Do you think we should refuse SCD's help out of some twisted sense of pride?*'

'I... Well, no, but—'

'*I will pursue and exploit* every *avenue available to me if I think it will help catch the person responsible for Claire Young's death. Next?*'

Huntly moved on to another pizza. 'Ah, *finally*. Something with salami on it.' He dumped the box on one of the pub tables and settled into a chair. He pulled a triangle of dough, cheese, and greasy meat from the carton and pointed at Ness with it. 'Good, isn't she? Promoted and transferred up from Tayside. Giving the local bumpkins a shake-up by all accounts.' He stuffed a mouthful in and chewed. Eating with his eyes

45

fixed on the screen. Then dabbed at the corner of his lips with a handkerchief. 'I did a case with her, back when she was a DS. Serial rape, very nasty... You wouldn't think it, but she's quite the *femme fatale* when she's not wearing her game face.'

'*Has the Inside Man sent another letter?*'

'*Let me repeat myself: we're not speculating about who's responsible. Next?*'

'*Yes, but has a letter—*'

'*Next?*'

Dr Constantine pulled out a chair and sank into it. The thick layers of her padded jacket ballooned out around her. 'I've checked with Ness and Knight – we can have the deposition scene first thing tomorrow morning, and the body any time after two.'

'*What kind of doll was it?*'

'*We're not releasing that information. Next?*'

Huntly took another bite. 'When do I get at the physical evidence?'

Sheila scowled at him. 'Not till you pay for that pizza.'

'Oh for goodness' sake...'

'*Was it a Tiny Tears, or a Baby Bunty doll?*'

'*I've already answered that question. Next?*'

'*These independent experts, do they report to you, or SCD?*'

Ness looked off to the side. '*Detective Superintendent Jacobson?*'

'Ah.' Huntly plucked the remote from my fingers. 'Here we go.' He turned up the volume.

The briefing room smeared across the screen as the camera turned, and there was Jacobson, standing off to the side, staring out into the pub. He'd put on a brown tie, but hadn't bothered with a suit, sticking with the tan leather jacket instead. '*My team are all at the very top of their field, each one hand-picked for their ability to bring decades of experience and a unique perspective to any case.*'

A moment's silence. Then whoever asked the question in the first place tried again. *'Yes, but do you report to Oldcastle CID, or the Specialist Crime Division?'*

'An excellent question.'

More silence.

'Er... Would you like to answer it?'

'The Lateral Investigative and Review Unit will feed its results, through me, to whichever Major Investigation Team is best suited to act upon them.'

Alice sooked the grease from her fingers. 'And now everyone thinks we're in charge.'

Sheila nodded. 'You were right. Good suggestion.' The camera swung back for a reaction shot from the top brass: cue coughing and spluttering.

Then Ness pulled on a hard smile. *'Having worked with Detective Superintendent Jacobson on several investigations, I'm pleased to welcome his LIRU team onboard.'*

The Superintendent sitting next to her stuck his chest out. It was covered in silver buttons, a row of multi-coloured ribbons above his left pocket: Golden Jubilee medal, Diamond Jubilee, and a Long Service & Good Conduct. All of them awarded for nothing braver than just being in the job long enough, but there he was, wearing them with pride. That would be Superintendent Knight, then. He jerked his chin up, the strip-lights flashed off his bald head. *'The Specialist Crime Division is also pleased to work with Detective Superintendent Jacobson's team.'*

Ness knocked on the tabletop, taking control of the briefing again. *'Next question?'*

Huntly jabbed the remote at the screen and the volume ticked down until it was barely more than a mumble. 'Excellent. That'll put the *felis catus* amongst the *columba palumbus*. Deserves a celebratory drink, don't you think, Sheila?'

A sigh. Then she reached into the carrier-bag and came out with a bottle of red wine and one of white. 'That's an extra fiver each.'

Huntly jumped up and produced a half-dozen dusty glasses from behind the bar. Huffed a breath into each, then polished them with his pink tie. Lined them up on the bar.

Sheila handed me a pizza box, the DinoPizza's T-Rex logo speckled dark with grease. 'Don't worry about the money. I'll get yours off Bear. Now, would you like a glass of wine?'

'Can't: pills. But thanks.' I opened the box. Mushrooms, ham, sweetcorn, and pineapple. Still, it could have been worse.

Huntly clapped his hands. 'That just means more for us!'

Tiny white dots curled into the pub airlock as I stepped outside and thumbed Detective Inspector Dave Morrow's number into Alice's mobile phone. I pressed the green button and listened to it ring, breath billowing out in a pale grey cloud where it caught the streetlight. Say what you like about prison, at least they keep the place relatively warm...

A rough voice crackled out of the earpiece. Slightly breathy and clipped. *'Alice, this ... this really isn't a good time.'*

'Shifty, it's me. You OK?'

A pause. *'Bloody hell, she actually did it. When did you get out?'*

'Couple of hours ago. I'm going to need a favour.'

He sniffed. *'You know I'd have done Mrs Kerrigan if I could, right?'*

'I know.'

'Last thing I need is Andy Inglis coming after me. Specially with the Rubber Heelers on a mission. Otherwise she'd be the filling in a shallow-grave buttie...'

I stepped out into the evening chill, taking a few lumbering steps away from the pub door. Glanced back to make sure no one was listening. 'Tonight: you, me, gun, her. Better get some petrol and a couple of shovels too.'

A pause. *'Ash, you know I'd—'*

'You're wimping out?'

'Am I buggery. You know what Andy Inglis is going to do when he finds out you've topped her though, don't you?'

'He's not going to find out.'

'Oh come on. You get out of prison and the very same night she gets shot in the face? How long's that going to take him to work out?'

True.

Another couple of paces, looking up at the billboard on the other side of the road with its never-to-be-built retirement home. 'So I don't hang around afterwards. I kill her, we burn the body, and I get out of Oldcastle. Hop a boat to Norway. You still friends with that fish guy in Fraserburgh?'

'Passport up to date, is it? Cos I kinda get the feeling the Border Agency will be keeping an eye out for you.'

A clunk behind me. I turned and there was Dr Constantine, all bundled up in her padded jacket, a cigarette clamped between her jaws. She sparked it from a lighter, then waved.

I waved back. Pointed at the phone against my ear. Turned away. 'What about Biro Billy?'

A sigh. *'I'll see what I can do.'*

Detective Superintendent Jacobson shrugged his way out of his leather jacket. A thin dusting of white flakes clung to the shoulders and the top of his head, melting away in the warmth of the defunct pub. He hung the jacket on the back of a chair. 'Well?'

Huntly swept his arms out, as if he was going to hug him. 'You were *magnificent*!'

'Don't push it, Bernard, you're still in my bad books after this morning.'

'Oh...' He dropped his arms.

'Any pizza left?' Jacobson crossed to the bar, opening and closing the grease-speckled boxes. 'Crusts, crusts, crusts...'

Sheila pointed to the stack of chairs and tables in the corner. 'I hid yours over there, so the human waste-disposal-unit couldn't find it. It'll be cold though.'

He pulled out the box, opened it, scooped out a slice and shoved one end in his mouth. Closed his eyes and chewed.

'Ahh... That's better. They never put on anything decent at press conferences any more. It's all bottled water and horrible coffee. What's wrong with a plate of sandwiches?'

Huntly poured red wine into a tie-polished glass. 'Speaking of the press conference...' He cleared his throat. 'Was Donald there?'

Sitting back in her seat, Sheila groaned. 'Not this again.'

He stiffened. 'There's no need to be like that.'

She put on a posh plummy accent. 'Was Donald there? Did he ask about me? Did he look like he'd been crying? Has he put on weight? Is he seeing someone?'

'There's no need to be homophobic.'

'I'm not homophobic, I'm grown-men-acting-like-jilted-teenage-girls-ophobic. And you still owe me seventeen pounds sixty-three.'

Jacobson took the glass of red and wolfed half of it down in one go. 'Donald wasn't there. Superintendent Knight's put him in charge of finding out which of Ash's ex-colleagues tipped off the press about the Inside Man killing Claire Young.'

Bet that went down well. Some tosser, from another division, investigating Oldcastle CID for misconduct? They'd have closed ranks so fast you could hear the sonic boom in Dundee.

The rest of Jacobson's wine disappeared down his throat. He held the glass out for Huntly to refill. 'I had a chat with a couple of guys from uniform. Seems Claire set off for work at seven fifteen on Thursday night, and never turned up. Her flatmates reported her missing Friday afternoon when she didn't come home. The geniuses at Oldcastle Division only took it seriously when Claire's body turned up yesterday morning.' He took a sip, swooshing the red back and forth through his teeth, then nodded in my direction. 'That's going to look *great* when the papers find out.'

I crossed my arms, staring at him. 'Why me?'

'Why you, what?'

'If Oldcastle CID's full of corrupt morons, why am I here?'

He smiled. 'Now that's an *excellent* question.'

But he didn't bloody answer it.

7

We stopped off at the twenty-four hour Tesco in Logansferry, Alice scurrying away into the aisles to buy breakfast supplies while I headed for the electronics bit. One dirt-cheap mobile handset and three pay-as-you-go sim cards. All paid for out of the hundred-quid sub I'd got from Jacobson.

On the other side of the checkouts I dumped the phone's packaging in the bin and tore open the cardboard and plastic entombing one of the sim cards. Popped it in. Clicked the cover back on. Powered it up and punched in Shifty's number.

Listened to it ring as I limped out into the car park.

The snow hadn't come to anything more than a thin crust of ice on the windscreens and a sheen of water on the salted tarmac.

A suspicious-sounding voice came on the line. *'Hello? Who is this?'*

'How you getting on with that gun?'

'God's sake, Ash, I'm on it, OK? Give us a chance – not like I can just waltz down to the nearest ASDA and pick one up, is it?'

'We're going to need a car too. Something flammable.'

Silence.

'Shifty? Hello?' Only just bought the damn phone and already it was—

'*What do you think I've been doing while you've been sodding about with your new mates? Got us a Mondeo. One careful owner, who's got no idea it's missing.*'

Ah... 'Sorry. It's...' I rubbed a hand across my chin, making the stubble scratch. 'Been a while, you know?'

'*This isn't my first rodeo, Ash. We'll be fine. Trust me.*'

Alice struggled half a dozen carrier-bags from the back seat of the tiny red Suzuki four-by-four. The thing had a big dent in the passenger-side door and looked more like a kid's drawing of a car than an actual real-life vehicle. Drove much the same way too. She'd parked it beneath one of the three working streetlights, between a rusty white transit and a sagging Volvo. 'Mmmnnnffffnngh?' She nodded at the Suzuki, the keys dangling from the leather fob gripped in her teeth.

'Yeah, no problem.' I got the last of the shopping, and the bin-bag they'd given me when I left prison, then took the keys from between her teeth and plipped the locks.

'Thanks.' Her breath streamed out in a thin line of mist. 'We're just there.' She nodded towards a front door two-thirds of the way down the terrace.

I shifted the bags from one hand to the other. Leaned on my cane.

Ladburn Street had probably been attractive once – a cobbled road lined with tall trees and cast-iron railings. A sweeping row of proud sandstone homes with porticoes and bay windows...

Now the trees were blackened stumps, surrounded by litter and vitrified dog shit. The houses all converted into flats.

Three buildings on this side were boarded up; four on the other, their gardens thick with weeds. Rock music belted out of somewhere down the row, a screaming argument a few doors up. Sandstone turned the colour of old blood. Railings blistered with rust.

Alice shifted from foot to foot. 'I know it's disappointing, I mean let's be honest it's not far off being a slum, but it was cheap and it's pretty anonymous and we can't stay with Aunty Jan because they're having all the wiring ripped out and—'

'It's fine.'

Her nose was going red. 'I'm sorry, I know Kingsmeath's not great, but it's only temporary and I didn't think you'd want to stay in the hotel with Professor Huntly, and Bear, and Dr Constantine, and Dr Docherty, and—'

'Seriously, it's OK.' Something scrunched beneath my shoes as I limped up the path towards the house. Broken glass, children's teeth, small animal bones... Around here, anything was possible.

'Right. Yes.' She lumbered along beside me, the bags banging against her legs. 'You see, a lot of people think Kingsmeath was thrown up in the seventies, that it's one big council estate, but there's bits of it go back to the eighteen-hundreds, actually, until the cholera outbreak in 1826, this would have been all sugar barons, of course the whole industry ran on slave labour plantations in the Caribbean, and can you get the lock, it's the Yale key.'

I leaned my cane against the wall, picked my way through the keys. 'This one?'

'No, the one with the red plastic bit. That's it. We're on the top floor.'

I pushed through into a dim hallway that had the eye-nipping reek of a pub urinal. A small drift of leaflets, charity letters and takeaway menus spread across the cracked tiles from behind the door. 'CAMMYS A WANKA!!!' scrawled in magic marker on the peeling mildewed walls.

Not far off being a slum?

The stairs creaked beneath my feet all the way up to the third floor, walking cane thudding on the mangy carpet.

Alice dumped her carrier-bags on the floor and took the keys back, working them through her fingers like a string of rosary beads. Then undid each of the door's four security locks – their brass casings all shiny and un-scratched. Newly fitted.

She tried on a smile. 'Like I said, it's not exactly great...'

'It's got to be better than where I've been for the last two years.'

Then she opened the door and flicked on the light.

Bare floorboards stretched away down a short corridor, lined with gripper rod, little tufts of blue nylon marking where the carpet had been, exposing a dark brown stain that was about eight pints wide. A single bare lightbulb hung from a flex in the ceiling – surrounded by coffee-coloured blotches. It smelled meaty, like a butcher's shop.

Alice ushered me inside, then closed the door behind us, locking and snibbing each of the deadbolts. 'Right, time for the tour...'

There wasn't enough room for both of us in the kitchen, so I stood on the threshold while Alice clattered and clinked her way through making a pot of tea for two. Cardboard boxes formed a wobbly pile next to the bin – one for the toaster, one for the kettle, another for the teapot, cutlery...

She unpacked two mugs from a box and rinsed them under the tap. 'So, is there anything you want to do tonight, I mean we could go to the pub or the pictures, only it's a bit late for the pictures, unless they're doing a late-night showing of something, or there's some DVDs I could put in the laptop, or we could just read books?'

After two years of being stuck inside, in a little concrete room with the occasional accident-prone cellmate, there should've been no contest. 'Actually … I'd rather stay in. If that's OK?'

The living room wasn't exactly huge, but it was clean. Two folding chairs – the kind sold in camping shops – sat on either side of a packing crate in front of the fireplace. She hadn't taken the price-tag off the rug, leaving it to flutter like an injured bird in the draught of a small blow heater.

The curtains were a washed-out blue colour that still wore the chequerboard creases from when they were in the packet. I pulled one side back.

Kingsmeath. Again. As if last time hadn't been bad enough.

Mind you, it didn't look quite as awful in the dark, just a sweeping ribbon of streetlights and glowing windows stretching down to the Kings River – the train station on the other side of the water shining like a vast glass slug. Even the industrial estate in Logansferry had a sort of fairy-tale mystery to it. Security lights and illuminated signs. Chain-link fences and guard dogs.

To be honest, most of Oldcastle looked better at night.

And then a trail of gold streaked into the sky. One... Two... Three... BANG – a glowing sphere of red embers punctured the night sky, throwing a pair of gravestone tower blocks into sharp relief, washing them with blood.

It slowly drained away until everything was in darkness again.

Alice appeared at my shoulder. 'They've been letting them off for a fortnight. I mean don't get me wrong I love fireworks as much as the next person, but it's nearly a whole *week* after bonfire night and soon as the sun goes down it's like Beirut out there.'

Another firework burst in a shower of blue and green. The change of colour didn't improve anything.

She handed me a cup of tea. 'You know, it might help to talk about what happened to Katie and Parker, now you're not inside, because you're safe here and you don't have to worry about being recorded or people—'

'Tell me about Claire Young.'

Alice closed her mouth. Bit her lips together. Then sank into one of the folding chairs. 'Her mother blames herself. We're not making it public, but she's on suicide watch. Tried it twice before, apparently and—'

'No, not her mother: Claire.'

'OK. Claire.' Alice crossed her legs. 'Well, she's definitely in the target range of the previous Inside Man victims – nurse, mid-twenties, very ... fertile looking.'

The tea was hot and sweet, as if Alice thought I was suffering from shock. 'So if it *is* him he's still hunting at the hospital. Security tapes?'

'Claire didn't go missing from work. As far as we can tell, she never made it further than Horton Road. With any luck they'll let us have the security camera footage from the area tomorrow.'

I turned back to the window. Another baleful red eye exploded over the tower blocks. 'Is it him?'

'Ah...' Pause. 'Well, that really depends on what happens tomorrow. Detective Superintendent Ness thinks it isn't. Superintendent Knight thinks it is. Bear's sitting on the fence till we've had a chance to examine the body and the physical evidence.'

'That why we're here: to decide if he's back or not?'

'No, we're here because Detective Superintendent Jacobson is empire-building. He wants the Lateral Investigative and Review Unit to be a full-time thing. This is his test case.'

I pulled the curtains closed. Turned my back on the world.

'So... What DVDs have you got?'

'No, you listen to me: we're going to fight this!' She stops, shifts her grip on the holdall, and stares up at the dark-grey ceiling. Her hair's like burnished copper, a dusting of freckles across her cheeks and nose. Pretty.

A fluorescent tube clicks and pings above her head, never quite getting going, making strobe-light shadows that jitter around the underground car park.

No place for a woman to be walking alone in the middle of the night. Who knows what kind of monsters might be lurking in the shadows?

Her breath plumes around her head. *'We won't let them compromise patient care to save a few grubby pounds.'*

Yeah, right. Because that's how it works.

Whoever's on the other end of the phone says something, and she stops for a moment, surrounded by manky vehicles, parked in miserable rows of dents and chipped paint. Raises her chin. '*No, that's* completely *unacceptable.*'

That's when the music starts – violins, low and slow, marking time with her footsteps as she walks towards her car: an ancient Renault Clio with one wing a different colour to the others. '*Don't you worry, we'll make them rue the day they decided people didn't deserve their dignity. We'll...*'

A crease puckers the gap between her neatly plucked brows. Her eyes are bright sapphire, set in a ring of ocean-blue.

There's something wrong with the passenger window of her car. Instead of being opaque with dried road spray, it's a gaping black hole, ringed with little cubes of broken safety glass.

She peers inside. All that's left of the stereo is a handful of multi-coloured wires, poking out of the hole where it used to be.

'*For goodness' sake!*' The phone gets clacked shut and stuffed back into her pocket. Then she stomps round to the Renault's boot and hurls her holdall inside.

Footsteps sound somewhere behind her, echoing back and forth as she stands there trembling and spiky. Some other underpaid nobody, making for their crappy car so they can go back to their crappy flat after a crappy day at their crappy job.

The violins get darker, joined by a minor chord on the piano.

She roots through her handbag, then pulls out a jangling mass of keys more suited to a prison officer than a nurse. They fumble through her fingers and tumble to the damp concrete. Cling-clatter their way under the car.

The footsteps are louder now.

She thumps her handbag on the bonnet and squats down, reaching into the oily blackness beneath the patchwork Clio, searching, searching...

The footsteps stop, right behind her.

Dramatic chord on the piano.

She freezes, car keys just out of reach.

58

Whoever it is clears his throat.

She lunges for the keys, grabs them, holds them jagged between her fingers like a knuckle duster, then spins around, back against the driver's door...

A man frowns down at her, with his big rectangular face and designer stubble. '*Are you all right?*' He's wearing a set of pale-blue nurses' scrubs, his top pocket full of pens. Castle Hill Infirmary ID tag hanging at a jaunty angle. Broad-shouldered. His blond hair, gelled into spikes, glints in the buzzing strip-light. Like something off *Baywatch*.

The grimace dies on her face, replaced by a small smile. She rolls her eyes, then sticks out her hand so he can help her up. '*Steve, you frightened the life out of me.*'

'*Sorry about that.*' He looks away, deeper into the fusty gloom, eyebrows knitting. '*Listen, about this meeting tomorrow: Audit Scotland.*'

'*My mind's made up.*' Laura picks through her keys, then unlocks the car door.

Seems like a waste of time, when she could reach in through the broken passenger window and open the thing, but there you go.

'*I want you to know that we're all behind you, one hundred percent.*' He doesn't just look like something off *Baywatch*, he sounds like it too.

'*Thanks, Steve, I appreciate that.*' She brushes broken glass from the driver's seat, and climbs in.

Steve pulls his shoulders back, chest out. '*If there's anything you need: I'm here for you, Laura.*'

For God's sake, who actually *talks* like that?

'*They'll have to give us more staff. Decent equipment. Cleaners that actually clean things instead of moving the filth around. And I'm not going to give up until they do.*'

He nods. Poses for a second more. '*I'd better get back. These sick people aren't going to heal themselves.*' He turns and struts away into the shadows, shoulders swinging like John Travolta.

Brilliant. Oscar-winning stuff.

Laura jiggles the keys in the ignition and cranks the Renault's engine into life. Then she pulls on her seatbelt, checks the rear-view mirror and—

She screams.

A pair of dark eyes glitter back at her from the rear seat, *staring*.

It's a big blue teddy bear, wearing a red bow around its neck, cradling an oversized card with 'HAPPY 6TH BIRTHDAY!' on it.

The air hisses out of her as she slumps back in her seat, arms loose in her lap.

Jumping like a frightened schoolgirl; it's a sodding teddy bear, not Jack the Ripper.

Idiot.

Then someone knocks on the car roof and the pale blue of a nurse's scrubs fills the driver's side window. Probably Steve, back to mangle some more dialogue.

She presses the button and lowers her window. *'Can I help—'*

A fist slams into the camera and the screen goes dark.

Alice hit pause. 'I'm going to make another pot of tea, do you want some, or there's juice, and I got biscuits too, do you like custard creams or jammie dodgers, stupid question really, who doesn't love jammie—'

'Surprise me.'

She nodded, collected the teapot and headed off to the kitchen.

The DVD case lay on the makeshift coffee table, beside her laptop: 'WRAPPED IN DARKNESS ~ ONE WOMAN'S JOURNEY TO HELL AND BACK!' The subtitle was about as melodramatic as the reconstruction.

Obviously the director really wanted to make a feature film of the story, but didn't have the budget, or talent, to pull it off.

OK, so he'd got the idea more or less right, but the details?

If Laura Strachan and her mate Steve had actually talked like that the day she went missing I'd eat my chair.

I fast-forwarded through some beardy type talking in front of a whiteboard while the kettle rumbled in the kitchen. Never trust a man with a beard – sinister devious bastards the lot of them.

Army ants marched in a line around the top of my left sock.

Bloody thing. I pulled my trouser leg up and raked my nails back and forward along the lip of the ankle monitor, scrabbling at the plastic edge. Blessed relief.

Alice emerged from the kitchen with the teapot and a plate of assorted biscuits. 'You shouldn't scratch it, I mean what if you break the skin and it gets all infected and then—'

'It's itchy.' I pressed play again.

Laura Strachan – the real one, not the actress playing her in the reconstruction – has her hands dug deep into her pockets, the wind whipping her curly auburn hair out behind her, ruffling the ankle-length coat as she picks her way along the battlements of the castle. She pauses, looking down the cliff, across Kings River towards Montgomery Park and Blackwall Hill beyond. Sunlight glints on the broad curve of water, turns the firework trees into explosions of amber and scarlet.

Her voice comes in over the background music, even though her lips don't move.

'From the moment I was attacked, to the moment I woke up in Intensive Care, everything was a blur. Some fragments are clearer than others, some just ... it was like peering into the bottom of a well, with something sharp glinting at the bottom. Sharp and dangerous.'

She leans on the battlement peering down. Then the camera switches so it's looking back up at her.

The scene jumps to a bright white room, lined with what looks like clear plastic sheeting. It's hard to tell – they've sodded about with the picture, making the highlights stretch vertically across the screen, as if everything's in the process of being beamed up. The room throbs in and out, then lurches to one side until a large stainless-steel trolley sits in the middle of the shot, with the younger, prettier, actress version of Laura lying on it. Her hands and feet are tied to the trolley's legs, two more bands of rope – one across her chest, under her armpits, the other across her thighs – hold her tight. Naked, except for a pair of strategically placed towels.

'I remember the smell, more than anything else. It was like detergent and bleach, and something … a bit like hot plastic? And there was classical music playing.'

Beethoven's Moonlight Sonata fades up.

'And he…' Her voice breaks. A pause. *'He was wearing a white apron, on over… Over… It might have been surgical scrubs. I can't… It was all so blurred.'*

A man walks into shot, dressed exactly like Laura described him. His mouth is hidden behind a surgical mask, the rest of his face blurred – reduced to an unrecognizable mess by the video effect.

Then a close-up of a syringe, the needle huge as it moves towards the camera. Fade to black. Then we're in what looks like a private hospital room.

'The next thing I know, it's four days later and I'm lying on a bed in intensive care. And I'm choking on the ventilator, and I'm wired up to half-a-dozen monitors, and this nurse is running around screaming that I'm awake.'

Alice poured the tea.

'All my life, ever since I was a little girl, I wanted to have babies. A family of my own to love and cherish the way my father never did for me.'

I helped myself to a custard cream.

'But the doctors said it wasn't possible any more. The Inside Man took it away from me when he… When he ripped me open.'

Cut to a posh-looking office, lined in wood, with a heap

of framed certificates on the wall. A thin balding man sits behind a big oak desk. He's wearing a dark-blue suit and a bright-red tie. A caption scrolls across the bottom of the screen: 'Charles Dallas-MacAlpine, Senior Consultant Surgeon, Castle Hill Infirmary'.

His voice is all public school pomp and barely concealed sneer. *'Of course, when Laura came to me her insides were a mess. It's a miracle she didn't exsanguinate in the ambulance.'* A tight-lipped smile. *'That means, "bleed to death".'*

Really? Wow, hark at him with his posh-boy big words.

'Luckily, she'd had the good fortune to be on my operating table. Otherwise—'

Three short thumps broke in on Dr Patronizing's monologue.

Front door.

Alice flinched. 'Are you expecting someone, because I don't—'

'I'll get it.'

'—shudder to think. You see, her uterus was—'

I closed the lounge door behind me. Limped across the hall's stained floorboards, walking stick clunking with every other step. Peered out through the peephole.

A bald head filled the lens with a swathe of pink and grey.

I undid the four security locks and opened the door. 'Shifty.'

He'd obviously not shaved his head for a bit: a fringe of gunmetal stubble stuck out above his ears. More stubble shaded his collection of chins. Folds of skin drooped beneath watery bloodshot eyes. A bruise rode high on his left cheek. The smell of aftershave oozed out of him, mingling with the rotten oniony whiff of the day's sweat.

A couple of orange carrier-bags sat on the floor by his feet.

Shifty blinked at me a couple of times, then a massive grin split across his face and he lunged, wrapped his arms around me, pinning my arms to my sides, and squeezed. Laughed. 'About bloody time!' He leaned back, lifting my feet off the floor. 'How've you been? I'm gasping here. Any chance of a drink?'

Couldn't help but smile. 'Get off me, you big Jessie.'

'Oh, don't be so repressed.' One more squeeze, then he let go. 'Thought we'd never get you out of there. You look like crap, by the way.'

'Did you get it?'

He reached into his crumpled jacket and came out with an envelope. Handed it over.

OK. Unexpected.

I tried again, nice and slow. 'Did – you – get – the – gun?'

8

Shifty dragged a hand down his face, pulling it out of shape. 'Alec wouldn't sell it to me, said it'd be bad karma.'

I opened the envelope. It was stuffed with creased tenners and twenties. Had to be at least three, maybe four hundred quid. Not bad at all. Shifty's shoulder wobbled when I patted it. 'That's a lot of walking around money. You're—'

'Don't be a divot. It's for the gun. Alec won't sell it to me, but he'll sell it to you. He's got bloody weird since he came down with Buddhism.' One podgy hand went back in Shifty's jacket and came out with a yellow Post-it note. He stuck it to my chest. A mobile phone number in scratchy red biro. 'But it's going to have to be tomorrow. Now are we having that drink or not?'

'Tomorrow? I wanted—'

'I know. It's not that easy finding someone who'll sell a gun to a cop, OK? Alec's a pain, but he's discreet.' Shifty pulled his shoulders up to his ears. Let them fall again. 'We'll do her tomorrow. I *promise*.'

Well, after two years was one more night really going to make that much difference? So she got another twenty-four hours, so what? She'd still end up dead.

Fair enough.

I nodded back towards the flat. 'Tea?'

'You're kidding, right? Tea? When you've just got out of the nick?' A wink. Then he dipped into one of the carrier-bags at his feet and came out with two bottles. 'Champagne!'

He followed me into the flat, standing in the hallway while I snibbed all the locks again then showed him into the living room.

Alice was out of her chair, standing like a fencepost, all pulled in and straight. She smiled. 'David, how nice to see you again. Is Andrew well?'

'I know we said tomorrow, but I couldn't wait.' He loomed over her, leaned in, and gave her a peck on the cheek. Then plonked one of the champagne bottles down beside the laptop and started picking the foil cap off the other. 'You don't have any decent glasses, do you?'

'Ah, yes, right, I'll see what I can dig up, sure there's something lurking in the cupboards...' She pointed at the kitchen, then disappeared through the door.

Shifty worked the wire cage off the cork, pacing as he did it. Never standing still. The floorboards creaking and groaning away beneath his feet.

Silence.

He stared at the laptop screen, where Laura Strachan was frozen halfway down a flight of stone steps, the pause icon overlapping her feet. 'I ... went round to see Michelle.'

'Did you now?' Two years, and not a single visit from her. Not so much as a letter.

'She came to the door and she was all...' He wiggled one hand beside his head. 'You know? Hair all over the place, really pale and thin, bags under her eyes. Been drinking.'

I sank back into my camp chair. Folded my arms. 'So?'

'She's got the house up for sale. Big sign in the front garden. Moving down south to be with her sister.'

Yeah. Well ... she was a grown woman. Not as if we were

married any more, was it? Could do what she liked. Didn't have to tell me. 'There a point to this?'

'Just thought you'd … I don't know.' He stared down at the bottle in his hands. 'Andrew threw me out. *Apparently* it's not him, it's me. Says I'm suffocating him.' Those fat fingers tightened around the neck of the bottle, squeezing until their joints were pale as bone. 'I'll bloody suffocate him…'

Alice appeared in the kitchen doorway, carrying three generic wine glasses. 'Who's getting suffocated?'

'Shifty's boyfriend's chucked him out.'

His bottom lip popped out an inch, then he shook his head.

'Oh, David, I'm so sorry.' She patted one of the camping chairs. 'Here, you have a sit down and tell me all about it.'

Oh God, here we go.

'Maybe later.' He twisted the cork in one meaty paw, pulled and – it *poomed* out from the bottle bringing a coil of pale gas with it. He filled two of the glasses, then dipped back into his plastic bag and handed me a can of Irn-Bru.

Fair enough. I clicked off the tab and filled my glass with fluorescent-orange fizzy juice.

Shifty raised his. 'A toast – to Ash, to friends, and to freedom.'

To revenge…

We clinked glasses.

He knocked back a mouthful. Sucked in air through his teeth. Gave a little shudder. Then sank into the chair. Slumped. 'Sodding Andrew. Two years. Two sodding years. I came *out* for him.'

'No… No, this'll … this'll be ffff … be fine.' Shifty blinked one eye at a time, then wobbled down into a squat, falling forward so he was on his hands and knees. Arse up. Wearing nothing but a pair of black Calvin Klein pants. He wobbled a bit more, then half lowered himself, half collapsed onto his side. It was just a sheet laid out on top of the new rug, but it was going to have to do. At least he had a pillow. Throw in a couple of bath sheets for blankets, and...

Well, it wasn't great, but after all the booze the pair of them had put away, he wasn't likely to notice.

The sound of retching echoed out of the bathroom, amplified by the toilet bowl.

Shifty twitched a couple of times, then let out a long, low groan. Followed by a pause. A snuffle.

I draped another towel over him then picked up the two empty champagne bottles and what was left of the supermarket whisky. Took them through to the kitchen and ditched them next to the kettle. Grabbed the washing-up bowl from the sink.

By the time I got back to the living room he was flat on his back, snoring hard enough to make the air vibrate. His towel-blankets were all rucked up on one side, exposing a hairy expanse of pale belly. The rumbling drone stopped for a couple of beats... Then he grunted something that sounded like a name, and went back to snoring again.

'Silly sod.' I tugged the towels into place. 'Try not to choke on your own vomit in the middle of the night, OK?' I turned out the light. Closed the door. Left him to it.

The toilet flushed. Then gargling. Spitting. And finally Alice lurched out into the hall.

She'd done her tartan pyjamas up wrong, the left side one button out of synch with the right. Hair sticking out in a tangled mess. 'Urgh...'

'Come on: bed.'

She clasped a hand to one side of her face. 'Don't feel so good...'

'Well, whose fault is that?'

Her bedroom door opened on a small room with a single bed, a flat-packed wardrobe, and a small bedside table. A Monet poster dominated the room, all greens and blues and purples.

She clambered into bed, hauled the duvet up around her chin. 'Urrgh…'

'Did you drink a pint of water?' I put the washing-up bowl on the floor by her head. With any luck there wouldn't be sick all over the floor in the morning.

'Ash…' She smacked her mouth a couple of times, like she was tasting something bitter. 'Tell me a story.'

'You're kidding, right?'

'I want a *story*.'

'You're a grown woman, I am *not* reading—'

'Pleeeeeease?'

Seriously?

She blinked up at me, grey bags under her bloodshot eyes.

Sigh. 'Fine.' I settled onto the edge of the bed, taking the weight off my right foot. 'Once upon a time, there was a serial killer called the Inside Man, and he liked to stitch dolls into nurses' stomachs. But what he didn't know was that a brave policeman was after him.'

She smiled. 'Was the policeman's name, Ash? It was, wasn't it?'

'Who's telling this story, you or me?'

Eight Years Ago

I hit the door hard, battering it open. Dodged a crowd of old fogies in their dressing gowns and slippers, surrounded by their own personal fog-bank of cigarette smoke.

Where the hell did he...

There – on the other side of the low wall that separated Castle Hill Infirmary from the car park. A pregnant woman screaming abuse, banging on the window of an ancient-looking Ford Fiesta as it roared away from the kerb.

More swearing erupted behind me as PC O'Neil staggered through the OAP smokers, his face flushed, sweat glistening on his cheeks. 'Did you get him?'

'Do I bloody look like I got him? Get the car. NOW!'

'Oh God...' He lumbered over the low wall – making for our rusty Vauxhall, parked on the double yellows.

The pregnant woman stood in the middle of the road, sticking two fingers up at the back of the Fiesta as it fishtailed out through the hospital gates and onto Nelson Street. 'I HOPE YOU CATCH AIDS AND DIE, YOU THIEVING BASTARD!'

I staggered to a halt beside her. 'Did you get a good look at his face?'

'He stole my bloody car! Did you see that?'

'Would you recognize him if you saw him again?'

71

'My dog's in the boot!' She cupped her hands around her mouth. 'COME BACK HERE, YOU WANKER!'

The pool car screeched out from the kerb, coming to a stop in a squeal of brakes on the wrong side of the road, opposite us. O'Neil buzzed the window down. 'He's getting away.'

I pointed the woman at the hospital. 'You don't go anywhere till someone's taken your statement, understand?' Then I ran around to the passenger side and clambered in. Slammed the door. Slapped O'Neil on the shoulder. 'Put your foot down!'

He did, and the Vauxhall surged forward in a squeal of tyre smoke.

Left onto Nelson Street, just missing a Mini, the driver leaning on his horn, eyes wide, mouth stretched in horror.

O'Neil got the slide under control, both hands wrapped tightly around the steering wheel, teeth biting down on his bottom lip as the car raced up the hill. Newsagents, carpet shops, and hairdressers streaked past the windows.

I scrambled into my seatbelt, then flicked the switch for the blues and twos.

The pool car's siren wailed above the engine's bellow, forging a path through the lunchtime traffic.

We screeched up the hill while I pulled out my Airwave handset and called it in. 'Charlie Hotel Seven to Control, we are in pursuit of the Inside Man. Eastbound on Nelson Street. Get someone out there blocking the road. He's in a brown Ford Fiesta.'

A pause, then a hard Dundee accent came on the line. '*You been drinking?*'

'Get backup out there now!'

The Vauxhall cleared the brow of the hill, flew for at least ten feet, then slammed back down onto the tarmac. O'Neil had his shoulders curled forwards, arms locked straight ahead, as if pushing the steering wheel would actually make the car go faster.

'There he is!' I jabbed a finger at the windscreen.

The Fiesta disappeared into the underpass.

We were there less than thirty seconds later, the dual carriageway rumbling above us as O'Neil kept his foot to the floor. The siren echoed back from the concrete. Out into the daylight again. 'Almost there...'

Couldn't have been more than four seconds between us now.

The Fiesta jumped the lights where Nelson Road cuts across Canard Street, narrowly missing a woman on a bicycle, and right into the path of a bendy bus. It ploughed straight into the Fiesta, grabbing the front passenger-side and wrenching it three feet into the air, spinning the whole thing around and into a streetlight.

'Shite!' O'Neil stamped on the brakes. Hauled the wheel left, sending the back end squealing out across the cobbles. And everything slipped into slow motion. All the colours and shapes bright and sharp in the thin December light. A woman with a pushchair, mouth hanging open; a man up a ladder outside Waterstones, painting over graffiti; a little girl coming out of Greggs, frozen mid-pasty. A Transit van, the driver leaning on his horn as we slammed into him.

The bang was like a shotgun going off – cubes of safety glass exploded across the Vauxhall's interior. The car kicked up on my side, hurling me into the seatbelt as the airbags detonated. Filling the world with white and the stench of fireworks. Then down again, bouncing, safety glass pattering against my skin like rain. Nostrils filled with the smell of dust and spent airbag and petrol.

Everything clicked back to normal speed.

O'Neil hung forward against his seatbelt, arms dangling at his sides, blood seeping down his face from the gash in his forehead and broken nose. The Transit van's radiator blocked his window.

I fumbled with the seatbelt, a high-pitched ringing filling my head.

Out... I shoved open the door and stumbled into the road, holding onto the pool car's roof to stay upright.

Someone screamed.

The Fiesta was bent around the lamppost, the passenger side all buckled in. The lamppost hadn't fared much better. It was bent and twisted, the glass head dangling from a couple of wires.

Yellow and black dots swirled around me, dimming the street.

I blinked. Shook my head. Cracked my jaw. And the ringing dropped from deafening to just painful. Christ, what a mess...

Glass crunched under my shoes as I picked my way across the road.

Whimpering came from the back of the Fiesta – a pair of brown eyes stared out at me, wet nose pressed against the cracked hatchback glass. Then the driver's door creaked open and the bastard fell out onto the road: baggy blue tracksuit, trainers, big woolly hat pulled down over his ears. Couldn't see his face, just the back of his head.

'You! You're under arrest!'

And that was it. He was up on his feet like he was on springs, not looking back, arms and legs pumping as he sprinted towards the blue-and-white monolithic Travelodge on Greenwood Street.

No you bloody don't.

I lurched after him, dragging my handset out again. 'I need an ambulance to the junction of Canard, Nelson, and Greenwood. Officer hurt. And get the Fire Brigade too – there's a dog trapped in the wreckage.'

Moving faster, pulse thudding in my throat, roaring in my chest.

Around the corner of Greenwood. The train station loomed ahead – a big Victorian upturned boat in wrought iron and glass, with a blocky 1970s concrete portico stuck on the outside for taxis and smokers to loiter under.

I shoved my way through the main doors, into a din of people shouting and pounding music. The interior was one big open-plan space, with walkways arching over the tracks, connecting the half-dozen platforms. Light filtered down through the dirty glass roof.

Someone had set up a big tent-stage thing by the ticket office – the Castlewave FM logo emblazoned on either side with 'TURNING MILES INTO SMILES!!!' in the middle. A table at the front was draped in black, a pair of tossers standing behind it clapping their hands above their heads in time to the music, still holding their microphones.

A sea of bodies clapped back at them, shoulder to shoulder, crowded into the concourse.

'Ha, excelente mi amigos!' The music faded out. 'What's the total, Colin?'

'Well, Steve, we're all the way to Calais in France already, how cool is that?'

'Megatastic coolio!' Followed by a grating honk from an old-fashioned horn.

Where the hell was he?

No sign of anyone running, or of anyone getting up, swearing, shaking their fists because they'd been knocked out of the way.

'You're listening to Sensational Steve and Crrrrrrrazy Colin. It's five past one, and we're live, live, live from Oldcastle train station in Logansferry!'

The crowd roared out a cheer.

Had to be here somewhere...

'You're not wrong there, Steve, and we're here cycling all the way to the Philippines to raise money for the victims of Typhoon Nanmadol! Six thousand, six hundred and seventy-four miles!'

I pushed into the crowd. There – blue tracksuit. 'You! Don't you dare run!'

'That's a lot of miles, Colin.'

'It's a lot of miles, Steve!'

People complained as I shoved them out of the way and grabbed the guy by the arm. Spun him around… Only it wasn't a he, it was a she. A lumpy woman with a short haircut.

She wrenched my hand from her arm. Glared at me. 'What the hell is wrong with you? Get away from us, you freak!' She backed up a pace, baring her teeth. 'God, what happened to your *face*?'

Sodding hell. There was another woman in a blue tracksuit over by the automatic ticket machines. And a couple of men too – all wearing blue tracksuits with the Oldcastle Warriors logo stitched onto the left breast. Bloody local football team colours.

'So if you're listening at home, why not come on down to the train station and take a turn on one of our stationary bicycles? Help us turn miles into smiles for those poor Philippine people!'

'Guv?'

I turned.

Constable Rhona Massie had her hands in her pockets. Blue tracksuit top on over a sweat-stained red T-shirt and a pair of stonewashed jeans. The bags under her eyes were shiny with sweat, cheeks hot-pink against her long pale face. 'You OK? Jesus, what happened? You're bleeding…'

What? I put a hand against my forehead, it came away red. That's when it started to sting. And not just my head, a wave of aches and pains rolled up my right side, crashing at the base of my neck. Something sharp throbbed deep inside my left wrist. 'Where is he?'

'Right, time for another stellar tuuuuuune. I want to see everyone getting their funky thang on for Four Mechanical Mice and their "Anthem for a Shining Girl"!' A big wobbling piano chord blared out of the speakers.

Rhona grimaced, showing off a row of perfect white teeth. 'You look like you've been in a car bomb, or something!'

'A guy, ran in here a minute ago. Woolly hat, white trainers, blue tracksuit.'

76

She stepped closer and brushed a flurry of safety glass off my shoulder. 'We need to get you a doctor.' She turned. 'I NEED A DOCTOR OVER HERE! SOMEONE'S HURT!' Then back to me. 'You're probably in shock.' She held up a hand, the fingers splayed. 'How many fingers am I—'

'Get that out of my face.' I slapped her hand away. 'I want all the exits sealed. No one in or out. Get everyone in a blue tracksuit rounded up. And why aren't you in uniform?'

'She's incandescent, she's all ablaze...'

Rhona stared at me. 'It's my day off, I'm down raising money for the typhoon victims.'

'She is the sound of a million glass grenades...'

'Not tomorrow, Constable, *now*!'

'Yes, Guv.' She turned and ran off to the front entrance, waving her arms at a couple of guys in fluorescent yellow waistcoats with 'SECURITY' printed across the chest.

'She is the shattered dawn, tearing round the world...'

Knots of broken concrete rolled their way through my spine. Jagged bars of rusty iron jabbing through the base of my neck. My knees refused to hold my weight.

Bloody Rhona. Felt fine till she started rabbiting on about how battered I looked.

'She's dark and light and home tonight, cos she's the Shining Girl...'

I sank down, till my backside was on the cold tiled floor. Curled my throbbing wrist against my chest.

God, everything *ached*...

A circle of people formed around me, all of them staring. A couple had their mobile phones out, filming me sitting there, covered in broken glass and blood. Then someone shouldered their way through the cordon.

'Come on, give the man some room to breathe. Back up.'

'Who died and made you God?'

'I'm a nurse, you moron, now back up before I put you on your arse in front of all your friends.'

I blinked up at her. A familiar face: broad forehead, small eyes, hair in a ponytail – blonde wisps sticking to her shiny face. A T-shirt with sweatmarks under the arms and between her breasts, white shorts and trainers. Wide hips and thick legs. A 'Turn Miles Into Smiles!!!' towel draped around her neck.

She blinked back. 'Inspector Hutcheson? Bloody hell... What happened?'

'Henderson. Not Hutcheson.'

'Of course, yes, sorry.' She knelt on the ground beside me. Took my head in her hands and stared into my eyes. 'Are you experiencing any nausea? Dizziness? Ringing in the ears? Headache? Confusion?'

I grabbed her hand. 'Who are you?'

'OK, that's a yes on the confusion. It's Ruth. Ruth Laughlin? Laura Strachan's friend? You came to the flat after they found her, remember? Talked to all the nurses?'

'She's still alive.'

'Of course she is. They let her out of hospital two weeks ago.' Ruth shifted herself around, placed one hand on the back of my neck, pressed her other against my chest. 'Come on, let's get you lying down... There we go. You know, you're lucky I was here. Concussion can be very serious.'

A distorted voice burbled from the station's loudspeakers. The words echoing back and forth until they were little more than a smear of syllables fighting against the song. '... *the train now departing from platform six is the one seventeen to Edinburgh Waverley...*'

For God's sake – why didn't Rhona tell them to cancel the trains? Fifteen minutes from now he could be in Arbroath. Dundee in twenty-five.

Not too late – call Control and get patrol cars to the nearest station. Have the bastard picked up right off the train...

'Inspector Henderson?'

Bloody fingers wouldn't work, Airwave handset was all slippery...

The wail of sirens cut through the end of the announcement. That would be the backup I called for. Late as always.

'Hello?'

Yellow and black dots bloomed in the siren's wake, growing, spreading, blanking out the glass ceiling behind Ruth Laughlin's head as she frowned down at me. A halo of darkness.

'Inspector Henderson? Can you hear me? I want you to squeeze my hand as hard as you can … Inspector Henderson? Hello?'

Monday

9

I eased Alice's door closed and crossed the corridor to my own room. It was small, but functional, just big enough for the double bed against one wall, the chest of drawers, and wardrobe. A pair of dark-blue curtains that still had the same creases as the ones in the lounge. A cheap-looking alarm-clock radio on the floor beside the bed, glowing 00:15 at me.

My cell was bigger than this.

An old-fashioned brass key sat on top of the duvet, with a cardboard tag attached to it by a red ribbon. Spidery handwriting: 'THOUGHT THIS MIGHT COME IN HANDY'.

Ah...

I turned. There was a lock fitted to the bedroom door, specks of sawdust dandruffing the floorboards underneath it along with a few quavers of shaved wood. The key slipped right in, and when I turned it, the bolt slid home with a clack.

After two years inside, it was strange how comforting that sound was. Especially combined with the muffled rattle of Shifty's snores coming through the wall.

The laptop went on the bed, while I stripped, folded all my clothes, and placed them in the chest of drawers. Old habits.

I took out my shiny new mobile phone and thumbed in the number on Shifty's Post-it note. It rang, and rang, and rang...

Crossed to the window, eased one side of the curtains open a couple of inches. Just concrete, gloom, and streetlights. Someone crept their way across the garden opposite with a torch. Good luck finding anything worth stealing around here.

Then a click, and a muzzy voice crackled from the earpiece. *'Hello? Hello, who's this?'*

'You Alec?'

Some rustling, a hissing noise, then a clunk. *'Do you have any idea what time it is?'*

'I need a piece. Tomorrow. Semiauto—'

'There must be some mistake. I offer spiritual guidance to wayward souls. Are you a wayward soul in need of guidance?'

Ah. Right. Cautious. Probably a good trait in a gun dealer. 'What do *you* think?'

'I think... I think that you're on a dangerous path. That your life hasn't turned out the way you hoped. That darkness surrounds you.'

Why the hell else would I need a gun? 'So, what now?'

'I think you should come see me. We can meditate on your predic-ament. Drink some herbal tea. Find a core of peace within you.' A muffled yawn. *'Now, do you have a pen and paper?'*

I stuck Shifty's Post-it to the windowpane. Went back to the wardrobe and pulled a pen from my jacket pocket. 'Go.'

'Thirteen Slater Crescent, Blackwall Hill, OC12 3PX.'

'When?'

'I shall be available for spiritual guidance between the hours of nine and five tomorrow. Well, I might head out to the shops around lunchtime, but other than that...'

'OK: tomorrow.'

'Peace be on you.' And he was gone.

A rogue firework screamed up into the sky from a couple of streets over, booming and crackling in a baleful eye of scarlet.

Peace wasn't exactly what I had in mind.

I let the curtains fall closed, slipped in beneath the duvet and powered up the laptop. Propped it up on my chest and settled back to watch the rest of *Wrapped in Darkness*.

Laura Strachan picks her way along the High Street, ignoring the olde worlde charms of the surrounding buildings – now converted into charity shops, bookies, and places you could get a payday loan or pawn your jewellery. *'What happened to me that night, and over the next couple of days … it's slippery – difficult to hold onto. Like… Like it never really happened to me. Like it was happening to someone else, in a movie. All larger than life and shiny and fake. Does that make sense?'*

Which might explain Baywatch Steve and the cheesy dialogue.

'I wake up some mornings and I can almost taste the operating room. The disinfectant, the metal… And then it fades, and I'm left with this feeling like something's crushing my chest.'

Then the scene shifts to the briefing room at Oldcastle Force Headquarters – the old one with the sagging ceiling tiles and sticky carpet. Before the refit. Journalists pack the seats, cameras, microphones and Dictaphones bristling towards the four men sitting behind the table at the front. Len's at one end – bald even then – in his ancient double-breasted black suit. Next to him is the Media Liaison officer, ramrod-straight and sweating. And next to him…

Something popped deep inside my ribcage, letting out a little grunt of pain.

Dr Henry Forrester stares out of the laptop screen at me. He's got more hair than he did at the end. More life about him. Before his cheeks sunk and the wrinkles stopped looking distinguished and started looking haggard. Before the guilt and the grief and the whisky hollowed him out.

'Henry. You silly, silly bastard…'

The man sitting next to Henry – the last person on the table – can't be much older than twenty-four. Slope-shouldered, a fringe of curly brown hair hanging over his eyes, a nimbus of it fluffing out around his head, coiling over the shoulders of a grey suit, shirt, and tie. Get a sensible haircut and he would be invisible.

A voice-over talks above the muted babble of questions and answers. *'But while Laura was struggling to come to terms with the horrific events that had left her stricken with nightmares and scar tissue, the operation to catch the Inside Man faced struggles of its own.'*

Cheesy, but correct.

A reporter sticks his hand up. *'Detective Superintendent Murray, is it true you're bringing in a psychic to help kick the investigation back to life?'*

Someone else's voice cuts in before Len can answer. *'Think they'll be able to contact your career?'*

Laughter. Swiftly brought to a halt as Len hammers his fist down on the table. *'Four women are dead. Three others will be scarred for life. Exactly* what *about that do you find funny?'*

Silence.

Len jabs a finger at the crowd. *'Any more of that and I won't just clear the room, I'll have you all barred. Are we clear?'*

No one speaks.

The footage jumps forward, and someone else is having a go. *'Is it true you almost caught him, but let him get away?'*

Len's face darkens. *'No one "let him get away". An officer was forced to abandon chase due to serious injuries sustained during the pursuit. If I see* anything *in print suggesting we "let the Inside Man go", I will come down on you like the wrath of God.'*

The scene cuts to wobbly mobile-phone footage of a large man slumped to his knees on a tiled floor, surrounded by a cordon of legs and mobile phones. Blood makes a red smear down the left side of his face, oozing out of gashes in his scalp and forehead, darkening his collar and suit jacket. Then a woman pushes into shot and takes his face in her hands. Lowers him down to the ground. Folds a tracksuit top and puts it under his head. Makes him comfortable.

Whoever's doing the voice-over says something, but it's just noise…

Did I really look that awful? No wonder Rhona wanted to call an ambulance.

I rewound a bit.

'... *down on you like the wrath of God.*'

It's not surprising I couldn't stay upright – it looks like someone's taken a baseball bat coated in broken glass to my head. Then Ruth Laughlin appears in her shorts and T-shirt and makes me lie down before I *fall* down.

Poor bloody woman. If I hadn't let him get away...

'*Details are thin on the ground about what actually happened that day in Oldcastle, but what we do know is a high-speed chase across the city ended in a near fatal collision. Detective Inspector Ash Henderson pursued the Inside Man into the train station, but collapsed from his injuires and was rushed to Castle Hill Infirmary suffering from concussion, two cracked ribs, a broken wrist, and whiplash. The irony is that the woman seen helping him is Ruth Laughlin, who went on to become the Inside Man's final victim.*'

Because I didn't stop him.

The mobile-phone footage is replaced by something slightly more professional with the Oldcastle Fire Brigade ident in the top-left corner. One team's cutting the driver's door off the battered pool car, while the other is spraying water on the burning Fiesta. '*The driver of the unmarked car, Police Constable O'Neil, suffered a broken arm and a fractured skull.*'

There's no mention of what happened to the dog in the Fiesta's boot.

Another jump and we're back at the media briefing. Another question. Another angry answer from Len.

And then the voice-over oils in over the top: '*With the investigation floundering, they went public with their psychological profile...*'

The guy with the grey suit and perm looks at Henry. Henry nods.

A caption appears on the bottom of the screen: 'Dr Fred Docherty – Forensic Psychologist'.

Dr Docherty clears his throat. 'Thank you.' He's obviously trying to sound posh, but those two words are carved in the sandstone of a Glaswegian tenement. *'We believe the person responsible for these crimes is in his late twenties, probably an unskilled worker who's got difficulty holding down a job. He was very close to his mother, who's probably died recently. His hatred of women stems from her smothering influence. He'll be dishevelled in his appearance, and most likely has a history of mental illness, so we expect him to have been through police custody at some point in his life.'*

Which didn't exactly narrow the pool. Not in Oldcastle.

The rest of the DVD was a bit of a let-down. The police can't catch the Inside Man, blah, blah, blah. The Crown Office refuse to release the first four victims' bodies, so the relatives have to have a symbolic burial and wait for the investigation to be finalized.

Poor sods were probably still waiting.

Dr Docherty reappears for a follow-up segment on Laura Strachan. He's fidgeting in a big leather armchair, eyes flicking to a spot just left of the camera, as if he's looking for approval from whoever's standing there. His Glaswegian burr is slightly less pronounced than it was at the press conference. He's obviously been practising. *'Of course, it was an intensely traumatic experience for Laura. We have weekly sessions exploring her feelings and helping her come to terms with what happened. It's a long path to wellness, but she's getting better.'*

An off-camera voice: *'And do you think she'll ever be normal again?'*

Dr Fred Docherty goes still in his seat. *'Normal is a relative concept that has no value in psychology. We're all individuals – there's no such thing as "normal". What we're trying to do here is help Laura get back to a state that's normal for her.'*

'And what about Marie Jordan?'

His fingers pick at the seam of his trousers. *'Sadly, Marie isn't responding quite as well. As I said, everyone's different, we all cope differently.'*

'She's been committed to a secure psychiatric facility, hasn't she? She's on suicide watch.'

'The human mind is a complicated animal, you can't just...' He looks down, into his lap. Stills his hands. 'She's getting the care she needs. As is Ruth Laughlin.'

Cut to CCTV footage of a woman collapsing in a supermarket's fruit-and-veg section, arms wrapped around her head, rocking back and forth while people steer their trolleys around her, not making eye contact.

Voice-over: 'Unable to cope with the nightmares and anxiety attacks following her abduction, Ruth Laughlin had a nervous breakdown in the Castleview Asda and is currently receiving treatment at the same facility as Marie.'

And the Inside Man is still at large.

Not exactly an upbeat ending.

Welcome to the real world.

10

'... and that was Mister Bones with "Snow Loves A Winter". You're listening to Jane Forbes, holding the fort till Sensational Steve kicks off the Breakfast Drive-Time Bonanza at seven. Stick around for that, it's going to be ... awesome!'

I blinked at the ceiling. It wasn't the right shape, the light was all wrong. Why the hell was...

A breath shuddered its way out of my chest and the thumping in my ears faded, slowed. Another breath.

Right. Not in a cell any more.

'We've got the news and weather coming up – spoiler alert, it's going to be a wet one – but first here's Halfhead, with their Christmas single "Sex, Violence, Lies, and Darkness"...' The sound of distorted piano and mournful guitars oozed out of the radio alarm clock's speakers.

The lead singer's voice was like barbed wire dipped in molasses. 'Bones in the garden, they sing like an angel...'

I rolled over and checked: quarter past six. What was the point of getting out of prison if you couldn't even have a lie-in? Bloody Jacobson.

'The shadows are sharp and they burn deep inside...'

Morning prayers at Force Headquarters. That was going to be fun. Perhaps I'd get lucky and not have to break anyone's jaw...?

Keep it calm today. Nothing rash. No lashing out. Nothing that could get me sent back to prison before Mrs Kerrigan could meet with that unfortunate accident.

'Her body is cold, her voice hard and painful...'

No hitting anyone. Eyes on the prize.

Come on, Ash. Up.

In a minute.

I spread out beneath the duvet, taking up the whole double bed. Just because I could.

'A knife-blade of bitterness, spite, and hurt pride...'

Then the pressure in my bladder had to go and spoil everything. Groaning, I levered myself up, swung my legs out of bed, sighed. Rolled my right foot in small circles from the ankle. One way, then the other. Flexing the toes. Making little blades of hot iron grate along the bones – scraping away beneath the puckered knot of scar tissue the bullet left. A metaphor for my whole bloody life, right there.

'Sex, lies, and violence, a love filled with sharpness...'

No point putting it off any longer. Up.

I limped over to the chest of drawers.

'Stoking the fires to stave off the darkness...'

A brief search turned up a couple of big towels in the third drawer. I wrapped one around my waist, grabbed my cane, then unlocked the bedroom door as the song headed into an instrumental break. All minor chords and misery.

The sound of someone murdering an old Stereophonics tune rattled down the corridor, with a boiling kettle as backup. Shifty poked his head out of the living room and grinned at me. His eyes were all shiny and bright, despite the fact he'd put away enough champagne and whisky last night to fill a bathtub. He'd even shaved. 'Hope you're hungry, we've got enough here to feed a family of six. Breakfast on the table in five, whether you're there or not.' And then he was gone again.

'Morning, Shifty.' I tried the bathroom door handle. Locked.

91

Alice's voice came from inside, the words all muffled and rounded as if she had her mouth full. 'Hold on...' Then some spitting and a running tap. The bathroom door opened and there she was, wearing a fluffy bathrobe, a towel wrapped around her head. A cloud of orange-scented steam billowed out behind her. 'Are you not dressed yet, only we've got the morning briefing at seven and it's—'

'What happened to the hangover?'

'Coffee. Coffee's great it really is and it's just, like, *pow* first thing in the morning and I think I got up in the middle of the night to drink some water, I was having the strangest dream and I was in a car crash and there was a dog and I'm chasing someone into the train station only it turned into a rock concert and there was a woman in a blue tracksuit and everyone was all sweaty, isn't that weird?' She squeezed past, and opened the door to her room. Froze on the threshold. A crease formed between her eyebrows. 'Maybe it was the pizza, probably shouldn't eat a *quattro formaggio* that close to bedtime, only it wasn't really bedtime was it, it was a slightly late dinner, and I *like* cheese, don't you, it's—'

'OK.' I held up a hand. 'No more coffee for you.'

'But I like coffee, it's the best, and Dave brought this little metal teapot thing with him that you put on the cooker and coffee goes in one end and water in the bottom and you get great espresso—'

'Shifty says breakfast's in five minutes.'

'Oh, right, better get dressed and really you should try his espresso it's terrific, it—'

I slipped into the steamy bathroom and locked the door behind me.

Alice leaned in close, her voice cranked right down to a whisper. 'So it wasn't a dream?'

The briefing room must have been given a coat of paint recently, the cloying chemical smell still coiling out of the walls.

92

Uniform and plainclothes had arranged themselves in a semi-circle of creaky plastic chairs around the table at the front of the room, the distance between them marking out the individual tribes. Front left: the men and women who'd have to go out and patrol the streets. Front right: the boys and girls from the Specialist Crime Division, looking prickly in their sharp suits. Behind them: Oldcastle CID, looking like a riot in a charity shop. Everyone with their pens out and notebooks at the ready.

And at the rear of the room: Jacobson's Lateral Investigative and Review Unit, all in a line: Jacobson, PC Cooper, Professor Huntly, Dr Constantine, and Alice. I'd grabbed the seat next to her, on the outside. Right leg stretched out, walking stick hanging on the back of the chair in front as the duty sergeant monotoned his way through the day-to-day assignments.

'... car thefts up fifteen percent in that area, so keep your eyes peeled. Next, shoplifting...'

I shifted in my seat. 'Of course it wasn't a dream, you wanted a bedtime story so I told you one.'

Alice looked up at me. 'You did? That's so sweet.'

'About how the Inside Man got away.'

'Oh.' The smile slipped a bit. 'Still, it's the thought that counts, isn't it. So you really did round up all the people in blue tracksuits?'

I nodded. 'Rhona got all nine of them. Two hours earlier and there would've been dozens – the whole sodding football team came down to ride on the bikes. The Super checked everyone's stories and alibis. Nothing.'

She glanced at the front of the room.

The duty sergeant was still droning on: '... break-in at the halls of residence on Hudson Street...'

'What about the train to Edinburgh?'

'Just missed it at Arbroath, but they were waiting for it at Carnoustie. No one in a blue tracksuit. *But* the in-carriage security camera caught someone matching the description getting off at the first stop.'

'... to remember, that just because they're students it doesn't mean you can treat them, and I quote, "like workshy sponging layabouts". Fitzgerald, I'm looking at you...'

'It was him, wasn't it?'

'We put out an appeal, got an ID, and did a dawn raid. Turned out it was a religious education teacher up to do the charity cycle.'

'Oh.'

Professor Huntly leaned over, glowered past Dr Constantine, teeth bared around a hissing whisper. 'Will you two shut up?'

'... Charlie went missing sometime between half eleven last night and six this morning. He's only five, so keep your eyes peeled. He's run away twice before, but his mum's still frantic. Best efforts, people.'

I stared back at Huntly until he licked his lips and looked away. Sat back in his seat.

Should think so too.

I leaned into Alice again. 'But we searched his house anyway. Came up with a stash of child pornography and an unlicensed firearm. I think he's on life-support now – someone cracked his head open on a washing machine in the prison laundry.'

'... but not least: lookout request for one Eddie Barron. He's got form for GBH and assault with a deadly, so don't say I never warned you...'

On the other side of Alice, Dr Constantine sat up. 'Oh-ho, here we go.'

At the front of the room, the duty sergeant brought things to a close. 'Right, if you're not on Operation Tigerbalm, you're excused.' He held up a sheet of paper with 'HAVE YOU SEEN CHARLIE?' in big letters above a photo of a wee dark-haired kid – sticky-out ears, a squint smile, and a face full of freckles. 'Pick up one of these, then get your backsides out there and catch some villains.'

Half the room shuffled out, Uniform and CID moaning

about being told to sod off, bragging about their weekends, or muttering dark curses about having to support Aberdeen or Dundee now the Warriors were gone. The duty sergeant marched after them, arms full of paperwork.

Detective Superintendent Ness took the floor. 'Someone get the lights.'

A couple of clicks and gloom settled into the room. Then Ness pointed a remote at the projector mounted on the ceiling, and two photos appeared on the screen behind her. The one on the left was a painfully pale woman on the beach at Aberdeen, grinning away in a green bikini and goose pimples. The other was the same woman, curled on her side in a thicket of brambles. Her white nightgown had got caught up on their barbed-wire coils – riding up to show off the purple slash across her belly. The wound's sides held together with crude black stitches over the distended skin.

'Doreen Appleton, twenty-two, the Inside Man's first victim. Nurse at Castle Hill Infirmary.'

Ness jabbed the remote again. Doreen Appleton was replaced by a happy brunette in a wedding dress, and the same woman lying flat on her back in a lay-by. She was dressed in a similar white nightdress to the first victim, the fabric stained with blood all across her swollen abdomen. 'Tara McNab, twenty-four. Victim number two. Nurse at Castle Hill Infirmary. Someone called nine-nine-nine from a public phonebox a mile from where she was found...'

Click, then a hissing old-fashioned audio-tape noise, and a man's voice filled the room, clipped and professional. '*Emergency Services, which service do you require?*'

The woman who answered sounded as if she'd been caught in the middle of a two-day bender, the words thick and slurred. Distorted. '*A woman's been ... been dumped in a lay-by, one ... one point three miles south of Shortstaine Garden Centre on the Brechin Road. She's...*' A small catch in her voice, as if she was holding back a sob. '*She's not moving. If you ... hurry, you can save her. She's, very weak, possible internal bleeding… Oh God… Blood type: B-positive. Hurry, please…'*

'Hello? Can you tell me your name? Hello?'

Silence.

'Sodding hell.' A scrunching noise, as if the controller had put a hand over the microphone on the headset, muffling his voice. *'Garry? You won't believe what I've just—'*

Ness held the remote up. 'Ambulance crew arrived fifteen minutes later, but she was dead when they got there. Audio analysis showed that the voice on the nine-nine-nine call was hers.'

One of the Specialist Crime Division team stuck his hand up. 'She made the call herself?'

There was a pause, then Ness pulled her brows down, bit her lips together. Closed her eyes for a moment. 'Does anyone want to take that?'

Professor Huntly laughed. 'How, *exactly*, do you imagine a woman with extensive blood loss and internal trauma managed to make a call from a public phone box, then walk a mile to the bus stop where she was found? It was obviously taped prior to her being dumped there. He drugs them, then makes them record their own SOS before he cuts them open.'

The guy from SCD put his hand down. Cleared his throat. Fidgeted. 'Perfectly valid question…'

Ness pointed at the photo of Tara's body. 'Original investigation tracked down the nightdresses: all from a stall down at Heading Hollows Market. Three for a fiver. The stallholder had no idea who he'd sold them to or when.'

She pressed the remote and victim number two was replaced by a sheet of paper from a yellow legal pad. Blue ink scrawled along the lines, the handwriting barely legible. 'Two days after Tara McNab's body turned up, this letter was delivered to Michael Slosser at the *Castle News and Post*. In it the writer complains about the papers calling him "the Caledonian Ripper", says there'll be more bodies to come, claims the police

96

are powerless to stop him, and signs off as "the Inside Man".'
She raised the remote again. 'Next.'

Victim three appeared. Her caramel skin was thick with bruises across one side, her slack face staring up from a ditch, both arms up above her head, one leg twisted to the side. She'd been dressed in another white nightdress, torn on one side and drenched almost black with blood. In the other photo she was frozen at what looked like a birthday party, laughing, her red silk dress swung out as she danced. 'Holly Drummond, twenty-six. Nurse at Castle Hill Infirmary. Emergency Services got the pre-recorded nine-nine-nine call at half-two in the morning. Voice was the victim's. She was pronounced dead at the scene.'

Holly Drummond was replaced on the screen by another sheet from a legal pad. 'This arrived at the paper the day we found her body. He's getting into his stride now: telling us all about how powerful and clever he is, and how we'll never catch him. From here on, all the letters are much the same.'

Victim four was a large woman in a strapless dress and mortarboard. Then face down at the bottom of a railway culvert, her nightdress scrunched up around her waist, pale buttocks on show. Skin flecked with green and black. 'Natalie May, twenty-two. Nurse at Castle Hill Infirmary. No call this time. She was found by a railway maintenance team who were out replacing a section of cabling.'

Click, and another letter filled the screen. 'It complains that she was, and I quote, "not pure enough to receive his bounty".'

Pause.

The screen went black. 'And then we got lucky.'

Laura Strachan's broad smiling face appeared, freckles glowing on her nose and cheeks, a Ferris wheel in the background. The other photo was her being lifted into the back of an ambulance, face slack and waxy, freckles partially obscured by an oxygen mask.

Ness pointed at the picture. 'Our first survivor. Call was made from a public phone in Blackwall Hill. They had to start her heart twice on the way to the hospital and she came this close,' Ness pinched two fingers together, 'to bleeding out, but they saved her.'

Ness clicked the remote again and Marie Jordan's face filled half of the screen. On the other side she lay in a hospital bed, wires and tubes connecting her to about half-a-dozen bits of machinery. 'Marie Jordan, twenty-three, nurse. Another pre-recorded call. Found wrapped in a sheet just off the road in Moncuir Wood. There was a bit of brain damage caused by hypoxia and blood-loss, but she lived. The letter compliments her on being a "good girl".'

Pause.

'Final victim.' Click. And there was Ruth Laughlin, sitting on a stationary bicycle in her shorts and sweaty T-shirt, both hands up as if she was crossing the finishing line. A circle of people cheered in the background, beneath a 'Turning Miles Into Smiles!!!' banner. Must have been taken the day she took care of me.

The day I let the Inside Man get away.

'Ruth Laughlin, twenty-five, paediatric nurse. No call this time because he didn't make it past the initial incisions. Far as we can tell he was disturbed during the operation, ran off and left her to die.'

All because she stopped to help me.

11

'Settle down.' Ness pointed off to the side. 'Dr Docherty?'

'Thank you, Detective Superintendent.' Fred Docherty had changed his look a bit since the initial investigation. The concrete-coloured suit was gone, as was the curly hair. Now he sported a sharp black Armani-looking number with a red shirt and white tie, his hair short and straight, swept back from his forehead. The boyish looks and nervous voice had been replaced by a strong jaw and stainless-steel gaze. No trace of a Glaswegian accent.

He paused, letting everyone get a good look at him.

Alice grabbed my hand and squeezed. 'This is so exciting...'

'Ladies and gentlemen, let us consider Unsub-Fifteen. He's clearly... Yes, Inspector?'

Shifty had his hand up. 'Aye, who's "Unsub-Fifteen" when he's at home?'

'An excellent question. "Unsub" means "Unknown Subject" and "Fifteen" differentiates him from the fourteen other active homicide investigations currently underway in Oldcastle. I think it's unwise to give the target of an investigation like this what might be considered a,' Docherty stuck his fingers in the air and mimed quote marks, '"cool nickname". It can contribute to their perception of themselves as something apart from, and *above*, the norm. Something to live up to. And, as we've yet to confirm a connection between Unsub-Fifteen and the offender known as the Inside Man, I want us to clear our heads of any preconceptions about what's going on here.' A smile. Bright, but not cheesy or sarcastic-looking. 'Does that help?'

Shifty shrugged.

'Good. Now, having reviewed the evidence, I'm pegging Unsub-Fifteen as being in his mid-to-late thirties. Chances are he's had a string of mediocre jobs and never really excelled at anything. He'll have been in your cells before, probably more than once and probably for petty crimes. A little wilful fire-raising, perhaps vandalism. *Possibly* cruelty to animals. Certainly we should be checking out anyone with a history of mental illness.'

Docherty folded his arms and tilted his head to the side, eyes narrowed. As if all this was just coming to him as he spoke. 'He's come from a close family – that's a definite – but chances are that he's all alone now. His mother probably abused him emotionally rather than physically, belittled him, criticized him, controlled every aspect of his life. That's the source of his rage against women. When we find him, everyone will be surprised that he's been capable of this kind of horrendous act. And they'll describe him as introverted, someone who kept himself to himself and never caused a fuss.'

Docherty nodded towards a short stack of paper on the table at the front. 'I've made up a list of the kind of red-flags you should be looking for, and a couple of follow-up questions you can ask to narrow the field.' The smile was back. 'And speaking of questions: does anyone have any?'

Sitting near the front, a hand appeared above the rows of heads. The voice that went with it was flat, and nasal, and instantly recognizable: Rhona. 'How come he never sent a letter after Doreen Appleton?'

100

'Well, that's actually more about the offender known as "the Inside Man" than Unsub-Fifteen, but it's still valid. He didn't send a letter because she was a trial run, a warm-up. She doesn't count. He hasn't *quite* worked out what it is he wants yet. So, he dumps her body, doesn't use the nine-nine-nine call he forced her to record, and moves on to Tara McNab. That's when it really begins.' Dr Docherty nodded, agreeing with himself. 'Anyone else? Don't be shy.'

Alice's hand shot up, fingers splayed, waving slightly. 'Me, me!'

'Yes…? I'm sorry, I don't know your name.'

'Alice McDonald. First: huge fan, I thought you were *great* in that documentary about the Tayside Butcher.' She still had her hand up.

Docherty preened. 'Oh, you saw that. Great. Thanks. So, what's your question … erm … Alice?'

'You say he's attacking women as sublimated revenge against an emotionally manipulative mother figure, but that doesn't explain the significance of the dolls, does it?'

'Well, that's another good question, you see—'

'By stitching the dolls into their abdomens, the Inside Man is making them pregnant, isn't he? *Literally* putting a baby into their tummies…' She wrapped one arm around her middle, lowered her hand and twisted the fingers through her hair. 'Of course then he muddies the water by dressing them in white nightgowns which are *clearly* symbolic of innocence and virginity, but if this is revenge against an unloving mother, why is he trying to impregnate her? I mean I'm not saying it doesn't happen, I helped Northern Constabulary catch someone who did just that, then stabbed her sixty-four times in the throat, her head nearly came off when they tried to load her into the body-bag, the pictures were really quite disturbing.'

'I see.' Docherty's smile chilled a good five degrees. 'So in your *opinion* my profile is wrong?'

Alice tilted her head to one side, mirroring his. 'I didn't say it was wrong, I just don't think it's entirely right.'

On the other side of Alice, Dr Constantine's voice was barely audible. 'Fight, fight, fight, fight...'

Docherty's jaw worked from side to side, chewing on something bitter.

'No offence.' Alice pressed a hand against her chest. 'Like I said, big fan. *Huge.*'

Ness stood. 'Perhaps it would be more productive if Dr Docherty and...' she checked her notes, 'Dr McDonald could take this discussion offline and report back to their team leaders with the outcome. In the meantime: I find myself having to remind you all that there is a *strict* media blackout in force. The Powers That Be are *not* happy someone broke the moratorium and told the press about Claire Young. I don't care who you are, or who you report to, the only information that gets out of this investigation is in the official press briefings. Are we all clear on that?'

Some shuffling from the crowd.

Superintendent Knight stood, wearing his dress uniform at half seven in the morning, as if that was going to impress anyone. 'On that note, one of my team from the Specialist Crime Division, DI Foot, will be inviting certain of you to assist him in uncovering who was responsible for feeding details to the *Daily Record* yesterday. I expect honesty and integrity. And if I don't get it there – will – be – trouble.'

Ness nodded. 'Right, that's it, people. Individual team meetings commence in five. Grab a cigarette or a cup of coffee if you can. It's going to be a long day.'

'... looking good, my man.' DS Brigstock patted me on the back, grinning with his mouth open, cheeks and forehead stippled with impact-crater acne scars. 'Don't he look good, Rhona?'

Rhona smiled at me, exposing a mouth full of thick grey teeth. 'Great to have you back, Guv.'

Half of Ness's Major Investigation Team had stayed behind, while their SCD rivals bustled out to cram in a quick cigarette or get something from the vending machines.

Jacobson's team had drifted apart: PC Cooper off running an errand; Dr Constantine on the phone in the corner; while Huntly was having what looked like a very intense conversation with a tall thin man in a grey suit – one of Superintendent Knight's SCD lot. The discussion all big arm gestures and hissing whispers.

Rhona stuck her hands in her pockets, hunched her shoulders. 'Listen, Guv, I was thinking of throwing a wee party, you know to celebrate? And—'

'I'm not sure if we'll have time, will we, Ash?' Alice stepped in close, slipped her arm through mine, and smiled at Rhona. 'I'm really glad I was able to arrange his release, I mean you wouldn't believe the hoops I had to jump through at the prison, but there was no way I was going to let him rot away in that place.' The smile got sharper. 'That would've been horrible, wouldn't it?'

Rhona squared her shoulders. 'We did our best.'

'Yes, I know. Still, never mind, he's out now.'

Not this *again*…

'I didn't see *you* visiting him every week.'

Alice raised her eyebrows. 'Didn't you? Well, they don't give members of the public access to the official—'

A jagged Aberdonian accent cut across the room. 'DS Massie, Brigstock: you heard the Super. Team meeting starts at eight, s*harp*.' It didn't look as if Smith's people skills had improved any in the last two years. He made a big show of pulling back the sleeve of his grey Markie's suit and checking his watch. Wrinkles stood out in thick stripes across his forehead. Big nose twitching. Close-cropped hair. A chin so small it was barely there.

Brigstock's face curdled for a second, then his voice dropped to a whisper. 'Why did they have to make the sheep-shagging bastard a DI?' Then louder: 'Yes, Guv.'

'*Now*, Sergeants.'

Rhona didn't move. Just stood there staring at Alice. 'Yes, Guv.' Then she turned her back. 'Come on, Brigstock. And the rest of you – backsides in gear. You heard DI Smith!' She shepherded the rest of the team towards the front of the room, where Ness was fiddling with her remote again.

Smith stared at us, then marched over, back straight, shoulders back. 'Do I need to remind you, *Mr* Henderson, that you're no longer a serving police officer? You have no powers in Oldcastle, or anywhere else. And if I hear you're throwing your weight around, I'll come down on you like a ton of broken glass. Are we clear?'

I took a step closer, shutting down the gap till we were almost touching. 'You think you're a big man because they made you a DI, don't you? Think that makes you invulnerable. Well, that massive nose of yours will break just as easily as a detective sergeant's.'

He took a step back. 'Threatening a police officer is a criminal offence and—'

'DI Smith?' Ness's voice came from the front. 'We're ready to start.' She pressed a button and the screen behind her filled with a map of Oldcastle, a red circle marking a patch of ground behind Blackwall Hill. She nodded at Jacobson. 'Simon, your team's welcome to join us if you like?'

'I appreciate the offer, Elizabeth, but there's a couple of things that need our urgent attention.' He flicked his arm out and peered at his watch. 'And if we don't get a shift on, we're going to be late.'

'Can't feel my toes...' Dr Constantine stomped her feet. She had her scarf wrapped around her neck and mouth, woolly hat pulled down over her ears, Parka coat zipped up to her chin.

Jacobson leaned against the waist-high wall, hands in the pockets of his brown leather jacket, breath streaming out in a line of fog. 'It's good for you. Builds character.'

Kings Park stretched away on both sides of us, the grass crisp with frost. Blue shadows reached down from the granite wedge of Castle Hill, the ruined battlements jagged against the pale sky. A blade of sunlight pierced the gloom – serrated around the edges where trees gouged it – making the Kings River sparkle.

The smell of onions frying in grease oozed through the cold air, thick and sweet and dark, spreading out from the burger van at the edge of the car park. PC Cooper had almost made it to the front of the queue.

Huntly stood with his back to the rest of us, staring out across the river, arms folded, camelhair coat wrapped around him, polished brogues sticking out at ten-to-two. Sulking.

Jacobson turned to Alice. 'Well? What do you make of our Dr Docherty?'

'He's a lot shorter than he is on TV.' She wrapped one padded arm around her padded waist, the other hand fiddling with her hair where it poked out from the hood of her Arctic jacket. 'On the basis of what we know so far, it's reasonable to be cautious and say this *might* not be the Inside Man. The papers are full of Laura Strachan's impending "Miracle Birth" – maybe someone saw that and it sparked a fire inside them, I mean if you're sitting at home full of rage and impotence and looking for some way to vent everything on a world that hates you, and then you see all this stuff about the Inside Man and maybe you think: that's what I'll do, I'll be just like him only better, and it'll make the angry things in my head leave me alone for a while...'

She turned, eyes narrowed, mouth pinched. 'But it's not going to work because this isn't *my* fantasy, this is someone else's, but until I try I don't know what I really want, and maybe there's something about it that makes me feel powerful and in control and aroused for the first time in years and I take that one thing and I relive it over and over in my mind till it's polished sharp, and I go out and I do it again, only

105

properly this time.' She let go of her hair, looked up at me. 'I mean, if it was me, that's what I'd do.'

I nodded. 'So you're saying it isn't him?'

'That depends on the next body. If it's someone else the MO will diverge as he experiments, trying to find his personal groove. If it stays consistent it's *probably* him.' She turned to Jacobson. 'At the press conference Detective Superintendent Ness wouldn't answer the question: *did* he send a letter about Claire Young?'

'Well ... yesterday was Sunday, so if he posted it after he killed her, it wouldn't get collected till today, and it won't be delivered till tomorrow. If we're lucky, we'll find out before the paper prints it.'

Alice shuffled closer. 'Superintendent, can I speak to the original survivors and review the victimology reports? I want to look at the Inside Man letters too. The photocopies in the case file are barely readable. I'll need access to the originals.'

He patted her on the shoulder. 'For you, anything. And please, call me Bear.'

Yeah, I probably shouldn't have laughed. 'Seriously? Thought that was meant to be a joke. You want us to call you "Bear"?'

'Dr McDonald has pleased me by putting that jumped-up publicity-hungry TV tart in his place this morning. Bernard?'

Professor Huntly kept his gaze on the water, still sulking.

'You made the boy from SCD who asked about the phone call look like a moron. So you're forgiven for yesterday.'

Huntly raised one shoulder, stared at his shoes. 'Thank you, Bear.'

Jacobson poked me in the chest. 'So far all you've done is limp about, taking up space and eating Sheila's pizza. *You* can call me, "Sir", "Guv", or "Super".'

One step forward and I was inches from his nose, looming. 'How about I call you—'

'Ash...' Alice tugged at my sleeve. 'Remember what we talked about? Going to see the deposition scene? I think we

106

should really go now, don't you, I mean there's a lot to get through today and we all want to do our best for the investigation so we can stay out of prison, don't we? Please?'

And miss a chance to rip the little git's face off and...

Don't be so bloody *stupid*.

Blink. Step back. Deep breath. 'Right.' I forced a smile into place and patted Jacobson on the shoulder. 'Sorry, still getting used to not being inside. You know.'

Jacobson tilted his head back, grinning up at me. 'And you can take Bernard with you. He doesn't drive.'

Huntly cleared his throat. 'Can we at least wait for my sausage sandwich?'

'... quite ridiculous, *surely* it's appropriate to observe a decent period of mourning.' Sitting in the back seat, Huntly took another bite of his sausage buttie, tomato sauce oozing out of the roll and onto his fingers. He chewed, with his mouth turned down, as if it was full of ashes. 'You didn't see *me* jumping into bed with the first person I saw, did you? Civilized people just don't do that.'

Alice clicked on the car radio. 'Maybe some music will cheer you up?'

'*... have confirmed that the family of four found dead in the wreckage of their burning home in Cardiff on Wednesday were subjected to a brutal hammer attack. Local news now, and the search for missing five-year-old Charlie Pearce continues as police—*'

She switched the thing off again. 'Maybe not. We could play I-spy?'

Outside the Suzuki's window, Oldcastle ground its way through the rush hour. Cars, vans, and buses crawled along the streets in a slow-motion metal conga line, blaring horns making a post-dawn chorus.

Huntly gave a big, theatrical sigh. 'I spy something beginning with bleakness, darkness, and lonely *crushing* cold. Give up? It's the rest of my life.'

I ground the tip of my cane into the passenger footwell. Gritted my teeth. 'How about we all just sit in silence till we get there?'

Alice looked across from the driver's seat and grimaced at me, both eyebrows up.

He shifted, leaning forward until his head poked through the gap between the seats. Enveloping everything in his sausagey breath. 'Have you ever loved someone, Henderson? I mean, really, really loved them? And then … then they're just gone, and there's nothing you can do to bring them back?' He grabbed my shoulder and squeezed. 'God: the *agony*.'

Alice stared at me, mouth hanging open. 'Err... Actually, maybe we should—'

I slammed my hand on the dashboard. 'Bus!'

'Eeek!' She stamped on the brakes, wrenched the wheel to the right, nearly battering into a taxi coming the other way. We screeched to a halt in the middle of the road.

An old woman with a tartan shopping trolley stopped on the pavement to gape, her Westie terrier barking at the car – tail stiff and upright.

The taxi driver wound down his window and belted out a mouthful of expletives, before sticking up two fingers and heading off.

Alice puffed out a breath. 'Right. Let's try that again.' She eased past the bus and back onto the left side of the road. 'Sorry.'

Huntly gave my shoulder another squeeze. 'Women drivers, eh?'

'If you don't get your hand off me *right* now, I'm going to tear your fingers off and ram them down your throat till you choke.'

He let go, licked his lips, then settled back onto his seat. 'I was only joking.'

'And no more talking either.'

Silence.

Go on, say something. *Anything*.

But he didn't. Not as thick as he looked after all.

12

A ribbon of blue-and-white 'POLICE' tape twisted in the wind, growling like a finger dragged across the teeth of a comb. Scrubland surrounded the deposition site on three sides, a patch of wood reaching up like a dark green wall behind it. The sky was a solid swathe of granite. The long grass whipping in a frigid wind.

I turned my back on the gusts and jammed a finger in my ear. 'No, not... Look, all I want is access to the Inside Man letters. How hard can it be?'

A loud sigh came down the phone. *'Seriously? Come down here and take a look; it's like a bring-and-buy sale for cardboard boxes down here. You know that bit at the end of* Raiders of the Lost Ark? *That.'* Another sigh. *'Did you check with the Major Investigation Teams?'*

'Come off it, Williamson, who do you think put me on to you? They haven't seen them.'

One of Oldcastle's collection of dented and scarred patrol cars blocked the path down to the scene, a pair of uniforms guarding the place by sitting on their backsides inside, out of the wind.

'Well, I don't know what I'm supposed to do. I'm not Santa. I can't just magic up a set of letters if I've no clue where the damn things are.'

110

'So go ask Simpson. He'll know.'

'*Look, I'm telling you there's—*'

'Hold on.' I pressed the phone against my chest and rapped on the driver's window.

The guy behind the wheel puffed out his cheeks, then buzzed the window down. He didn't look old enough to vote, never mind arrest anyone – with a threadbare moustache and a scabby pluke on his forehead. Bored eyes and a droopy mouth. Crumbs and flakes of pastry all down the front of his stab-proof vest. He took another bite out of whatever was wrapped in the paper bag from Greggs, talking with his mouth full. 'Sorry, mate, this bit's shut. Gotta go walk somewhere else.'

I leaned on the roof. Stared down at him. 'First off, *Constable*, I am not your "mate".'

He obviously recognized the tone of voice from previous bollockings, because he sat bolt upright in his seat and dropped the paper bag into the footwell. A blush erupted across his face, flushing his cheeks, making the tips of his ears glow. 'Sorry, sir, I didn't mean—'

'Name?'

'Hill, sir, erm … Ronald. I didn't—'

'Second: I don't care how long you've been sitting here, you're a bloody police officer, so try to look like one. You're a disgrace. Third,' I pointed at Alice and Huntly, 'get your arse out of this car and show these people the deposition scene. *Now*, Constable.'

'Yes, sir, sorry, sir.' He scrambled out of the car, ramming his peaked cap down on his head. 'This way, and—'

'Check their bloody identification first!'

Alice looked over her shoulder. 'You enjoyed that, didn't you?'

I turned. Constable Hill was standing to attention with his back to us, guarding the path down to the deposition scene as if his life depended on it.

'Might have done.' I might not have been a police officer any more, but that didn't mean I couldn't have fun putting the fear of God into lazy PCs.

The Scenes Examination Branch had laid out a common access path, marked off with more blue-and-white tape, the jaundiced grass crisp with frost and trampled flat. The path curled around the scene, looping back on itself towards an inner cordon of yellow-and-black tape: 'CRIME SCENE DO NOT CROSS'. A handful of triangular yellow flags punctuated the undergrowth, all of them marked with a letter and number.

Huntly stood, chest out, shoulders back, nose swinging left to right as if he was scenting the place. 'I see...' And then he was off, working his way along the trampled path. Sniffing as he went.

I stuck my hands in my pockets. 'They're having difficulty locating the original Inside Man letters. *Apparently* the archives are a mess. No one knows what's in what box. Sure you can't make do with the photocopies Jacobson gave you?'

She curled her top lip. 'They've been copied so many times they're barely legible. I *need* to see the originals. I want to feel the ink on the page, see the weight he's put behind the words, the scratch of the pen, I want to *touch* something he has. Something that didn't end up dead or damaged.' She turned, her eyes following Huntly as he ducked under the inner cordon. 'Did you get anything off them eight years ago?'

'We ran every test we could on the letters *and* the envelopes, but there was nothing. All six were postmarked Oldcastle. The only fingerprints we could lift belonged to the journalist he sent them to. All that's left is the words.'

For a moment, it looked as if she was about to say something. But she dug into her leather satchel instead and came out with a manila folder and a carrier-bag. She jiggled the folder. 'Photos.' Then held up the bag. 'And this is your investigation kit. Dr Constantine made one for everyone.'

I took the bag. Rummaged through the contents. A

112

decent-looking camera – small but high-res, large memory card. Five or six pairs of blue nitrile gloves in individual sterile packages. A handful of evidence bags. A ruler. A notepad. A sheet of instructions. And a smartphone. I pulled it out, turned it over in my hands. 'Let me guess: it's all monitored and GPS tracked so they know where I am and what I'm up to?'

Alice just looked at me. Then, 'No, it's a phone. It's for making calls and uploading stuff to the LIRU server, see there's a slot in the side that'll take the camera's memory card? They've got the ankle monitor if they need to find you.'

Good point. I distributed the investigation kit between my pockets.

Huntly's voice brayed out from the other side of the crime-scene tape. 'I do love a good deposition scene. But this isn't one of them. I mean *look* at this, honestly.' He swept his arms up and out. 'Everyone and their rancid mother's picked the place clean, leaving dirty big footprints everywhere. And why, oh why, oh *why*, didn't they put down a walkway? It's all compromised. How am I supposed to work like this?' He turned around, doing a slow one-eighty, left the cordoned-off area, then stomped and crackled away into the woodland.

So much for Jacobson's hand-picked, decades of experience, top of their game, experts.

I ducked under the tape marking off the access path and scrunched through the knee-high grass towards the inner cordon. Stopped. Looked back to where Alice was standing with her arms wrapped around herself. 'You coming?'

'Aren't we supposed to stick to the authorized path?'

'You heard Huntly. Operation Tigerbalm have tromped all over it with their size elevens. There's nothing left to compromise.' I went back to wading through the frosty grass. Paused at the line of tape. Opened the folder and pulled out the photos.

They were the same ones Jacobson had given me in the Range Rover, the colours a lot more vibrant in the daylight.

It took a little back and forth, but eventually I found where the photographer must have stood to take the first couple of shots. I stood in the same place, holding the pictures out.

Claire Young's head lay pointing back towards the path we'd started on, her skin pale and veined like marble.

'She died somewhere else...'

Alice hadn't moved, still hiding behind the blue-and-white line. 'What?'

'I said, she didn't... Will you get your backside over here?'

I pointed as Alice picked her way across to the deposition scene. 'There's not enough blood. He slit her open, stitched a doll inside, and sewed her up again. Ground should be saturated with it. And the positioning's wrong too.'

'But we know the Inside Man has an operating room, it was on the DVD and—'

'Supposed to be keeping an open mind, remember? And Unsub-Fifteen didn't drag her here from the car park either, he carried her. Otherwise there'd be drag marks on the path.' I planted my feet apart and hefted an imaginary Claire Young's dead body up onto my shoulder. 'So: you've got her in a fireman's lift. You stagger down the path, till you think you've gone far enough that no one will see you from the car park. You don't dump her at the side of the path, do you? No, you strike out at ninety degrees, put some distance between you and the path. Then you dump her.' I mimed it, tipping the body off my shoulder and onto the grass. 'Her head would be pointing that way, towards the woods, not away from them.'

'Well ... maybe he turned around and *then* dumped her body?'

Possible.

Then again, we'd already established that Professor Huntly couldn't be as daft as he looked.

He was still crashing about out there, breaking branches and singing what sounded like opera to himself.

Alice picked at her satchel. 'Ash, the big car chase... You

114

ended up all covered in glass and blood and you broke your wrist and your ribs – I looked it up in the case file – but it doesn't say why the Inside Man wasn't all bashed up in the crash.'

'Luck? Angle of collision? Not having a moron like O'Neil behind the wheel? How should I know?' I put the photos back in the folder. 'Listen, once we've dropped Rain Man back at the Postman's Head, I need to run a little errand.'

Alice took a sudden interest in the path. 'Oh.'

'Nothing important. Just need to pop in on an old friend.'

'Right...'

'You can stay in the car if you like, I probably won't be long.'

'Ash, do you think we could talk about what happened with you and Mrs Kerrigan, I mean I know you're not—'

'There's nothing to talk about. What happened, happened; there's nothing I can do to bring Parker back.'

'Ash, it's perfectly normal to—'

'She had him shot twice in the head, then framed me for it. What's normal about that?'

Nothing.

Silence.

And then Huntly was back, stumbling out of the woods a good twenty yards further down than where he'd gone in. 'Behold!' He held a small digital camera aloft. 'The Mighty Bernard Huntly has returned.'

Oh, lucky us.

He turned back towards the woods. Then froze. Looked over his shoulder at me. 'Well, don't just stand there – come, witness my brilliance.'

'Gah...' Alice stumbled, staggered forwards a few paces and thumped into a tree. 'This is stupid.'

The forest floor was rutted, littered with roots and fallen branches. Dark with rotting pine needles and the brittle bones of dying ferns. Heady with the smell of earth and decay. Cold enough to make our breath fog as we picked our way deeper into the woods.

Huntly kept going, ducking under the jagged thicket of branches. 'On the contrary, it's infinitely sensible.'

She lowered her voice to a mutter. 'Infinitely stupid, more like.' Then back to full volume again. 'There's no way the killer came this way – there's no path. How would you carry a body through all this? It'd get snagged in the branches, you'd drop it, you'd leave a big trail of snapped stuff and my hair keeps getting caught on these horrible twigs. Gahh!'

Huntly smiled back at her. 'You are, of course, perfectly correct. We're wading through the thicket here *precisely* because Unsub-Fifteen didn't. There's a track, ten foot to our right, that we're walking parallel to. I don't want either of you treading in any evidence.'

He shoved his way into a clump of broom and disappeared. The gap snapped closed again, dark green tendrils shivering behind him, seedpods rattling and angry.

Alice stopped. Stared at the bushes. Then stared at me. 'I'm not a violent person. But if I look the other way, can you break his legs for me?'

I hauled a handful of broom back, making a gap. 'Put your hood up, it'll be fine.'

She did. Sighed. Then lowered her head and pushed her way into the bushes, setting the rattling going again.

Three, two, one. The branches snatched at my hair and shoulders, as I clambered in after her, ducking and weaving through the thicket, following the sound of swearing.

More rattling, and the bush opened out at the bottom of a ditch. Damp earth squelched beneath my feet, slippery as I scrambled up and onto a grass verge.

A road stretched away left and right, disappearing into the woods. Ten or twelve yards from where I'd emerged was a bus shelter, alien and battered beneath the reaching claws of more pine trees. Graffiti tattooed the phone box next to it – a sickly, twisted thing with a buckled door and half the Perspex missing. Snakes of soot curled up the remaining panes, the plastic warped and pitted by heat.

Huntly stood in the middle of the road, hands on his hips, a grin stretching his stupid little moustache wide. 'Well? What did I tell you?'

Alice pulled a burr of pine needles from her hair. '... just washed it this morning...'

I stopped, twenty feet from the bus shelter. 'So you're saying the killer took the bus here, hauled the dead girl over his shoulder, and stomped off into the woods? Do dead bodies have to pay full fare, or do they count as luggage?'

A sigh. 'You may mock, but what about this...?' He made his way around to the back of the bus shelter, giving the side a wide berth, and pointed. 'See?'

I followed, placing my feet in his footsteps, minimizing disturbance to the scene. A single smear of red-brown ran for six inches along the shelter's bottom edge, just above the grass.

'See? How much would you like to wager that it's a DNA match with our victim?' He moved over to the left, peering at a flattened patch in the scrubland. The grass was stained and darkened. 'She probably died here. There's not enough for a full bleed-out, but I imagine a lot of it would have clotted inside the body cavity by the time she got here. Hence the relative cleanliness.'

Alice hadn't moved from the roadside. 'Why bother though?' She curled an arm around herself, the other hand playing with her hair again. 'I mean he could've just left her there, behind the bus shelter, why pick her up again and carry her all the way through the woods to the bit of waste ground where she was found, doesn't that seem like a bit of a waste of time?'

I reached into my pocket and pulled out a pair of gloves from Dr Constantine's investigation kit. Tore open the sterile

117

packaging, and snapped them on. Scuffed through the weeds and grass to the far side of the flattened area – taking the long way around to avoid treading on any evidence. 'Have you got a photo of this?'

Huntly sniffed. 'Of what?'

'Syringe.' It lay in a clump of dockens, lined with frost, its yellow cap about a foot away.

'Ah...' He followed the path I'd made, his digital camera at the ready. 'Say cheese.'

Alice still hadn't moved. 'Unsub-Fifteen tried to save her. He got Claire all the way out here, then he takes the cry for help he made her record and goes to call an ambulance, but she crashes. She's not breathing. So he gives her ... maybe something like adrenaline? Tries to start her heart again. He doesn't want them to die, he wants us to get to them in time, like Laura Strachan, Marie Jordan, and Ruth Laughlin. Claire was meant to live. This was a failure.'

Huntly took another couple of shots. 'And he didn't want us to connect her body with this place, in case he'd left something of himself behind. So he moved the remains.' The digital camera went back into Huntly's pocket. 'Of course, he didn't reckon on tangling with someone of *my* calibre. They never do.' He grinned. 'Here's a fun fact for you: one of the ambulance men who saved Laura Strachan, himself went on to become the last ever victim of another serial killer: the Nightmare Man. Personally, if I lived in Oldcastle, I'd move.'

Damp grass scuffed around my ankles as I made for the telephone box. The door squealed as I dragged it open. A new-car stench of burnt plastic slumped against me, underpinned with a bleachy tang. The phone itself looked reasonably intact, under all the black-marker swearwords and cocks scratched into the metal. I picked the handset up and held it so the mouthpiece was nowhere near my lips. The dialling tone burred in my ear.

Still working. I punched in 1471, looking for the last number

118

dialled, but the LCD display came up '— BARRED NUMBER —' The handset went back into its cradle then I stepped out into the unburnt air again. Pulled out my new official phone and powered it up. It'd been pre-programmed with a half-dozen numbers, '~ THE BOSS!' sitting at the top of the list, above 'ALICE', 'BERNARD', 'HAMISH', 'SHEILA', and 'X – DOMINO'S PIZZA'. My finger hovered over the first entry. Of course, by rights it should be Control, *not* Jacobson getting the first call. Then again, Control couldn't send me back to prison.

And there was no way I was risking that. Not when I was so close...

The phone rang for a bit, then Jacobson picked up, listened while I filled him in. Then, *'Excellent. Bernard might be a pain in the arse, but he's worth it. Get as many photos as you can, then call Ness – get her to send out a Scenes Examination Branch team. I want that scene cordoned off and picked over with an electron microscope. Tell them Bernard's in charge, and if they give him any grief I'll have them. OK?'*

13

Alice looked back over her shoulder as I pulled into Slater Crescent. 'Are you sure it's OK to leave Professor Huntly there, I mean what if he upsets all the—'

'He's a grown man.' And besides, maybe getting punched on the nose by one of the Scenes Examination Branch would take the edge off him a bit. If we were lucky.

The Suzuki jerked and juddered as my right foot slipped off the accelerator. Bloody idiot. Oh, no *I'll* drive this time. It's been far too long. Need the practice...

Need my sodding head examined, more like.

Teeth gritted, I put the aching foot back down, on the brake this time. Eased Alice's car up to the kerb. Killed the engine. Folded forward and rested my forehead on the steering wheel. Hissed out a breath.

'Ash? Are you OK?'

'Fine. Perfect. Never better.' God that *hurt*. 'Just ... been a while.'

I straightened up, dug a pack of paracetamol from my jacket and dry-swallowed three of them. Pulled in a few deep breaths. Then opened the driver's door. 'I'll only be a couple of minutes.'

She stared at me. 'And he's an old friend.'

'It'll be fine.' I grabbed my cane and struggled out of the car. Closed the door.

Slater Crescent curled away down Blackwall Hill, giving the road a decent view across the valley to the Wynd. Over there, the sandstone terraces were arrayed like soldiers on parade. Expensive houses surrounding little private parks. Picturesque and historical beneath the heavy grey sky.

And a lot prettier than the seventies maze of cul-de-sacs and dead ends that surrounded us. Blackwall Hill: a twisting nest of grey-harled bungalows and terracotta pantiles. Gardens jealously guarded behind leylandii battlements. Knee-high wrought-iron gates with nameplates bolted to them: 'DUNROAMIN', 'LINDISFARNE', 'SUNNYSIDE' and half a dozen variations on 'ROSE', 'FOREST', and 'VIEW'.

Number thirteen – the address I'd got from the mysterious Alec – had an archway of honeysuckle wound up and over a stupid little gate, like brittle strands of beige barbed wire. The nameplate had 'VAJRASANA' on it, picked out in gold letters. Gravel made a twisting path through bushes and dead flowers, seedheads heavy and drooping on either side. A concrete Buddha sat beside the path, his grey skin speckled with lichen.

A little girl knelt before him, trundling a bright yellow Tonka tipper truck back and forwards, scooping up gravel and dumping it at the Buddha's feet. Making the beep-beep-beep noises every time the tipper reversed for another load.

I creaked the gate open and limped in, clanging it shut behind me with my cane. Pulled on a smile. 'Hi, is your daddy in?'

She jumped to her feet, clutching the Tonka against her stomach. Can't have been more than five or six, but she had a single thick eyebrow stretching across a mealie-pudding face. She smiled, showing off a hole where the two bottom middle teeth should have been. 'Yeth.'

'Can you run and get him for me?'

A nod. 'But you have to look after my tiger for me.' She pointed at an empty patch of grass, then lowered her voice to a whisper. 'He'th thcared of clownth.'

'OK, if any clowns come along, I'll keep him safe.'

'Promith?'

'Course I do.'

'OK.' She patted a hand up and down, in mid-air. 'You be good Mithter Thtripey, and don't eat the man.' And then she was off, skipping up the path and into the house.

I limped over and rested against the Buddha's concrete head.

She was back two minutes later, dragging a small middle-aged man by the hand: dumpy, central parting, chinos and a cardigan. He fiddled a pair of glasses from his pocket and slipped them on. Blinked at me. Then beamed. 'Ah, you must be Mr Smith. How nice to see you, Mr Smith.' He turned to the little girl. 'Sweetie, why don't you take Mr Stripy through to the back garden so I can talk to Mr Smith?'

She stared at him, face hard and serious. 'Are there any clownth?'

'They all ran away when they heard Mr Smith was coming over.'

A nod, then she wrapped an arm around thin air and pulled it towards the side of the house. 'Come on, Mithter Thtripey...'

The man watched her go, head on one side, a wide smile on his face. Then sighed. Turned back to me. 'Now then, Mr Smith, Alec believes you're looking for some spiritual guidance?'

'Where is he?'

He placed a hand against his chest and gave a small bow. 'This one has the questionable honour of being Alec.'

'OK...' Shifty was right, the man was a nutter. 'In that case: semi-automatic, clean, at least thirteen in the clip, and a box of brass. Hollowpoint if you've got it.'

'Hmm, that's a lot of spiritual enlightenment.' He joined

me at the Buddha, leaning back against the statue. 'Tell me, Mr Smith, have you truly contemplated the consequences of your actions here today? Because Karma is watching, and it's never too late to change one's path.'

'Have you got it, or don't you?'

He placed both hands against his chest, fingertips spread. 'Take Alec for example. Accepting the Buddha into his life made a world of difference to Alec. Alec was a sinner – it's true – and his life was hard and dark… Well, until Alec had his little *incident* and decided to let the teachings of the Buddha into his cold, cold heart.'

I pushed off the statue and stood, resting most of my weight on the cane. 'You're going to have another "little incident" if you don't make with a gun in the next fifteen seconds. And it better be clean – I find out it's been used in a hit, or a Post Office job, or some sectarian drive-by shite, I'm going to come back and introduce you to your god personally.'

'Ah, Mr Smith, there is no "God". The Buddha teaches us that Mahâ Brahmâ did not create all things. We come to being instead through *paticcasamuppada*, and—'

'Do you have the bloody gun, or don't you?'

The smile hadn't slipped an inch. 'Patience, Mr Smith. Patience. Before we can proceed, Alec needs to know why you want it. What your intentions are.'

'None of Alec's bloody business.'

'Ah, but it *is* a *bloody* business, is it not?' He stood too, crunching along the gravel path, between the dying plants. Following the circle. 'Alec struggled long and hard with the essential dichotomy of continuing in his chosen profession, given his beliefs. Alec meditated. He appealed to the Buddha for guidance. And in the end he came to realize that his place in the karmic cycle is to facilitate a moral choice on behalf of people like yourself. And so he achieved another step upon the road to enlightenment.'

'Fine. Forget it.' I made for the gate.

'Alec can give you what you ask for, but he needs you to understand that *right now* you've got the option to just walk away from the darkness surrounding you. Take a plus in the Karma column. Be a better man.'

'Yeah. Well I'm more of an Old Testament kind of guy. Eye for an eye. Bullet for a bullet.'

'Ah, revenge...' Alec stopped, head bowed. Then nodded. 'Wait here.' He headed back inside, and when he emerged again he held out a plush Bob the Builder doll – about the same size as a rugby ball, a grin stitched across its face, over-sized yellow spanner in one hand. 'Here.'

'Are you seriously looking for a kick up the...' There was something hard inside Bob. Something L-shaped. More some-things in his legs, as if they'd been stuffed with finger bones.

'Mr Smith, are you certain Alec can't convince you to turn from this?'

At least a dozen bullets in there, possibly more. Wouldn't know until I slit him open.

Now all I had to do was keep my head down until I could introduce Bob to Mrs Kerrigan tonight. Twice. In the face.

'Mr Smith?'

I looked up, just as the clouds gave up their first drops. They struck the Buddha, darkening the concrete around his eyes, more and more joining them as the wind picked up. Rolling down his fat cheeks.

'How sad.' Alec shook his head. Sighed. Let his shoulders fall. 'You've made your mind up, and the world weeps for you.'

Nothing like being pitied by an arms dealer who talked about himself in the third person to really put a shine on the day.

I handed over Shifty's envelope full of cash, then limped back to the car, Bob the Builder tucked tightly beneath my arm.

Can we fix it? Yes, we bloody well can.

* * *

'... *for three days has been found in a disused quarry in Renfrewshire. Police are appealing for anyone who might have seen the six-year-old since she went missing on Thursday evening ...*'

Rain smashed against the tarmac, bouncing back to make a knee-high spray of mist as Alice pulled into the car park. The Suzuki pitched and rolled through water-logged potholes, sending Bob the Builder sliding across the back seat.

'... *refusing to confirm or deny that there are similarities with three other children abducted since Halloween...*'

She picked a parking space not too far from the entrance, and sat there, the windscreen wipers scraping across the pitted glass. 'It doesn't look very promising...'

'It's the overflow facility for a mortuary, what did you expect: palm trees and marble?'

'... *an appeal from the mother of missing five-year-old, Charlie Pearce—*'

Alice killed the engine.

The overflow facility was a low concrete bunker in a run-down industrial estate on the outskirts of Shortstaine – a mean line of grey and black, scowling behind chain-link fences festooned with warning signs about guard dogs, CCTV, and razor wire. Loading bay at one end, reception at the other. Shielded from the road by a barricade of green bushes.

There was a clatter, and a couple staggered out through the mortuary doors: the man's face ripped open by grief, wet with tears; the woman walking as if her knees wouldn't bend any more. As if what she'd seen inside had fossilized them.

The rain drummed against my shoulders.

Alice stood with the keys in her hand, turning to watch the couple lurch into the car park. Him collapsing against an old Renault Clio, her walking around in small, stiff-legged circles. 'Maybe we should do something?'

A beat later, a uniformed constable crashed out into the rain, skidded to a halt on the top step, face flushed. A lumpy stain spread from the edge of her stabproof vest down one leg and the sharp, bitter smell of bile clung to her like a shroud. 'Sorry...' She gave me a pained smile, then went over to join the sobbing man and clockwork woman.

Inside.

Dr Constantine stood facing a blow heater, the sides of her Parka jacket held open, basking in the warm air.

The room was small, bland, and functional: a stubby reception desk made of stainless steel; an easy-clean lino floor; walls covered with public health and information posters; a rack of leaflets about bereavement services; two security cameras – one watching the front door, the other the entrance to the mortuary proper; a dozen or so business cards from a funeral director's strategically tucked where grieving relatives could see them: 'UNWIN AND MCNULTY, UNDERTAKERS EST. 1965 ~ DISCREET PROFESSIONAL CARE FOR YOUR LOVED ONES'. A rubber plant loomed in the corner, its thick waxy leaves covered with a layer of dust. The air sagged beneath the cloying floral scent of too much air freshener, that still wasn't strong enough to obliterate the dark smear of decay.

The door swung closed with an electronic bleep, and Dr Constantine looked over her shoulder at us. Rolled her eyes. 'They've only gone and lost the body.'

Alice shook the water from her shoulders. 'How could they lose the body, I mean this is supposed to be a major murder investigation and the whole world's going to be—'

'You know what I think?' Constantine went back to the heater. 'The natives are playing silly buggers, because they're scared we'll show them up.'

I pressed the bell on the reception desk, and ringing sounded from somewhere behind the double doors leading deeper into the facility. 'Yeah, I don't think it's quite that sinister.'

No reply from the bell. So I tried again.

She shook her head. 'I don't think it's sinister, I think it's petty bloody-mindedness.'

One more go on the bell.

Still nothing.

Alice turned to stare at the door we'd come in through. 'Actually, do you think it'll be OK if I...?' She pointed out towards the car park. 'They seemed really upset.'

'Go on then.'

Last chance. I mashed my thumb down on the bell and held it there as she hurried back outside. The ringing stretched on and on and on and on... And still no answer.

I crossed to the double doors. Frosted glass panes offered no view into the interior. I flattened my hand and slammed my palm against the wood.

BANG! BANG! BANG!

'DOUGAL, YOU USELESS FLAP OF SKIN, GET YOUR ARSE OUT HERE NOW!' Then went back and leaned on the bell again. 'This isn't a conspiracy, they're just morons. It's *always* like this.'

BANG! BANG! BANG!

'DOUGAL, I'M BLOODY WARNING YOU!'

One side of the door creaked open and a wrinkled face peered out, eyebrows raised above a pair of dark, glittering eyes. Silver hair yellowing at the tips. 'Ah... Yes...?' A smile made of greying dentures. 'Well, I never: Detective Inspector Henderson, how nice to see you again. I thought you were ... *away*.'

'What have you done with Claire Young's remains?'

His eyebrows drooped. 'I *was* sorry to hear about your daughter, I can only imagine— Ulp!'

I reached through the gap in the doors and grabbed a handful of white lab coat. Dragged him out into the reception area. 'Where is she?'

'Ah, yes, Claire Young...' His eyes darted to Dr Constantine, then back to me again. 'Actually, that's a funny story, well, maybe not funny *per se*, but it's—'

I gave him a shake. 'Last time, Dougal.'

'We're looking, we're looking! It's not my fault, it—'

Another shake. 'Get the book. *Now.*'

He staggered back, straightening the front of his lab coat, refastened the poppers. 'Yes, the book, I'll get the book...' Then he ducked behind the reception desk and came out with a thick ledger, flopped it open at a leather bookmark about five-sixths of the way through. Pulled on a pair of big round glasses that magnified his dark rat-like eyes. Ran a finger down the name column. 'Young, Young, Young... Ah, here we are, yes, right: Claire Young. She should be in Fifty-Three A, but we've looked and there's no one there...' He cleared his throat. 'But we're pulling out all the stops, searching every drawer in *every* unit, I'm sure she'll turn up eventually. Right?'

I burled the book around a hundred and eighty degrees, till it was the right way up for me. Scanned the rows and columns. 'Says here she was PM'd yesterday morning. Have you checked she's not still lying in the cutting room?'

Dougal stuck his nose in the air, pulling the loose wattles of skin around his neck tight. 'We're not idiots.'

'You do a bloody good impersonation of one. What about Thirty-Five A, have you tried there?'

'Of course we...' He stopped, his mouth hanging open. Then his lips contracted to make a wrinkly 'O'. 'Excuse me a moment...' And he was gone.

The front door bleeped again and Alice shuffled in, face all flushed, hair dripping wet, wiping her eyes on the sleeve of her stripy top. She didn't say a word, just crept up to me, wrapped her arms around my torso and pressed her face against my chest. Sniffing.

I hugged her back. She was soaked. 'You OK?'

Another sniff. Then a deep breath. One last squeeze of my ribs, and she stepped back. Wiped her eyes again. 'Sorry.'

'Detective Inspector?' Dougal was back, flashing his dentured smile again. 'I'm pleased to announce that we've managed to locate Claire Young. Give me a couple of minutes and she'll be in the cutting room ready for you.'

'Someone got the numbers the wrong way round, didn't they?'

'Well, the important thing is that Miss Young's still here, all safe and sound.' He pushed the door all the way open, holding it there as he gestured us in. 'Was beginning to think our ghoulish friend had come back...'

14

'Now you're sure I can't get you a tea? Coffee?' Dougal tilted his head on one side, hands in front of his chest, the finger-tips stroking each other as Dr Constantine picked her way around all that remained of Claire Young. 'I've got some fig rolls, if you like?'

Alice shook her head. 'Thanks, but ... with the post mortem and everything...'

'Ah, yes, right. Detective Inspector?'

I nodded. 'Tea. Milk. Two biscuits. And a proper mug – *not* polystyrene.'

He scuttled off, leaving us alone in the cutting room. The thing was at least six times the size of the mortuary at Castle Hill Infirmary. A dozen stainless-steel tables were arranged in a grid of six by two, complete with drains, hoses, scales, and hydraulics. Each one sat beneath its own CCTV camera – the black globes hanging from the ceiling like fruiting bodies.

A long glass wall ran down one side of the room, above a row of sinks and taps. Work surfaces covered the opposite wall, beneath anatomy posters and health-and-safety notices.

Alice shuddered. 'Why do they always have to hire creepy guys to work in mortuaries? Did you see his eyes? All dark and shiny...'

'He looks like an oversized rat in a lab-coat doesn't he? He's overpowered the scientists and it's their turn to be experimented on.' I leaned back against the cutting table next to Claire Young's remains. 'One summer, when the girls were wee, it was just *bakingly* hot. For a week Oldcastle was like living in an oven, so we'd leave the windows open the whole time; trying to get a bit of cool air into the place. One night I went to check on the girls – both sound asleep – and there's this big brown rat inching its way up the blankets towards Rebecca's face. That's what Dougal looks like.'

'You forgot to say, "Once upon a time".'

'Sorry.'

Alice shuffled her little red Converse trainers, turning on the spot, staring out at the cutting tables and sinks. 'It's very big.'

'Comes in handy when a busload of school kids turns up, or something unpleasant happens at a nursing home, or the council unearths a mass grave...' I twisted my fingers together until the joints burned. Looked away. 'It comes in handy.'

Dr Constantine wheeled a stainless-steel trolley over and dumped an oversized Gucci handbag on it. Delved inside and picked out a roll of fabric – unfurled that to reveal a glittering spread of knives, clippers, pliers, and shears. The tools of her trade. 'You know, in the good old days I used to get first crack at a body.'

She pulled on a lab coat, then crossed to a dispenser mounted above the sinks and tore a green plastic apron from the roll. Slipped it over her head and tied it at the back. Snapped on a pair of purple surgical gloves. 'Would someone mind starting my Dictaphone? It's in the bag.'

I got it out and pressed the red button, hanging it by its strap from the lamp above the table.

Dr Constantine worked her fingers across Claire Young's abdomen.

131

Two sets of scars dimpled the waxy skin, one punctuated with little black stitches, the other with the thick nylon thread beloved of pathologists everywhere. The little black stitches held together the cruciform cut, the thicker ones closing the Y incision that reached from Claire's collarbones to her pubic hair.

Constantine made humming noises behind her mask. 'Well, at least they were bright enough not to disturb the Inside Man's surgery.' She took a pair of needle-nosed scissors and snipped through the thick thread. Peeled back the pre-loosened skin, exposing the ribs. 'I suppose, in some ways, it's nice not to have to do all the heavy lifting.' She wrapped her fingers around both ends of the breastbone and popped the ribcage out; laid it on the trolley next to her implements. 'Of course, *this* isn't so good.'

Claire's chest and abdominal cavity were filled with clear plastic bags, each one full of something dark and glistening. Constantine rummaged through them, then plucked out one with what looked like a heart in it. 'A not-so-lucky dip.' She tipped the contents out into a metal bowl. 'Mr Henderson, would you grab your wrinkly idiot friend and ask him if he's still got the original victims in storage? Might as well, while we're here…'

I tracked Dougal down in the staff room, feet up on the coffee table, watching an old 'Miss Marple' film on the TV, and necking a bottle of Lucozade.

'The pathologist wants the original victims' bodies.'

He pulled a face. Took another swig. 'Might be a *teeny* bit of a problem there. We've only got one of them left. One went … missing, and we had to surrender two to their families for burial. I can dig number four out and defrost her, if you like? Take a while for her to get up to temperature though.'

'Natalie May's still frozen? Operation Tigerbalm haven't been in to look at her?'

A shrug. A swig. 'Who can fathom the workings of Police Scotland? Anyway, she didn't have any family, so no one came to claim her. Been here all cold and alone for eight years...'

'Dig her out.'

'Might be able to scare up some tissue samples and X-rays from the others. Depends if they survived the winter of twenty-ten.' He looked away. 'I really *was* sorry to hear about your daughter. And your brother.'

On the TV screen, Margaret Rutherford tricked a young man into confessing to murder in a drawing room. Then had a cup of tea as the police took the guy away to be hanged. All nice and cosy.

Dougal squeezed the Lucozade bottle, making it squeal. 'When the leukaemia got our Shona... Well...' Another swig. 'Just wanted to say I know what it's like.'

Yeah, because losing a child to cancer and losing one to a serial killer were *exactly* the same thing.

I didn't say anything. Just turned and walked from the room.

At least he got to say goodbye.

The corridors squealed beneath my feet as I worked my way back towards the cutting room, walking cane thumping out a slave-galley beat against the grey terrazzo, phone pressed against my ear. 'How long?'

Shifty's voice wheezed out of the mobile's earpiece. '*Yeah, well, you know, only till I get on my feet... I wouldn't ask, but ... you know.*'

'Andrew still being a dick?'

'*You won't even know I'm there. Swear. I'll get one of those blow-up mattresses from Argos, a duvet and all that. No trouble.*'

'I want to interview the Inside Man's surviving victims – you text me their details and I'll ask Alice about you bunking down in the lounge. Deal?'

'*Deal.*'

'And keep it low key. Don't want Ness to know we're speaking to them.' I paused, one hand on the door back through to the cutting room. 'I went to see your mate for some spiritual guidance.'

'*Oh.*' Pause. '*And are you all enlightened?*'

'How does tonight sound?'

The wheezing dropped to a whisper. '*Pre-dawn raid?*'

'I want details about the address – security, dogs, access points, when she's going to be there. The usual.'

'*Deposition site?*'

'I think the classics are the best, don't you?' I hung up. Dialled another number.

It rang, and rang, and then *click*: '*You've reached Gareth and Brett. We can't come to the phone right now, but you can leave a message after the beep.*'

'Brett? It's Ash. Your brother? Brett, you there?'

Silence. Screening his calls, or genuinely out? Didn't really matter either way.

'I...' I what? What could I possibly say that would make any difference? 'I just wanted to let you know that ... I'm taking care of it. You guys be good to each other, OK?' Awkward silence. 'Anyway, that's it. Bye.'

The phone went back in my pocket.

Deep breath.

Then I pushed through into the cutting room again.

Dr Constantine's trolley was covered in clear plastic bags, arranged in order of largest to smallest. She dug about in one containing a slab of purpley-black, humming the theme tune to *The Archers* as she went.

Alice was sitting on the cutting table furthest away from the action, red shoes dangling three feet off the floor, one arm wrapped around herself, the other hand twiddling with her hair. Gazing up at the CCTV camera hovering over her head.

'There's a lot of cameras.'

'Whole place is wired. About six years ago, they noticed bodies going missing from long-term storage. No idea who did it, or what they did *with* them.' I shrugged. 'Welcome to Oldcastle.'

'Hmm...' Alice went back to playing with her hair. 'I've been thinking about Dr Docherty's profile, I mean I can understand why he's proposing Unsub-Fifteen's a lone male hunting—'

'It's the same profile he drew up with Henry eight years ago. He's fluffed the wording up a bit, but the only thing he's really changed is the guy's age. Used to be in his "late twenties", now it's "mid-to-late thirties".' A harsh electronic ringing noise cut through the musty air like a rusty scalpel: the mortuary phone, mounted on the wall by the samples fridge. It rang, and rang, and rang, then fell silent again. I stared at it. 'Docherty obviously thinks Unsub-Fifteen's the Inside Man.'

Phones... I stared at the one by the fridge. How did he know? How did he know they'd work?

Alice swung her feet. 'I'd like to talk to the survivors, we can do that can't we, Bear said we could and—'

'Soon as Shifty sends through their details.' I waved my cane at Dr Constantine. 'Hoy, Doc? You going to be long?'

She took a long-bladed carving knife to the slab of liver. '*Please*, don't call me "Doc". Makes me sound like one of the Seven Dwarfs.' She took the slice of liver and cut it into bite-sized chunks. 'And I'll be at least another three hours. Maybe more. Depends if your pal Wrinkles can find those other victims.'

'Who's your computer guy?'

She dumped a chunk of glistening purple into a sample tube. 'Don't have one.'

'Thought you were supposed to be all leading edge.' I pulled my team mobile out and pressed the entry for '~ THE BOSS'.

Jacobson picked up on the fifth ring. '*Ash?*'

'Why haven't you got a forensic computer specialist on the team?'

'Why, do we need one?'

'Detective Sergeant Sabir Akhtar – used to work with the Met, don't know if he still does, but he's the best.'

'Listening.'

'Tell him to get hold of the call log from the phone box we found this morning – the one where he tried to dump Claire Young. The Inside Man doesn't just pick his deposition sites at random; he needs a working phone box within easy reach so he can call an ambulance. So...?'

'So he's got to be scoping them out and making test calls.'

'Have Sabir run down every call for the last six weeks. Perhaps there's a pattern. And give him the nine-nine-nine calls from the original victims as well. I want them cleaned up and any background noises isolated – we don't care about anything from where they were played back, but if we can get something from where he recorded them in the first place... Might be worth a punt.'

Silence from the other end of the phone.

'You still there?'

'Maybe you're not so useless after all. I'll let you know.' And he was gone.

About three seconds later my mobile buzzed. A text message from Shifty.

> Marie Jordan: Sunnydale Wing, Castle Hill Infirmary
>
> Ruth Laughlin: 16B, 35 First Church Rd, Cowskillin
>
> & U fancy curry for tea?

Marie Jordan and Ruth Laughlin. Nothing for Laura Strachan.

I texted him back, then stuck the phone in my pocket. Held out a hand for Alice and helped her down from the cutting table. 'Constantine's big enough to look after herself for a few hours. We'll go see those survivors.'

As we pushed through into the reception area, Dougal gave a little squeal. Grabbed the death book and clutched it against his chest. 'Frightened the life out of me...'

I paused, one hand on the door to the outside world. Pointed at him. 'Find those samples and Natalie May's body, or next time we meet you'll be the one getting post-mortemed. Understand?'

He tightened his grip on the book. 'Yes, right, finding her now, not a problem.'

'Better not be.' I hauled on the handle and followed Alice out into the grey morning.

Rain bounced off the tarmac and hissed against the mortuary's concrete walls. A lake was forming in front of the loading bay, spreading out from an overflowing gutter.

The little portico didn't offer a lot of protection from the downpour, but it was better than nothing.

Alice pulled up her hood. 'You wait here and I'll get the car.' She skittered between the puddles, knees high, back hunched. Plipped the locks and scrambled in behind the wheel. The Suzuki's lights flickered on, followed by the engine. Then it spluttered its way to the mortuary door, twitching with palsy tremors.

I limped over, climbed in.

Mist thickened the windows, eating the day until there was nothing left but blurry shapes and vague shadows. Alice cranked the blowers up full. Their roar drowned out the rain drumming on the roof. 'Sorry... It'll only take a minute.'

A knock on the driver's window made her flinch. A man's chest filled the glass, barely visible through the fog – suit jacket, shirt and tie.

She buzzed the window down. 'Can I help you?'

A high-pitched voice slithered into the car. 'Felicitations, dear lady. May one enquire where you're taking our good friend Mr Henderson this fine morning?'

Shite.

I clambered out of the car, hands balled into fists. 'Joseph.'

He looked across the bonnet at me and smiled. Big sticky-out ears, Neanderthal forehead, prominent chin, and a crewcut that did nothing to hide the scar tissue lacing back and forth across his scalp. The rain played a drum solo on his big black umbrella. 'Mr Henderson, how splendid to see that you're no longer incarcerated. We *have* missed you. Are you well?'

Rain flattened my hair to my head, a trickle making its icy way down the back of my neck. 'What do you want?'

'*Moi*?' He placed a hand against his chest – a DIY swallow tattoo in faded blue marked the web of skin between his thumb and forefinger. 'I wanted to make sure that you'd come through your period of incarceration with your spirit intact, ready to take on the world once more with your *legendary* vigour.'

I cricked my head to the left, then back again, tendons making popping noises at the top of my spine. 'Are we going to have a problem?'

'Oh, I do so hope not, Mr Henderson. I would so *hate* for us to have a falling out when we've always been the best of friends.' He looked over my shoulder. 'Isn't that right, Francis?'

Two years in prison. You'd think I'd have learned to keep an eye out for someone sneaking up behind me.

Francis appeared at my shoulder, his reflection in the passenger window smiling down at me from behind his John-Lennon sunglasses. Curly red hair pulled back in a ponytail, big wild-west moustache, and little soul-patch. ''Spector.'

His umbrella cut into the rain, looming above me like the wings of a massive bat.

I stayed perfectly still. 'Francis.'

His mouth barely moved. 'Got a message for you, like.'

'Indeed we do, Mr Henderson. Our mutual friend is glad to hear that you've re-joined the land of the free, home of the Braveheart, and she looks forward to renewing your acquaintance at the earliest possible convenience.'

I bloody bet she did. 'How did you know I was here?'

Joseph's hand traced a lazy figure eight through the air. 'Let's just say that we've been the beneficiaries of a fortuitous happenstance.'

I glanced back towards the mortuary doors and there was Dougal. His eyes widened, then he ducked down out of sight. Two-faced little sod. 'Tell her, next time I see her, we're going to have a long hard chat about what she did to Parker. And then I'm going to bury her vicious arse in a shallow grave in Moncuir Wood.'

Francis leaned in close, the words breaking against my cheek on a waft of peppermint. 'What about the rest of her?'

'Oh dear.' Joseph's smile slipped a bit. 'I fear Mrs Kerrigan is going to be ... somewhat *disappointed* by your less than warm response to her kind invitation.'

The blowers had made a dent in the fogged-up car windows. Enough to reveal Bob the Builder grinning up at me from the back seat. Typical bloody tradesman, never there when you needed them. 'She'll be more than disappointed when I get my hands on her.'

'I see.' A nod. 'Then we shall leave you to enjoy your freedom. While it lasts. Francis...?'

Something exploded in the small of my back, jagged needles ripping through my left kidney. Breath hissing out between clenched teeth. My knees buckled ... but I got them in line, stood tall. Shoulders back. Stuck my chin out. Ground my teeth. 'Big man, aren't you?'

Francis made a little sooking noise. 'Nothing personal, like.'

Strictly business.

Joseph raised his umbrella, like he was doffing an imaginary cap. 'If you change your mind, you know you can always get in touch.' Then he leaned down and smiled through the open driver's window. 'It's been a pleasure, dear lady. I'm sure our paths shall cross again.'

They better bloody not.

I stayed where I was until they'd got into their big black BMW 4x4 and growled their way out of the car park. Then I opened the Suzuki's door and eased into the passenger seat. Hissed out a breath as my ribs touched the backrest. Bloody innards were packed with ice and barbed wire.

Two against one, just like every time in prison. Every sodding time.

I balled my right fist and slammed it into the dashboard. 'BASTARDS!'

The noise overpowered the blowers for a moment, then their roar took over again. Now the barbed wire was threading through my knuckles, every movement tearing through flesh and cartilage. When I stretched out my hand, it wouldn't stay still, fingers quivering and trembling in time to the blood bellowing in my ears.

'Ash? Are you OK, only you don't look so—'

'Just...' I clicked on the radio. 'Just drive.'

15

'Look, Marie, you've got visitors.'

Marie Jordan didn't get up, just sat in her high-backed seat, gazing out of the rain-pebbled window – out through the wire mesh to the doctors' car park and the concrete-and-glass block of the main hospital. Her hair was hacked off short enough to show her scalp in patches, tufts sticking out over one ear, a smattering of dark-red scabs visible in the thinner bits. A slack face, mortuary pale, with sunken red-rimmed eyes and a thin, almost lipless mouth. Dressed in a grey cardigan and jogging bottoms. Her bare feet weren't flat on the floor, they rested on their outside edges, toes curled in towards each other like claws.

Alice glanced back at me, then pulled up a chair with 'DON'T TRUST THEM!!!' scratched into the orange plastic. Sat down with her knees together, hands motionless in her lap. 'Hi, Marie. I'm Dr McDonald, but you can call me Alice. Marie?'

The room was big enough for half a dozen large padded chairs, a handful of cheap plastic ones, a coffee table covered in drifts of *National Geographic*s, and a TV mounted high on the wall where no one could get at it. If anything, the place was even less comfortable than the rec room back at the prison.

None of the other patients were here, leaving just Alice, Marie Jordan, an orderly, and me in the antiseptic silence.

141

I leaned back against the windowsill, blocking Marie's view of the car park. Didn't seem to make any difference to her, she just stared right through me as I flexed my right hand. In and out. The bones and cartilage grinding and grating.

My own stupid fault for punching a car...

Alice tried again. 'Marie?'

The orderly sighed. According to the ID badge pinned to his breast pocket, he was 'Tony' and 'Happy To Help'. A big lad with round cheeks and a saltire tattoo poking out of the neck of his scrubs. 'She's got good days and bad days, I'm afraid. Yesterday *wasn't* one of the good ones.'

'Marie, can you hear me?'

Her head came around. Tilted to one side as if it wasn't really on properly. A blink.

'Marie, we need to talk to you about what happened eight years ago. Do you think you can do that?'

Another blink.

Tony, the orderly, shrugged. 'She saw that thing on the telly last night, on the news, about You-Know-Who being back and went for one of the other patients. Bang, just like that. No warning, no nothing. Poor sod's got a broken nose and half his ear bitten off.'

'It's OK, Marie, we're here to help.'

'Took four of us to pull her off him. Had to dose her up a bit. Then this morning she got hold of scissors from God-knows-where and gave herself a short back and sides. Lucky she didn't hack her wrists open again—'

'Actually,' Alice looked back over her shoulder, 'you know, this might go a little easier if we had some water. Do you think you could go fetch that for us?'

He blew out a breath between pursed lips. 'Not really supposed to leave patients unsupervised with—'

A bright shiny smile. 'Don't worry, I'm sure we'll be fine. My friend Mr Henderson's a police officer, after all.'

'Well... Suppose so. Jug of tap water OK?'

142

Alice waited until the door swung shut behind him. 'Marie, I know it's upsetting to think about the man who hurt you being back, but he can't get to you in here. You're safe.'

Marie blinked a couple of times, pale lips twitching. And when her voice came, it was a whisper of broken glass. 'It's all my fault…'

'No it isn't, it's nobody's fault but his.'

'It was me. I shouldn't have … made him angry.' Her fingers ended in stubby ragged nails, the skin around them bitten back to the raw pink quick. They fluttered across her stomach. 'He put it in me, but it didn't grow…'

'Marie, have you ever been hypnotized?'

'It wouldn't grow because they took it out.'

Alice tried a smile. 'I think it would help you, if we tried. Are you OK with that?'

'They took it out and it died and it was all my fault for not making it grow.'

She reached out and picked Marie's right hand out of her lap. Placed it on top of her own, palm to palm. 'I want you to sit back in your chair. Isn't that comfortable?' Alice's voice dropped: a little deeper, a little quieter. 'Can you feel all your muscles starting to relax?' Deeper still, slower too. 'Can you feel how warm and comfortable it is?'

'No.' Marie turned her head to face me, eyes like pools of blood-rimmed darkness. 'He was there. Watching…'

'I was part of the investigation. I tried to catch the man who did this to you.'

Marie's eyes flicked back towards Alice for a moment. 'I don't like him. Make him go away.'

Noel Maxwell glanced back over his shoulder, down the empty corridor, then slipped a box of pills from the pocket of his blue scrubs and into my hand. 'Just between us, right?' A frown lined his wide forehead. A tuft of black hair clung to the middle, the rest of it receding out of view; sticky out ears;

143

and a pointy chin. Thick brows above a pair of watery blue eyes. 'You sure you're OK?'

I popped a couple of the Prednisolone from their blister pack and knocked the little round pills back. Then reached for my wallet, but he waved me off.

'Nah: old times' sake, and that.' He cleared his throat. 'I was sorry to hear about your daughter. Crappy thing to happen. Really crappy.'

I flexed my hand a few more times. Still felt as if there was something inside, gnawing at the joints.

He shrugged. 'Give it a few minutes.' Then checked the corridor again. 'You need anything else? You know, medicinally?'

'I'm fine. Thanks.'

'Don't mention it. You know, cos we're friends, like. Right?' A greasy little smile. Then he turned and swaggered off the way he'd come, whistling.

There was a clunk behind me and Alice slipped out of the rec room. 'Maybe best to give her fifteen minutes or so.'

A small glass pane sat in the middle of the door. On the other side of it, Marie Jordan was curled into herself, feet up on her chair, knees against her chest, sobbing.

Alice placed her fingertips against the glass. 'It's been a lot for her to process, but I think we've made real progress, and I know that rhymes, but it isn't meant to, she's never actually walked through what happened to her before and—'

A voice rang down the corridor. 'What the bloody hell do you think you're doing?'

A tall thin man in three-piece tweed marched towards us, strip-lights glinting off his bald head and big black-framed glasses. 'You!' He jabbed a finger at Alice. 'Who said you could interfere with my patients? How dare you!'

Tony the orderly scurried along behind him. 'Honestly, Professor Bartlett, they never said they were going to do stuff to her! I was only trying to help, and—'

'I'll deal with *you* later!' Bartlett stomped to a halt in front of Alice, towering over her. 'I don't know who you think you are, but I can assure you—'

She stuck her hand out. He didn't take it. Alice's smile didn't slip an inch. 'You must be Professor Bartlett, I've heard *so* much about you, it's a pleasure, lovely secure ward you've got here, I mean of course the décor's a bit depressing, but there's only so much you can do with these old Victorian asylums, isn't there?'

'Miss Jordan is extremely vulnerable and I will *not* have people wandering in off the street and interfering with—'

'Marie needs time to process what happened. Doping her to the eyeballs and sticking her in a padded room isn't making her better.'

'That's simply not—'

'It's been eight years; I think it's time to try something new, don't you?' Alice produced a business card and slipped it into the breast pocket of his jacket. 'I can see her Wednesday afternoons and Friday mornings. Make sure she's clear of medication for at least four hours beforehand. Oh, and Aberdeen are running a trial treating Post Traumatic Stress Disorder with MDMA, it looks promising, you should try getting Marie into the study.'

'But—'

'And if you *really* want to help her, stop making her wear that hideous cardigan.'

'Cardigan?' I reached down into the footwell and had a scratch at the ankle monitor as we swung around the Ptarmigan roundabout into Cowskillin.

'It was horrible, how could that possibly be good for anyone's mental health?'

The downpour had faded to a misty drizzle that turned the approaching cars' headlights into orbs of gold. 'Left up here at the junction.'

The City Stadium loomed on the other side of the road, all exposed metalwork and angular glass, wrapped in dark-blue metal and painted concrete. Castle Hill rose up behind it, the sides covered in dark buildings with slate-grey roofs, the castle lost in the rain.

Alice glanced over from the driver's seat. 'Do you want to talk about it? You know, before we see her?'

This part of Cowskillin was all post-war council houses, semi-detached boxes built for a brighter tomorrow, turned drab and saggy by the intervening years. Crumbling harling and drooping gutters.

'Ash?'

'There's nothing to talk about. He cut her open, something happened, and he abandoned her. Didn't call it in, just left her there to die.'

'I meant, talk about her relationship with you.'

'She woke up from the anaesthetic in a patch of waste ground: no idea how she got there, covered in blood, middle of the night, pouring with rain. And somehow she manages to stagger as far as the main road. Drunk driver stopped and gave her a lift to hospital.'

'She must be very brave.'

A large corrugated-iron building slid past on the driver's side, the six-foot lettering fixed to it spelling out 'The Westing', with the silhouette of a sprinting greyhound tacked on the end. Mrs Kerrigan's lair...

I turned away. 'Yeah, well, that was a long time ago.'

'I know you still blame yourself, but—'

'She helped me and he saw her. If she hadn't done that...'

'If she hadn't done that, he'd just have picked someone else. Maybe someone not so brave. Someone who wouldn't have survived.'

That didn't exactly make me any less to blame.

I pointed at the junction ahead. 'Right here, then again at the end of the street.'

Two-up-two-downs lined the road: salt-and-pepper harling bristling with satellite dishes; neat gardens out front, bordered by knee-high brick walls. A row of three shops stood side by side halfway down – a butcher's, a grocer's, and a vet's – their windows boarded up and plastered with fliers and posters for a circus that passed through town six weeks ago. The signs above the sheets of chipboard were barely legible, weather-bleached, peeling, and grimy.

Alice took the right at the end. The gardens were a little less tidy here, the windows and doors in need of a fresh coat of paint.

'And down to the left.'

She pulled onto First Church Road.

More post-war boxes. Patches of harling had crumbled around their windows. Weeds poked out above the garden walls. Black-plastic bags piled up the side of wheely-bins. A Renault Fuego was up on bricks at the kerb, the bodywork more rust than steel. A terrier snuffled around the brake discs.

Three-quarters of the way down it looked as if four or five houses had been demolished and replaced with a four-storey block of flats. Orange brickwork stained with grime and scrawled with gang tags: 'KINGZ POSSE MASSIV FTW!', 'BANZI BOYZ ROOL', and 'MICKYD SUX COX!'

Past that, at the end of the road – where the tarmac was blocked off with concrete bollards – rose the blood-red spire of the First National Celtic Church. Barbed with gargoyles and spines, curved black slates like the scales on a dragon's tail.

Half a dozen kids did lazy figure-of-eights around the bollards on BMX bikes, all baggy jeans and hoodie tops, cigarettes leaving curling contrails where they stuck out between their teeth. Half twelve on a Monday – little sods should've been in school.

I checked the text message on my phone again.

Thank you Shifty. Speaking of which...

'That's it, three doors from the end.' I put my phone away. 'Erm ... you know Shifty's boyfriend's thrown him out? Would it be OK if he crashed with us for a couple of nights?'

Alice bit her top lip for a breath, then blinked a couple of times. Pulled her smile back on. 'Of course. We like David, don't we, I mean he was always there trying to help get you out, why would I have a problem with that, it's no problem at all.'

'Are you sure, because—'

'No, he's your friend and he needs your help, and is this it?'

I nodded and she pulled up opposite the block of flats. Then sat, tapping her fingers on the steering wheel, frowning.

'Look, if you don't want him there, it's OK, I can—'

'It's fine. I said it was fine, didn't I? It's fine.' She undid her seatbelt and climbed out into the drizzle. 'Coming?'

One of the kids peeled away from his mates and cycled towards the car.

I grabbed my cane.

Drizzle leached the warmth from my face and hands, greying my jacket as I worked my way around the Suzuki and out onto the road.

Alice didn't wait, just marched over to the flats and up the stairs to the front door. Peered at the buttons by the intercom.

The kid on the bike went by, grinning on one side with picket-fence teeth, the other side clamped around a cigarette. His blond fringe stuck out from beneath a red hoodie with 'Banzi Boyz' printed on it in black marker pen. A face full of freckles. Couldn't have been much more than seven or eight. He circled around me. 'Hoy, granddad?'

I kept on going.

148

'Hoy, limpy, talking to you. Got any fags?' He drifted round slow enough to wobble. 'Come on you auld fart, got any cash?'

'Get lost, you wee shite.'

The kid widened the circle, sooking on his cigarette, making the tip glow bright orange. 'You got a pension, right? Don't want to be a greedy bastard, do you?'

'Not telling you again.'

He popped the BMX up on to the pavement, stood upright on the pedals and drifted closer, standing almost as tall as me. 'Welfare state's for everyone, right? So come on then, hand it over.' He grinned at his little friends, still weaving their way slowly back and forth between the bollards. 'Or you more a Werther's Original paedo? Eh?'

Alice was bent over, face close to the intercom. Listening or speaking – it didn't really matter which, as long as she wasn't looking this way…

The BMX went around me again. 'Peeeeee-do, peeee-do.'

I grabbed the little git by the throat and shoved him off his bike. Bent down, grabbed a handful of fringe and thunked his head off the pavement. Not hard enough to do any permanent damage, just enough to set his ears ringing. 'Listen up, you little shite, I'm going to give you five seconds to bugger off back to your cesspit before I kick your arse.' Loomed in close. 'We clear?'

He blinked up at me, mouth hanging open.

I reintroduced his head to the pavement. 'I said, are we clear?'

'Gerroffus!' He scrambled to his feet, grabbed his bike and legged it. Hopped onboard and jumped the BMX off the pavement. Freewheeled off with one hand on the back of his head and the other making wanking gestures.

Big and brave with a bit of distance on him.

He re-joined his mates at the end of the road and they stood there, giving me the finger, waving them back and forth, before laughing and cycling off.

Their mums and dads must've been so *proud*.

Alice's voice cut through the drizzle. 'Ash?'

'Right.' I turned my back on the church and limped up the steps to meet my past.

16

Ruth Laughlin's living room didn't look as if it saw much in the way of living. A three-bar electric fire pinged and glowed against one wall, making the air scratchy and dry. Hot enough to prick sweat across the back of my neck. A small portable TV sat on a battered nest of tables, the plug pulled from the wall, the screen thick with dust; a brown corduroy couch draped with tartan blankets; a couple of faded family photos in clipframes; a standard lamp with tassels on the shade. As if someone had transported an old lady's house into a block of soulless flats.

She sat in the only armchair, knees together, arms limp in her lap. Her left wrist was cocooned in a bandage, stained grey with dirt. Creases lined Ruth's broad forehead, her hair hanging down over her shoulders in a mousey-brown frizz. Deep-set purple folds lurked beneath her small eyes. Sunken cheeks. She didn't look anything like the woman who'd taken care of me till the ambulance came.

Only thirty-three and she looked sixty – as if someone had reached deep inside her and hauled something out, leaving her empty and broken.

Alice shifted on the couch, rearranging her arms and legs until she mirrored Ruth. Smiled. 'How are you feeling?'

Ruth didn't move, her voice small and crackly. 'They spit at me sometimes. When I go to the shops.'

'Who do?'

'The kids. They're feral. They spit at people and they break into houses. Steal things. Smash everything up.' Her eyes drifted down to the bandage on her wrist. 'I had to stop volunteering at the vet's.'

'Did something happen?'

'It... I thought it'd be nice to go back to it, you know, when I got out? But it's...' Her face pinched. 'We had to put down six dogs in one day. I cried for a week.' She reached up and wiped her eyes on the dirty bandage. 'I'm stupid.'

'You're not stupid, Ruth.' Alice let that hang in the air for a bit, then: 'Did you see the fireworks last week? I went down to Montgomery Park and watched the council display on the other side of the river. It was beautiful, all reds and blues and greens, the cascade of gold down the cliff from the castle.'

Heavy metal sounded in the flat below, distorted by too much volume on cheap speakers, making the floor thrum.

Ruth kept her gaze fixed on the window. 'They should've let me die.'

I cleared my throat. 'I'm sorry.'

She blinked up at me.

'You don't remember me? Ash Henderson? I was chasing the Inside Man, in the train station? There'd been an accident?'

'Oh.' She looked out of the window again. 'I'm tired.'

'I'm sorry he got away. If he... If I'd been stronger, I could've got him.'

A long sigh rattled its way out of her. 'You were bleeding.'

That didn't mean it wasn't my fault.

Alice leaned forward, placed a hand on her knee. 'You were very brave, Ruth, you helped him.'

'I was a nurse. We...' A frown. 'There was lots of us there, on the bikes, raising money for the people in that storm. We did it for Laura.'

Silence.

'We'd like to ask a few questions about what happened to you, Ruth, is that OK? Do you think you can do that?'

She pulled up her jumper, then the grey vest underneath, exposing her bare stomach. A puckered line of scar tissue disappeared into the waistband of her jeans. Another ran left to right under the edge of her bra. 'Ever since I was little, I wanted to be a mother. Two boys and a girl. And we'd go on holiday, and I'd help them with their homework, and we'd be the happiest family in the world... All I ever wanted.' The jumper fell back into place. 'It's all ruined now. They should've let me die.'

'You know, there's always hope. Remember Laura Strachan?' Alice dug into her leather satchel and came out with a copy of the *Castle News and Post*. Held it out. It was the one from last week: '"CHRISTMAS MIRACLE!" BABY JOY ON THE WAY FOR INSIDE MAN VICTIM'. She placed it on Ruth's lap. 'The doctors said she could never have children, and now look at her: nearly eight months pregnant.'

Ruth blinked at the paper for a couple of breaths. Then there was a soft thump – like a tiny punch – and a droplet spread out in a ragged circle of grey into the newsprint. Then another. She sniffed. Picked the paper up and pressed it against her chest as if she could absorb the words through her jumper and into her scarred skin.

Alice put her hand back on Ruth's knee. 'You've not spoken to Laura since the attack, have you?'

She shook her head, cheeks glistening, a dribble of silver shining on her top lip.

'Well, what would you think if I arranged for you to see her again? Would you like that? And, maybe, afterwards we could make you an appointment with the fertility clinic – see what they say?'

'I can't believe it...' Ruth wiped a hand across her trembling lips.

153

Alice reached into her satchel again and produced a couple of tissues. Held them out. 'Now, I'd like to talk about what happened eight years ago. Could we do that?'

She took the tissues in one hand, the other still hugging the paper, and bunched them against her eyes. Then nodded.

'OK, so just you sit back in your seat and relax. And—'

'What if I can't remember?'

'Well, I've got a technique that can help, if you're OK with it? Is that OK?'

Another nod.

'Great. So I need you to make yourself comfy and take a deep slow breath and take us back to that day.' Alice's voice dropped, just like it had in the secure ward that morning. 'Picture the smells. The sounds. The noises as you wake up that morning.' Lower and slower. 'You're lying in bed and you're warm and comfortable, drowsy with sleep, your muscles all relaxed and warm and you're so comfortable and warm and you're safe and nothing can hurt you...'

... and then I'm standing in the corner of the room, crying while they wheel her out and down to the mortuary. She's forty-nine but there's nothing left but tumours and yellow skin stretched over jagged bones.

'God's sake, Ruth. Get it together, yeah? It happens.' Andrea squats in front of the bedside cabinet and empties it into a cardboard box. Perfume, a fuzzy monkey, a toilet bag, supermarket moisturizer. The end of a life. 'You going to help, or what?'

So I do. Not saying a word. Trying not to sniffle in case it sets her off again. And then we strip the sheets off the bed, remove the pillowcases, spray the plastic-shrouded mattress with disinfectant and wipe it clean.

She's the fourth woman to die tonight. Two cancers, one septicaemia, and a pneumonia. All thin and rattling and alone.

The lift jerks and shudders, like it's crying, all the way down to the locker room. Names and swearwords are scratched into the stainless-steel walls.

It's the end of night shift, but I'm the only one here. Everyone else bunked off dead on time to stomp down to the Severed Leg in Logansferry for Janette's leaving do. A dozen haggard, hollow-eyed women hammering cocktails at five in the morning.

But Janette's never liked me, so here I am. Alone.

Up above – in the triangle between the main building, the admin block, and the old Victorian part where they keep the psychiatric patients – the sky's thick and deep-deep purple, like when you trap your fingernail in a door.

The doctors' car park is full of BMWs and Porsches, all covered with a crisp layer of white frost that sparkles in the glare of security lights, but the entrance to the underground bit they make us use is shrouded in darkness. Even with four nurses dead and two in intensive care, they *still* haven't put up lights. Just a notice printed in thick red letters, 'WARNING: LONE WOMEN SHOULD NOT ENTER PARKING AREA UNACCOMPANIED'.

Because *that's* going to help.

Still, it's not as if I have to worry about it – I don't have the car with me today. Some bastard robbed it on Old Year's Night and left it burning in a lay-by near Camburn Woods. Which makes getting to the twenty-four-hour Asda a pain, but there's nothing in the fridge but Bacardi Breezers and olives. So I take a left, through the broken security gate, beneath the lifeless gaze of a security camera with the wires dangling from its blackened casing, and onto St Jasper's Lane.

Half the streetlights are out. The cold air smells like pepper and lemons.

The pavement crunches beneath my feet. Little piles of grit make goose-pimple patterns on the slabs, dirtying the ice. I dig my hands into my pockets.

My breath mists out in front of me, pulled away on the wind like a ghost from my mouth.

Cross the road.

Should really go the long way round: past St Jasper's, along to Cupar Road and down to the bus stop, but it's much quicker to nip down Trembler's Alley.

When I was at school – can't have been more than six or seven – they told us the Earl of Montrose trapped the town council there, caught in the narrow slit between the granite church wall and the apothecary's. His men butchered them like hogs and painted the walls with their blood. Mounted their heads above St Jasper's door for everyone to see ... I had nightmares for months.

I... They haven't... The council hasn't gritted the alley. Maybe it's too narrow for the machine, or maybe they just can't be bothered? It's icy, slippery. Mounds of crunchy snow you have to pick your way through and try not to fall flat on your arse.

And it's *dark*. Just a couple of lights for the whole length, and they can barely work up a faint glow.

And... And I'm halfway down...

Please...

'It's OK, Ruth, you're safe, remember? You're in bed and you're warm and you're comfortable. So very comfortable and safe and warm and nothing can happen to you, because you're safe.'

And there's a noise. Behind me. Crunching. Like feet.

Oh God, someone's following me. There's someone there.

Faster. Get away.

Oh God, oh God...

'Ruth, it's OK. Take a deep breath. We're here. Nothing can happen to you, you're safe and—'

It's Him! He's right behind me and I try to run, but the ground's like glass beneath my feet and I slip and stagger and try to stay up. Get away, run away! RUN AWAY!

'OK, Ruth, I need you to come back to us. It's OK, we're here, you're—'

And the pavement rushes up and cracks across my knees and my arm goes out, but I can't stop myself and my head smashes into the ice and everything smells of old pennies and meat, and I'm crying and I can't get up and he's on top of me pressing me into the snow and there's something over my mouth. Hot breath in my ear, sour like sick. Stubble rasps against my cheek. His hand grabs my belt, undoing it... Fingers jabbing into the zip of my jeans. Yanking them down. Grunting.

Please, don't. No. Someone help me!

HELP ME!

'Ash, slap her. Not too hard! Just a gentle—'

'*You* hit her. I'm not—'

HELP ME!

Alice lurched out of her seat and whipped an open palm across Ruth's cheek, hard enough to snap her head to the side. Hard enough to stop her screaming. Hard enough to leave a perfect five-fingered print on her tear-streaked face.

Then Alice was on her knees, pulling Ruth into a hug. 'It's OK, it's OK. Shhh... You're OK. We're here. Nobody's going to hurt you.'

Ruth's shoulders shook, vibrating in time with her howling sobs.

'It's OK, it's OK...'

I stepped back, the tips of my ears burning. Looked away – out of the window and down at the street below. At Alice's

157

rattled Suzuki. At the three-legged dog tripoding its way down the pavement in front of a T-shirt-wearing skinhead. At a pair of vulture-sized seagulls tearing into a mound of black bin-bags. Up at the blood-streaked spire of the First National Celtic Church. Anywhere that wasn't Ruth.

Anywhere that wasn't pain and suffering and my bloody fault.

A harsh buzz trembled in my pocket, followed a moment later by a high-pitched ringing. I snatched out the phone that came in my investigation pack. Pressed the green button. Swallowed. 'Henderson.'

Shifty's voice rattled out of the earpiece. *'Ash? You need to get your arse—'*

'Hold on.' I put my hand over the mouthpiece. 'Sorry, I have to take this.' Yes, it was cowardly, but at least I wouldn't be just standing there, wallowing in Ruth Laughlin's pain...

Yeah, because it was *her* fault I'd let the Inside Man get away. Her fault that he'd gone after her. Way to be a prick, Ash. Great work.

I slipped out into the hall.

Must've been one o'clock, because the church bells chimed out their warm-up peal, followed by a single massive note. Dark and hollow.

'Ash? You there?'

'Have you got that address for Laura Strachan yet?'

'Doesn't matter where you are, or what you're doing – you want to get over to... Hold on...' His voice became muffled. *'Where are we?'* Then back to full strength again. *'Wishart Avenue. It's behind the—'*

'I know where it is. Why?'

'The Inside Man strikes again.'

17

Wishart Avenue made a redbrick arc between the condemned bingo hall on Mark Lane and the vacant business centre on Downes Street. It'd been residential once. Then shops. And now it was a gallery for badly spelled graffiti tags.

Most of the terrace was boarded up, thick sheets of plywood bloated with rainwater and swelling beneath the spraypaint. The handful of houses that were still occupied had steel front doors and bars on the windows. Puddles dotted the potholed tarmac.

Alice stayed close, her little collapsible brolly held over us both. 'Did you know Ruth was raped, I didn't know she was raped, why wasn't there anything in the file about him raping his victims?'

'We didn't know.' I sidestepped a pool of greasy water, the surface rippled by rain and rainbowed with diesel. 'Ruth didn't say anything about it when we questioned her eight years ago. Nor did Laura, or Marie... Though to be fair, we didn't really get much out of Marie full stop. Not with the brain damage.' I gave Alice a nudge with my shoulder. 'You're the only one who's managed to get the truth out of Ruth.'

That got me a smile and a blush.

A white Scenes Examination Branch marquee sat two-thirds of the way down the road, in front of an alley through to Henson Row. A double layer of blue-and-white 'POLICE' tape cut the street in half, a white Transit van and two patrol cars blocking either end.

Two figures stood in front of the tape barrier: Shifty in his cheap black suit – scowling beneath a red-and-green golf umbrella – and a short man in a waxed jacket and trainers. Baseball cap on his head, hands deep in his pockets. Shoulders up against the rain.

He squinted at us as Shifty pulled the tape up so Alice and I could duck under.

'Ash *Henderson*? Dear Lord, when'd they let you out?' The wee man grinned, stuck out his hand... Then used it to give his baseball cap a tweak when I didn't shake it. 'Good to see you. Sorry to hear about your daughter.' He pointed at Alice. 'Who's this lovely creature?' He gave her a little bow. 'Russell Kirkpatrick, *Castle News and Post*, old friend of Ash's. So you're here about the murder?'

Alice opened her mouth, but I got in first. 'Don't say anything: he's fishing. No comment, Russell.'

His face drooped. 'Come on, Ash, be fair. No one else's got wind of this yet – bottle of Glenfiddich if you help me out?'

'It's a blackout, Russell. No one's talking.'

'It's not Charlie Pearce's body, is it? Off the record?'

'Bye, Russell.'

Shifty lowered the cordon and hurried after us. 'So, you guys are up for a curry tonight? I'll pick up a takeaway if you get the beers in.'

Russell's voice echoed out behind us. 'Bottle of whisky *and* a ticket to the Aberdeen–Dundee match. Corporate box!'

No chance.

As soon as we were out of earshot, Shifty made a big show of patting down his pockets. 'Damn. Alice, any chance I can grab Ash for a minute?'

160

A small crease appeared between her eyebrows, then she nodded.

He gave Alice the umbrella. 'Just be a minute.'

We stood there, in the rain while she walked off towards the SEB tent.

Shifty gave it a couple of beats then leaned in, his voice low and garlicky. 'I've been onto my mate with the boat – you might need to hole-up in Fraserburgh for a couple of days, but you'll be in Norway by the weekend. And Biro Billy says he can have the passport ready tomorrow, but he needs a headshot. Mobile phone won't do: needs to be one of those approved photo-booth jobs.'

'What was all that business with the pockets?'

Shifty shrugged. 'Thought it'd be more convincing if it looked like I'd lost something.' He nodded towards Alice as she reached the SEB marquee. 'You taking her with you?'

I stood there, in the rain, mouth open for a bit. Hadn't thought about that. If I sodded off to Norway on my own, Mrs Kerrigan's goons would go after Alice sooner or later. And they wouldn't care if she had nothing to do with the death or not, someone would have to pay.

Shifty could take care of himself, but Alice?

No way I was letting that happen.

I cleared my throat. 'She'll be safer with me.'

His face scrunched up on one side, the eyes narrowed. 'Might be difficult. You know: abandoning her career and all that.'

Sodding hell. 'It'd only be a couple of years.'

She'd understand, wouldn't she?

One of Superintendent Knight's team poked his head out of the SEB tent. Looked around until he was staring straight at Alice. Frowned. He stepped out into the road. Middling height with a slight paunch bulging the checked shirt out over his suit trousers. He bared his top teeth. Ran a hand along his monk's tonsure. 'DI Morrow, what's this *civilian* doing here?'

161

I marched over. 'What do you think, you baldy wee—'

'Actually,' Alice pulled out her widest smile, 'we're all on the same team really, aren't we, I mean it's not about jurisdiction or brownie points, is it, it's about catching this guy before he has a chance to hurt anyone else, and my name's Dr McDonald, but you can call me Alice if you like, what's your name?'

He backed up a couple of steps, until he was right against the SEB tent. 'Err... Nigel... No, erm ... Detective Constable Terry.'

'Nigel Terry, wow, that's super, was it strange growing up with two first names, or did you not let that bother you, I know it can really undermine a person's confidence if people keep getting their name wrong, I mean everyone probably gets confused and ends up calling you Terry, don't they, and that's got to feel really rude, so who's running the scene?'

'It... We... Em... I am?'

'That's just great, so if you'd like to sign us in we'll take a look and then we can all get together and talk it through, is that OK, Nigel?'

'But... Yes?'

'Super.'

We scribbled our names into the log and stepped into the tent. Inside, the air was muggy and a good ten degrees warmer than outside, thick with the familiar smell of SEB marquee. A mix of Pot Noodle, coffee, and last night in the pub – sweated out into a white Tyvek suit and left to percolate for a couple of hours as they worked the scene in their own private saunas.

A couple of the SEB techs stood by a folding table, oversuits peeled off to the waist, chugging bottles of water. Steam rose from their shoulders in oily ribbons.

One turned and puffed out her cheeks at me. 'Hope you're not expecting anything exciting.' She pointed towards a flap at the back of the tent. 'We've got one alley and one handbag. It's not exactly *Gone with the Wind*.'

'Is that all?' Alice stood on her tiptoes and peered at the flap. 'Why isn't there a body, I thought there'd be a body, if there's no body then how do they know it's the Inside Man?'

The tech raised an eyebrow. 'You're kidding, right?'

I grabbed a couple of bagged Tyvek suits and handed one to Alice. Tore my own from its forensic sheath. 'He leaves a calling card. First couple of times we missed it, but it's always there.'

'A calling card? Why wasn't it—'

'Suit up. You'll see.' I struggled my shoes through the suit's legs, leaning on Shifty for balance. 'You've done a sweep for DNA?'

The tech nodded. 'Well, stickytaped the bit around the bag and the baby.'

I got my arms in and shrugged the oversuit over my shoulders. Zipped it up. 'Any semen?'

A snort. 'You're kidding, right? Wishart Avenue is a *Mecca* for young lovers. Long as you've got the cash, or a wrapper of brown.'

I pulled up my hood. Grabbed an oversized evidence bag. 'Just go back and look, OK?' The cane went into the evidence bag, held on with a couple of elastic bands. One more to fix a blue plastic bootie over the rubber tip. Bit makeshift, but it'd work.

Alice hopped on one leg, the other tangled in her suit. 'We just found out that he raped Ruth Laughlin before he abducted her, so he probably did it to the other victims too.'

'He did?' The tech's face soured. 'Great. *Thanks* for that.' She turned and hauled back the tent flap. 'HOY, RONNIE: DO A SWEEP FOR PUBES AND SPUNK! OUR BOY'S A FIDDLER.'

Alice hauled on the suit and did up the zip. 'He's unlikely to wear a condom, given the fact it's all about putting a baby in the victims' tummies, and why isn't the calling card in the case files, how am I supposed to produce coherent behavioural evidence analysis if I don't have all the facts, it's—'

'It's not in the file because of Sarah Creegan. Now, get your gloves and booties on and let's go take a look.'

She did, then followed me out through the flap at the back of the tent, leaving Shifty behind. Two suited SEB techs knelt on the alley floor, one dabbing away with a cotton bud, the other pressing a wide strip of clear stickytape against the ground.

A third figure stood in the background, leaning back against the brick wall, arms folded.

Alice did a quick three-sixty. 'He forced her in here, I mean it's not on the way to or from anywhere is it, and it's not like a young nurse is going to nip into a filthy alleyway for a pee, and who's Sarah Creegan?'

'Once upon a time, there was a little boy called Bob Richards, he was a very naughty little boy and his mummy and daddy didn't like him very much. So they beat him with a thick leather belt; broke his fingers and ribs; put their cigarettes out on his naked back; and once, for fun, they poured boiling water over his genitals. Sarah Creegan was little Bob's social worker.'

'So she reported the parents?'

'Nope. She put him out of his misery with a pillow over the face. Then she got his mummy and daddy drunk and gave them both an overdose of heroin. She cut it with slug pellets and caustic soda, just to be sure.'

The tech with the stickytape transferred the strip he'd been pressing against the ground onto an acetate sheet. Labelled it. Then got out more tape.

'When the second set of shitty parents turned up with a dead kid and veins full of poisoned drugs, we knew we had a problem. The third time it happened we noticed the calling card. Sarah Creegan was leaving tiny teddy bears at the scene – really small, maybe an inch-and-a-bit tall with a safety-pin on the back. Didn't spot it at first, because Cancer Research were handing them out if you put a quid in the tin for child-hood leukaemia.'

A yellow marker with 'A' printed on it sat next to the alley wall. Another marked '8' was on the other side. I walked over. 'So it went in the report: "charity teddy bear left at the scene by killer". And the next morning it was all over the papers. After that, every crime scene in the city was festooned with the bloody things.'

Marker '8' lay beside a pile of scrunched-up newsprint. I squatted down and looked back at the stickytape tech. 'You bag and tag it yet?'

An anonymous face looked back at me: bottom half hidden by the mask, top half by the safety goggles. 'The boss wanted to see it in situ. All photographed though.'

'Good.' I raised one corner of the pile. And there it was: one plastic key ring. A little pink baby, the chain coming out of the top of its head with a single Yale key attached to the ring at the end. '*That's* how we know the Inside Man abducted someone.'

I straightened up as Alice peered at it.

'The big question is: how did we find it in the first place?' The bootie on the end of my cane scuffed against the ground as I hobbled over to the figure leaning against the wall. 'Well?'

Detective Superintendent Ness's voice came out through the facemask. 'We got an anonymous call on Crimestoppers.' She pointed at marker 'A'. 'Working girl found the handbag lying here after servicing one of her clients. Says she thought a purse-snatcher probably dumped it, but maybe there was still something worth having inside. Got to the ID and freaked.'

Ness held up an evidence pouch. It contained a Castle Hill Infirmary identification badge – still attached to its green lanyard: 'MATERNITY HOSPITAL ~ MIDWIFERY SERVICES'. The photo showed a woman in her mid-to-late twenties, wearing cherry-red lipstick but no other makeup. Her mousey-blonde hair was pulled back in what was probably a loose ponytail. Striking blue-grey eyes and neat eyebrows.

It was the name that brought me up short. I blinked at it. 'Jessica McFee? Not *the* Jessica McFee? The bastard grabbed Wee Free McFee's daughter?'

165

'That's why our anonymous working girl called it in. Didn't want Wee Free to find out she'd come across the bag and done nothing.'

Wee Free McFee's daughter. For Christ's sake...

As if things weren't bad enough already.

'Bet he *loved* that. His little girl, grabbed off the street, raped, slit open...' I stopped. 'What?'

'He doesn't know. Not yet.'

Alice stood, brushed imaginary dirt off the knees of her SOC suit. 'Who's Wee Free McFee?'

'Good luck with that. He's going to go absolutely mental.'

Ness cleared her throat. 'Funny you should mention that. When I tried to get a Family Liaison Officer to go break the news, they all came down with dysentery. Everyone from CID disappeared, and uniform have called in their Federation rep.'

'Yeah, well, they're not daft.'

'Normally I'd *make* the lazy bastards go – send a firearms team in to break the news, if he's really as bad as they say – but the Powers That Be want this handled sensitively. Which is why I got DI Morrow to call you.'

I backed up a pace, tightened my grip on the cane's handle. 'Oh no you don't.'

'Apparently you have some sort of relationship with the man.'

'No chance – I'm not even a police officer any more, I don't have to—'

'I've spoken with Bear and he feels it would be appropriate for you to assist us in contacting the bereaved family and questioning them about Jessica's last known movements.'

'Well, Detective Superintendent Jacobson can pucker up and—'

'*And* he says to tell you that you can either get over there and break the news, or I can get someone to give you a lift right back to prison.' She shrugged, making her SOC suit rustle. 'Up to you.'

Alice tugged at my sleeve. 'Why's everyone afraid of this Wee Free McFee?'

Shifty backed up, keeping pace. 'Look, it's not my fault, OK? She made me—'

'You are *not* in my bloody good books.'

'Aw, come on, Ash, it—'

'Wee Free McFee. Yeah, thanks a lot, *Dave*. You set me up!' I stopped, dragged out my official mobile and called Jacobson.

'*What?*'

'Did you lend me out to Ness?'

'*Ah…*' A small pause. '*I was led to understand you've got a relationship—*'

'I arrested him a couple of times, we weren't moving in together!'

'*All you have to do is go round, tell him his daughter's been abducted, and get him to answer a few questions. How hard could it be?*'

'How hard?' I lowered the phone, limped off a few steps, then back again. 'He's a psychopath. I'll need some muscle.'

'*Ash, Ash, Ash…*' A sigh. '*That's your job. Your prison record is one long list of fights and broken bodies. Why do you think I sprung you?*'

'Oh, that's great. Well done. The guy with arthritis and a walking stick is the team muscle. What *stellar* planning.'

'*I'm sure it won't be as bad as all that, you just—*'

'And there's no way in hell I'm taking Alice in there. No muscle, no visit.'

A long rattling sigh. '*Fine, you can have some muscle. Constable Cooper will be with you in—*'

'The boy couldn't beat up a damp nappy.'

'*Well who* do *you want then? And it better not be one of your Oldcastle cronies.*'

I told him.

18

Bad Bill's Burger Bar was a rusty Transit van – painted matt black, with the menu chalked on the bodywork beside the open hatch. He'd parked it in the far corner of the B&Q car park, the air around it heady with the smell of onions frying in the fat that oozed out of the burgers and Lorne sausage.

Alice wandered back towards the car with her shoulders hunched, woolly hat pulled down over her ears, curly hair escaping to sprawl down the shoulders of her padded jacket. The fog of her breath mingled with the steam rising off the Double Bastard Bacon Murder Burger clutched in both hands. She curled in for another bite.

I popped the Suzuki's boot and loaded the contents of the trolley into it. Shovel. Pick axe. Stanley knife. Three-and-a-bit-foot-long iron crowbar.

Alice chewed – tomato, marie rose, and brown sauce made a Joker-from-Batman smile that nearly reached her ears. The words were barely audible through the mouthful of bun and meat and lettuce and crisps. 'Sure you don't want a bite? S'good.'

Duct tape. Bolt cutters. Compost accelerant. Heavy-duty rubble sacks. Firelighters. Lump hammer. Five-litre container of methylated spirits.

'Not hungry.'

Tarpaulin, plastic washing line, pliers.

'I've never had a burger with Bacon Frazzles on it before.' More chewing. Then she frowned at the boot full of tools. Shuffled her feet. 'I still don't see why you made me buy all this stuff just to go visit Mr McFee.'

'Because that's how the law works: if you batter someone to death with a crowbar, it's assault with a deadly weapon. Why did you have a crowbar? You must have taken it with you to attack the victim. You're going to prison.' I clunked the boot shut. 'But if you've got a car full of DIY stuff, because you're going to do up your new flat in Kingsmeath, you can batter the same person to death and call it self-defence. All about context. And I *will* pay you back.'

Alice froze, mid-bite. 'Are we planning on doing that? Killing him?'

Not him, exactly... But it'd make for an evening Mrs Kerrigan was going to remember for as long as she lived. Which would be about two hours if I could keep the blood loss to a minimum.

I turned the trolley around and gave it a shove towards the battered orange pipework corralling a few of its mates. Letting it find its own way in. 'I don't care what Jacobson says, muscle or not, there's no way we're going to see Wee Free McFee without a bit of hardware.'

And if the crowbar didn't work, there was always Bob the Builder. He smiled up at me from the back seat, that bright yellow spanner clutched in one hand.

'Ash...' She licked a smear of sauce from the side of her mouth. 'You were really quiet at Ruth Laughlin's and I think it'd be a good idea if we talked about how you feel about the—'

'Can you do me a favour?' I looked back towards Bad Bill's, where the man himself was hammering a chicken into bits with a cleaver. 'I know I said I wasn't hungry, but now I think about it, I could go a stovies. Only, my foot's killing me, and you know ... would you mind?'

She sighed. Took a bite. Chewed. Swallowed. 'Tea?'

'Yeah, please.'

But Alice stayed put. Tilted her head to one side. 'When you were on the phone with Bear, why didn't you tell him about Ruth being raped?'

Why? Because knowledge was power. What was the point of giving it away without getting something back?

I pointed at the Transit van. 'And make sure Bill doesn't skimp on the beetroot.'

Another sigh. Then she ripped a bite from her burger, turned, and munched her way back to Bad Bill's.

When she reached the counter, I ducked into the Suzuki and grabbed Bob the Builder. Gave the car park a quick scan – no security cameras pointing this way, but better safe than sorry. Got into the passenger seat and turned Bob face-down in the footwell. A seam ran up the middle of his back, but it was stitched tight. I flipped him upside down.

A line of Velcro ran up the inside seam of his dungarees. It scritched open, revealing wads of kapok stuffing. The stuff snagged on my nails as I pushed my fingers inside Bob, grabbed the gun, and pulled it out.

Black. Small enough that when I wrapped my hand around the grip and pointed my index finger the tip poked out past the end of the barrel. Light, too. I thumbed the release and the clip slid out into my open palm. Empty.

A quick check over my shoulder – Alice was standing at the hatch of the burger bar, talking to the dark rounded bulk of Bad Bill while he ladled something into a polystyrene container.

I dipped back into Bob and gave him what had to be the world's roughest full body-cavity search: rummaging through his innards till I had thirteen bullets in my lap. They were tiny – not even as long as the last joint of my thumb – steel-bodied with a copper tip, like a small metallic lipstick.

The first one was a struggle to get into the clip and it just got worse after that as the spring inside compressed. When the final one snapped into place I slipped the magazine into the handgrip again. Hauled back the slide and racked a round into the chamber. Made sure the safety catch was on.

Then gave Bob a loaded-handgun suppository and returned him to the back seat where he'd come from.

A knock at the window: Alice, her face now free of sauce, a polystyrene carton in one hand, a couple of wax-paper cups in the other.

Lunchtime.

Stovies. Couldn't remember when I'd last had proper ones, made with lamb instead of prison gristle and stock-cubes. The beetroot sat in one corner of the carton, staining the potato like spilled blood. I forked up another mouthful and shovelled it in while Alice sat with her phone pinned to her ear.

'Uh-huh… No, I don't think so…' Her satchel lay in her lap, a makeshift desk for one of the Inside Man letters. Its grainy, badly photocopied scrawl was streaked with yellow highlighter pen and red biro. The rest were stretched across the dashboard. Waiting their turn.

The view from the lay-by wasn't as bad as it could've been: out across a ditch, then a couple of fields, a garden centre, a static caravan park, a patch of woodland, ending at the sprawling boundary of Shortstaine. From here, the suburb was a soulless swathe of gingerbread houses crammed into twisting cul-de-sacs. Eight years ago, it was all fields.

'Yeah… Uh-huh… I'll ask.' She put her hand over the mouthpiece. 'Bear wants to know where we are.'

I lifted my left shoe from the footwell and jiggled it. The ankle monitor shoogled against my skin. 'Thought that was the point of the GPS.'

Alice's face turned down at the edges. 'But he's—'

'Tara McNab.' I sooked my plastic fork clean and pointed it at the bins by the side of the lay-by, overflowing with

McDonald's bags and empty drink cans. 'The Inside Man's second victim was found right there. Flat on her back, staring up at the dawn.'

'Ah...' Back to the phone. 'We're revisiting the deposition sites from the original investigation... Yes... No, I haven't met with Dr Docherty yet...'

A tangent of beetroot clipped off beneath the fork, got skewered, then loaded up with mushy grey potato and a lump of meat. Say what you like about Bad Bill's grubby van, hairy arms, and collection of tattoos, he made a mean stovie. Lots of meat, sod-all gristle, and comforting as a lover's embrace. I chewed around the words, 'Ask him what's happened with Sabir.'

'Yes ... I know, but we've been... No, Chief Superintendent Jacobson...'

Chief Superintendent Jacobson. Sounded as if she'd lost her 'call me Bear' privileges.

'Has he got those numbers from Sabir yet?'

'What?... No... Em, Ash wants to know if you've heard anything back from Detective Sergeant Akhtar?... Right...'

The carton squealed as I scraped the last morsels up with the fork. 'And while you're at it, when do we get our muscle?'

'Yes, I understand that, Chief Super—... No, it's... Yes. Soon as we can. Now, about getting someone to come with us to Mr McFee's house, is... Ah, right, yes...'

'Well?' The last dobs of mushy potato gravy got wiped up on a fingertip.

'No, I understand... Yes.'

I scrunched the carton up and opened the car door. 'Tell him to get his finger out, we're supposed to be catching a killer here.'

'What? Yes... It's...'

At least the drizzle had stopped. I climbed out and limped between the puddled potholes to the bins. Jammed the polystyrene container in with the shells of dead Happy Meals.

Was it raining that night – when we found Tara's body? Difficult to remember. Probably. All of us standing around in our white SOC suits, caught in the spotlights' glow like ghosts at a party for the dead. The guest of honour laid out, with blood thick and dark on the front of her nightdress...

Tara McNab's mother never got over the death of her little girl. She went on the drink. Started hanging about outside Force Headquarters with a thermos full of tea and a placard with 'POLICE INCOMPETENCE ~ CAN'T CATCH MY DAUGHTER'S KILLER!' on it in big black letters. Three weeks later she jumped off Dundas Bridge.

Couldn't really blame her.

The worst thing about losing your child was having to go on living every day. Everything else was a bloody cakewalk compared to that.

'Ash?'

I blinked. Turned.

Alice was half out of the car, clutching the satchel to her lap with one hand, holding her phone out in the other. 'Detective Superintendent Jacobson wants to talk to you.'

I hobbled back and took the mobile. 'What's the result on the phone box?'

'Why the hell are you sodding about at old body-dump sites? It's—'

'Dr Fred Docherty is an idiot. We're putting together an independent profile: the Inside Man picked these deposition sites for a reason, Alice needs to see them if she's going to work out what it is.'

'I'm not happy she's—'

'And while we're on the subject, I want to limit her exposure to Docherty. He's got an agenda to push – that's why his profile for Unsub-Fifteen's pretty much identical to the one he came up with eight years ago. He's not interested in the truth, he's interested in being right.'

An eighteen-wheeler thundered past the lay-by, tyres kicking up a mist of dirty spray.

'*I see.*'

'If Professor Huntly's about, get him to put a fire under the lab for those samples from Wishart Avenue. Probably a waste of time checking if Castle Hill Infirmary did rape kits on the original survivors, but you never know.'

Silence.

'Jacobson?'

'*Normally* I'm *the one who gives the orders round—*'

'Sorry if you've got sore toes, but we're looking for someone who's killed five women, mutilated three, and right now Jessica McFee's out there waiting to be slit open like an Arbroath Smokie. We don't have time to sod about with niceties. We're doing our jobs, and I need *you* to make sure everyone else is doing theirs.'

Laying it on a bit thick, but what the hell. Look at me, I'm a team player.

Don't send me back to prison.

'*All right, but I'll be expecting results.*' He hung up.

I switched the phone off and handed it back to Alice. Climbed into the car and pulled on my seatbelt.

She picked the photocopied letter from her lap and held it up. Some of the blurred spidery words were circled with red biro. She pointed at a line she'd highlighted in yellow. 'Does that say "fusillade", or "forward"?'

It was little more than a squiggle of grainy grey. 'Looks like … maybe "funwarde"? Thought these were transcribed years ago. It'll be in the case file.'

'Always go to the source material. It's not just about the words, it's how they fit together on the page – what happens on the lines above and below.' Alice squinted at the paper for a bit. 'Maybe that's a "T" not an "F". "Terrified"?'

'Next time we're at FHQ we'll go see Simpson. The man's like a cadaver dog – if the original letters are in the archives, he'll find them.'

Another eighteen-wheeler thundered past.

She started the car, then sent the windscreen wipers groaning through the dirty spray covering the glass. 'I'm supposed to go discuss the profile with Dr Docherty.'

'Screw him. We're going to take a look at where Doreen Appleton was dumped.'

The jagged sea of brambles, where we'd found Doreen Appleton eight years ago, wasn't there any more. An electricity substation stood in its place, secured behind a chain-link fence with bright yellow 'DANGER OF DEATH' notices.

Bit late for that.

Alice peered out through the windscreen. 'Do you think we could arrange for Ruth to meet Laura Strachan? I think it'd be good for her.'

'Don't see why not. Have to find Laura first though – she's gone to ground somewhere, ducking the media.'

'Ash?'

'What?'

'If Doreen was his first victim, why didn't we come here first?'

'Because I didn't want to eat my lunch looking at a sub-station.'

'Oh...' She started the car again.

Holly Drummond's ditch was still there, running along a winding country road leading northeast from the Wynd. The regular Edwardian terraces glowed like rows of sandstone teeth, small private parks glimmering green in the afternoon light.

From here, standing at the side of the road, Oldcastle was laid out like a 3D map. Blackwall Hill to the left, rising up in a mound of grey housing developments and trendy shops. Kingsmeath beyond it, with its tombstone tower blocks and crumbling council housing. Then across Kings River to Logansferry: industrial estates, the big glass-roofed train station, and abandoned riverside developments. Castle Hill in the middle: twisting Victorian streets curled around the blade of granite where the ruins sulked. Part of Shortstaine just visible behind it. Then Cowskillin to the right: all seventies houses and an abandoned football stadium. And back across the river to Castleview, the spire of St Bartholomew's Episcopal Cathedral rising like a rusted nail from the surrounding streets, catching the last rays of a dying sun.

Nice place to dump a body. Heft your victim into a ditch, then stand here admiring the view for a bit, before heading off into town to pick up the next poor sod.

I got back in the car. 'Across the river, then take a left.'

The view from where he'd dumped Natalie May wasn't nearly as impressive. A railway culvert – just a small stone arch beneath the single line heading north – with a burn running through it. The embankment rose up on both sides, following the tracks, but the burn cut across it at right angles, like a cross.

Alice joined me on the grass verge at the side of the road, one hand on the barbed-wire fence, peering down into the shadows. The drop had to be at least fifteen feet to the water. She stood on her tiptoes. 'This isn't like the others.'

'There isn't a phone box for eight or nine miles.' I picked up a stone and tossed it over the fence and down into the burn. 'Everyone else was dumped where an ambulance could get to them in ten to fifteen minutes, clear directions, nice and easy to find. Natalie gets dumped in the middle of nowhere. If that maintenance team hadn't come out to fix the wiring, she could've stayed hidden for years.'

'No nine-nine-nine call.'

'No point, she was already dead. Same with Doreen Appleton and Claire Young. Dumped off the beaten track. Failures. If he thinks they've got a chance, he makes the call...'

Alice scuffed her foot along the verge, drawing a line in

the mud with the toe of her Converse trainers. 'Except for Ruth.'

'Except for Ruth.'

'It's not your fault. She was a nurse, she lived in the same halls as the other victims, it was just ... bad luck.'

I hurled another stone in after the first. It splashed into the dark water and disappeared. 'There's what, thirty nurses in each building? Three halls in total. Ninety nurses to choose from and he grabbed the one who'd helped me. Luck?' My walking stick squelched through the grass as I limped back towards the car. 'Of course it's my fault.'

19

'… *train now departing from platform six is the delayed three forty-five to Aberdeen…*'

I stuck my finger in my other ear and leaned back against the photo booth. 'What?' The word came out in a fog of breath.

On the other end of the phone, Sabir's Liverpool accent was like hairy treacle. '*I said, you've got a bloody cheek. My guvnor wasn't exactly made up when I got yanked off Operation Midnight Frost.*' Chewing noises came down the phone, and Sabir's accent got even thicker. '*Like it's my fault youse whackers up there in Jockland can't work computers?*'

The railway station's ironwork had faded from green-and-gold to rust-and-grey, the anti-pigeon netting sagging and torn, speckled with feathers. The floor beneath the thicker beams streaked with droppings. The big, domed glass roof was thick with caked-on dirt, painted orange and red by the setting sun. A crowd of people shuffled through the automatic barriers, trundling suitcases and sour faces.

'Did you find anything?'

'*Course I did: properly genius, me.*' The sound of thick fingers hammering away at a keyboard rattled through from the other end. '*Got thirty calls in the last four weeks. Ten are to local* residential numbers, two to the speaking clock, and eighteen to a business in Castle Hill – Erotophonic Communications Limited. Gave 'em a call and spoke to some biddie calling herself "Sexy Sadie". Premium-rate sexline. Had a nice long chat and a ciggie afterwards.'

'Hope you didn't put that on expenses.'

'You gorra email address now you're out the nick? I'll send you the numbers, names, addresses, and that.'

'Hold on...' I pulled out the instruction sheet that had come with Dr Constantine's investigation kit, and read off the address. The arrivals and departures board flickered, updating itself. Sodding Perth train was going to be *another* ten minutes late. 'Do me a favour and cross-reference the residential numbers with anyone on the sex-offenders' register. Doubt there'll be anything, but better safe than sorry. Then see if you can have a rummage through the HOLMES data for the original investigation. Might be a match there.'

'Bleeding heck, not after much, are you? Fancy a foot-massage while I'm at it? I've—'

'How are you getting on with the background noise on those recorded messages?'

'Give us a chance! They've only just—'

'And I want an address too: Laura Strachan. Still in Oldcastle, but might be living under an assumed name. Local plod can't seem to find her.'

Munching came down the line again.

'Sabir? Hello?'

'Oh, have you finished? Thought you might've been after a pony as well. One that farts rainbows and pukes glitter.'

'Sometime today would be good.'

'You know the problem with youse Jocks? You're all a bunch of—'

I hung up and stuck the phone back in my pocket.

The photo booth whirred and a strip of glossy pics dropped into the hopper. Me, looking like death had come early, staring

179

straight into the lens. A horrible photograph, but it'd be just right for a fake passport.

I let it dry for a minute, then slipped it into my jacket as Alice emerged from WH Smiths with a carton of milk and a packet of extra-strong mints.

She crunched a couple, chasing them down with a swig of milk. 'They were out of antacids.'

'Should've had the stovies.' I unhooked my cane from the lip of the photo booth. 'Sabir says hi.'

Alice placed the palm of her hand below her breastbone and rubbed at the stripy sweater. 'Is he coming up, because if he's coming up we should all go out for a meal or something, well, not all of us, I mean Sabir's not going to get on with Professor Huntly, but then I don't think many people do, he's a bit of an acquired taste and—'

'Sabir's going to track down an address for Laura Strachan. Just as well, because Shifty's hopeless.'

The distorted voice crackled out of the station's tannoy again. '*The next train to arrive at platform one is the four seventeen from Edinburgh.*'

She shifted from one red-shoed foot to the other. 'About this, are you sure—'

'Positive. Come on.' I lumbered toward the automatic barriers, joining a boot-faced bloke in a suit, and a teenage girl with big hair and a homemade 'WELCOME ♥ HOME ♥ BILLY!!!' banner.

I leaned on the barricade separating the platforms from the concourse. 'Alice...'

She crunched another mint, staring at me.

'Alice, what would you say if I told you I had to go away for a bit?'

'I won't let them send you back to prison. We're going to catch the Inside Man and—'

'I don't mean back to prison, I mean ... away. Maybe Spain, or Australia?'

Her eyebrows pinched. 'You're leaving me?'

I cleared my throat. Looked away down the line heading south. 'You could come with me, if you like.'

'To Australia?'

'Just... Just until things calm down a bit. You know, with Mrs Kerrigan.'

Alice stepped in close, stood on her tiptoes and planted a kiss on my cheek. 'Could we get a house with a swimming pool? And a dog? And a barbecue?'

'Don't see why not. Money might be a bit—' There was a warbling bleep and my official mobile vibrated in my pocket. I pulled it out – an envelope icon blinked in the middle of the screen above 'You Have One New Email'. That'd be Sabir. I poked the icon and read the message... Ten names, complete with telephone numbers and addresses. He'd even annotated them with the results of a Police National Computer search. Say what you liked about Sabir, he didn't mess about.

Alice peered over my arm at the phone. 'Anything good?'

'Every call made in the last four weeks from the phone box where Claire Young died. Two of the numbers are for people with form. One for housebreaking and assault, the other's on the Sex Offenders' Register.'

'What for?'

'Doesn't say.'

A distant rumble resolved itself into the grubby diesel roar of the Edinburgh train as it hauled its blue-white-and-pink carriages into the station.

The girl with the banner bounced up and down on her tiptoes. Mr Suit-and-Tie checked his watch.

Alice hunched her shoulders. 'What does Detective Superintendent Jacobson think?'

'No idea – didn't tell him.'

'Ash...'

'We'll pay the sex offender a visit soon as we've broken the news to Wee Free McFee. Don't need Jacobson or anyone else sodding it up before we get there.'

Bleeping, then the train doors hissed open and a dozen people stomped out onto the platform. And there she was – our muscle.

Officer Barbara Crawford had abandoned her prison uniform black-and-whites for a pair of jeans and a Raith Rover's football top – tattoos on full display. Leather jacket tucked under one arm, big rucksack over the other shoulder.

She hung back, letting everyone else get through the barriers first.

The guy in the suit grumbled off with a nervous-looking woman in a beige twinset. But the teenage girl just stood there, looking up and down the empty platform, her banner wilting till the tip was on the floor. Then she turned and dragged it away.

Babs stayed where she was. Nodded. 'Friends in high places, eh, Mr Henderson?'

'Ash. We're not in prison any more.' I jerked my head to the left. 'You know Dr McDonald.'

'Alice, please, it's nice to see you out of your uniform, Officer Crawford, oh, I don't mean that in a suggestive way, I mean it's not that I've been picturing you naked or anything, though I'm sure you'd look lovely, I'm not actually coming on to you, only it's nice, isn't it, to get a feel for people away from their work context?'

Babs's right eyebrow climbed an inch. 'She's a lot more talkative than she was inside.'

'Babbles when she's nervous, Babs. Must be the thought of you in the nip. You ready?'

'You got my money?'

'Nope. Whatever deal you've got going, it's between you and Detective Superintendent Jacobson.'

'Fair enough.' She pulled out her ticket and squeezed through the barriers. 'I call shotgun.'

* * *

Alice pulled the Suzuki up to the kerb and hauled herself forward, chest pressed against the steering wheel as she squinted out at the eight-foot high wall of rust-streaked corrugated metal that stretched away into the darkness. Coils of razor wire looped around the top of the barricade; faded yellow signs declaring, 'WARNING: These Premises Patrolled By Big Vicious Dogs!' and 'Pray For Salvation For HE Is Coming!'

Babs filled the passenger side of the car like a ton of cement and broken bottles. She sniffed. 'Got a squint at his jacket from a mate in Barlinnie. Nice bloke. Very family orientated.'

The horizon was on fire: a burning slash of gore and brass, trapped beneath a lid of coal-dark cloud. And in front of us, the junkyard loomed. A pair of tall gates – made of the same corrugated metal sheets – marked the entrance, topped with barbed wire and spikes. The words 'Frazer McFee and Son, Reclamation Specialists Est. 1975' were daubed across them in white paint, just visible in the headlights.

'Big vicious dogs...' Babs sat back in her seat again. A smile crept across her face like blood on a kitchen floor. 'Cool.' She winked at me in the rear-view mirror. 'According to my mate, Mr McFee's got a biscuit tin full of severed human ears in there.'

I undid my seatbelt. 'Ears?'

'All dried and smoked, you know, like beef jerky? And every time he tortures someone, he takes one of the ears out the tin and eats it right in front of them. So they know what's coming.'

'Did your mate tell you about the time Wee Free took a chainsaw to PC Barroclough's patrol car? Had half the roof off before they could stop him. Barroclough's cowering in the well between the front and back seats, hands over his ears, screaming for his mother. Never really got over that...'

'Way I hear it, there's *police officers* with restraining orders out against this guy.'

'Runs in the family. You should've seen his dad: "Blowtorch" Frazer McFee.' I sucked a breath in through my teeth, making it hiss. 'One man demolition crew.'

Alice licked her lips. Fidgeted in her seat. Cleared her throat. 'And we're certain this is a good idea?'

Of course it bloody wasn't. 'Babs, I think it'd be best if none of us end up in A&E tonight, so I'm going to leave you to take care of Fire and Brimstone.'

She half turned in her seat and squinted at me. 'Fire and…?'

'Alsatians. Big ones. You're good with animals, aren't you?'

The smile was back again. 'Wonderful.' She climbed out of the car, stomped around to the boot and clunked it open.

I pulled out my phone and called Shifty. Let it ring.

The boot thumped closed, and Babs appeared at the driver's window, a stab-proof vest on over her Raith Rovers top. She pulled on a pair of heavy leather gloves. There was a sawn-off shotgun tucked under one arm. 'We ready?'

The Suzuki rocked as I clambered out into the cold night. A faint whiff of diesel and fish underpinned the coppery smell of rusting metal. I nodded at Babs's gun. 'Holding up a Post Office later?'

She flicked the catch and the barrels hinged forwards, exposing their innards. 'You'd be surprised how often Thatcher comes in handy. She's very loyal.' Two chunky red cartridges slipped into the holes, then she flipped the shotgun shut again. 'Why, you going to report us?'

I blinked a couple of times. 'Fine, but if anyone asks, you found her on the premises, understand?'

A shrug. Then Babs rolled her shoulders and lumbered off to the gates. Planted her feet wide, and mashed her thumb against the doorbell.

Nothing.

Alice climbed out of the car as I limped round to the boot and got the crowbar out. Thing was just about long enough

184

to use as a walking stick. At least it'd leave me a hand free. I checked the Stanley knife was loaded and slipped it into my trouser pocket.

Yammering sounded from somewhere deep inside the junk-yard. Barking and snarling, getting louder and closer on sharp pattering feet. Then BANG something big slammed into the other side of the gate at chest height, making the metal sheeting rattle. Whatever it was scrabbled backwards and had another go: BANG.

Alice backed away from the fence, palms flat against her chest, as if the heartburn was back. 'Maybe it'd be a good idea to call for backup, I mean it's not as if we've actually got any official powers here, is it...?'

Fur appeared in the four-inch gap between the corrugated-iron doors, teeth flashing. The second dog smashed into the gate again: BANG.

Fire and Brimstone.

Good job the gate was chained shut.

Babs sucked her cheeks in and raised an eyebrow. 'Any chance he's not in?'

BANG.

'He's in.'

'Good. No point copping a sicky to come rattle some scally, only to find he's not there.' She frowned up at the razor wire. 'Can't go over. Have to go through. Come on, Crowbar Boy.'

BANG.

Yeah... Maybe not. 'That chain's the only thing between them and us.'

Babs lowered the sawn-off shotgun till it was at waist level. 'Don't you worry your pretty little head, Mr Henderson. Me and Thatcher will look after you.'

I lifted the crowbar, slipped the curved end in between the padlock and the hasp. Hissed out a breath. Bob the Builder was just sitting there, on the back seat. He'd probably like to help. Certainly it'd be a hell of a lot safer with him on our

185

side. But that would make Babs a witness – *yes, Officer, now you mention it, I did see Mr Henderson with an illegal handgun.* And when Mrs Kerrigan turned up with her face blown off…

Yeah, maybe not.

I pointed back towards the Suzuki. 'Alice, get in the car.'

The chain rattled as a huge furry body slammed into the other side of the gate.

'Are you sure we shouldn't just—'

'Car. Now!'

She fumbled with her keys and scrambled inside. Slammed the door behind her. Thumbed the locks down. Stared up at me with wide eyes.

I turned back to the gate. Deep breath. 'Right, on three. One. Two. Th—'

A harsh voice cut through the night. 'FIRE! BRIMSTONE! SHUT UP, YOU WEE BUGGERS, OR I'LL SKIN YOU ALIVE!'

Framed in the gap between the gates, the two dogs froze: mouths hanging open, tongues lolling over jagged teeth, muscles in their haunches twitching. Then they turned their heads and looked back into the scrapyard.

A tall, thin man, wearing nothing but a pair of torn jeans padded out of the shadows. Bottle of Glenmorangie in one hand, a huge meat cleaver in the other. His chest and arms were smeared with scarlet and black, more blood on his jeans and bare feet. Scars criss-crossed his torso – some old and pale, others angry red-and-purple – stretched tight across muscle, the skin like tanned leather between the gore. A mane of dark hair reared up from his lined forehead, a grey moustache covering his top lip. Hooded eyes, narrow as stab wounds. A face carved from granite and other people's pain.

He bared his teeth and whistled.

The dogs loped off to join him, silent and compliant.

Babs lowered her shotgun, one side of her mouth twisted up. 'He's a lot … better looking than I imagined.'

Never thought I'd be happy to see Wee Free McFee.

20

Wee Free padlocked the gate shut behind us.

Alice tugged at my sleeve, her voice low as the dogs prowled silently around us. 'It's like something out of a horror movie...'

The junkyard was a dark maze of partially crushed cars, stacked into monolithic blocks; mounds of scrap metal; and a sagging Cheops of washing machines, cookers, and fridge freezers.

A shipping container sat in the middle, surrounded by these towering piles, 'The Chapel' painted in chipped white on the side. It was bolted onto a ramshackle collection of two caravans, an ancient Oldcastle Transportation Company bus – sitting on six flat tyres – and the boxy bit off the back of a Transit van. All stitched together with more sheets of rusting corrugated metal. Strings of multi-coloured fairy lights hung in drooping lines, marking out a two-storey-high crucifix, looming over everything. Twinkling red and yellow, with all the festive welcome of an infected wound.

Home sweet home.

Wee Free wrenched open a wooden door set into the container's wall, and lurched inside, the cleaver screeching along the rust-streaked metal.

Fire and Brimstone squeezed past him, feet scrabbling on

the linoleum, and Wee Free looked back over his shoulder at me, top lip curled, showing off those little white teeth. Now he wasn't shouting any more, his voice was quiet. Well-spoken. Bordering on posh. 'You'll have had your tea.'

Babs slipped Thatcher through a couple of Velcro straps fixed to the front of her stab-proof vest, the gun nestling against her stomach. 'Actually, I wouldn't mind a coffee if—'

'We're fine.' I ignored the glower that got me. 'We need to talk to you about Jessica.'

Wee Free's back stiffened for a moment. Then he grunted, took a swig from his bottle of whisky and marched away down the hall.

Inside, the shipping container's walls were hung with striped wallpaper, slowly fading to a uniform filthy grey, darkened by patches of mould. A saggy brown sofa squatted in the middle of a Turkish rug – surrounded by drifts of paperbacks, newspapers, and beer cans – facing a small TV propped up on a stack of tyres. More books lined the walls, some in bookcases, but most just piled up in heaps.

The coppery smell of raw meat filled the place, so thick I could taste it.

Wee Free prowled straight past the sofa, towards the back of the container where a light bulb dangled from a cord above a wooden table covered in sheets of newsprint. The paper was clarted in blood. A large chunk of meat – about the size of a small child – sat on a crumpled patch of dark red. Whatever it was, there was no skin on it, just thick veins of white fat. He took another swig of whisky, then slammed the cleaver into the meat, hacking a chunk off the end.

Fire and Brimstone padded around his bare feet, eyes on the table, mouths open.

The container's metal floor was a patchwork of rust and scuffed paint. It rang every time my crowbar-walking stick clanged against it, like the toll of a funeral bell.

Alice clasped her hands in front of her. 'Your home's very …
distinctive.'

Wee Free gave her a tombstone smile. Drew the cleaver's
edge along the chunk of raw meat, carving off a thin slice.
'What's your name, girl?'

'Dr Alice McDonald. This is Ash Henderson, and that's
Officer Crawford.'

He took the slice of meat and tossed it over the edge of the
table.

The dogs scrambled forwards, jaws snapping, one of them
grabbing it just as it slapped against the metal floor, leaving
the other to lick up the smear of blood it left behind.

Wee Free transferred the cleaver to his left hand, and stuck
the right one out. The smile died. 'William McFee.'

Alice looked down at the blood-smeared fingers – scarlet and
brown, flecked with clots of black. Swallowed. Shook his hand.

Then he offered it to me.

The palm was sticky, the fingers cold and slick, leaving
smears of red on my skin. He squeezed, making my knuckles
groan. I squeezed back. Kept my teeth gritted and my face
dead till he let go and moved on to Babs.

I adopted the Standard Police Officer's Bad News Pose: feet
shoulder-width apart, hands behind my back. 'Mr McFee, we
have reason to believe your daughter, Jessica, has been—'

'She's a whore.' His mouth turned down. 'Fornicating with
that Godless … *Dundonian*.' The cleaver battered down into
the meat again. 'Dishonouring her father in his twilight years.
Turning her back on the Lord.' He bared his teeth at the bottle,
daring it to contradict him. 'Bitch is no daughter of mine.'

'Have you heard of the Inside Man?'

Wee Free stared at me for a beat, then carved off another
slice. Only he didn't toss this one to the dogs, he bit it in half.
Chewed. Knocked back another swig of whisky. 'Then it's
God's judgement. He's punished her for her sins. He punishes
us *all*, in time.'

Something wet brushed my right hand and I flinched – couldn't help it. One of the Alsatians was right beside me, sniffing my stained fingers. No idea if this one was Fire or Brimstone, but it was massive. Its wedge-shaped head moving back and forth, muscles rolling beneath the broad hairy back as it shifted from side to side. Ears forward.

'The bitch deserved to die.' He turned the cleaver, pressed the blade against his chest – in amongst the other scars – and drew it slowly from left to right. Nothing happened for a heartbeat, then blood welled up along the line, spilled over the edge of the cut and trickled down his skin. A sigh shuddered free from his lips.

Alice opened her mouth an inch, then shut it again. Looked at me. Then back at the line of scarlet dripping its way down his chest. 'Actually, she's not dead, well probably not, I mean she might be, but the other women abducted by the Inside Man were kept for at least three days before they were dumped, so there's every reason to believe she's still alive—'

'She's not dead? How can she not be dead? Of course she's dead, it's God's *judgement*.'

The Alsatian's tongue rasped against the back of my hand, warm and slippery. Tasting me...

Stay perfectly still.

Alice cleared her throat. 'Well, she *might* be, but there's a very real chance she's still—'

'You saying she's beyond God's judgement? That what you're saying?' He carved off another slice, the knuckles of his hand white around the cleaver's handle. Voice low and cold. 'You saying she's above God?'

'I didn't—'

'No one's above God. No one!' The cleaver slammed into the meat.

Alice squeaked and backed up a pace.

The dog stopped licking my hand and growled, hackles rising, teeth bared.

Babs put a hand on Thatcher's stock. 'Easy now.'

I inched away from the Alsatian. 'All right, let's all calm down. Dr McDonald didn't say anything about God, she just said—'

'No one's above God's judgement. NO ONE!'

Growling, snarling.

Babs pulled Thatcher out and pointed her at Wee Free's face. 'Time to put the knife down, Mr McFee.'

I nodded. 'Let's all just calm down, OK? We can talk about it.'

Babs clicked off the safety catch. 'No need to get uncool. We're cool, aren't we, Mr McFee? Cool?'

'"Hold not thy peace, O God of my praise; for the mouth of the *wicked* and the mouth of the *deceitful* are opened against me: they have spoken *against me* with a lying tongue."' Getting louder with every word.

'That's *not* cool, Mr McFee. That's another way of saying, "Shoot me in the face, please."'

He snatched a sheet of newsprint from the table. The front page of the *Telegraph* was half obscured with blood, the headline: 'Serial Killer Strikes Again' above a big photo of an SOC tent in the scrubland behind Blackwall Hill, inset with a camera-phone snap of Claire Young at some sort of Christmas do. Wide smile, shiny green party hat perched at a jaunty angle, snowman earrings with lights in them. '"They compassed me about also with words of *hatred*; and *fought against me* without a cause. For my love they are my adversaries: but I give *myself* unto prayer."'

The dog took a step closer, saliva dripping onto the metal floor. The other one emerged from beneath the table.

I tightened my grip on the crowbar. 'Come on, Mr McFee, put the knife *down*.'

'Be cool, Mr McFee, do the sensible thing.'

He padded out from behind the table. Threw the paper at his feet. '"And they have rewarded me *evil* for good, and *hatred* for my love. Set thou a wicked man over him: and let *Satan* stand at his right hand."' Wee Free's face was swollen and flushed, the sinews in his neck sticking out like cables, the cleaver snaking back and forth – glittering in the light of the bare bulb.

Babs braced her legs. 'Mr Henderson, Dr McDonald? You might want to back up a bit...'

'No one is above God's judgement!'

I smashed the crowbar down on the table top. 'All right, that's enough!'

And Fire and Brimstone weren't just growling any more: they were coming at me.

One second the world was full of fur and teeth and the next: BOOM! The shotgun kicked up in Babs's hands, spewing out a cloud of smoke. One of the dogs slammed into my chest. We crashed backwards onto the floor, in a tangle of arms and legs, a ton of yowling Alsatian pinning me to the cold metal floor. My ribs burned, the whole right side of my body throbbed. Oh Jesus, she shot me...

Alice screamed.

The other dog leapt, and Thatcher barked again.

The sound was deafening in the container, reverberating back and forth, a sledgehammer battering my skull flat as the animal crashed sideways into the table, yammering and whining.

She bloody shot me!

Alice stumbled over and shoved the Alsatian off my chest. Then grabbed my face. 'Ash? Oh God, Ash, are you OK?'

This was it: blasted at point-blank range. Bleeding out on the metal floor of the manky, cobbled-together, shanty-town house of a vicious nut-job, in the middle of a junkyard...

Next to me, the dog wriggled then he and the other one were on their paws, scrabbling away, tails between their legs. Whimpering.

'Ash?' Alice's face swam in and out of focus. 'No, please,

come on, you'll be OK, won't you, please say you'll be OK.'
She glared over her shoulder at Babs: 'You shot him!'

The real pain would kick in any second now, soon as the
initial shock faded. All that crap, all those deaths and pain,
and this was how it ended. It wasn't *fair*. Not like this. Not
while Mrs Kerrigan was still breathing…

Wee Free gaped at Babs as she broke Thatcher open and
the spent cartridges flew out. She slipped in another pair.

'You shot my dogs!'

Clack, and the gun was closed again.

Sprawled flat on my back, I checked for the huge gaping
hole pumping my life out onto the rusty floor. Fingers trembling against my jacket… Maybe they could get a tourniquet
on? Apply pressure, staunch the bleeding, get me to the
hospital?

Where was all the blood?

'Ash? Can you hear me?'

There was no way Babs had missed me at that range, not
with a sawn-off.

A gnawing ache clawed its way up and down my side,
where the pellets had torn through my flesh, ripping my lung
apart like…

Hold on a minute.

How could there be no blood? Not even a drop. Not so
much as a hole in my jacket. How the hell…?

Wee Free trembled, spittle flying from his mouth. 'You shot
my dogs! No one shoots my dogs but me!'

Babs brought Thatcher up till she was pointing at Wee Free's
face again. 'Drop the knife, Mr McFee, or you'll find out how
they feel.'

I batted Alice's hands away and hauled my way up one of
the table's legs. Struggled to my feet. 'ARE YOU INSANE?
YOU COULD'VE KILLED ME!'

'Inside voice, eh, Mr Henderson?'

'You *shot* me!'

She grinned. 'Rocksalt and tampons. Not exactly rubber bullets, but good enough at close range. Tell you what though: stings like an utter bastard.' She waggled the gun at Wee Free. 'Fancy a go? Or are we cool now?'

He lowered the cleaver. Licked his lips. 'They... Maybe God's using this Inside Man to give my little girl a second chance. It's a test of my faith. I'll find her and save her for a higher purpose.' A nod. 'Yes, that's it. It's God's will.'

Alice stepped in close and wrapped her arms around me, her face pressed into my shoulder. 'Don't *do* that to me.'

Knives and bullets ripped through my ribs as she squeezed. 'God ... please ... get off...'

'Sorry.' One more squeeze and she let go.

Wee Free placed the knife on the table, next to the meat. Picked up the whisky bottle instead and drank deep, then threw his arms wide. 'Praise be to God!'

Babs clicked Thatcher's safety catch back on and tucked her away. 'There we go. Now we're all cool again, I'll have that coffee. Three sugars. And have you got any decent biscuits?'

21

A lone firework streaked into the dark sky on a line of silver, then burst in a rattle of green and yellow.

Wee Free took another draw on his cigarillo and trickled a line of smoke from his lips. The security light turned it into a ribbon of solid white. 'She was always a pain in the back-side. Lippy.' He shifted his naked feet, elbows resting on the roof of a rusting VW Beetle. Where he'd cut himself, the blood had hardened into a scabby black line across his chest, the dribbles merging with the gore. 'Never did what I told her.'

Above us, the sagging fairy lights twinkled, drawing up towards that vast rusting cross. The rest of the junkyard lay thick with darkness, piles of dilapidated machinery looming around us like the bones of metal dinosaurs.

'"Honour thy father and thy mother: that thy days may be long upon the land which the Lord thy God giveth thee."'

I took a sip of my tea. 'Doesn't it also say something about thou shall not kill?'

Another line of smoke got caught in the security light's glare. 'That was thrown out of court. Insufficient evidence.'

The Beetle sat up on bricks. Both front doors were gone as was all the glass, the interior stripped bare except for the back seat where Fire and Brimstone lay, ears twitching, glittering eyes like polished marbles. Staring at me.

'According to the hospital, Jessica was doing a split shift, clocked out at midnight. We found her handbag on Wishart Avenue. He probably followed her there.'

In the shadows, over by the shipping container, Babs leaned against the corrugated metalwork, steam rising from her coffee, one hand on Thatcher's stock.

Wee Free took another drag. 'I've read the papers. He slits them open, stuffs a doll inside, stitches them up again, then dumps them at the side of the road to die.'

'Did your daughter say anything about strangers hanging around the dorms or the hospital? Anyone bothering her?'

'You strike me as someone who's let darkness into his heart.'

Me? 'You can bloody talk.'

A shrug. 'Like I said – I read the papers, I take an interest. If she's alive, I want my daughter back.'

'That's what we're trying to do.'

The tip of his cigarillo glowed like a malignant orange eye. 'Didn't manage it with your own, what makes you think you can do it for mine?'

I thumped my mug down on the Beetle's roof. Tea sloshed out onto the rusty paintwork. 'Fuck you.'

Inside the car, Fire and Brimstone sat up, ears pricked.

'Finally: a bit of passion.' A smile twitched the corners of Wee Free's moustache. 'Jessica hasn't said anything to me for years. Oh, I try, because I'm a good parent, but she's wilful. Got that from her mother, God rest her tortured soul.'

My knuckles ached, pulled tight into fists. Burning in anticipation. 'You don't *ever* talk about my daughters.'

'She was seeing someone, I know that. A godless man with a tattoo.'

Over by the container, Babs sniffed. 'You got something against tattoos, like?'

196

'Leviticus 19:28, "Ye shall not make any cuttings in your flesh for the dead, nor print any marks upon you."'

'Says the man with the moustache: Leviticus 19:27. *And* you cut yourself – we all saw it.'

He raised an eyebrow. 'But not for the dead.' Then went back to his cigarillo. 'You've no idea where he takes them, do you?'

I stepped back. Took a deep breath. Unclenched my teeth and fists. 'We're following a number of leads. I'll see if we can get a Family Liaison officer to keep you up to date, be your point of contact for the investigation.'

'In fact, you don't know a single thing about him.'

'We *will* catch him.'

The smile disappeared. 'Not if I get there first.'

Babs stretched her arms forward, till her fingertips touched the windscreen. Then slumped back. 'Thought that was going to be a total waste of time, but turned out pretty sweet in the end.'

Alice took the Suzuki down York Street, past the knot of halal butchers and dry cleaners, heading for the border with Castle Hill. The rush-hour traffic thickened the closer we got to the centre of town. 'You should maybe think about getting some help for your emotional expression mechanism, an overt reliance on violence for serotonin release isn't healthy.'

'Meh. Each to their own, right? Sometimes it does you good to shoot things.'

I shifted in the back seat, but the ache in my ribs wouldn't go away. Someone slammed a fist into them every time I breathed.

'So,' Babs turned and grinned at me, 'what's next? Anyone else needing a rattle?'

Alice stiffened. 'The intention wasn't to "rattle" Mr McFee, we were there to break the news about his daughter, and anyway, don't you have to get back to work or something, I

197

mean it's been lovely meeting you again, but we don't want to be a burden, do we, Ash?'

'Nah, don't worry about it. Told them I'd come down with that norovirus, they're not wanting me back till it's all cleared up. Can you imagine a prison full of guys with vomiting and the squits? Nightmare.'

I shifted again, but it still didn't help. So another couple of Prednisolone got popped from their blister pack and swallowed dry. Probably should have read the instructions about maximum dosage and side-effects, but it was too late for that. And besides, everything hurt...

Alice tapped her fingers around the outside edge of the steering wheel, one at a time, like a centipede's legs. 'Tell me about the calling card.'

'The key ring? Cheap plastic from China, sold through cash-and-carries at something like a hundred for a fiver. Nearest wholesale outlet is Colonel Dealtime's in Logansferry. Retails from corner shops and pound-stores. We checked out all the retailers, but no one matched the profile.'

'Hmm...' Alice took the third exit on the Keller roundabout and onto Dundas road, where the traffic slowed to a crawl. 'What about the key?'

'Yale. YA-Sixteens. They're all for different locks. We took the key profiles to every locksmith in the city, and got laughed at. No way to trace what lock they were for.'

The traffic finally ground to a standstill, a long line of red tail-lights stretching away from us. Probably backed up all the way to the bridge.

She pulled on the handbrake and wrapped one arm around herself. Using the other hand to fiddle with her hair. 'The keys and key rings are symbolic – obviously the little plastic baby represents the bigger plastic baby he's going to stitch inside Jessica, it's fertility, *fecundity*, which means he's probably sterile himself, I mean if he could get someone pregnant the normal way he wouldn't have to go through the whole surgery routine, would he, he'd chain them to the floor and rape them.' A frown. 'But he *did* rape Ruth Laughlin, so maybe it's belt and braces, or he's mentally compartmentalized sex away from procreation?'

Babs rolled her head from side to side, stretching the cords in her neck. 'Maybe he's just a nutter? Maybe he *likes* cutting women open?'

'If we want to get all Freudian the key represents the penis and the lock the vagina, it's a metaphor for penetration and unlocking what's hidden, but then I always thought Freud was a bit of a pervert, all that stuff about wanting to have sex with your mother is just plain disturbed.'

I tapped her on the shoulder. 'Can we cut to the chase, here?'

'What if it's not a metaphor, what if it's an invitation...? What if it's a case of, when you get out of hospital and you've had my baby, here is the key to get back to me so we can be together?'

A snort came from the passenger seat. 'He's asking them to move in with him? Yeah, real romantic.'

'Maybe he doesn't hate women, maybe he loves them, and this is the only way he can express it: by giving them a baby...'

I tapped her on the shoulder again. 'We're moving.'

'What?'

Behind us a symphony for angry car horns filled the night.

'Oh, right...'

And we were on our way again.

My phone rang – Sabir's number. I picked up. 'What have you got?'

'*What, no pleasantries? No, "Here, Sabir, you're my favourite bizzie, you are, a star among men and killer with the ladies"?*'

Alice slid the car forward ten foot, then came to a halt again.

'Finger out, we're none of us getting any younger here.'

199

A pause. Then, *'Fine. Be like that. Got an address for one Laura Strachan: Thirteen Camburn View Crescent, Shortstaine. And you want to know how I got it? It was doing my head in – they're not living at the family home, probably cos of all the journos, so—'*

'The short version, Sabir.'

'You know, I used to like you.'

'No you didn't.'

'Bloody long time ago, mind. They're not registered at the address, it doesn't belong to a relative, and they're paying the rent in cash. Playing properly hard-to-get. But her bloke... Now, I accidentally *got hold of his credit-card details – don't ask. He's getting stuff delivered off the interwebs. And when I accidentally got access to his Amazon account too, guess what he's using as a delivery address?'*

'Now you see, *this* is why I stick up for you when people start mouthing off about your general lack of personal hygiene. What about the audio?'

'Personal hygiene? Cheeky bugger. You'll get the audio when it's ready. If I'd known you were going to be this big a pain in the arse, I would've had a word with your mam when I was shagging her last night. Got her to give you a clip round the lug.'

'Bye, Sabir.' The phone went back in my pocket.

So we finally had an address for Laura Strachan. Mind you, if the calls from that phone box panned out, we might be able to leave the poor woman alone after all... Still, it'd be nice if Ruth Laughlin *could* talk to her. God knew I owed Ruth that much.

I pointed through the windscreen. 'Take the next left, we'll cut along Slaine Road. Should miss the worst of it.'

'... I'm not asking you to kill anyone, George, I just want you to check your records: why's Cunningham on the sex-offenders' register?' I shifted my mobile from one ear to the other as Babs squeezed herself out of the Suzuki's passenger door and into the rain.

200

There was a pause. Then George's nasal monotone droned out of the earpiece. *'Why do you want to know?'*

'Just interested.' Because there was no way I was going to tell him Cunningham had been on the receiving end of a call from the phone box where the Inside Man tried to dump Claire Young's body. It'd be all over the station by the time I hung up the phone, and as soon as Jacobson found out... Well, he wasn't likely to be very pleased at being kept in the dark, was he? 'A quick search on the computer, how hard can it be?'

'It's not like it was in the old days, we've got a duty of care to the dodgy bastards. We can't just go handing out their personal—'

'Are you forgetting what happened in Falkirk?'

His voice jumped up an octave. *'You promised!'*

'Then get me Cunningham's details.'

Sitting in the driver's seat, Alice widened her eyes, mouthing the word back at me. 'Falkirk?'

I waved her away. *'Now* would be good, George.'

'Wasn't even my fault...' The sound of fingers clattering across a keyboard. *'Cunningham, Cunningham, Cunningham... Right. Here: done eleven years ago for having nine-gig of naked wee boys on a laptop. Two counts of indecent exposure about a month after release. Three assaults on pregnant women. And...'* More typing. *'And unlawful sex with two minors, six years ago. What sort of idiot puts someone like that in charge of a primary-school swimming club? On the register for life. Gets a visit every other week from McKevitt and Nenova.'*

'How long for the kiddie porn?'

'Erm... Four years, released on licence after two.'

'Thanks, George.' I stuck the phone back in my pocket. 'Here's something interesting: our sex offender has form for assaulting pregnant women.' I climbed out of the car.

After a beat, Alice did too, closed the door and plipped the locks. Put up a little collapsible brolly. 'Are you sure we shouldn't tell Detective Superintendent Jacobson?'

201

'If this works out, we go to him with a result. If it doesn't pan out, he doesn't need to know. Everyone wins.'

Carrick Gardens looped away down the hill – two rows of bland, respectable bungalows, some with loft conversions, all with neat front gardens and estate cars in the driveways. Not the poshest bit of Castleview by a long way, but infinitely better than the crappy flat Alice had rented in Kingsmeath. Decent view as well: over the river, Dundas Bridge, and up the cliff to the castle, streetlights twinkling in the darkness.

I hobbled after Babs, up the garden path to number nineteen. The blinds were down on the two front windows, the door painted red, with a semi-transparent stained-glass panel. 'Cunningham's been in and out of prison for the last eleven years, but was *definitely* at large during the Inside Man's first spree.'

Babs thumbed the doorbell.

Alice stopped halfway down the path. Fiddled with her hair for a bit as the rain drummed on her umbrella. 'I'm still not convinced we should be deviating so far from the profile.'

'We're not here because I think Cunningham's the Inside Man, we're here because someone called this number from the phone box where Claire Young was dumped. So perhaps Cunningham knows him? Long shot, but we've got sod-all else. Besides, you said it yourself: the profile's wrong and Dr Docherty is a dick.'

'I didn't exactly use those words, I mean he's a very well-respected psychologist and I'm just a—' Her mouth shut with a click as a light came on inside. Then the front door opened and a puffy face peered out through the gap.

Mid-thirties, long blonde hair rumpled on one side, small mouth, a flash of what looked like a red towelling dressing gown. 'Look, I'm not wanting solar bloody panelling, my drive re-tarmacked, a free quote for double glazing, help with a PPI claim, to talk about Jesus, Tupperware, Avon, or a sodding Anne Summers party. For the last time: leave – me – alone!'

I stepped up. 'Actually—'

'Go away. I'm not in.'

'Miss Virginia Cunningham?' I reached into my pocket and hauled out my old warrant card. The one I wasn't supposed to have any more. 'We'd like a word about where you were last night.'

She took one look at the warrant card and her mouth fell open – round and red, like a bullet wound. 'Oh shite...' She slammed the door shut before I could get the tip of my cane in the gap. Her voice came through, muffled from inside. 'Shite, shite, shite...' The bolt clacked home. 'Shite, shite, shite...' Then she turned and lumbered off down the hall, just visible through the stained glass.

Babs clapped her hands. 'You want me to force entry?'

Alice blanched. 'But we don't have a warrant and we're not—'

'Do it.'

22

Babs slammed her elbow into the stained-glass panel, turning it into a multi-coloured spider's web of cracks. One more and it burst inward with a bang, shards clattering down on the floor. Then she jammed her whole arm through the hole, face flat against the door as she fiddled with the locks. 'Bing!'

The thing swung open and we tumbled inside.

All of us except for Alice. 'Don't we need a police officer and a warrant and—'

'Watch the front!'

Inside, the hallway dog-legged around to the right. The lounge door was open, the sounds of some sort of kids' programme on the TV blaring out its cheesy cheeriness. '... oooh, that is a spooky looking haunted house, isn't it? But don't worry, we can sing the "Bravery Song"!' No one there – just two couches, a coffee table and a large sheepskin rug in front of an electric fire. Video camera on a tripod beside the television.

I pointed down the hall. 'You take the door on the left, I'll get the right.'

'When things seem dark and scary, there's no need to be afraid...'

Babs squared her shoulders and stomped down the corridor, hauled her door open as I hobbled to the next one. She stuck her head inside. 'Boxroom: clear.'

'Just think of lots of lovely things, like crisps and lemonade...'

Mine opened on a small bathroom that reeked of ammonia. A towel hung over the side of the salmon-pink bath, stained with brown streaks. A couple of small plastic bottles lay in the corner along with a box of hair dye. 'Clear.'

'Airing cupboard: clear.'

The last door opened on the kitchen: fitted units, pink fake-marble work surface, peach tiles on the floor. The back door hung open. The window above the sink looked out over a rain-soaked garden caught in the glow of a security light...

'And you can sing the "Bravery Song", whenever you get a fright...'

Virginia Cunningham was clambering up onto a set of plastic garden furniture arranged against the back fence. Her red towelling dressing gown flapped out behind her, showing off a pair of pale legs, massive spotty pants, and a pregnant bulge. Had to be at least seven months gone.

'And, before you know it, everything will be all right!'

'Babs! Back garden.'

Babs pushed past me, stomped across the kitchen. 'Come back here!'

'So forget the ghosts and goblins – no they can't scare us today...'

'And go easy. No violence.'

'Cos we can sing the "Bravery Song", and make them go away...'

Cunningham got one pasty leg hooked over the fence before Babs grabbed a double handful of dressing gown and pulled. Cunningham wobbled, then threw her arms back – the dressing gown slipped right off and Babs ended up on her arse in the wet grass.

'The "Bravery Song", the "Bravery Song", sing it and you'll feel big and strong...'

I limped out onto the top step as Cunningham pulled herself up the fence, now wearing nothing but mismatched under-wear. 'Seriously? You're doing a runner in your bra and pants? Think it's going to take long to catch you?'

205

She froze. 'I didn't do anything.'

Babs scrambled to her feet, reached out, and grabbed the strap at the back of the industrial grey bra. 'Slip out of that. Go on, I *dare* you.'

Cunningham shut her eyes. Rain plastered her hair to her head. 'Shite...'

She stood in the kitchen, dripping onto the peach tiles, clutching the dressing gown shut over her pregnant belly. 'Can I at least get some clothes on?'

I leaned back against the fridge freezer. 'Soon as you tell us where you were last night.'

Pink flushed her cheeks, hot against her pale fleshy face. 'I was at home. Here. All night. Didn't go out.'

'And you can prove that, can you? Got a witness?'

Alice cleared her throat. 'What do the Offender Management Unit think about you being pregnant?'

Cunningham just stared at her. 'I want some clothes. And I need a pee. This is against my human rights.'

'Right.' The fridge freezer was covered in kid's drawings. I pulled one free of its Blu-Tack. A happy stick-man family, grinning beneath a smiley yellow sun. 'Home alone. No witness. No alibi.'

She raised her chin, taking the swell of skin underneath with it. 'Didn't think I needed one. Want me to pee on the kitchen floor? That what gets you off? Pregnant women peeing?'

'Oh, for God's sake. Fine. Go: pee.' I pointed at the hallway. 'Babs, stand outside the door and make sure she doesn't try anything.' Well, it wasn't as if she'd be able to wiggle out the bathroom window.

Cunningham waddled off with Babs in tow.

As soon as the toilet door clunked shut, Alice pulled a face. 'I'm very uncomfortable with the thought of her having a child, I mean what if it's a boy, do they think she won't sexually abuse it just because it's hers, because most abuse happens within the family and I really don't think the child's going to be safe, well, unless it's a girl, and even then... Where are you going?'

'Living room.'

'Oh. Can I come too?'

The kids' show was still playing – a pair of idiots in fluorescent dungarees dancing with a third idiot dressed as Jacob Marley, chains rattling as he went. *'Oh, I used to be quite scary, but I'd much rather be nice. Because having friends and having fun—'*

I dumped the kid's drawing on the coffee table, picked up the remote and jabbed pause – the trio froze, mid-song.

The tripod by the TV had a small camcorder mounted on it, the kind with the little screen that swivelled out of the side. It was pointing at the sheepskin rug in front of the electric fire.

The sound of a flushing toilet filtered down the corridor, followed by a clunk – that'd be the bathroom door – then another clunk. Bedroom.

Probably hadn't even washed her hands.

Alice stood by the door, looking back over her shoulder, both arms wrapped around herself. 'Do you think we should have a word with her social worker and the monitoring team, only she really shouldn't be—'

'I think they probably already know she's dodgy.' I moved around behind the camera and tilted the screen up a bit. Pressed the power button.

'Virginia Cunningham. It's a bit ironic, isn't it, given her track record: the cunning virgin?'

Maybe not so cunning after all. The screen lit up blue, with a row of icons along the bottom: rewind, play, forwards, record. I pressed play and the screen filled with the sheepskin rug and fire, obviously shot from here.

'Ash? Don't you think it's ironic?'

Cunningham waddled into shot, dressed in a matching set of black bra and pants, the blue veins on her legs visible

207

through her pale skin, bellybutton popped to an outie. She lowered herself to the rug in three awkward grunting steps, clearly having trouble with her pregnant bulge. Then she pouted at the camera and started rubbing herself, licking her lips, peeling off her bra.

I hit rewind and she jumped to her feet, lurched backwards out of shot.

Singing came from somewhere down the hall outside. Not a great voice, but not awful either. *'When things seem dark and scary, there's no need to be afraid. Just think of lots of lovely things, like crisps and lemonade…'* That would be Cunningham – somehow Babs didn't seem like the kind who'd need to sing the 'Bravery Song'.

'And you can sing the "Bravery Song", whenever you get a fright. And, before you know it, everything will be all right…'

Someone else reversed onto the screen – a small boy, blond, wearing nothing but a vest. Red welts on his bare arms and legs. Couldn't have been much more than four or five. I jabbed the pause button and there he was, staring at the camera with wide blue eyes, tears on his cheeks, snot glistening on his top lip.

'So forget the ghosts and goblins – no they can't scare us today…'

I set it rewinding again. Cunningham backed into shot, naked except for two black leather gloves.

'Cos we can sing the Bravery Song, and make *them go away…'*

And then she was… I switched the thing off. Stepped away from the camera.

'Ash? Are you all right? You've gone all red.'

'The "Bravery Song", the "Bravery Song", sing it and you'll feel big and strong…'

I turned away, stared at the closed blinds. 'Get her. Get the rancid bitch in here. *Now.*'

'And you can sing it all night long, till good things come along.'

The plasterboard rattled as I slammed my palm against it. 'And tell her to SHUT THE FUCK UP!'

Silence.

Alice shuffled her little red shoes, then hurried out. There was some muffled conversation in the hallway, then Babs's voice boomed out. '*All right, that's enough. Get your bloody clothes on already!*'

Two minutes later, Alice was back with Cunningham. Babs brought up the rear, blocking the doorway.

Cunningham had changed the dressing gown for a maternity dress: dark blue, with little red flowers. A pair of greying trainers. White cardigan. She lowered herself into the couch, flexing her hands into fists, then out again, as if she was trying to work out a cramp. 'I didn't do anything.'

I grabbed the camcorder, complete with tripod and thrust it under her nose. 'YOU WANT TO REPHRASE THAT?'

She flinched back, pushing herself into the upholstery. 'You didn't show me a search warrant. You can't use that as evidence.' A smile. 'I know my rights. I want a lawyer.'

'Oh, I know what you want...' I put the camera back by the TV. 'Who is it: neighbour's child? Bet it is. Some nice trusting family that doesn't know you like to fiddle with little boys. What do you think they'll do when I show them that film? Think they'll invite you round for drinks and nibbles?'

'I know my rights.'

I smiled down at her. Took some doing, but I got one on my face. Let it sit there, cooling. 'You seem to be confusing us with *police* officers. We don't have to give a toss about evidentiary procedure, because we're not bound by it.' I leaned in close. 'You see my friend in the doorway? She's got a shotgun in the boot of her car. How much fun do you think she'll have taking your kneecaps off with it?'

'You're not the police?' Cunningham tore her eyes away from mine for a moment to glance back at Babs. 'You can't touch me. I'm preg—'

'Actually,' Babs rolled her shoulders, flexed her fists, 'don't

209

think I'll bother wasting shells. Use that crowbar instead. Can make a *lot* of mess with a crowbar.'

'I don't believe you.' Her chin came up. 'You're trying to scare me and you're failing.' A chainsaw grin. 'I'm pregnant. You really going to kneecap a pregnant woman? Nah. Didn't think so. Now get the hell out of my house.'

Alice settled onto the other end of the couch. Knitted her fingers together in her lap. 'Virginia, you're right. They won't hurt you. How can they? But you see, we're after a very bad person who's cutting women open and stitching things inside them. And we think you might know who he is. Wouldn't it be nice to be on the inside for a change?'

'I want you out of my house.'

Alice glanced up at me. 'Ash, when was the call?'

A quick check on the email from Sabir. 'Last Wednesday – five days ago. Half four in the afternoon. Call lasted for fifteen minutes.'

Cunningham crossed her arms beneath her swollen breasts. 'Get out, or I'll scream.'

'Virginia, it's not your fault society doesn't understand your love, is it? You love those boys and they love you, don't they? But the man who's out there isn't a nice man. What's happening *is* his fault. We wouldn't be here if it wasn't for him. He made us look at you.'

'I...' She shut her mouth. Pulled one shoulder up almost to her ear. 'I didn't do anything.'

'I know you didn't, Virginia, but we need you to be a hero and help us catch him. You want to be a hero, don't you? Have people look up to you for a change? They've got it all twisted in their heads, haven't they? Think you're a monster, when that's not you at all. Wouldn't it be nice to show them? Nothing bad will happen to you, I promise.'

'I...' A sigh. Then she looked up, into the corner of the room, as if the answer was written there. 'They don't know me. Not the *real* me.'

'So, someone called you last Wednesday at half-past four. Was it someone you knew?'

'I... I don't remember. Got a lot of calls last week. Setting things up for the birth, you know? Want to make sure everything's OK.'

'Think back to last Wednesday – half-past four: what were you doing then?'

This time her eyes flickered to the camera on its tripod. 'I was ... baking a cake. Chocolate. Everyone likes chocolate.'

'Was that when the phone rang, Virginia?'

A frown. 'Someone wanting me to fill out a survey? You know, one of those, "On a scale of one to five, how would you rate your assigned midwife?" kind of things. Goes on and on and on?'

Alice put a hand on Cunningham's knee. 'Was there anything else? Anyone else call?'

She shook her head. 'No, it was just a stupid survey, I know cos I was in the middle of ... baking that cake.'

'Are you sure?'

'Said, didn't I?'

'OK. I believe you.' Alice patted the knee. Then looked up at me. 'That's it.'

'Virginia Cunningham I'm arresting you under Scots Common Law for the taking and possession of indecent images of children and at least one case of Sexual Assault on a Young Child by Penetration, as defined in the Sexual Offences, Scotland, Act 2009.'

She turned and glared at Alice. 'You said nothing would happen. I *trusted* you!' Then howched and spat – a gobbet of frothy phlegm that spattered against Alice's cheek. 'Bitch!'

'All right, Mrs Cunningham.' Babs stepped forwards, grabbed her by the shoulders and hauled her up from the sofa. Turned to me. 'You want her in the car?'

'Get off me!' Eyes wide, spittle frothing at the side of her mouth. 'I'm doing you for assault, you can't—'

'Oh, shut up. It's called reasonable force.' I pulled out my phone. 'Put her in the kitchen: if we remove her from the premises it's abduction. Want this all above board.'

'I want my bloody lawyer!'

'Sure you do.' Babs swung her around and steered her out through the lounge door. Pulled it shut behind them.

A box of Kleenex sat on the coffee table, beside a pile of scribbled colouring books. I pulled a couple of tissues out and handed them to Alice. 'You all right?'

She wiped at her cheek, face contorted into a grimace. 'I think Virginia was telling the truth about the phone call. Obviously the cake business was a lie.' The tissue got crumpled and for a moment it looked as if Alice was going to throw it to the floor. Then she pulled out one of the Investigation Kit evidence bags and dropped it in there instead. 'Never know when you might need a DNA sample.'

I stuck my hand out and helped her up from the couch. 'So who conducts midwifery surveys from a public call box in the middle of nowhere...?'

Alice stared at me. 'What?'

I poked Control's number into the phone.

'Oldcastle Division, how can—'

'I want the Offender Management Unit: McKevitt or Nenova, don't care which.'

Alice frowned at me.

'One second... Putting you through.'

'Come on.' I hobbled out of the lounge and into the hall, making for the kitchen as Vivaldi's Four Seasons crackled out of the phone's earpiece.

Babs stood by the fridge, arms folded across her chest while Cunningham slumped at a tiny breakfast bar. Pot of yoghurt on the worktop in front of her.

I loomed over her. 'Who's been looking after you at CHI?'

She bared her teeth. 'Think you're clever, don't you? Well you're not. You're stupid and you'll be *sorry*.'

'I'm already bloody sorry, now answer the question: who's your midwife?'

'It's all your fault. That's what I'll tell them. All – your – fault.'

'Fine.' I stepped back and stood up straight. 'I'll get it from the hospital. You can go rot in prison for the rest of your life.'

A hard-edged female voice hacked its way out of the phone. *'Nenova.'*

'I've got one of your clients here with a camcorder full of homemade kiddie porn.'

A small pause, then a groan. *'Who is it this time?'*

Cunningham glowered up at me. 'What's it worth?'

'Doesn't bother me if you don't want to do yourself any favours.'

'Favours? Hello?'

'Not you: Virginia Cunningham.'

'God's sake, we only visited her three days ago!'

'Then you know the way here: get your arse in a car.'

A scrunching noise, and the voice was muffled just enough to take some of the harshness off. *'Billy? We're going out.... No, sodding Virginia Cunningham...'*

The star of the show held my gaze for a couple of breaths. Then looked away. Jabbed her spoon in the yoghurt. 'My midwife's Jessica someone. McNab, or McDougal? Something like that. Kind of mousey, but she's got these lovely eyes...' A smile. 'I knew a wee boy with eyes like that, once. Just the brightest blue.'

Mousey with blue eyes. 'Not McNab: McFee. Jessica McFee?'

A shrug. Then the smile got sharper. 'Just remember: it's all your fault.'

Not this time.

23

I stood back, holding the door open. 'Took your time.'

The detective constable standing on the step stuffed her warrant card back into the vast handbag slung over her shoulder. DC Nenova barely came up to my shoulder, the frown on her face making crow's feet around her eyes. Jeans, denim jacket, and some sort of monochrome animal-print T-shirt. Curly brown hair, not quite shoulder-length. Her voice was even sharper in real life. 'If we're more than ten minutes late, you get to keep your sex offender for free.' She looked back over her shoulder. 'Billy, arse in gear, eh?'

She stepped inside, out of the rain. Lowered her voice. 'Just between the two of us, this porn Virginia's made…?'

'Little blond boy, about four or five years old.'

'Oh God.' Something painful crossed her face. 'She didn't … you know?'

'Thought you were supposed to be *monitoring* her.'

'We are. We were.' A shrug. 'Oh, don't look at me like that: you know what it's like. We've got more sex offenders per capita than anywhere else in the country. Can't watch them *all* twenty-four hours a day. Haven't got the resources or the budget. We do what we can.'

A small thin bloke hurried up the path behind her. Stopped

just outside. 'Shift over, Julia, it's sodding bucketing down out here.'

Nenova did and he squeezed into the hallway. Stuck his hand out. 'Billy McKevitt, OMU. Thanks for calling us, Mr…?'

Julia thumped him. 'It's Ash Henderson. Remember? Used to be a DI till they busted him to DC over that Chakrabarti stuff? His wee girl got grabbed by that…' She stopped. Licked her lips. 'Ah. Sorry. What I mean is: he's one of us.'

'Ah, OK.' McKevitt nodded. 'So, what we got?'

I handed Nenova the camcorder and she turned it over in her hands. Flipped open the screen. Then went hunting for the 'ON' button. 'You haven't touched the tape or anything, have you? Should be plastered with her fingerprints…' The frown was back. 'Did she say where she met him? The kid? Only— Ah, there it is.' The screen flickered into life, speakers muffled by the palm of her hand. Grunting. Groaning. A high-pitched sobbing.

All the life sagged out of Nenova's face. Her lips pinched together. Shoulders dipped. 'Son of a bitch.'

She handed the camera to McKevitt. 'What?' His face did the same thing. Then he poked at the screen, sending it flickering into reverse again. Stood there in silence for nearly a minute. 'We've got at least three kids on here.' He slammed the door shut. What little glass was left in the thing tumbled to the floor. 'Aaaaargh! Two years monitoring her, right down the bloody drain!'

Nenova clutched her handbag to her side. 'Where is she?'

'Kitchen.'

'OK.' The chin came up, the shoulders back as Nenova marched down the hall. 'Virginia Cunningham, what the sodding hell do you think you're playing at?'

I followed her into the kitchen, McKevitt right behind me.

Cunningham was still at the breakfast bar, the counter littered with discarded chocolate wrappers and crumpled yoghurt pots. A half-bottle of Gordon's well on its way to empty. She took another swig. 'I want my lawyer.' Her finger pointed at me, then Alice, and finally Babs. 'These bastards impersonated police officers and forced their way into my house. Assaulted me, conducted an illegal search, and detained me against my will.'

Nenova raised an eyebrow at me.

'That's not how I remember it. When we arrived Ms Cunningham seemed distressed. Worried for her safety, we secured entry, fetched her in from the rain, and encouraged her into dry clothes. We discovered the camcorder playing in the lounge displaying images of child pornography. At that point I placed her under citizen's arrest and contacted you.'

Cunningham's mouth hung open. 'You're not actually going to *believe* that shite, are you? He told me he was a policeman. Had ID and everything!'

'Ms Cunningham's mistaken. Perhaps she heard me refer to my associate as "Officer Crawford",' I nodded at Babs, 'and assumed I meant police officer?'

Babs grinned. 'Prison officer, actually. Must've been mistaken identity.'

'They're lying!'

Nenova placed the camcorder on the work surface, the screen flipped out and playing.

'*Come on, darling, do it for Mummy...*'

Cunningham looked away.

'Thought so.' She closed the screen and switched the thing off. 'Virginia Cunningham, I'm arresting you for the possession of indecent images of children...'

I made a porthole in the fogged-up Suzuki window. 'Yeah, they're just taking her away now.'

McKevitt marched out of Cunningham's house, turned off the lights, locked the front door, then hunched his shoulders and ran for the unmarked Vauxhall parked outside. Soon as he was in the back with Cunningham, Nenova climbed out of the car and into the downpour. Walked across the road to where we were parked. Knocked on the window.

I wound it down. Held my phone against my chest, so the mouthpiece was covered. 'Something wrong?'

She leaned one arm on the roof and poked her head into the car. 'That was all bollocks, wasn't it? You impersonated a police officer, forced entry, and conducted a search without a warrant.'

'Us?' I hauled on my best innocent face. 'No, it all happened exactly as I said, didn't it, Babs? Alice?'

Alice looked up from another one of the Inside Man letters, a yellow highlighter sticking out the corner of her mouth like a neon cigar. 'Oh yes, definitely, I mean why would we lie about something like that?'

Babs grinned. 'Word perfect.'

'You see, Detective Constable? We're all on the same side here.'

Nenova sniffed. Looked back at the Vauxhall. 'Just make sure you stick to the story, OK? And stop telling people you're a police officer. That shite's illegal.'

Rain drummed on the car roof, almost loud enough to drown out the blowers going full pelt.

'Right.' She straightened up. Stuck a hand through the open window for shaking. 'Thanks. At least now we can make sure she gets banged up where she belongs.' Then Nenova turned on her heel and stomped back to her own car.

The Vauxhall's headlights snapped on as it pulled away from the kerb – Cunningham glaring at us from the back seat. I returned to the phone. 'You hear that?'

On the other end, Jacobson sounded as if he was chewing on something. *'That you've been impersonating a police officer? No, not a word.'*

'According to Cunningham, the hospital allocated Jessica McFee as her midwife. Cunningham gets a call asking

217

questions about Jessica from the very same phone box where Claire Young's body is dumped three days later.'

'*And?*'

'Perhaps Virginia Cunningham isn't the only one he called for info. Get Sabir a list of everyone on Jessica McFee's books. Then stick Cooper on finding out if any of them got phone calls too. Do the same with the parents of Claire Young's patients. Alice thinks the Inside Man's checking to see if they'll be good with children – good mothers.'

There was a pause.

Alice turned in her seat. 'Tell him we're going to drop Barbara back at the train station.'

Sitting next to her, Babs shook her head. 'Oh no you don't. I got a night in a hotel coming to me, and a brown envelope stuffed with cash. Dinner would be nice too.'

'Jacobson, you there?'

'*Now would you care to explain why,* exactly, *you didn't bother to keep me informed about what you were up to?*'

'You want me to bring you problems or solutions?'

'*They teach you that on some management course?*'

'Here's one for you: how did the Inside Man know Jessica McFee was Cunningham's midwife? Where did he get her telephone number?'

There was a pause, then, '*Ah…*'

'Claire Young was in paediatrics. Jessica McFee is a midwife. Shall we play join the dots?'

'This is it?' Babs stood on the pavement, rucksack in hand, looking up at the Travelodge on Greenwood Street. 'Really?'

I shrugged. 'Don't look at me, I didn't book it.'

'Supposed to be swanky…'

Behind us, the diesel rattle of black-cab taxis mingled with safety announcements about not leaving your luggage unattended or it'd be taken away and destroyed. The rumble of a train pulling out of the station.

'If you're hungry, they do a decent fry-up.'

She hefted the rucksack over her shoulder. 'Cheapskate police scumbags...' Then lumbered in through the automatic doors. 'Better be a double room.'

I got back in the car and on the phone. Checked in with Shifty. 'You got that info I was asking for?'

'Did you really do an illegal search of that paedo's house?'

'Don't need a warrant if you're a private citizen, Shifty. No way it's getting thrown out of court.'

'There's a wee ned owes me a couple of favours. Meeting him in an hour to go over what kind of security She Who Must Not Be Named's got. My money's on big dogs and barbed wire. How about you?'

Bob the Builder smiled up at me from the back seat, yellow spanner in hand. 'We can fix that.'

'Only problem is: we're screwed for tonight. My bloke says she's away through to Edinburgh for some charity boxing thing. Not back till tomorrow.'

Sodding hell...

Still nothing we could really do about it. If she wasn't here, she wasn't here. 'OK, I've had enough of big dogs for one day anyway.'

Alice tugged at my sleeve. 'Is David still getting the curry, or do we need to pick it up on the way home?'

'We're not going home.' Back to the phone. 'We've got a couple of things to take care of. You can let yourself in. And Shifty...?'

'What?'

'A decent curry, OK? The Punjabi Castle, not some dodgy rathole.'

It was after eight by the time we pulled into Camburn View Crescent. The housing estate curled around us like a brick cyclone: identical houses with identical front gardens and identical 4x4s in their identical driveways, all lit by identical lampposts that turned the rain into shimmering droplets of amber. The trees of Camburn Woods were thick silhouettes behind the houses. Solid black clouds, lurking in the darkness.

Ruth leaned forward in the passenger seat, staring out through the windscreen wiper's arcs. 'I can't...'

Alice smiled at her. 'Just picture yourself standing in the sunshine, like we practised. Feel its warmth seeping all the way down to your bones. Comfortable. Calm. Relaxed.'

Ruth shifted in her seat, fingers trembling on the black-plastic dashboard. 'Maybe we should just go home...?'

I put a hand on her shoulder and she flinched. 'It'll be OK. You were friends, remember?'

'It's just... I don't *know* her any more...'

'You'll be fine. Comfortable. Calm. Relaxed.' Alice climbed out into the night. Then after a beat, Ruth did too, leaving me to struggle with the seat.

Finally, I found the little lever – folded the thing forward, clambered over it and onto the street. Scents of woodsmoke and sulphur drifted on the damp air, underpinned with something musky. Wet soil and rotting leaves.

Rain seeped through my hair, cold and damp, trickled down the back of my neck.

Ruth sidled closer to Alice, then fumbled for her hand. Holding it like a small child afraid of getting lost.

'Comfortable. Calm. Relaxed.'

'OK...'

I followed them up the driveway, past the chunky oversized Mini, to the front door. Leaned on the bell.

No answer. So I tried again.

Ruth fidgeted, her breath a cloud of pale grey. 'She's changed her mind, she doesn't want to speak to us...'

'Trust me.' One more go.

Finally, the door cracked open a couple of inches and a man peered out. Short auburn hair, round cheeks, pale eyebrows above a pair of twitchy eyes. He looked Alice up and down, as if he was trying to memorize her. 'Are you ...' He'd moved on to Ruth. Stood there with his mouth hanging open.

'You remember Miss Laughlin.' I pointed at her. 'She was Laura's flatmate.'

His eyes narrowed. 'Good God... Ruth?'

What was probably meant to be a smile flickered on and off. 'Hello, Christopher.'

'Bloody hell...' Some blinking. Then he opened the door all the way and stepped out into the rain. Hugged her.

Her arms stayed at her sides.

'How *are* you? God it's been years.' More blinking. 'You ... come in, please, God, I'm sorry. Standing out here in the rain. We'll... I'm sure Laura's dying to see you.'

He ushered Ruth inside, stood back to let Alice in, then closed the door behind me. 'I'm sorry, we have to be careful.' A shrug. 'Journalists. Excuse me...' He squeezed past the three of us. 'Can you all just wait here a minute. I need to make sure Laura's OK. She can be a bit... With the pregnancy.' Christopher scurried off down the hall, and through a door into what looked like a kitchen, shutting it behind him.

Ruth twitched. 'What if she throws us out? What if she never wants—'

'Feel the warm sun on your face. Comfortable. Calm. Relaxed.'

Silence.

The hallway was anonymous, plain cream-coloured walls and laminate flooring, a single bland landscape painting screwed to the wall. As if it was a hotel room.

The kitchen door opened again. 'Come in, come in... I've got the kettle on.'

Christopher backed out of the way and Ruth crept her way into the room. We gave it a beat, then followed her.

A heavily pregnant woman stood at the sink, peeling potatoes. Her bright-copper curls were tied back in a frizzy ponytail that reached halfway down her smock top. Laura Strachan looked over her shoulder. Didn't smile. 'The bloody media's been hounding us ever since that scumbag got hold of my medical records. What bloody good was Leveson? Answer me that.' She hurled a naked potato into a pot, and a dollop of water splashed out onto the working surface. 'Can't even stay in our own home any more, it's like a siege – cameras and microphones and journalists everywhere.'

Christopher opened a cupboard and fetched out some mugs. 'Well, we could always take *Hello!* up on their—'

Laura Strachan's face soured. 'We're not talking about this again.'

'Wouldn't hurt to *think* about it, that's all I'm saying. Sooner or later someone's going to find us and the photos'll be all over the papers anyway. At least this way we'd have some control.'

Ruth looked about two sizes smaller than she had in the car – all hunched over, her hands worked into knots against her chest. 'Laura, I...' She stared at her feet. 'I'm sorry.'

Another potato got hurled into the pot. 'I was going to come see you, in hospital, but they said you weren't up to visitors. Said you tried to kill yourself in the loony bin. Said you'd gone mental.'

Ruth's mouth goldfished for a moment. 'I... It...'

Alice put a hand on her arm. 'Everyone copes with stress differently.'

She looked away. 'I knew this was a mistake. I'm sorry, I'll go.'

'Sweetheart, God, come on.' Christopher rubbed at Laura's shoulders. 'Bet it's taken a lot for Ruth to come here, after what she's been through. You don't have to be...' He cleared his throat. Turned. Opened the fridge. 'Who takes milk?'

'I don't have to be what? A bitch? A cow? Come on, Christopher, what don't I have to be?'

Ruth rubbed a palm across her eyes. 'I should never have come.'

I stepped up. 'This was important to Ruth. She thought you were her friend.'

Laura glared at me. 'She tried to kill herself and leave me on my own! Do you have *any* idea what that feels like?'

I just stared back.

She dumped the potato peeler in the sink, then turned and pulled up her smock, exposing her swollen belly. 'Look at me!'

Had to be what: four, six weeks to go? She was massive.

A puckered line of scar tissue reached from about a hand's-width below the line of her greying bra to somewhere below the waist of her elasticated trousers. A shorter scar crossed it at a right angle, a third of the way down – the angry pink lines stretched taut and shiny by the child growing inside her.

The kettle rumbled to a boil, then clicked itself off in the silence.

Then Ruth unbuttoned her padded jacket. Pulled up her sweatshirt. Did the same with the blue T-shirt underneath, showing off her identical cruciform scar.

The two women nodded, then lowered their tops, connected by an unenviable bond: members of an exclusive and horrible club.

Laura picked up the potato peeler again. 'Christopher, take the others through to the lounge. Ruth and I have stuff to talk about.'

24

'Thank you for organizing that.' Alice turned the key in the ignition.

Sitting in the back seat, I shrugged, then deleted Shifty's text message about not forgetting to pick up some beer. 'Ruth deserves better than she got.' Promising career slashed short by some scumbag with a scalpel, a private operating theatre, and a thing for torturing nurses.

The windscreen wipers squeaked back and forth in slow-motion arcs, clearing away the drizzle. Outside, the door to number thirteen opened, spilling warm light across the driveway. Ruth and Laura hugged, the physical contact looking awkward as they tried to accommodate the pregnant bulge. Then some laughter. A kiss on the cheek. And Ruth walked towards the car, pausing twice to look back over her shoulder.

Alice smiled at me in the rear-view mirror. 'What if people found out you weren't the scary grumpy old horror you pretend to be?'

'Less of the cheek.'

Ruth clunked open the passenger door and climbed in. Wiped her shining cheeks. 'Thank you.'

Alice pulled away from the kerb, skirting Camburn Woods, heading back towards Cowskillin while Ruth babbled about how great it was to see Laura again and how they were best of friends and wasn't it wonderful about the baby and there was hope for everyone when you thought about it and wasn't it lovely...

My phone went while we were negotiating the Doyle round-about: Professor Huntly.

'What?'

'Ah, Mr Henderson, tell me, are you planning on gracing us with your presence at the Postman's Head this evening?'

'What do you want, Huntly?'

'It's traditional for the team to get together to discuss the day's adventures. It's how we keep abreast of developments.'

Great – an extra couple of hours listening to everyone droning on about how little they'd actually managed to achieve today. Perfect.

And there was no way I could just skip it... Was there?

Worth a go.

'Is Jacobson there?'

'Hold on.'

The City Stadium drifted by on our right. Dark and barren. Someone had strung up a couple of bed sheets from the metal superstructure. 'BRING BACK THE WARRIES!' and 'SUPPORT FOOTBALL NOT CUTS!' daubed in blood-red paint. They'd obviously been there for a while – the fabric grimy and tattered, frayed at the edges by the wind.

Ruth just stared out of the window, a big soppy smile on her face.

Jacobson came on the line, sounding as if he was in the middle of chewing something. *'Ash?'*

'Yeah, this team meeting – any chance I can give it a miss? I got a sawn-off shotgun's worth of rocksalt in my ribs at Wee Free's place. Every time I breathe it's like being stabbed. Need to go home and soak in the bath before I seize up completely.'

'He shot *you?'*

225

'No, Babs did. But to be fair, Wee Free's dogs were trying to tear my throat out at the time.'

'*I see…*' A sigh. '*Well, if you've been in the wars, I dare say we can probably manage in your absence.*'

'Sorry.' Show willing. Don't give him any excuse to send you back. 'Anyway, do you want to give me an update? Let me know where we're at?'

Jacobson's voice got all echoey, as if he'd turned away from the phone. '*Bernard? Bring Mr Henderson up to speed. He's not joining us tonight.*'

A rustling clunk, and Huntly was back. '*Well, while you've been off larking around I, as usual, have been a superstar. That syringe I found contained Labetalol Hydrochloride, it's a beta-blocker frequently used to treat hypertension in pregnant women. Lowers the blood pressure. Just the ticket if you're planning on hacking someone open, but aren't too keen on them bleeding to death. Not exactly widely available at your local Boots the Chemists.*'

He found it?

'What does Doc Constantine say about the PM?'

'*I could give you the full medical details, but I doubt you'd under-stand them, so we'll try the CBeebies version. Claire—*'

'You think I won't kick your arse, don't you? First thing tomorrow morning you and I are going to have a wee chat, you pompous little prick.' Just because I had to keep in with Jacobson it didn't mean everyone else got a free pass.

'*Ah… Well, perhaps I did misjudge your sense of humour there.*'

'Post mortem.'

'*Sheila says Claire's got four cracked ribs and bruising consistent with an extended period of CPR: Tim* really *didn't want to let her go. Her last meal was a bacon cheeseburger with fries and pickles and some sort of maize-based crisps? Followed by chocolate cake. Consumed sixteen hours before she died.*'

The spire of the First National Celtic Church rose above the surrounding houses, scratching at the burnt-orange sky. Ruth wrapped her arms around herself and let out a long sigh, as if she'd been holding something in for years and finally let it go.

All that hurt and pain...

I frowned at my reflection. 'Who the hell is Tim?'

'That's what we're calling him now. T.I.M. The Inside Man. Tim. Sixteen hours means he's probably waiting for the food to clear their stomachs so they don't choke on their own vomit under the anaesthetic.'

Bacon cheeseburger with crisps. No prizes for guessing where her last meal came from. A little nugget to keep in my pocket until it was time to throw Jacobson a treat. Look, Detective Superintendent, I have been working after all, not just killing time till I could do the same to Mrs Kerrigan.

'Sheila also compared the stitches from Claire Young and the young woman they've still got in storage from the first time.'

'Natalie May.'

'In Sheila's opinion they're similar enough to assume they were made by the same person. The only difference is that the newer set are rougher than the ones holding Natalie together. She thinks whoever's doing the stitching is out of practice. And whilst Sheila is frequently a barb in my flesh and a pain in my posterior, I will, reluctantly, accept that she's a damn fine pathologist.' He cleared his throat. *'Just never tell her I said that.'*

There wasn't a single person on the streets, just parked cars and empty windows. 'What about CCTV?'

'Bear got them to pull the Closed-Circuit Television footage all the way along Jessica McFee's route to work. Cooper's about halfway through. So far all he's done is whine about it. The boy's quite useless.'

'Well tell him to get his finger out. This isn't playschool. And make sure Jacobson gets Sabir access to the HOLMES data too.'

'And while we're on the subject of useless, did you really ask Bear to see if they did rape kits on the previous victims?'

Alice pulled onto First Church Road, slowing to let a rogue Alsatian lope across the street, tail down as it disappeared between two parked cars.

'Far be it from me to rain on your parade, Mr Henderson, but even a basic grasp of biological science should tell you that semen doesn't remain viable in the female body for long. These women are abducted three to five days before they're dumped, they're all washed and the incision site cleaned down with chlorhexidine prior to their operations. So unless you're suggesting he goes to all that trouble to keep things sterile, carries out major surgery, then clambers on-board for a quickie before calling the ambulance, a rape kit isn't going to pick up much, is it?'

Huntly might be a prick, but he was right.

Didn't mean he wasn't crying out for a punch in the mouth though.

Alice stopped outside Ruth's building. 'Here we go.'

Ruth turned, leaned across the gap between the seats, and gave her a hug. 'Thank you so much.'

'Mr Henderson?'

'What about combings – they might have got pubic hair from him.'

'Ah, now that is a possibility.'

Ruth turned in her seat and waved at me. 'It's like ... like a light's come on in my life again. It's been dark for so long...' She reached back and placed a hand on my knee. 'Bless you.'

'Glad we could help.'

'The only drawback being, they didn't do any rape kits. I checked with the hospital staff – they were too busy trying to stitch them back together to do anything else.'

Ruth blinked. Placed a hand flat against her chest, as if she was pushing her heart back into place. Then she nodded and climbed out of the car.

'Of course, in an ideal world we could just check with the dead. But, Sheila tells me two of them were cremated, one disappeared, and – looking at her post-mortem photographs – it's clear that Natalie May favoured... Shall we call it a "Yul Brynner bikini line"?'

I folded the passenger seat forward and struggled my way into the front. 'What about Claire Young?'

'*Ah yes, a woman favoured with a full and lustrous mons pubis. One moment.*' A soft bleep and the phone went silent.

Ruth stood on her top step, turned and waved at us, before letting herself in.

Soon as the building's door swung shut again, Alice did a three-point turn. 'We need to get some wine and beer, or should we just get beer, probably we should get both, I mean better safe than sorry, and—'

'OK, OK: we'll get some wine.'

'*Hello, are you still there? Sheila says the Tigerbalm pathologist did a rape kit. But, just in case the man's an idiot, she's done one too and sent it off along with the tissue samples and bloods. We should hear back in a few days. In the meantime I shall ask Sheila to unleash herself upon the old post-mortem reports.*'

Why couldn't it be like it was on the TV, where DNA and lab results only took fifteen minutes? 'OK, let me know when they're in.' I hung up, before he said anything else that deserved a thumping.

The neon sign above the abandoned cash register buzzed and flickered as rain pelted the off-licence window. Bottles of violently coloured alcopops and minimum-unit-price booze lurked inside wire cages screwed to the wall, filling the six-foot gap between the front door and the short black counter that segregated the shop into two bits. Behind the counter, the whisky, wine, vodka, and beer were kept out of reach of the natives.

Alice opened her satchel and pulled out her Inside Man letters, placed them in a pile by the register. 'While we're waiting.' The yellow highlighter came out to join it.

She streaked a fluorescent line across two-inches of scribbled handwriting.

I turned my back on the counter, leaned against it. 'Henry thought he called himself "the Inside Man" because of stitching things inside the nurses. What if it's not, though? What if it's because he's on the inside?'

'Mmm?' More searing yellow streaks.

'What if he's one of us?'

'Mmmmm…'

'What if he's *literally* on the inside: screwing things up, falsifying evidence, burying the truth so we can't catch him?'

'Hmmm…' A sigh. She tapped the plastic end of the highlighter against the paper. 'Listen to this: "The panicked surge of her breathing makes my nerves sing. A choir of power and control…"' She narrowed her eyes. 'At least, I *think* it says "panicked surge" – could be almost anything.'

'What about it?'

Wrinkles creased her forehead. 'Not sure.'

Dear Lord, a two-word answer. That was a first.

She squeaked on another line of fluorescent yellow. 'Doesn't it seem a little *verbose* to you, like whoever wrote it was trying to make everything sound salacious, or like it was part of a book or something? All that imagery: the "panicked surge", "choir of power", "singing nerves"…'

'So, he's a pretentious nutter with literary delusions.'

'Hmmmm…' The highlighter picked out another sentence, then Alice stuck the tip of her tongue between her teeth. 'Have you ever read the letters the police got from Jack the Ripper? Some are definitely fakes, but the "Dear Boss" and the "From Hell" ones are the most plausible.'

Still no sign of the useless sod. The door at the back of the shop remained resolutely shut. 'This is taking for ever.'

'The "From Hell" letter goes: "Mr Lusk, Sor, I send you half the Kidne" – no "Y" – "I took from one women prasarved it for you tother piece I fried and ate it was very nise" – N.I.S.E. – "I may send you the bloody knif that took it out if you only wate a whil longer, Signed Catch me when you can Mishter Liusk." No punctuation: no commas, apostrophes, or full stops.'

'For God's sake.' I rapped my walking stick on the counter, raised my voice to a shout. 'Did you fall in and drown, or something?'

No response from the closed door.

Alice took her red biro and circled a couple of highlighted adverbs. 'Anyway, the handwriting in the "From Hell" letter is nothing like the "Dear Boss" ones. Neither have any punctuation, but the "Dear Boss" one's three hundred percent neater, and the spelling's way better. Lots of people think the "Dear Boss" letters are genuine – because they describe events that you could only know if you were Jack, or on the investigation – but "From Hell" came with half a human kidney preserved in wine.'

'Michelle used to get hers delivered from Tesco.' I banged on the counter again. 'Get a bloody shift on!'

'They can't *both* be from Jack the Ripper, can they? He goes from super-neat handwriting to badly spelled scrawl, and you can't just pick up half a human kidney from the corner shop, so clearly that's come from a very disturbed individual who's probably killed and mutilated someone, but that doesn't mean they're the same person.'

'Is there a point to this?'

The sound of a toilet flushing filtered out through the door at the back.

She circled another pair of words. 'So what we have to ask ourselves is was "Dear Boss" the real Jack the Ripper and "From Hell" a copycat, or was it the other way around? Or were neither of them really him?'

'Still not seeing how this helps.'

'Just thinking out loud. "A choir of power and *pain*"... That's how I'd put it. Power and pain.'

The back door opened and the guy left in charge of the shop lurched out, face pale beneath the short spiky haircut and designer stubble. He had one hand pressed against the middle button on his chunky cable-knit cardigan, cheeks puffed out, a black spike sticking out of his left earlobe. Donald's name badge was squint, a gold star stuck to the plastic. 'Sorry about that... You wanted half a dozen Cobra and some alcohol-free lager, right?' He crossed to the shelves on the right and picked up a pair of six-packs. Placed them on the counter beside Alice's letters. 'God knows what I ate, but dear God...' He rubbed at the button. 'Anything else?'

She nodded. 'Bottle of shiraz, a chardonnay – Australian if you've got it – and a bottle of Gordon's. And some tonic.'

'Right. Cool.' Donald peered down at the photocopy with its whorls of red biro and streaks of yellow highlighter. 'You see the documentary? I did it for my media studies dissertation. Some people think the hyperrealism of the re-enacted segments breaks the implicit contract of truth between director and viewer, but I think it represents a more fundamental *inner* truth by mirroring Laura Strachan's emotional narrative.' He pulled a little smile, waggled his head from side to side. 'Got a two-one.'

I picked up the Cobra and tucked it under my arm. 'Glad to see that's working out for you.'

He shrugged. 'Recession.' A bottle of red and a bottle of white got dumped on the counter, followed by one of gin. 'Most people just don't understand that the documentary works on so many levels. Take the characters: they're not just people, they function as fable archetypes. Laura Strachan is the Imprisoned Princess, Detective Superintendent Len Murray is the Troubled Knight, the psychologist Henry Forrester is the Venerable Mage, and Dr Frederic Docherty is the Wizard's Apprentice, isn't he?' Donald took a step towards the chiller cabinet. 'You want regular tonic, or diet?'

Alice slipped the letters back into her satchel. 'Regular.'

'He's even got his own narrative arc, hasn't he? From bumbling curly-haired sidekick to this slick TV personality in a suit, right? And we all know what Nietzsche says about staring into the abyss. Wouldn't it be the perfect transformative actualization if it was classic Thomas Harris – the psychologist battles his patients' inner monsters, but in real-life *he's* the monster. You want a bottle or tins? Bit more expensive, but they don't go flat as quick.'

'Erm… OK, tins.' She tilted her head to one side, staring at him as he got the tonic from the chiller cabinet. 'So, you think Dr Frederic Docherty is a cannibal?'

'Metaphorically – consuming his mentor's knowledge and legacy to emerge reborn as a media celebrity.' Donald returned with a box of six tiny tins. 'And the Inside Man: he's the Dragon. Lurking in the darkness, taking virgin sacrifices. Yes, I know they're not actual virgins, but the analogy's sound because he gets them pregnant with the dolls. Do you want to stick your card in the chip-and-pin thing?'

The brand-new microwave droned its electronic monotone in the corner of the kitchen while Shifty popped the top off a bottle of Holsten and passed it over, then opened a Cobra for himself. Clinked it against my lager and swigged back a couple of mouthfuls. 'Ahhh…' Then nodded at the bottle in my hand. 'A soft drink's one thing, but alcohol-free lager? Bit gay, isn't it?'

'You can talk.'

The working surface was littered with plastic carryout containers. Curries, rice, dals, side dishes, a silvered paper bag with garlic naan poking out of the top. A plastic bag of salad. Little polystyrene containers of dips and sauces.

I had a sip of the lager. Malty and hoppy and bitter. Five years on the wagon and it was like being eleven again, trying it for the first time and wondering what all the fuss was about. Should've just got some more Irn-Bru. 'So, where does *she* live?'

Shifty peered through into the lounge, then lowered his voice. 'Cullerlie Road, in Castleview? Victorian townhouse with private parking and big back garden. Mind that family where the dad stabbed them all to death in their sleep, then slit his throat in the bathroom? Just down the street from that.'

Tendrils of cumin and coriander reached out into the kitchen as Shifty pulled open the microwave door, before it went bleep.

'Security?'

'Bluelight special. Window locks and three-point UPVC door with deadlock.' The containers in the microwave got replaced by another set. 'According to my bloke, she's got a pair of dogs too – Doberman-Alsatian cross. So I win.'

'Need a couple of tasers then.'

Shifty sucked on his teeth as he programmed the microwave and set it going again. 'No chance. They're a lot stricter about that kind of thing since the merger. Could just pop the dogs, but … noisy. And bit of a shame too – not their fault their mistress is a bitch, is it?'

Alice stuck her head in from the lounge. 'Who's a bitch?'

'Erm…' He pulled on a frown. 'We raided a bondage dungeon in the Wynd this morning. Shocking language off the woman running it.'

'We about ready to eat? I'm starved.'

'Just got the rice and naan to do.'

'Great. I'll set the table.' She opened three drawers before she found the cutlery, then went back through.

'How about pepper-spray then?'

He nodded. 'That I *can* do. Been squirrelling it away for months: Andrew…' Shifty cleared his throat. 'Bastard was cheating on me. He'd come home reeking of Paco Rabanne, but he only ever wore Lacoste. Like I couldn't tell the difference? Really?' A shrug. Then Shifty stared down at his hands, the kitchen light reflecting off his bald head. 'Was going to swap them over – you know, booby-trap his aftershave with it. Didn't have the guts in the end. Didn't want to confront him about it, in case he picked whoever it was over me. How pathetic is that?'

The microwave bleeped time.

I patted him on the shoulder. 'He was an arsehole. And you were too good for him.'

'You're a lying bastard.' A little smile curled the corner of Shifty's mouth. 'But I'll take it.'

'How about this – soon as we've dealt with Mrs K, we'll pay him a visit with a baseball bat.'

The smile became a grin. 'Deal.'

I swapped the containers in the microwave for the rice. Stopped with a finger on the controls. 'One more thing: we'll need a sedative. Something to keep Alice … comfortable in the car while we're at—'

'Nah, no way. You're not taking her with you. Me, I don't mind helping you kill the old bag, but Alice? No. You can't.'

I reached down and pulled up my left trouser leg. Flashed the grey plastic ankle tag. 'Don't have any choice. If the two of us are more than a hundred yards apart, this'll bring the full force of the law down on me like a ton of incompetent lard. She's coming.'

Shifty started the microwave going again. 'It's not right. Alice—'

'Will be *fine*. It'll be clockwork: we drive over there… What?'

Shifty's grimace turned into a blush. 'Bit of a wrinkle: we need another car.'

'What happened to the Mondeo? I thought you—'

'I parked it round the corner, yesterday.'

Oh that was just brilliant. 'You left it in Kingsmeath?'

'Well, how was I supposed to know?'

'It's Kingsmeath!'

He picked at the label on his beer bottle. Stared at the floor. 'Yeah.'

Deep breaths. OK… Not the end of the world. 'We steal another car. Go over there, disable the alarm, in, stun the dogs, grab the murdering cow, out, woods, shallow grave, burn the car, home.

'But what if—'

'Nothing's going wrong. Trust me.'

Tuesday

25

'... that great? And they'll be live at the King James Theatre in December. You've got Castle FM on the dial, I'm Jane Forbes, and you're fabulous. Sensational Steve's coming up at seven, but first here's Lucy's Drowning with their new single, "Lazarus Morning".'

I blinked at the ceiling, heart beating like a brick in a washing machine. Where the hell...

Right. The flat in Kingsmeath. Not prison.

Got to stop doing that.

Closed my eyes. Let my head fall back against the pillow. Hauled in a deep trembling breath.

A guitar jangled from the clock-radio, upbeat and jarring. Then a man's voice: 'It's Monday morning, eight a.m., and my head's on fire again, for you. For you.'

Today was the day. Finally. After all this time.

'Another night of cheating death, living with your final breath, for me. You see?'

Bob the Builder grinned at me from the bottom of the bed.

'And all the people on this bus, don't know about the end of us...'

Mrs Kerrigan's last day on earth.

'Can't see the way I'm torn inside, my hollow heart is all untied...'

The clattering in my chest settled down to a dull ache. It

239

was one thing to fantasize about killing someone, another to plan and prepare for it, but to do it?

'Like Lazarus crying, his soul to the stars...'

To actually stick the barrel of a gun against the back of their head and pull the trigger?

Couldn't help but smile.

'Filled up with strangers from desolate bars.'

Of course Mrs Kerrigan deserved something a lot slower and more intimate. Something with knives and pliers and drills... But would that bring Parker back? Course it wouldn't.

'Lazarus morning, all wrapped in decay...'

Come on, Ash. Up.

'I will rise from this darkness, but just not today...'

I stayed put, warm beneath the duvet.

The gun cold in my hand, the barrel blazing as the bullet seared into her forehead, the boom mingling with the wet explosion as the back of her head splattered its contents out across the floor.

Take her kneecaps first.

Listen to her begging for mercy.

Like she deserved any...

The song played out. Was replaced by another one. Then one more after that.

At least we didn't have to go to morning prayers today. For the first time in two years I could stay in bed as long as I liked.

'... new single from Closed for Refurbishment. What do you think? It's growing on me. Anyway, it's coming up for half past, and that means it's Donald with news, travel, and weather. Donald?'

I sat up, swung my legs out of bed.

'Thanks, Jane. Oldcastle Police have appealed for volunteers to help search for missing five-year-old Charlie Pearce. The schoolboy went missing on Sunday night, and officials are becoming increasingly concerned for his safety...'

240

My foot crackled and burned as I rolled it one way, then back again. Back and forth until it didn't hurt *quite* as much. Shame the same wasn't true about my ribs. The skin was purple, blue, and black – stretched all the way down my right-hand side, from armpit to knee. More on my shoulder and arm. As if I'd been battered with a two-by-four.

'*… car park at Moncuir Wood from eight this morning. In other news, a source close to Operation Tigerbalm, investigating the death of Claire Young, has revealed that the Inside Man has abducted another victim. Jessica McFee, a midwife at Castle Hill Infirmary, was snatched on her way to work yesterday…*'

'Good work, guys.' Oldcastle CID didn't so much leak information as haemorrhage the bloody stuff.

'*… declined to be interviewed, but Police Scotland issued the following statement…*'

Blah, blah, blah.

It took a bit of effort, but I managed to lever myself upright, hissing and groaning all the way. Breakfast first, then a quick shower, then off to the Postman's Head to let Jacobson know about Claire Young's last meal. Maybe go interview Jessica McFee's colleagues after that – ask if anyone had seen anything suspicious, anyone hanging about.

Keep myself busy until it was time to bid Mrs Kerrigan a hollowpoint farewell. Right between the eyes.

I struggled my way into a fresh set of clothes, unlocked the bedroom door, and limped out into the corridor.

Yesterday there had been singing and showering, today there was silence.

In the lounge, Shifty was hunched over, sitting on the edge of the inflatable mattress, his weight buckling it out shape. He had the duvet wrapped around his middle, fat fingers fumbling with the skin on his flushed cheeks, bags under his eyes.

He grunted something, then scrubbed his face with his hands.

'What, no cheery chappy coffee-making today?'

'Urnnng…'

The kitchen was awash with takeaway refuse, empty bottles and little scrunched-up tins of tonic. I stuck the kettle on and dragged out some mugs. 'How does three in the morning sound?'

'Urnnnng…'

'Can't decide if I want to take my time, or make it last.' Stuck my head back into the lounge. 'You ever tortured someone?'

He hadn't moved. 'Why did you let me drink all that gin?'

'Probably quite messy, but I've got that tarpaulin.' A frown. 'Mind you, you'd have to be pretty sick, wouldn't you? It's different if you need to get information out of someone, but doing it for the sake of it…' Perhaps a couple of bullets in the head would be the safest thing after all. No need to drop to her level. Just as long as she ended up dead.

But still…

Shifty's mouth split open in a yawn, then he shuddered. Sagged even more than his mattress. 'You wimping out on me?'

'Am I hell.'

Back to the kitchen.

The fridge was full of half-empty takeaway containers, the untouched bag of salad and the five bottles of alcohol-free lager I didn't drink. No milk. Or anything else that wasn't curry-related. And lamb Rogan Josh wasn't exactly an enticing prospect for breakfast.

I clunked the fridge shut again. 'Shifty, fancy picking up some bread and milk?'

'Can't. Shave. Then shower. Then death.' He flopped back, bare hairy legs sticking out from under the duvet. 'Urgh…'

Fine.

Alice shuffled along beside me, eyes two bloodshot slits in her waxy face. Nose and ears heading from pink to red. 'I'm not

242

well...' The words came out in a pale cloud of breath – last night's onions and garlic and chillies mingling with the icy air.

'Bit of exercise will do you a world of good then, won't it?'

The street glittered in the darkness – a dusting of frost catching the streetlights' baleful glow. Glinting on the windscreens of parked cars. Above us, the sky was a patchwork of black and dirty orange, the approaching dawn just a smear of pale grey on the horizon.

She dug her hands deeper into her pockets. 'Cold...'

'Did you think any more about it? You know, Australia?'

'I think my brain died.' She sniffed. 'David's a bad influence.'

Up ahead, Mr Mujib's Corner Emporium shone like a grimy beacon on the darkened street. Not quite half six yet, and the shop's lights blazed in their wire cages. Bars covered the poster-filled windows, but the metal shutter over the door was up.

I paused on the threshold. 'Only I might have to leave sooner than I thought.'

Inside it smelled of furniture polish and washing powder, mingling with the sweet earthy scent of rolling tobacco. The place was lined with shelves, covered in tins and packets and sachets and bottles and jars. Sweets in a big display by the lottery tickets, opposite the newspapers and soft-porn lads' mags.

A radio sat up on a shelf behind the counter, some greasy politician on the *Today* programme banging on about the latest round of cuts.

Alice stared at me. 'But we haven't caught him yet...'

'It's complicated, OK?' A large glass-fronted fridge growled away to itself between the bread and the household goods. I cracked it open and grabbed a pack of smoked streaky, a pat of butter, and two pints of milk. 'You know what Mrs

Kerrigan's like. She's been screwing with me for the last two years, do you think she's happy I've got out?'

'But Jessica McFee...?'

'That's what her thugs were doing outside the mortuary yesterday: threatening me.' A loaf of sliced white from the rack by the fridge and a packet of tattie scones. 'It's no fun for her if I get away.'

Alice reached out and held my sleeve. 'We can't just abandon Jessica.'

'Jessica's...' Two steps away, then back again. 'I don't like it any more than you, but what am I supposed to do? Wait for her to come find me?' Turned my back. Tin of beans, carton of eggs.

'We can find her, I *know* we can.'

Sigh. 'We couldn't catch the Inside Man eight years ago, what makes you think we can do it now?' I placed the shopping on the counter, by the newspapers.

The *Castle News and Post* had 'LOCAL MIDWIFE NABBED BY SERIAL SICKO' plastered across its front page above a photo of Jessica McFee.

I rapped out a couple of beats on the wood with the head of my cane. 'Shop! Mr Mujib? Hello?'

Alice was tugging at my sleeve again. 'Please?'

Oh for God's sake... I folded forward until my head rested on the counter. 'It's not the movies. Sometimes the bad guy gets away.'

A rough voice sounded on the other side. 'What?'

When I looked up, a tall thin man was standing in front of me. Greying hair clung to either side of his head, skin the colour of curdled yoghurt – stained by a red patch on one cheek. A line of purple hooked at the corner of his left eye, the beginning of a proper shiner.

'Where's Mr Mujib?'

'Cancer. Now do you want this stuff, or don't you?'

I brought my chin up. 'You got a problem?'

'Me? No. Why would *I* have a problem? Not like I've been ripped off again, is it?' He totted up the total, lips moving as he counted. 'And the bloody police are a joke, aren't they? How am I supposed to run a business when scumbag crooks can just walk in here and demand protection money?'

I handed over the cash and he thumped my change down on the counter.

'Bloody city's a disgrace.'

Couldn't argue with that.

We took our shopping and headed back out into the pre-dawn chill.

Alice scuffed along the pavement in silence, clutching the bacon, eggs, and milk to her chest.

'I'm sorry, OK? I know it's…' I stopped. 'She killed my brother. She kept me in prison. She even arranged this.' I circled the tip of my cane over the top of my aching foot. 'If I hang around for too long, she's going to get bored and send someone after me.'

'Can't we, I don't know, get her arrested or something?'

I limped around the corner, back onto Ladburn Street. 'She's got Andy Inglis behind her, she's not going to stay banged up for long. And when she gets out she'll come right after us, worse than before.'

Light blazed from our flat windows – it was the only one lit up on the whole street. Obviously no one else had to be awake at seven on a Tuesday morning.

Alice passed me the bacon and beans so she could rummage for her keys. 'Then we have to find something that she can't talk her way out of. Something serious with a long sentence.'

God, the naivety of youth.

I nodded. 'Yeah, that's a good idea.' And then we could all climb aboard our unicorns and ride off into the lollypop sunset.

She clambered up the stairs, pausing at the first landing to let me catch up. 'I know it's not ethical to frame someone for murder, but surely there must be a real one we can connect her to, one she *did* do?'

My cane thunked on each step, like the beat of a faltering heart. 'Go ahead, get the kettle on. I'll catch up.'

'Milk, two sugars, coming up.' She smiled, turned, and scampered off, little red shoes disappearing up the stairs. Then the flat door rattled open and clunked shut again.

Pfffff... Closed my eyes. Rested my forehead against the wall.

OK, so she wasn't happy about just abandoning the case, but how the hell was I meant to hang about Oldcastle after putting Mrs Kerrigan in a shallow grave?

Unless I could fit someone else up for it?

I started climbing again.

That might work. Find some lowlife who deserved to be inside, and make sure there's enough evidence to point to him. A junkie perhaps, or one of her dealers?

Or a rival?

That was good. More believable.

Up the last flight of stairs and onto the top floor.

Just need to get a few names from Shifty and manufacture some evidence – fingerprints on the gun, bit of DNA, some fibres. Even better if he was dead at the scene.

A smile pulled my cheeks tight as I stepped into the flat and locked the door behind me.

It was perfect.

I shrugged my way out of my jacket and dumped it in my bedroom. Took the butter and tattie scones and beans out of my pockets. Gathered it all up along with the bread.

Alice would be happy, Mrs Kerrigan would be dead, and I'd be in the clear.

Absolutely perfect...

Someone cleared their throat out in the corridor and I froze. Turned. Swore.

There was a man, standing right outside my room, little pink eyes staring straight at me. Francis.

A nod. ''Spector.'

Damn...

'Francis.'

He jerked a thumb towards the living room. 'They're waitin' for you.'

26

I stepped out into the corridor – still holding the shopping – and Francis moved to one side, blocking the front door.

He was big, had to give him that. Broad shoulders. Some muscle working under the leather jacket, hands that looked as if they'd have no problems tearing someone's face off. Bit of a reputation too.

And I *definitely* owed him for that shot in the kidneys yesterday.

Blood fizzed in my throat, soothed out the pain in my ribs and chest. Nothing like an adrenaline buzz to take the sharp edges off a bit of bruising.

'Where's Alice?'

He just smiled.

I took a step towards him...

Then a voice oiled out from the corridor behind me. His other half: Joseph. 'Actually, Mister Henderson, it might be considered unwise to reduce this to a bout of pugilism. I fear I would be duty bound to intervene, and two against one wouldn't be sporting, would it?'

Sodding hell. And where was Bob the Bloody Builder when you needed him? Sat on his stuffed backside at the end of the bed.

I didn't look around. 'How did you get in?'

'Suffice it to say that my colleague, Francis, is not unskilled in the locksmith's arcane arts. Now, may I prevail upon you to join us in the lounge for a *tête-à-tête*?'

Francis didn't even blink.

One I could take. Two at the same time? Wedged between them in a corridor?

Like being right back in prison again. Trapped. Hemmed in. Waiting for two of Mrs Kerrigan's goons to beat the living shite out of me.

It … wasn't worth the risk. Not with Alice in the flat.

I cricked my head to the left, then the right. Held Francis's gaze for a couple of breaths, then turned my back on him.

Joseph nodded. 'An excellent decision Mr Henderson. Now, shall we…?'

'Let's get one thing crystal: if you've laid a finger on her, I'm going to break every one of yours. Then make you eat them.'

'Her?' A frown. Then his face opened out again. 'Ah, I see! The good doctor. Worry not, Mr Henderson, as far as I'm aware she's perfectly safe. Well, perhaps not *perfectly*. It was, regrettably, necessary to restrain her after she became obstreperous.'

Behind me, Francis sniffed. 'Had to give her a bit of a slap. Teach her some—'

I slammed my elbow back into his chest. Dropped the butter and the bread and the tattie scones. Twisted to the left then drove the tin of baked beans into his face, put all my weight into it too. Crunch. His head snapped back, mouth open, blood shining like tiny jewels in the light of the bare bulb.

Two.

Three.

And there was Joseph, head down, charging. Arms pumping as if he was running the hundred metres.

No point trying to dodge.

So I lunged forward instead, leaned to the right, let his head pass under my left arm. Then looped my arm around his neck as his shoulder hit my chest. Tightened it. Let my knees sag. My backside hit the bare floorboards and Joseph went up and over, head still trapped under my arm, making choking noises, setting the light bulb swinging.

Thump – he clattered into Francis and I let go. Scrambled to my feet. Took my weight on my right foot. A jab of pain. But it freed the left up to slam down on Joseph's face. Once, twice, three times.

Grunting.

The pair of them were a tangled mess of arms and legs, Francis struggling to get out from underneath.

Joseph's hands came up, fluttering over his blood-spattered face, so I aimed for his throat instead. Got his clavicle. Chest. Then bingo.

His eyes bugged, breath a ragged wheezing gasp.

Francis shoved Joseph off. Got as far as his knees. Scarlet streamed down his chin, dripped from the end of that stupid little soul patch.

I grabbed a handful of ginger ponytail and rammed my knee into his nose. A crunch. A spurt of blood. So I did it again, catching him right in the eye. Then brought the beans down like a hammer on the crown of his head, ripping off a flap of scalp. One more time for luck…

A sound, behind me. A dark, metallic *click*.

Ah.

Then a cold Irish accent clawed its way down the corridor. 'Have yez finished foostering about, or would ye like a bullet in the Gary Glitter?'

I let go of Francis's ponytail and he slumped sideways into the wall, bubbles of neon red popping between his lips, shoulders limp, arms dangling by his sides, blood oozing from his tattered scalp. Joseph gurgled and gasped, both hands wrapped around his throat, as if he was trying to force air into his neck through the skin.

I turned, hands out where they were nice and visible.

Mrs Kerrigan smiled back at me with sharp little teeth. Black suit, grey silk shirt buttoned all the way up, small golden crucifix hanging on a chain over the top. Her hair was almost solid grey, the ends still holding on to the last vestiges of brown where they escaped from the bun at the back. She had a semi-automatic in one hand, the metal dark as a tumour against her yellow Marigold gloves. The barrel drooped to point at my groin. 'Now are ye going to be a good little boy, or shall we get yez singing soprano?'

'What do you want?'

A lopsided smile. 'Yer a lucky man, Mr Henderson. I've got an offer for yez that'll take a bite out what you owe Mr Inglis.'

'I don't owe anyone anything.'

It was more like a bark than a laugh. 'Don't be a caffler. Thirty-two grand.'

My fist curled around the tin of beans. 'Go to hell.'

'A good Catholic girl like me, Mr Henderson? Don't think so. Why do ye think we invented confession?' The gun came up till it was pointing at the middle of my chest. 'Now, why don't ye drop the Heinz, and come join the party in the lounge? We'll discuss this like civilized adults.'

'And if I don't?'

At my feet, Joseph's breathing was beginning to sound a little less like he was trying to inhale a bowling ball.

She shrugged. 'That's OK. You hand over the thirty-two big ones, and we'll be on our way.'

'You killed my brother!' I pulled my shoulders back. Stepped forwards.

The gun came up again. Right between the eyes. 'So why the hell would it bother me to rip the head off ye? And then go through for a little fun with yer doctor girl?'

Don't move. Don't even blink. Don't let her know she's found a weak spot.

'Or maybe I won't kill yez? Maybe I'll just put a hole in your belly and drag you into the bedroom, so you can watch me tie her down and ride the arse off her? Would yez like that? Bet you would, ye dirty old sod.' The smile hardened. 'Only I'll be using a cordless drill with an eight-inch masonry bit. Oh, there'll still be writhing and screaming, but a *lot* more mess.'

Not so much as a twitch.

'Unngh...' Joseph rolled over onto his front, coughing and spluttering. Dragging in ragged breaths. Blood and spittle corkscrewed across the floorboards. 'Bastard...'

Mrs Kerrigan rolled her eyes. 'Serves ye right, yez were getting lazy. Mr Henderson's done yez both a favour.'

More coughing. Then he spat out a blob of frothy pink. 'Could've killed me...'

'You should be so lucky.' Then she stepped back into the lounge and twitched the gun at me. 'Right so.'

I let the baked beans thump to the floorboards, then followed her. Stopped. Swore.

Shifty sat in the middle of the lounge, on one of the folding chairs, in the slashed wreckage of his inflatable bed. He was stripped to his pants, shivering – but probably not from the cold. Coils of duct tape fixed his arms and legs to the chair. Another thick band of it around his chest. His nose was nearly flat, blood a dark smear down the duct tape gag. A small cut pierced the silver tape, just enough to let out hissing, shuddering breaths. Scarlet oozed from a gash on his forehead. Thick weals of red made parallel lines across his chest. Bruising on his face, neck and shoulders.

Two fingers on his left hand were bent back, sticking out like they were on the wrong way around. Blood pooled around his thighs.

Bitch.

Weapon. Grab a weapon and batter her skull flat. Anything would—

'Now, now. Let's not turn this torture into a mass murder.' She wiggled the gun at the open door to the kitchen.

Alice was just visible, sitting on the floor, backed up against the units, hands in front of her, the wrists wrapped in duct tape. Another strip across her mouth. Eyes wide and bloodshot, tears streaking her cheeks. Trembling. The soles of her Converse trainers were stained dirty brown and red, like she'd walked through blood...

Mrs Kerrigan grinned. 'That's a right kick in the bollocks, isn't it?'

Coughing rattled out of the hallway, then Joseph lurched into the room, rubbing at his throat. His left eye was already swelling shut, scarlet smeared around his mouth – more staining the sleeve of his jacket. His voice was a raw wheeze. 'Mr Henderson, it would be efficacious if you could put your hands on your head and kneel. Failure to comply would have the *most* unfortunate consequences for Dr McDonald And DI Morrow.'

Mrs Kerrigan brought the gun up and Alice flinched. 'Five. Four. Three. Makes no fecking difference to me. Two...'

I put my hands on my head. Then creaked down to my knees. Kept my mouth shut.

'There we go. All friends again.' She handed the gun to Joseph. 'If Mr Henderson moves, put a hole in his other foot, then ventilate his lady friend.' The wooden floorboards clacked beneath Mrs Kerrigan's boots as she wandered across the room to stand behind Shifty. Put her gloved hands on his shoulders. 'Fecky the Ninth here, on the other hand, needs a bit of an education. Did yez really think I wouldn't notice some feller asking after me? My house and my movements? What kind of security I've got? My dogs?' She lowered her lips to his ear. 'Dear, oh dear, oh dear.'

A low moan trembled out of the gap in the gag.

'Had a lovely little chat with the wee man ye sent to do yer spying. Just him, me, and my friend Mr Soldering Iron.' She squeezed Shifty's shoulders, her yellow rubber fingertips digging into the bruised skin. 'Ye must think a bigger bollox

253

never put her arm through a coat, right? Think I'd let yez get away with that?'

Keep it nice and level. Calm. In control. 'You've proved your point, now let them go.'

'Ah now, I've not even *started*.' She straightened up, patted Shifty on the bruised cheek. 'With ye all tied up to the chair like that, a lot of people would cut yer ear off and dowse yez in petrol. It's a classic. But for me, it's all about the eyes. No idea why. Some weeks it's fingers. The next it's toes. Or maybe I'm after taking a soldering iron to yer langer. But this week it's eyes.'

She moved around in front of him. Took his head in her hands. 'Left or right...?' Looked over her shoulder. 'What do ye think, Mr Henderson?'

Shifty moaned, blood bubble popping from his flattened nostrils. 'Nnnnnnngh!' He screwed his eyes shut.

'Leave him alone, or I swear to God...'

Something cold and hard pressed into the nape of my neck. Then came the delicate metallic click of a safety catch slipping off. Joseph cleared his throat a couple of times, but it didn't make any difference to the rasping voice. 'Trust me, Mr Henderson, your silence would probably be beneficial to all concerned at this moment in time.'

Mrs Kerrigan winked. 'Funny you should mention God. How does it go? "And if thine eye offend thee, pluck it out, and cast it from thee: it is better for thee to enter into life with one eye, rather than having two eyes to be cast into hell fire."' She slid her left thumb across Shifty's cheek. Pressed the yellow rubber against the socket. 'And if it's good enough for the baby Jesus...'

Behind the gag, Shifty screamed.

27

Shifty's left leg trembled to a halt. His shoulders slumped. Head hung forwards.

Mrs Kerrigan dropped something to the floorboards, then stood on it. Worked the toe of her boot back and forth, as if she was grinding out a cigarette. 'Right so. Shall we talk about that offer I was going to make yez?'

In the kitchen, Alice was rigid, eyes wide and round.

I took my time. Cleared my throat. 'We need to get him to a hospital.'

'There's a certain gentleman of Mr Inglis's acquaintance that we need taking care of. That's yer job. Take care of him, and yez'll get four grand off the top.'

'He's in shock, he could die.'

'Think about it: four grand down, twenty-eight to go. And the warm fuzzy feeling of doing Mr Inglis a solid. All ye have to do is deliver the thieving fecker's body to the old chandler's warehouse on Belhaven Lane at nine tonight. Don't even care how you do it, long as it gets done.'

'Just call an ambulance and—'

'Now, I know yez're probably thinking, "Why the feck should I kill someone I don't even know? What's he done to me?" So I'm going to give ye a little incentive.' She pursed her lips, tilted her head to one side. 'How about we take ourselves a hostage? That good for you, Mr Henderson? That incentive enough?'

I just stared at her.

'Now, obviously I can't take yer doctor friend: that'd set off yer ankle monitor.' A smile. 'Mind you, I could always hack Miss McDonald's foot off and leave her tracker with you. Would yez like that? Bit of freedom from the old ball-and-chain?' She let the silence stretch. 'Come on, Mr Henderson, yez're after burying two daughters already, what's one more dead girl? Should be used to it by now.'

Don't even blink.

'No? In that case, we'll just have to take yer pal, Detective Inspector Morrow, with us. Seeing as he's all started and everything. Bit messy, but we've got plastic in the boot of the car.'

She smeared her bloody thumb across Shifty's neck. 'Oh, and just in case yez are thinking of calling yer thickie mates to come arrest us – I *own* Oldcastle CID. I get so much as a whiff of that and Fat Boy here goes through a bacon slicer. We clear?'

'He needs a *doctor*.'

'We all need something, Mr Henderson. Right now, Dr McDonald needs every one of her fingers. But these things change, don't they?' Mrs Kerrigan looked over my shoulder. 'Joseph, do yez have the pliers?'

'I believe my colleague is in possession of our toolkit. Would you like me to fetch them?'

'Well, Mr Henderson? Think we should start with a thumb or a pinkie?'

Alice moaned, feet slipping on the kitchen floor, pressing herself back into the cabinets. Going nowhere.

My tongue turned to sand in my mouth. It took two goes to get the words out. 'Who needs to die?'

*   *   *

256

'… ha, ha! Spectacularrrrrr. Right, we've got another heeeeee-larious wind-up call coming after Nigel News and Travel Trevor, but first: this one's for all you special people out there searching for little Charlie Pearce today…' A big orchestral intro, followed by an electric guitar.

I ran a hand across the Jaguar's passenger window, carving a trail through the condensation. 'Do we have to listen to this prick?'

Most of Jura Row sat behind high stone walls. Posh mansions with gravel drives and tall, barred, automatic gates. Imprisoning the kind of cars that cost more than the average family home. Fifteen years ago the Jag would have fit right in, but now – next to the street's collection of Ferraris and Aston Martins and Lexuses – it looked like a shabby old man. Tired, saggy, and anonymous. Which was the whole point of stealing it in the first place.

Fake period streetlights made pools of glittering light on the wet pavements. The rain had given up, leaving everything still and damp beneath the pewter sky. Waiting for the sun to come up.

Alice fidgeted, eyes fixed on the rear-view mirror. Staring at Bob in the back seat. He just sat there, smiling his stitched-on smile, yellow fabric spanner held in his hand. 'I still don't understand why *he* has to be here…' The words were slightly mushy, deformed by her swollen lower lip, the skin split, a bruise darkening around the crack of dried blood.

Francis was bloody lucky I hadn't caved his head in. I would next time.

She reached up and twisted the rear-view mirror, so it was pointing at the car's roof. Hiding Bob. 'I don't like the way he keeps staring at me. It's creepy. Can't we put him in the boot?'

'You don't put your lucky mascot in the boot.'

A woman's voice, harsh and warbling, cut over the guitar. I switched the radio off. Stared out at the six-foot wrought-iron gate securing number twelve from the road.

257

Alice cleared her throat. 'Can we please talk about what Mrs Kerrigan—'

'There's nothing to talk about. If we don't do this, she kills Shifty. End of story.'

'Please.' Alice's fingers trembled in her lap. She tucked them under her arms. Holding them still. 'We ... I can't kill someone.'

'You don't have to: that's my job.' My official phone rang in my pocket. I pulled it out and hit the green button. 'What?'

Jacobson sniffed. *'Where the hell are you?'*

Great. Just ... great.

Time to toss him that nugget.

'We've been chasing up a couple of leads. You need to get someone round to Bad Bill's Burger Bar with photos of Claire Young and Jessica McFee. Probably find him parked outside the B&Q in Cowskillin. The last thing Claire ate was from there.'

'You're sure?'

'It's called a Double Bastard Bacon Murder Burger, AKA: double cheeseburger with bacon frazzles. No one else is mad enough to make them.'

A scrunching noise came from the other end, muffling Jacobson's voice. *'Cooper – get your backside over here. Got a job for you.'* There was some muttering, too low to hear, but probably Cooper getting his orders.

Alice tugged at my sleeve. 'We should tell him.'

'Are you serious?'

'We need help!'

And Jacobson was back. *'Good work, Ash, I'm impressed. Initiative, I like that.'*

Good.

'I want to talk to everyone who lives in the same halls as Jessica McFee. Might take a while, but I think it's worth a go. And if there's any time left, we'll get stuck into her colleagues too.'

'I don't think so: any old plod can talk to witnesses. The Lateral

Investigative and Review Unit is meant to be about insight, outside-the-box thinking, and applied knowledge. Not *shoe-leather.*'

'Well, my applied knowledge says this is how we make connections. We gather information. We rattle people. We jog their memories. He's got access to hospital drugs and patient records – he's in there somewhere.'

Silence.

I wiped a hand across the glass again, making it cry. Teardrops of condensation dribbled down onto the rubber beading.

The light flickered on above the door of number twelve.

And then a sigh came down the line. *'Fine. But I want regular updates, and I expect you both back here at seven for the team debrief. While we're at it: I need to speak to Dr McDonald. She is there, isn't she?'*

Where the hell else was she going to be? I poked the button for speakerphone and held the mobile out. 'Wants to talk to you.'

'Dr McDonald?' Jacobson's voice echoed out into the old Jaguar. *'I've had yet another call from Detective Chief Superintendents Knight and Ness, wanting to know why you've still not met with Dr Docherty.'*

Alice licked the crack in her lip, setting it bleeding again. She cleared her throat. 'It's been—'

'He might be a pain in the backside, but they've made formal requests for your input. They're testing the team and I will not have anyone letting the side down. So you will damn well go and cooperate.'

Her bottom lip wobbled for a moment. Then she hissed out a trembly breath. 'Yes, Detective Superintendent.' Voice flat and dull.

'But any startling insights you get – you tell me first, understand? It all comes through me. No giving it away like a drunken teenager.'

I nodded at the phone, curled my other hand into an aching fist.

She shook her head. 'Yes, Detective Superintendent.'

Hairy little git.

I clicked off the speakerphone before he could say anything

else, and held the thing back to my ear. 'What's happening with Sabir? He been through the HOLMES data yet?'

'Why don't you phone him and find out? Believe it or not, Ash, my job's to run the team, not your errands. I'm actually beginning to think you're a half-decent police officer, don't spoil it.' Then *click* he was gone.

I slipped the phone back in my pocket. 'Ignore him, he's a wanker.'

Number twelve's door opened and a big man stepped out – tall and broad, hair swept back from his head, black overcoat, dark-grey suit, pastel lemon shirt, stripy tie. Hooked nose, high forehead. Distinguished looking. I checked the photo Mrs Kerrigan had left on the flat's mantelpiece. The name 'PAUL MANSON' was picked out in biro capitals on the back, along with his home address and a mobile number. Definitely him.

A woman popped up next to Manson, handed him a brief-case, then stood on her tiptoes to kiss him on the cheek. A wee boy appeared next, wearing the blue-and-gold blazer of the Marshal School. Manson reached down and ruffled the kid's hair. Then turned and marched down the steps and over to the Porsche parked on the gravel driveway.

'Look at them. Like something out of a bloody toothpaste commercial.'

Manson climbed into the car, set it growling like an angry Rottweiler. He must've had a remote in there, because the gates clunked then swung open.

Alice licked her lips. 'I… I don't think I can—'

'You heard what Mrs Kerrigan said: he's a mob accountant. All this – the house, the clothes, the car, the private school – it's all paid for with drugs and prostitutes and extortion and beatings and murder. That bastard, right there, is the grease that keeps the machinery turning.'

'It doesn't mean he has to die.'

'It's him or Shifty. Start the car.'

*   *   *

'It's OK, just ease up a bit, let him get another car ahead.'

Alice drifted the Jag to a halt at the roundabout, paused, then slid out into the stream of traffic.

'There you go, you're a natural.'

The river was a ribbon of concrete, following the road on the right. To the left, it was all Victorian sandstone, laid out in rigid geometric patterns. Prestige offices with double-barrelled names rubbing shoulders with Oldcastle's only five-star hotel.

Up ahead, Manson took a left, into the Wynd.

Alice followed him. Keeping her distance. Not racing or crowding the target. Doing well.

She licked her lips. 'Ash, we *have* to talk about—'

'Concentrate on driving. There, next right.'

She turned onto a leafy lane, lined with yet more sandstone. Only this time the pillars looked like marble and granite. The Porsche pulled into a marked space at the side of the road.

'OK, just go past it and take the next left.'

'But—'

'You drive, I'll worry about Manson.' I grabbed the rear-view mirror and twisted it, keeping him centre-stage as he climbed out of the Porsche and marched towards the building opposite. He was just starting up the steps when the Jaguar made the turn and he disappeared from view.

I tapped the dashboard. 'Park.'

She did, nose-in at the kerb beneath a bare rowan tree. Let out a long breath. Closed her eyes and folded over the steering wheel.

'You did good.' I reached across and rubbed her back. 'Made me proud.'

'I don't feel well. My pulse is elevated, I'm dizzy. Headache. Stomach churning.' Alice closed her eyes. 'I can see him, squirming and shaking and bleeding and she's gouging her thumb—'

'There was nothing you could do.'

'His eye...' A shudder, then she wiped a hand across her face. 'Thirty percent of people who witness a traumatic event go on to develop PTSD.'

I undid my seatbelt, stretched my leg out in the footwell. 'You're a forensic psychologist, you've seen much worse than—'

'Not in real life! In photos, at post mortems, crime scenes. Never actually ... *happening*.' She took a deep breath, then shook. 'You need a displacement activity, Alice, something to keep you occupied. You help people through things like this all the time, just treat yourself as any other patient. If it's too raw to revisit, put some distance between you and it and let your subconscious frame it.' A frown. 'Or you could try playing violent video games. Or does that only work when you do it before the event? I don't know, Alice, you should look it up on the internet...' She blinked at me. 'What?'

'You're talking to yourself.'

She stared at her fingers as they worked themselves into knots in her lap. 'I don't want to go back to the flat. I can't stay there any more. Not after...' Tears sparked in the corners of her eyes.

I rubbed her back again. 'It's OK. I'll sort something out. We'll get a hotel or a B-and-B or something.'

A little, sickly smile. 'Tell me something about the Inside Man.'

'Apparently we're supposed to call him "Tim" now.'

'No, something from the initial investigation.'

'All right.' I climbed out into the gloom, leaned on my walking stick. 'Once upon a time there was a young man called Gareth Martin. Gareth hadn't had the best of childhoods and spent a fair bit of time checking in and out of the local psychiatric ward. He set fire to a shop in Logansferry once.' The car door clunked shut. 'Jessops, I think it was.'

Alice got out the other side. Plipped the locks. 'What if someone spots the number plate?'

A shard of light slashed through the low clouds as the sun

finally made it over the horizon, leaving a scar of gold and scarlet across the grey.

'Why do you think I nicked the car from an old folks' home? No one's going to notice it's gone for weeks. And even then, they'll probably think they just forgot where they parked it.' I limped past, going back towards the street we'd turned off. 'Four weeks after Ruth Laughlin was found, Gareth walked into the police station on Grigson Lane, covered in blood, put a plastic baby doll on the counter, and threatened the duty sergeant with a carving knife.'

We turned the corner onto Aaronovitch Lane. Brass plaques lined the street on both sides. Solicitor. Accountant. Stockbroker. Solicitor. Solicitor. PR Agency. Solicitor. And then the building Manson had disappeared into: number thirty-seven. 'DAVIS, WELLMAN, & MANSON ~ CHARTERED ACCOUNTANTS.'

A flight of marble steps gleamed in the early morning light, leading up to a black wooden door with a brass knocker set dead in the middle of it.

Crime definitely paid.

'Gareth copped to all four murders and the three abductions too. Said he'd done it because his grandmother used to clean his genitals with bleach and caustic soda when he was five.'

Alice stopped at the foot of the steps. 'The poor boy...'

'All bollocks, of course: he'd read it in some crime novel.'

'Oh.' She stared up at the building's windows. 'Killing Manson is stupid.'

'What other choice do we have? It's—'

'That's not what I meant.' She looked up at me. 'If we kill him now, what do we do with him? Drive about town with his body in the boot till it's time to hand him over, I mean we're in a stolen car, someone's going to notice, what if we get pulled over and they search us and they find him?'

'Who says we're going to drive—'

'We can't just hole up somewhere, we're both wearing GPS locators on our ankles, if we don't go speak to Jessica McFee's colleagues like we told Detective Superintendent Jacobson he'll *know*. And he'll come get us, and we'll have a dead body in the boot of the car and we'll get arrested and I'll spend the rest of my life in prison...'

'That's why we're not doing it right now.' I started walking again, straight past the accountants'. 'Stand there too long and someone's going to notice.' I took a sharp left, hobbling across the road.

'Oh, OK, sorry...' She hurried to catch up. Scuffed along beside me, dragging her little red shoes along the damp pavement. 'But if we—'

'We're *not* getting caught. OK, so we have to pretend that nothing's going on: speak to Jessica McFee's flatmates, meet with that dick Fred Docherty, go through the motions. Fine: we can do that. We come back at close of business and grab Manson on the way home.' I paused beside the Porsche, grunted my way down to one knee, as if I was tying my laces.

The small triangular window behind the driver's door had a bright yellow sticker in it: 'THIS CAR SECURED WITH 24/7 GPS TRACKING' I copied the firm's name into my notebook – Sparanet Vehicle Security – along with the telephone number and the car's registration.

Time to go.

I stuck out a hand and Alice helped me up, then fell into step as we headed off down the pavement.

She glanced back at the accountants'. 'So what happened?'

'What, with Gareth? Turned out he'd broken into the petting zoo at Montgomery Park and hacked a lamb's stomach open to get the doll inside. That's why he was covered in blood. Confession was as fake as his bleach story.'

At the bottom of the lane, we took a right.

'Every year we'd get two or three people turning up at Force Headquarters claiming to be the Inside Man. And twelve months later they'd be back claiming to be DIY Dave, or the Blackwall Rapist, or Johnny Fingerbones.'

264

'Does he still confess to things?'

'His swansong was putting his hand up for a rape-murder. The victim's husband found out where Gareth lived, went round, out of his face on antidepressants, and beat him to death with a cricket bat. Got eight years – diminished responsibility.'

Another right, heading back towards the stolen Jaguar.

Alice slipped her arm through mine. Held on as if she was about to be swept away by the current. 'Do you think David's going to be OK?'

No. But I pulled on a smile anyway, gave her arm a squeeze. 'He's going to be fine. Trust me. Shifty's not as soft as he looks. We'll get him back.'

Or whatever was left of him.

28

Alice pulled her shoulders up to her ears, and turned her back to the wind. Brown curls lashed and writhed around her head like angry snakes. 'But I'm not *hungry*...'

The Old Castle visitor centre was shut, but Manky Ralph's – a dirt-streaked catering trailer with four flat tyres – squatted in the corner of the car park. Better than nothing. And besides, the food wasn't the reason most people handed over their money.

'I don't care.' I held out two napkin-wrapped parcels and a polystyrene container of hot, sweet tea. 'Eat those and drink that.'

'But—'

'This isn't a discussion. Come on, you need breakfast. You'll feel better afterwards.'

She puffed out a breath and took one of the butties. Unwrapped it. Pulled a face. Then took a bite. A small smile. 'Chips.'

'See?' I ripped into my sausage and onion, chewing as we wandered into the ruins.

This part was a collection of waist-high lines of crumbling masonry. Further in there were fire pits, an ice cave, and a staircase to nowhere. And, right at the very back, what was left of a three-storey tower. All of it washed in the golden glare of early morning light, glowing against the coal-dark sky.

We huddled in the lee of a section of battlement, a narrow arrow slit giving views out, down the cliff, past Dundas House, the river, and back towards the Wynd where Paul Manson was working out his last day on earth.

Alice finished the chip buttie, then creaked the lid off her tea, sipping as the steam was yanked away by the wind. She leaned against the wall. Kept her eyes on her little red shoes. 'I'm scared…'

The small, clear, plastic bag Manky Ralph sold me barely weighed a thing. Sat in the palm of my hand like it wasn't really there. I held it out. 'Here.'

She peered at it. 'Pills?'

'You told Dr Dimwit at the hospital he should get Marie Jordan on some MDMA trial in Aberdeen.'

Alice picked the tiny bag from my hand and held it up. Half a dozen pink heart-shaped pills nestled against each other in the bottom. 'You bought Ecstasy for me?'

'You know, for … taking your amygdala down a notch.'

A smile. She reached out and squeezed my arm. 'No one's ever bought me chips and drugs before.' Alice slipped the pills into her pocket. Then her face sagged. 'But we need to talk about David.'

'I told you: he'll be OK.'

She peeled the napkin back from her second buttie – bacon this time. 'I mean it doesn't make any sense to kill Paul Manson, if we do—'

'You're not killing anyone. You're not responsible for what happens. And if it wasn't for these bloody ankle monitors I'd make damn sure you had nothing to do with it.' Seagulls soared above the Bellows, dipping and wheeling over the hollow shells of the old sanatorium, cast adrift on their island in the middle of the river. 'But there's not a lot we can do about that now.'

She shuddered. 'If it wasn't for the ankle monitors Mrs Kerrigan would've taken *me* for a hostage instead of David.'

Perhaps they weren't so bad after all.

Alice peered up at me. 'You always knew it'd come to this, didn't you? That's why you were talking about running away to Australia...' Her eyes dropped. 'I should've guessed, shouldn't I? I mean, what else was going to happen?'

'I'm sorry.'

Wind whipped her hair around her face and she pushed it back, twisted it into a rope with one hand. 'Can't we ... I don't know. Can't we do *something*?'

'So everyone lives happily ever after?'

'Please?'

Off in the distance, a wee child scrambled over a pile of crumbled masonry. A young woman in a chunky jumper stumbled after her. 'Not too far, Catherine, be good for Mummy!'

I leaned back against the ramparts, closed my eyes. 'She wants Manson dead, and if I don't deliver him she's going to kill Shifty. And then what? What if she tries to hurt you?'

'It doesn't matter if he's a mob accountant or not, we can't—'

'I know, OK? I know.' A weight settled inside my chest, crushing me towards the ground. 'If I do this, she's got me connected to a murder. Doesn't matter how much money I pay back, I'll never get out of her pocket. She'll own me.'

'Then what are we—'

'Eat your bacon.'

'I'll just be a minute...' Alice unbuckled her seatbelt and climbed out into the windy morning, leaving me sitting in the passenger seat. The Suzuki's hazard lights clicked on and off, two wheels up on the pavement, the others straddling the double yellows outside the tiny convenience store on John's Lane: 'Justin's Twenty-Four-Seven ~ Licensed Grocer (For All Your Shopping Needs)'.

The stolen Jag was stashed in the old multi-storey car park on Floyd Street, behind the Tollgate Shopping Centre. The one with no security cameras. Where it could stay until it was time to collect Paul Manson.

I turned on the car radio and Kate Bush filled the speakers, wanting to make a deal with God.

If only it was that easy.

A newspaper billboard sat on the pavement outside the shop: 'Hunt Continues For Missing Five-Year-Old'. Another declared: 'This Friday's Euromillions Jackpot Is £89,000,000'. And a third: 'Inside Man Snatches Midwife – EXCLUSIVE!' Posters in the window advertised French lessons, missing cats, and bicycles for sale.

Normality.

No one getting tied to a chair, tortured, and their eye gouged out.

No one being bundled into the boot of a stolen Jaguar and driven out to the woods and murdered.

Bob the Builder grinned at me from the back seat.

What choice did I have?

'And that was little Katey Booooosh, busting those clouds for her dear old dad. Well, it's a smidgeon after half eight, and you know what that means...' Klaxons, honking, a choir singing 'Hallelujah' in the background. *'Another heeeeee-larious wind-up call!'*

Prick.

I turned 'Sensational' Steve down and got on the phone to Sabir instead. Listened to it ring. And ring. And ring.

When he finally picked up he sounded as if he'd just run a marathon – puffing, panting, wheezing. *'What the bleeding hell do you want?'*

'What's happening with the HOLMES data?'

'It's not even nine yet! I was in me bed.'

'In bed? Then what's with all the heavy breathing...?' Oh. 'Never mind. What about HOLMES?'

'*Are you kidding me? I'm in the middle of*—'

'If it was that important, you wouldn't have answered the phone. What did you find?'

'*You used to be less of a tit, you know that, don't you?*' Some rustling. Then a groan. What sounded like a hand over the mouthpiece, muffling his voice. '*Sorry, got to take this.*' More rustling. A clunk. And he was back again. '*Your mam says hello, by the way.*'

'She's still dead, Sabir.'

'*Thought she wasn't moving about much.*' More clunking. '*Your HOLMES data's a right mess, whoever managed that lot needs taking out and spanking. I'm having to go through the whole lot and reindex it. You got any idea how much of a pain in the plums that is?*'

'Did you run the telephone numbers against it?'

'*Course I did. Had to hack the database to do it, but I did it.*'

Silence.

'And?'

'*More chance of a three-way in a penguin house. Nothing came up. When I get the data sorted I'll run the names and addresses too. Not surprised you didn't get the bugger eight years ago: the bell-end who stuck this lot together couldn't have done a worse job if they tried. Crap in, crap out.*'

The shop door opened, and Alice lurched into the wind, a carrier-bag in one hand, a bar of chocolate in the other.

'Think it was deliberate?'

Sabir made sooking noises for a moment. '*Dunno. It's properly rank though.*'

'See if you can find out who did it.'

Alice climbed in behind the wheel, bringing a rush of cold air with her. 'Sorry. Took a little longer than I thought.' She reached back between the seats and dumped her carrier-bag on the floor of the footwell. It clinked.

I peered into the back. The label from a half-bottle of Grouse was just visible through the thin plastic bag.

'How did you manage to buy booze at half eight in the morning? That's not even legal.'

Alice turned the engine over. 'I can be quite persuasive when I need to be.'

On the other end of the phone, Sabir coughed. *'Now, if you don't mind, I'm not done banging your mam yet.'*

The sign outside Force Headquarters didn't say 'Oldcastle Police' any more, now it was 'Police Scotland ~ Oldcastle Division'. They'd even ditched the crest for some bland corporate saltire thing.

Shame they hadn't ditched the building. The large Victorian red-brick wart blemished the street's sandstone skin – its narrow windows dark and barred, as if it was expecting a siege. Just as well, because one had arrived.

A clan of reporters and camera crews hung around the front doors, smoking and joking, waiting to pounce and tear someone to shreds. Feast on their bones.

One of them looked up as we climbed the stairs, a heavy Nikon hanging around his neck, little brown cigarillo clamped between two fingers. 'Oy! You two got anything to do with the Inside Man?'

I gave him a big theatrical shrug. 'Someone broke into our shed and nicked the lawnmower.'

'Pity...' He took a couple of photos anyway, then went back to waiting.

I held the door open and Alice slipped past me into reception, carrier-bag clinking against her thigh.

Black-and-white tiles made the room look more like a train-station toilet than somewhere to report a crime. At least it was easy to hose the vomit and blood off the floor...

A raptor-thin man sat behind the desk and a slab of bullet-proof glass. The hair on his head was a close-cropped grey, about half as short as his bushy black eyebrows. Sergeant Peters puckered his mouth, narrowed his eyes. 'How come you didn't come in round the back?'

'Wouldn't give me the new access code.'

'Hmph. Tossers.' He nodded at Alice. 'Pardon my French, like.' Back to me. 'You want us to call someone?'

'Actually,' Alice stepped forward, 'I'm here to see Dr Frederic Docherty, it's Dr McDonald, well, I'm Dr McDonald, not him, I realized that would sound a bit confusing as I was saying it, but you can call me Alice.'

Peters raised a thick eyebrow. 'Right... I'll just do that. What about you, Guv?'

'Archives.'

He slammed the visitors' book down on the counter. 'Right, sign in, I'll knock you up a pass, keycode is three-seven-nine-nine-one. And you can tell the tossers upstairs they can stick their bloody job if they don't like it.' He grumbled over to the computer and battered the keyboard into submission with two-fingered hate. 'Like it's *my* fault I can't work nights. Don't see *them* looking after a sixty-year-old bedridden woman with cancer...'

'Ah, Dr ... McDonald, isn't it?' Frederic Docherty half rose from his seat and gestured towards the other side of the conference table. Another sharp suit, this time with a bright blue shirt and white tie. 'Please, do sit. And will your friend be joining us?' He looked at me.

I didn't move. 'Better things to do.'

'I see.'

Alice put her carrier bag down on the tabletop, then sat. Pulled out a half-bottle of Grouse and cracked open the top. 'Would you like one?'

'Ah...' He lowered himself back into his seat. 'Let me guess: you've worked with Henry Forrester, haven't you? He was a big believer in the empathic-slash-cognitive-enhancing power of caffeine and whisky.'

She poured a glug into her mug. 'Two years ago, we were hunting a serial killer. I ... was the one who found Henry's body in the hotel.'

Docherty's face pinched, as if something sharp had just burrowed its way beneath his skin. 'He was a good man. A good mentor. When I heard he'd died…' A sigh. 'That must have been horrible for you.'

Alice knocked back a mouthful of laced coffee, then dipped into her satchel and came out with the Inside Man letters, all six of them covered in highlighter strokes and red biro squiggles. She laid them out on the table top. 'I've been analysing the form and content and I think we need to revisit the profile. The Inside Man—'

'If you want to talk about it, I've done a considerable amount of work with bereaved families.'

She added another slug of Grouse to her mug. 'The language used, the imagery, it's all heightened, salacious, like he wants us to be there with him. That doesn't match someone—'

'It's nothing to be ashamed of. When Henry died, it took me months to work through my feelings with my therapist. We'd been very close. It's—'

'—kind of background in the profile, so we need to go back and—'

'—be highly beneficial to your on-going emotional health.'

I left them to it.

29

Another box. This one was scribbled with black marker pen, the case number crossed out three times and written in again. No wonder it was nearly impossible to find anything.

I dumped it on the floor with the others and reached into the row behind it. The shelves were scarred, the paint flaking away, rust spreading out from the joins. Dust covered everything with a blanket of fur, little puffs of the stuff drifting out every time something was moved. It glowed in the gloom, caught by the miserable gritty light of a fluorescent bulb.

PC Simpson had a scratch, setting the fat on his belly wobbling. Dumpy, balding, and coasting towards retirement in slow-motion. 'Of course, the real problem's the voting system, isn't it?'

Next row wasn't much better. All illegible numbers and corrections and why could no one ever file things properly? 'Are you sure this is the right section?'

'Take that Marilyn woman: can't sing for cheese, but there she is week after week, because people think it's funny. Thought Britain was meant to have talent?'

'Simpson, I'm going to count to five, and then I'm going to take this walking stick and ram it so far up you everyone'll think you're a bloody unicorn!'

He stopped scratching and hauled out another box. 'Should be in here *somewhere*. Tosspots from SCD and CID ransacked everything they could find when they started the investigation. But they lack the systematic approach, don't they? Charging about like idiots.'

I dumped another box on the floor – two completely separate crime numbers scrawled on the greying cardboard. 'How could you let the place get into this mess?'

'Oh no you don't; my system was working perfectly, thank you very much. I go off on the sick for a couple of months and some idiot puts that wee tosser Williamson in charge. When I get back everything's all over the shop.' He popped the top off a case file and rummaged in the contents. 'You let people run amok in your archives and they get used to it. Take advantage. Number of times I've come down here to find that prat Brigstock hauling stuff out of boxes, or Rutledge, or that psychologist git, or bloody Detective Superintendent "Why can't you get this place tidied up?" Knight. No one ever wants to sign for anything.' His voice jumped half an octave, put on a posh Glaswegian accent. '"Oh, I just need to check something, I'll put it right back." Does this look like a sodding library?'

The next box had a knife and an axe in it, both in their clear plastic bags with dried flakes of blood in the bottom.

'And how come it's always cover versions? You want to be famous: write your own songs. Otherwise it's just glorified karaoke.'

Another box, this time with no crime numbers on it at all.

'But no one cares, do they? Ah, here we go.' He thumped a box down in front of me. 'Inside Man, "K" to "N".' He took a deep breath and wheezed it out across the lid, sending up a little storm of dust. 'Told you it'd be back here, somewhere.'

I coughed, waved a hand back and forth. 'God's sake...'

'Course, I *could* sort it out. Start at one end and re-index everything till it was back in shape again, but why bother?

It'd take years. Come May, I'm retiring to sunny Perth to play golf and drink beer. Let whatever poor sod comes next sort it.'

I lifted the lid. Inside, it was stacked with evidence bags, paperwork, and notebooks. 'You got a table I can use?'

'Simpson said you were down here.'

'Hmm?' I looked up, and there was Rhona, leaning against the metal shelving, hands in the pockets of her suit trousers. Her shirt was unbuttoned to the bra line, a ring of orange-grey dirt around the inside of the collar, a grease stain darkening the green fabric.

She shrugged. 'Looking for anything in particular?'

'The Inside Man letters. Supposed to be in here.'

Rhona settled on the edge of the table and reached into the box. Pulled out an evidence bag. A scrunched up tissue sat inside, speckled with the dark brown dots of ancient blood. She put it on the tabletop and went back in for something else. 'Listen, about that party, it's not important. I was … you know: thought it'd be nice to celebrate you getting out.'

'Been through everything in the box twice and there's no sign of them. They're on the evidence log, but they're not here…'

'We could just grab a drink, or something? Maybe down the Monk and Casket? Like the old days. Or we could even do it in the hotel bar?'

'Hotel?'

'The Pinemantle. Aren't you staying with the LIRU and SCD lot?'

I settled back in my seat, stretched my right leg out. 'Why would the letters be missing from evidence?'

She sucked at her teeth. 'Maybe one of the other teams got there first?'

'No. They'd have checked them out.' I held up the sheet of paper with everything in the box listed on it. 'And it took

276

me and Simpson half an hour to find the sodding thing. It was clarted in dust – according to him, no one else's been near it for years. There's a scalpel missing too.'

I swivelled the chair all the way around, until I was facing the long, gloomy rows of shelves. 'The letters are gone, and the HOLMES data is all screwed up. What if someone's been covering their tracks?'

Rhona's eyebrows went up. 'You think the Inside Man's one of us?'

It made a twisted sort of sense.

She whistled. 'Bet it's that dick DI Smith. Never trust an Aberdonian, that's what my dad always said.'

'He's not been here long enough. Do me a favour: find out who was on the Inside Man HOLMES team eight years ago. Might be someone who transferred to another force for a while? That'd explain why we've got eight years with no Inside Man.'

'Speaking of people dropping off the radar: you seen Shifty Dave on your travels? Her Ladyship's not too impressed he skipped morning prayers.'

Damn.

I picked up the pile of notebooks and put them back in the box. 'He's sick. Said it was probably the norovirus or something.' Well, if it was a good enough lie to get Officer Babs off work, it was good enough for Shifty. 'Vomiting, diarrhoea, aching joints, the whole thing. Sounded dreadful. Thinks he won't be in for a couple of days.'

'Shifty's got the squits? Not surprised, the amount of kebabs he puts away. Should've told the Super though, she's in a bad enough mood as it is. You see that bit about Jessica McFee in the *News and Post* today? Tell you, half of CID couldn't keep their mouths shut if you superglued their lips together.'

I stacked everything else back where it came from and put the lid on again. 'I'll let him know next time I see him.'

'Anyway, about that drink, I was thinking after work?'

Couldn't carry the box and the cane at the same time, so I had to limp my way back to the shelf, needles digging their way through my right foot with every scuffed step.

'Guv?'

'I can't tonight. I've ... got a thing.'

'Oh.'

I slid the box through the dust to the rear of the shelf. Looked back at Rhona. 'How about tomorrow?'

Her head drooped. A thin smile like a bad taste on her lips. 'Yeah. Maybe tomorrow.'

A low buzz filled the canteen on the fourth floor. A PC stood in front of the glowing microwave rocking from side to side, as if he was slow-dancing with whatever ready meal he was nuking in there.

Other than him, and a civilian support officer eating a Pot Noodle, the place was empty. Just rows of ratty tables and creaky chairs. A communal fridge. Sink. Tea-and-coffee-making facilities. A vending machine that was fifty-percent chocolate and fifty-percent crisps.

The shutters were down over the service hatch. No chips till lunchtime.

I dumped a teabag in a mug and flicked the kettle on to boil.

Pulled out my phone and called Jacobson.

No answer. No answer from Huntly either. Or Dr Constantine. Typical.

Could try chasing Sabir up ... but then he'd only whinge about it.

The kettle rumbled to a halt.

Of course, what I really needed was a bit of muscle on my side when I introduced Bob the Builder to Mrs Kerrigan – in a run-down corner of an industrial estate, with a dead mob accountant in the boot of a stolen car. Perhaps Babs would like a little extra cash to get Joseph and Francis out of the picture for a bit, no questions asked?

Yeah, that'd go down well.

Hi, Babs, fancy keeping a pair of vicious bastards busy while I shoot their boss in the face a couple of times? What's that? You're calling the police?

Francis and Joseph would just have to take their chances with Bob the Builder too.

Shame Shifty wasn't here...

Teabag. Hot water. Milk in over the top.

The distant sound of shouting oozed in through the open canteen door. Muffled curses and not so muffled yells of pain.

Over by the microwave, the PC glanced back at the corridor then went on dancing with the microwave. No one gave a toss any more.

I stuck my tea on the table and limped out, cane thunking against the cracked terrazzo floor. The shouting was louder to the left, by the stairs. Four or five of them yelling at the top of their lungs.

'*Ayabastard!*'

'*Don't just stand there, you cabbage: get him!*'

'*Sod off, you get him!*'

'*Aaaargh! Oh Jesus that hurts!*'

'*Come on, you big bastard, try— Unf...*'

'*Shite, shite, shite...*'

By the time I got to the bottom of the stairs, there were half a dozen of Oldcastle's finest cowering against the corridor walls. Uniform and CID all pressing themselves into the battleship-grey paint. A Community Support Officer had his bum on the floor, one leg stretched out, a bloody hanky clamped to his nose.

The rest of them were staring at the door to the family room.

More swearing from inside.

'*Help me! Please, you can't just— AAGGHH!*'

I shoved past. 'The hell is wrong with you people?' Then wrenched open the door.

The comfy sofas were tipped over, the coffee table smashed to firewood, big dents in the plasterboard, the light fitting torn from the ceiling. Picture frames cracked, glass littering the dirty carpet. Curtains dangled from their broken pole – there wasn't really a window behind it. The whole place was a fake.

A uniformed officer was slumped against the far wall, scarlet glistening across her top lip, mouth, and chin. Another's leg poked out from behind one of the sofas. Two CID face down on the carpet.

Wee Free McFee stood in the remains of the shattered coffee table, blue V-necked jumper torn at the shoulder, white shirt collar smeared with blood. Both hands curled into fists. Breathing hard.

Two more uniforms charged him, both with their batons out.

The first got a fist in the face that lifted him right off his feet. The second slammed into Wee Free's chest, knocking him back a couple of paces. Raised the baton ready to take his knees out from under him—

But Wee Free was *fast*. He grabbed the arm, wrenched it back, yanked the officer towards him then slammed his forehead into the guy's nose.

A wet crack, a grunt, and the uniform's legs gave way. Wee Free caught him by the stabproof vest before he could go too far and battered a knee into his groin.

Let go.

The poor sod crumpled to the floor.

Wee Free raised his head and glared at me. Tiny spots of red dotted his cheeks and moustache. Chest heaving. 'You – said – they'd – find – her.'

I raised one hand, palm out. 'OK, I need you to calm down. Can you do that for me, Mr McFee?'

'It's – all over – the papers – but – but this lot – they – wouldn't – tell me shite.' He howched, then spat on the back of one of the CID bodies. 'Bastards.'

'Right now, someone's on their way down here from the armoury.' I checked over my shoulder, where the cowering idiots were just visible through the open door. 'Aren't they?'

One of the officer's eyes went wide then they scurried off. Morons.

'That what you want, Mr McFee? Spend the rest of the day with a bullet hole in you?'

His breathing was getting easier. Less violent. 'Supposed to be a Family – Liaison officer. Wouldn't – even talk – to me.'

The uniformed officer slumped against the wall twitched. Wee Free took two quick steps towards her, then kicked her in the stomach. 'RAN AWAY LIKE I WAS SCUM!'

'This isn't helping, Mr McFee, this is making matters worse.' I limped closer. 'Come on, let's you and me go sit down somewhere quiet and we can—'

A screeching wail burst into the room, high-pitched and jarring, like a ruptured car alarm. I froze. Sodding hell: the ankle bracelet. The family room was at the opposite end of the building from the conference suite, four floors apart. The only way I could get further away and still be in the same building would be the cell block in the basement.

Two hobbling steps back towards the door … and the noise didn't stop.

Brilliant.

'MR MCFEE, LISTEN VERY CAREFULLY, I NEED YOU TO LIE FACE DOWN ON THE FLOOR WITH YOUR HANDS BEHIND YOUR HEAD!'

'MY JESSICA DESERVES—'

'THEY *WILL* SHOOT YOU!'

He puffed out his chest. 'I'LL BATTER THE BLOODY LOT OF THEM!'

'DON'T BE A DICK!' No point backing away, it wasn't making any sodding difference to the volume. 'NOW GET DOWN! ON THE FLOOR! NOW!'

The door thumped against the wall behind me and a couple of firearms officers burst into the room, all done up in their SAS-style kit, complete with crash helmets and black scarves so their faces couldn't be seen.

They had their tasers out – the things looked like children's toys: bright-yellow plastic body, neon-blue cartridge on the end.

About time.

I held a hand up. 'IT'S OK, I'VE GOT THIS, I JUST NEED EVERYONE TO—' And then the bastards shot me.

30

'What the hell were you thinking?' DI Smith marched up and down the office, wearing a path in the ratty carpet tiles. 'Assaulting a victim's father in a police station, do you have *any* idea what the press are going to do with that?'

The duty doctor flicked the mini torch away from my left eye, then back again. His liver-spotted hand trembled as he switched it off and placed it in his bag. 'How's the pain: on a scale of one to ten?'

'Like having cramp and pins-and-needles at the same time.'

Smith did a one-eighty by the filing cabinet and headed back for another pass. 'Soon as you're finished, I want him processed and in a cell. Assault, destruction of property—'

'You'll live.' The doc smiled, showing off tar-stained teeth. 'Never been tasered myself. Always thought it best to avoid that kind of thing.'

'Didn't really have much choice.'

Smith jabbed a finger at me. 'You're lucky the response team saved you from a murder charge!'

All right. Enough was enough.

I levered myself off the desk. 'Don't see them here now, do you? Nothing to stop me ripping your head off, you chin-less bag of—'

A voice cut through the room. Female. Sharp. 'All right, Mr Henderson, that's enough.' Detective Superintendent Ness stood in the open doorway, arms folded.

Jacobson appeared in the corridor behind her, lips turned up in a little smile.

Ness waved a hand in the vague direction of the cells downstairs. 'Would someone care to explain to me why I've got a wrecked family room, six officers and one Community Support off to A&E, and Jessica McFee's father in custody?'

Smith stiffened his back, brought what little chin he had up. 'I was just saying exactly the same thing, Super. Mr Henderson here went on a rampage, broke the conditions of his release, assaulted—'

'I didn't lay a finger on anyone, you prick.' I turned to Ness. 'Wee Free only wanted to know what was happening with his daughter. Wakes up this morning and it's splashed over the papers, but your idiots wouldn't speak to him. He got ... agitated.'

'*Agitated*?' Ness's right eyebrow raised an inch. 'He went through the room like it was a wet paper bag.'

'His daughter's just been grabbed by a serial killer. It's not...' My jaw clenched. Deep breath. Closed my eyes. Hissed it out. 'They had no business treating him like a monster. Even if he is one.'

'Then there's the matter of my firearms team getting an urgent call to apprehend you, in *complete* violation of standard operating procedure and the command structure.'

Brilliant, not 'Friendly Fire' after all. So much for sending someone off to the armoury. Suppose it was too much to hope that anyone at FHQ would be bright enough to take Wee Free down on their own initiative. No, the bastards in black were there for me.

Behind her, Jacobson raised a hand. 'That was on my orders.'

I gave him a glower. Then back to Ness. 'Let Wee Free go,

drop the charges, and get him a Family Liaison officer that isn't scared of their own shadow.'

Smith sniffed. 'You're in no position to decide what action we do and don't take, *Mr* Henderson. You can pack your stuff up, Doctor, he's going—'

'Oh, give it a rest.'

'Ash Henderson, I'm arresting you for assault on one William McFee, and—'

'DI Smith!' Ness closed her eyes, pinched the bridge of her nose. 'That's enough. Go chase up the CCTV team. I'll deal with Mr Henderson.'

He worked his jaw from side to side for a moment, then turned and marched out of the room, back straight and stiff. Presumably because of the stick up his arse.

She gave the Duty Doctor a nod. 'Thank you, Dr Mullen. We'll be fine from here.'

As soon as he'd rumbled out of the room, Ness ushered Jacobson in and closed the door.

'I don't appreciate people going behind my back and appropriating my officers, Mr Henderson. A firearms team is not a toy.'

'Right, because *I'm* the one who called them. Said, "Come on down to the family room and shoot me in the chest with a taser. That'll be fun." You want to blame someone?' I pointed at the smirking git in the leather jacket. 'Blame *him*.'

Jacobson shook his head. 'Not this time, Ash. You knew the conditions of your release – you have to stay within a hundred yards of Dr McDonald. What happened is entirely your own fault for breaking that.'

'I wasn't trying to *run away*. I was stopping Ness's morons from getting themselves killed!'

Ness bristled. 'My officers are *not* morons.'

'Really?' I grabbed my walking stick. 'Well, if they'd been bright enough to treat Wee Free like a victim instead of a villain, I wouldn't have had to break my hundred-yard tether.

Cowering in the corridor like wee kids when they should've been talking him down!'

She rolled her shoulders. Then sighed. 'I will admit to being somewhat disappointed by the conduct of certain officers. Perhaps, as you have a rapport with Mr McFee, *you* should act as Family Liaison?'

'No chance.'

'I see. So it's all right to shout the odds when it's my team, but—'

'One: I'm not a police officer any more. Two: I'm not on the main investigation so I don't have all the facts. Three: I'm not qualified. It's not just making tea and handing out chocolate biscuits, it's—'

'I can assure you that I'm well aware of a FLO's duties.' She frowned at me. 'I understand you think the Inside Man might be one of us.'

Not like Rhona to blab. 'Do you now?'

'That you think they've been tampering with evidence and screwing up the HOLMES data to protect themselves.'

The smile disappeared from Jacobson's face, eyes narrowing as he stared at me. 'That's one possibility the LIRU team is investigating.'

Ness ignored him. Tilted her head to one side. 'The way I hear it: back in the day, you were the organ grinder around here. Was one of your monkeys the Inside Man?'

'They're your monkeys now, remember?' I stretched out my right leg, tested my weight on it. 'Anything else gone missing?'

Jacobson folded his arms, leaned against the wall. 'Well?'

She pulled out her notebook and flipped it open at the marker. 'The lace trim from the bottom of the nightdress Laura Strachan was found in. A heart-shaped locket necklace from Holly Drummond. A sample vial containing the stitches removed from Marie Jordan in the operating theatre. The little doll key ring recovered from Natalie May's abduction site.' Ness put the notebook down. 'In fact, there's something missing from every Inside Man victim. Do you have anything to say about that?'

I looked at Jacobson, kept my mouth shut.

He bared his teeth. 'Go ahead, Mr Henderson, we're all on the same side.'

OK: 'He's got access and he's taking trophies.'

Ness slipped the notebook into her pocket. 'Mr McFee assaulted eight people today, six of them police officers. If they're prepared to drop the charges, I'll let him off with a caution. Otherwise he's up before the Sheriff tomorrow morning.' She turned on her heel. 'Now, if you'll excuse me, I've got a considerable amount of paperwork to sort out.'

As soon as she was gone, Jacobson moved so he was blocking the door. He picked at his nails for a second. Then, 'Was I being obtuse, in the car when I picked you up, Ash? Was I vague, or unclear in my meaning?'

Here we go.

'You see, I distinctly remember telling you that you reported to me. Not Oldcastle, not the Specialist Crime Division, not Santa Bloody Claus, the Easter Bunny, or the sodding Tooth Fairy!' He thumped his hand on the desk. 'What the hell did you—'

'I didn't report anything to anyone, OK? I've been digging through the archives. I've been trying to find out who was on the original HOLMES team. Someone must've noticed and told Ness.'

He scowled at me in silence.

'Look, do you think I *want* to go back to prison? The only reason I didn't tell you about the missing stuff is there wasn't time. I had to rush off and rescue Ness's morons from Wee Free McFee. Then *your* morons tasered me!'

Silence.

Jacobson stepped away from the door. 'You need to stay within a hundred yards of Dr McDonald for a reason, Ash.

She keeps you out of trouble. She's your guardian angel.' He described a lazy circle with one hand. 'You know, it might be a good idea for you to make yourself scarce for a bit. Let things calm down here. Maybe even stop rubbing people up the wrong way?'

I scrubbed a hand across my face. Let my head fall back, till I was staring at the ceiling tiles. 'We need to get Sabir to check who'd have access to hospital records *and* police evidence.'

That little smile had returned. 'Did you enjoy being tasered, by the way?

'Funny. I'm laughing right now, can you hear me? Bastards didn't even issue a warning.'

'Look on it as a learning experience, Ash: this is what happens if you stray off your leash.'

I poked my head around the door – no one there. Good. Meant I didn't have to explain what I was up to.

The traffic office was a small room on the third floor, lined with desks and filing cabinets, 'SPEED KILLS!' and 'THINK BIKE!' posters on the walls. The 'BOX O' STUFF' sat where it always had: in the corner by the large steel locker where they kept the warning triangles and spare body-bags. I rummaged through the odds and sods that cycled their way between the various traffic cars and panniers. Helped myself to a couple of stickers and pair of biker gloves. Then headed upstairs to the conference room.

The place smelled like a distillery. Alice sat at the far end of the table, folded over her Inside Man letters.

No sign of Dr Docherty.

I knocked on the table and Alice jerked up. Blinked at me.

The words came out slow and careful, as if she didn't trust them. 'Why did you try to run away?' Not quite drunk, but not far off it. 'I don't want to be left behind...'

'How much whisky have you had?'

'Spilled some when the alarm went off. It was loud, wasn't it loud? I think it was really, really loud, then there was whisky everywhere, and it wouldn't stop, and the door battered in, and these guys were there and they had guns and they were all, "Where's Ash Henderson?" And I didn't know…' She made little wet smacking noises with her mouth. Frowned. 'Do I feel hungry, or a little bit sick?'

Had to admit, whoever was monitoring the ankle bracelets for Jacobson, they were keen. Prompt too. Which wasn't good.

Of course, the fact that we were in a police station when it happened probably helped the response time, but still…

'How long was it? Between the alarm going off and them turning up?'

Alice narrowed her eyes. 'I think it's a little bit of both.'

'Alice: how long?'

'Four, five minutes?'

Sodding hell, that was quick. They must've been already geared up, ready to head out to make someone's day special. No wonder Ness wasn't happy about them being diverted.

Still, as long as Alice and I stayed within a hundred yards of each other we would be fine. Unless they were recording all the GPS data – and they would be – which made abducting and murdering a mob accountant a bit more risky. But it was too late to worry about that.

'Ash?'

I blinked. Turned. 'Sorry, miles away.'

She pointed at her photocopies. 'I said, these are hopeless. Did you get the originals?'

'No. But I know who's got the next best thing.'

A life-sized oil painting of an old man glared down from the wall of the news room, dominating the rows of cubicles and their occupants. The words *Castle News and Post* were picked out in large silver and bronze letters along the opposite wall, above a row of clocks all set to different time zones.

Micky Slosser didn't look up from his monitor, fingers barely pausing as they clicked and clattered across the keyboard. A big man with wide shoulders, thick sideburns, and frameless glasses. Dundas Grammar School tie at half-mast, the top two buttons open, exposing one end of a thick pink scar. 'Bugger off.'

I settled on the edge of his desk. Puffed a couple of breaths. Sweat trickled down the gap between my shoulderblades. Someone was hammering rusty nails through the flesh and bone of my foot. Then hauling them out with pliers and thumping them back in again.

Well, I couldn't let Alice drive, could I? Not until she sobered up a bit.

It took some effort, but I finally managed to fake a smile. 'Come on, Micky, that's no way to treat an old friend, is it?'

'Not dignifying that with a response.'

'Are you refusing to cooperate with a police investigation? Obstructing the hunt for a serial killer? Seriously?'

He gave the enter key an extra-hard jab. Scooted his chair back a foot. 'After what *you* did?'

Ah. I ran a hand around the back of my neck, catching a pad of cold sweat. 'Len thought you—'

'I don't care what Detective Bloody Superintendent Lennox Murray thought. I wasn't the Inside Man then, and I'm not the sodding Inside Man now!' Micky grabbed an empty mug, ringed inside with brown tidemarks, and stood. 'Still hurts when it's cold.'

'He was...' Try again. 'Len went too far some times. But only because he was trying to save lives.'

Micky bared his teeth. 'Oh, how *noble* of him.'

'Yes, and I know he was wrong, but he's not here, is he? They banged him up for it. And I'm asking you to help me catch a killer.'

'Hmph...' Then Micky limped off towards the recess at the side of the room where the fridge and hot-water urn lurked.

I lumbered after him, jaw clenching every time my right foot hit the ground, cane trembling in my hand.

Prednisolone my arse. The four I'd dry-swallowed on the way over here hadn't even made a dent in it. 'You made copies of the originals, didn't you?'

Alice appeared at my shoulder, flashing her whitest of smiles. 'Alice McDonald, it's an honour to meet you, Mr Slosser, I have to say that I'm a *big* fan of your weekly column. *Slosser's Saturday Sessions* is compulsory reading in my house. And your work on the Inside Man case was revelatory, wasn't it, Ash?'

Revelatory? I stared at her.

She took a breath. 'Anyway, if you can let us have those copies of the letters and envelopes, that'd be great. Big assistance.' Alice held her hands out, as if she was holding an invisible beach ball. 'Huge.'

Micky pursed his lips and leaned back against the working surface. 'Did you know that before *I* printed the first letter they were calling him the Caledonian Ripper?'

Her eyes went wide. 'Really?' Even though it was in the sodding briefing notes she'd written.

'Oh yes: the *News of the World* gave him that nickname soon as Doreen Appleton's body turned up. Well, it was pretty obvious that the kind of guy who'd cut a woman open and stitch a plastic doll inside wasn't going to quit at just one, was he? Man like that needs a good nickname so people will know who we're talking about when the next one turns up.'

'Wow.'

'Then, one day, I get this letter from someone saying they're the bloke who killed Doreen Appleton. Said the papers should stop lying about him being sick and evil, he was only doing what had to be done. That calling him the "Caledonian Ripper" was disrespectful and rude. And he signed himself, "The Inside Man".'

'Gosh.' She stepped closer. 'So, if it wasn't for you, we'd never know his real name, I don't mean the name he was born with, obviously we don't know that, I mean the more important one – the one he picked for himself.'

Micky nodded. 'Exactly. You want a coffee?'

I nodded. 'Tea would be—'

'Didn't ask you.' He thumped two mugs down, snatched a jar of decaf from the countertop. 'I couldn't run for two years, you know that, don't you? Two sodding years.'

I rested my thumping head against the wall. 'Tell me about it.'

He spooned out gritty coffee granules into both mugs. 'Do you take sugar, Alice, or are you sweet enough as it is?'

She actually giggled. 'Two, please.'

Micky lumped in a couple of heaped teaspoons. Then frowned. 'You think it's him again, don't you? All that stuff at the briefings about not jumping to conclusions – you *know* it's him. Otherwise you wouldn't be here scrabbling about for copies of his old love letters...'

I went for nonchalant. 'Just tidying up a few loose ends.'

He put the milk down. 'What happened to the originals? You've got them on file, don't you? All boxed up somewhere safe in the archives?'

I sighed. Put in a shrug as well for good measure. 'You know what they're like. It's all about jurisdiction and infighting these days, one big unhappy family choking on its own bureaucracy.' Probably.

'So what's in it for me?'

Alice put a hand on his arm. 'It's important.'

'Hmmm...' He filled the mugs from the urn and stirred. 'How about we have a little reciprocity? My back's *very* itchy.'

'Well...' She looked at me, then back at Micky. 'How about I tell you where Claire Young's last meal came from?'

OK, so Jacobson wouldn't be happy about it, but screw him. Swings and roundabouts. And when it got splashed all over the *Castle News and Post* tomorrow morning, we could just blame PC Cooper. There is no 'I' in team.

Micky handed her a mug. 'What is it, McDonalds? KFC?'

I shook my head. 'Nope: local establishment, lots of history.'

He chewed on the inside of his cheek for a bit. Took a sip of coffee. 'Suppose we could play up the "condemned woman's final request" angle. "What would your last meal on earth be?" Get in a few local celebs...' He limped off to his desk again. 'What else?'

'Don't be greedy.'

'You're after the letters for a reason. I get first dibs on anything official that comes out of them. Twelve-hour lead.'

'Maybe. Now let's see the letters.'

31

On the other end of the phone, Jacobson made sooking noises. *'And Ness and Knight are delighted with Alice's work on the profile with Dr Docherty. So at least I've got* one *team member who's doing what they're meant to.'*

I glanced over to the passenger seat, where she was squinting at one of the photographs Micky had copied for us. Six full-sized, and six blown-up to double the original – cramped black handwriting spidering along the lines of a yellow legal pad. Another set with the envelopes. Her tongue stuck out of the side of her mouth, a crease between her eyebrows as she ran a finger back and forwards along the words.

Outside, rain whipped down across the car park, battering the four-storey block of redbrick flats, the concrete central stairwell marked with: 'Saxon Halls – Building C'. The other two halls lurked behind it, the three of them running in a diagonal line along the edge of Camburn Woods.

A handful of cars were parked in front of the entrance, all of them occupied, windows cracked open to let curls of cigarette smoke escape into the downpour. Telephoto lenses, Dictaphones, and chequebooks at the ready. An outpost of the siege in front of FHQ.

'I'll tell her.' I put a hand over the mouthpiece. 'They say you did great on the profile.'

She curled her top lip, not looking up from the letter. 'Nothing to do with me, Dr Docherty ignored nearly every one of my suggestions.'

'Oh... Well, he seems to be giving you credit, anyway.'

'Is he now...' Her mouth hardened. A highlighter was jabbed into the paper and dragged across a sentence. 'How *nice*.'

Back to the phone. 'What's happening with Wee Free?'

'Four of the officers he spanked have dropped the charges; still waiting on the other three. And I've got Sabir going through the journal entries on the HOLMES data. He thinks he can get a user ID from the mess.'

'Told you he was the best.'

'And while we're on the subject, don't forget we're having a team briefing this evening at seven. No excuses this time: you will *be there.'*

Seven o'clock.

If Huntly didn't run his mouth there would still be time to deliver Paul Manson's body to the dump site by nine. As long as we got everything prepared in advance.

'Wouldn't miss it for the world.'

I slid the phone back into my pocket. 'You ready?'

'Hmm...? In a minute.' She traced her finger to the end of the page, then sat back. Stared at the Suzuki's roof for a bit. Frowned. 'The more I read, the more I'm sure there's something ... off about these.'

'What, other than they were written by a nut-job who likes impregnating nurses with plastic dolls?'

She didn't move, just sat there staring at the ceiling.

'Alice?'

'Power and control.' She tucked the pictures into the large brown envelope, reached back and placed it in the rear foot-well. '"A choir of power and control" doesn't make any sense. I mean control *is* power, isn't it?'

295

I opened the door – grabbing the handle as the wind tried to rip the whole thing off the side of the car – and struggled out into the rain. Stood on my good foot and leaned back in to retrieve my cane. 'Try to look like a journalist.'

We hurried past the parked cars, both of us barely fitting under Alice's little black umbrella. Rain sparked and thrummed against the black material.

The security camera above the main double doors pointed down at the keypad, but someone had stuck a yellow smiley-face sticker over the lens. No wonder there was never any CCTV footage when someone got attacked.

I thumbed the button for flat number eight. The names 'McFee, Thornton, Kerr, and Gillespie' were printed on a plastic label next to it. No sign of Claire Young's name on the board, so she had to be in building A or B.

Nothing happened for a bit except the rain.

A couple of posters were sellotaped to the glass – 'Save Our Halls!', 'Jumble Sale In Aid Of Somalia', and 'Have You Seen Timmy?' above a photo of a ginger cat with a white bib.

Alice fidgeted next to me, her umbrella bucking and twisting in the wind as she glanced back over her shoulder at the hyenas huddled in their cars. 'Eight years ago, did Henry say anything about the letters? Any suspicions? Anyone on the periphery of the investigation who used lots of pompous imagery in their reports, or when they spoke?'

'To be honest, Henry really wasn't a lot of use.' I tried the bell again. 'Ellie had just been diagnosed. Most of the time he was plastered. And when he wasn't, he was on the phone to her oncologist. He and Docherty played mentor and student at the press conferences, but really the magician's apprentice was doing all the work.'

The intercom bleeped, and a low, clipped Scottish accent rode out on a wave of static from the speaker. *'She doesn't want to see you, Jimmy, take the hint.'*

I leaned in close. 'It's the police. We need to talk to you about Jessica McFee.'

'*Again?*' What might have been a sigh. Then, '*Hold on, frickin' buzzer's broken…*'

Alice shifted her grip on the brolly as the wind caught it again. 'I thought we weren't supposed to tell people we were the police any more?'

'It sounds better than, "Hello, we're not actually police officers, but we're part of a team of old-fart specialists who're *sort of* assisting the official investigation, only we're not allowed to tell them anything, because our boss is on a scheming power-trip."'

'True.'

There was a clang from somewhere inside, echoing down the stairwell.

Alice bumped her shoulder into my arm. 'So Henry didn't come up with the behavioural evidence analysis?'

'Could barely walk straight half the time. He reviewed everything Docherty did though… Or at least, he said he did.'

She bit her bottom lip, shuffled her feet. Then fiddled with her hair. 'I think we need to ditch the profile and go back to the beginning.'

A pair of shoes appeared at the top of the stairs inside.

'I mean if Dr Docherty came up with the original profile and Henry rubber-stamped it without really *reading* the thing, it's no surprise Docherty's just regurgitating it for Unsub-Fifteen, he's wedded to the ideas he came up with eight years ago because he thinks Henry agreed with them, but they've never been subjected to any real scrutiny.'

The feet descended the stairs, bringing a pair of jeans with them, then a red strappy top with a butterfly picked out in sequins, showing of a jiggle of cleavage. Finally the head – sun tan, cherry lipstick, eye shadow, blonde hair in a long bob with a fringe, a sparkling glass necklace around her throat. A bit done up for twenty-to-twelve on a Tuesday morning.

Alice dropped her hands to her sides. 'We need to pick up some more whisky.'

The woman stopped on the other side of the door and squinted at us, her voice muffled by the glass. 'Can I see some ID?'

I fished out my expired warrant card and she nodded, then pressed the button by the side of the door. A grating buzz. We pushed in, out of the rain. Stood, dripping on the mat.

Behind us, a ripple of flashes caught the glass door, as the hyenas finally realized we might be worth photographing.

The woman folded her arms, increasing the cleavage. 'You've found her, haven't you? You've found Jessica and she's dead.'

Nurse Thornton opened the bedroom door and wafted a hand towards it. 'This is Jessica's.'

The place was a mess: drawers pulled open, their contents spilled on the floor; wardrobe empty; mound of coats and dresses, trousers and shirts piled on the bed; duvet crumpled into one corner, pillows on top of it. The rainbow-coloured rug on the floor was barely visible.

She sighed. 'I tidied up after the first lot searched the place yesterday, but I've not got time to do it again. Taxi's coming at twelve.'

I stepped over the threshold. Did a slow three-sixty. Then pointed at a rectangular patch on the wall, delineated by dust. 'Them?'

'No, that was Jessica. Smashed the frame into a million pieces, tore the photo up, and burned it.'

Hmm... I picked my way through a drift of underwear to the window. The room backed onto Camburn Woods, thick and dark and glistening in the rain. A couple of paths wound away into the forest gloom. 'Miss Thornton, did Jessica mention anyone who'd been hanging around? Maybe someone who made her feel uncomfortable?'

'It's Liz. And your mates asked all this. Both lots.' She turned on her heels and click-clacked off down the corridor. Marking time with the music seeping out from the living room.

Alice sniffed, poked at the corpse of a green jumper with her toe. Her voice was barely audible as she frowned at the mess. 'Back to the start. What do we know about the Inside Man…'

I followed Liz Thornton through into the kitchen. It was big enough for an electric cooker, fridge freezer, small table, sink, and a washing machine. She opened the fridge door and pulled out a small yellow tin of tonic. Then delved into the freezer for a bag of pre-made ice cubes and a bottle of vodka. 'You want one?'

'Can't: pills.'

'Anything good?' A glass from the cupboard got half-filled with clinking ice.

'Arthritis and a gunshot wound.'

'Sorry to hear that.' A slug of vodka, topped up with tonic. 'And if you're thinking it's too early to be drinking, I've been on nights for a fortnight. It's about eight in the evening for me, so *technically* this is a sundowner.' She nodded at the cupboard I was leaning against. 'There's a bag of cashews in there.'

I pulled it out, ripped it open, then poured them into the proffered bowl. 'She was your friend?'

Liz's bare shoulders dropped an inch. 'Why do you lot always ask the same questions?'

'Because they're important, and we want to get Jessica back.'

A sigh, then she took a sip, closed her eyes. 'Happy birthday to me.' The nuts rattled in the bowl as she dipped into them. 'We're supposed to be off to Florida for Christmas. Her, Bethany, and me. Renting a villa.' Liz picked up the glass with her fingertips, holding it palm-down as she clacked through into the living room.

It was a decent size – posters and framed photos on the walls, a stack of DVDs by the TV, books in a case beneath the window overlooking the car park, two sofas covered with tartan throws facing each other across a coffee table littered with magazines and a random pile of bits and pieces. Rod Stewart crooned from the stereo, telling everyone how he was clueless about history, biology, science, and French.

The television was on, with the sound turned down. Dr Fred Docherty stood in the middle of the screen, talking to some serious-faced woman in a green suit. A ticker scrolled across the image beneath them: 'HUNT FOR SERIAL KILLER CONTINUES IN OLDCASTLE • JESSICA MCFEE CONFIRMED AS LATEST VICTIM • FORENSIC PSYCHOLOGIST SAYS KILLER IS GETTING REVENGE AGAINST MOTHER • …'

Little sod. So much for no information gets out except through formal press briefings.

Liz sank into the sofa. Picked up the remote and killed the TV. 'You've never rescued any of them, have you? I remember one of the poor cows coming in – I'd just started at CHI, only been on A&E a week, when…' A frown. 'What was her name, Mary Jordan?'

'Marie.'

'They brought her in and there was blood everywhere. I held her hand as they rushed her straight into surgery… That's what's going to happen to Jessica, isn't it?'

'Not if we can find her first. *Did* she mention anyone?'

'Pfff. You mean the "Camburn Creeper"?' Liz took another swig of pre-noon sundowner and made a couple of cashews disappear. 'Dirty sod was hanging about here for *weeks*. Taking photos. Caught him going through the bins one time, probably hunting for old pants and used tampons. Had to pelt him with the recycling to make him sod off.' A grin. 'Wine, gin, and vodka bottles. Should've heard him *scream*, running

300

off with hands over his head, glass exploding all around him.'

'Good for you. What else did he do, other than the rubbish?'

'Oh, the usual. What frickin' idiot thought it was a good idea to back the nurses' halls onto a chunk of woods? The number of times I've had to call security because some perv's up a tree with a telephoto lens or binoculars while we're changing.'

She reached beneath the coffee table and pulled out a big leather handbag. Picked a lipstick and a BlackBerry from the random pile of stuff and dumped it inside. Followed by a comb, purse, keys, pen... 'Of course, security come running straight away to chase the perverts off.'

'That's something.'

A laugh. 'Do they hell! If you're lucky they'll stick a form through the letterbox the next day asking for "details of the alleged offence".'

Alice appeared in the doorway. Shook her head.

I creaked into the sofa opposite. 'Did you give them a description?'

A card wallet, collapsible brolly, and another lipstick disappeared into the bag.

'I did better than that – I took a photo of the dirty sod when he was hanging about the car park one night.' Liz dipped back into her handbag and came out with the BlackBerry again. Fiddled with the buttons for a moment, then held it out.

A man – had to be at least six feet, going by the Fiat 500 he was standing beside – in a black bomber jacket, black woolly hat, black jeans, and black gloves. His face was blurred, caught in the middle of moving. The phone's camera hadn't been quick enough in the low light.

I squinted, moved the phone away from me and back again. Did he have glasses? Maybe a moustache-beard thing? Then again, it could've just been a shadow cast by the lamppost between the camera and the Fiat. Almost impossible to tell.

301

On the CD player, Rod launched into 'If You Don't Know Me by Now'.

'Did you show this to the other police officers?'

A blush turned her neck pink. 'The first lot spent the whole time staring at my breasts. I was getting ready to head off for my shift, and I was in a towel, and so *frickin'* angry with them... Second lot acted like they were James Bond or something. I...' She looked away, went back to stuffing things in her handbag. 'I forgot it was on my phone till just now.'

I handed the BlackBerry back. 'It's OK, probably nothing anyway. Any chance you can text the photo to my mobile?'

I gave her the number and she thumbed the buttons, still not looking at me. 'Jessica said he followed her to work a couple of times. Home too. Then, about a week ago, he just stopped coming around.' The phone in her hand bleeped. 'Or he just got better at hiding.'

Alice settled next to me on the couch. Picked up a couple of DVDs, turning them over in her hands. 'I like *The Bourne Identity*, but I'm not too keen on the *Girl with the Dragon Tattoo*, don't you think Daniel Craig looks a bit like a monkey, not that there's anything wrong with that, but I find it a little off-putting...'

'Suppose.'

The phone in my pocket trembled – that would be Liz's text. I pulled it out and forwarded it on to Sabir:

```
I need this cleaned up and sharpened

I want an ID ASAP — check sex offend-
er's register

And can you do something about these
bloody ankle tags???
```

302

Alice put the DVDs down. 'The photo Jessica smashed, was that the Jimmy you mentioned when you answered the buzzer?'

A grimace, then Liz knocked back a mouthful. 'No. Jimmy is Bethany's ex-husband. He doesn't seem to get that she's not his emotional punch-bag any more.' She looked at me. 'Don't suppose you could harass him a bit, could you? Pretend he was a paedophile or something?'

My phone trembled again:

> God, Ur not shy, R you? What did Ur
> last slave die of?

'He done anything to her? Smacked her around? Anything we could do him for?'

Liz blew out a breath. 'Never mind.'

'So,' Alice scooted forward, 'the photograph?'

'Jessica was going out with this bloke – well, *boy* really – from Human Resources. Darren Wilkinson. Very clingy and needy. All over her like she'd evaporate if he wasn't touching her.' A shake of the head and a roll of the eyes. 'Then one day he sends her a text saying he didn't want to see her any more and he was moving on with his life. Dumps her by text message. How frickin' pathetic is that?'

I put the phone back in my pocket. Sabir might be a moan, but he'd get on it. 'When was this?'

A little crease appeared between Liz's neatly plucked eyebrows. 'Last Thursday? No, Friday – I know because she'd been planning a trip to the pictures to see that new French film, and she'd got tickets and booked a table for dinner, and she was getting all dolled up to go out when the text came in. Standing there in her bra, new skirt, and four-inch heels swearing a blue streak.'

And two days later she goes missing.

Liz laughed, not loud, more of a small, slightly smoky chuckle. 'Tell you, her dad's some sort of lay preacher, but by

Christ that woman could curdle the air when she wanted to.' Then silence. 'I mean she can. Not could. *Can.*'

Alice nodded. 'It must be a bit weird, all living here together. Did you know Claire Young?'

'Not really. Yeah, I'd bump into her at work, or in the car park. Maybe once or twice at a birthday party, or a flat-warming.' She waved a hand at the window, where the rain lashed against the other two buildings. 'I know it's old-fashioned, but living here's about the only perk we get – cheap rent and a bit of community spirit. Course, the scumbags want to sell the place off for development. Cost-cutting my arse, it's profiteering.' She rummaged in her handbag and came out with a creased sheet of paper, half-covered with signatures. 'Don't fancy signing our petition to save the halls, do—'

A jingling ringtone blared out of the BlackBerry and she snatched it up from the table. 'Hello? … What, right now? … No, no, I'll be right down…. Yes.' She pressed a button, then sat there frowning at the blank screen. 'It's the taxi. Bunch of us are going to the King's Hussars for a curry. It was supposed to be a birthday treat.' She looked up at Alice, blinked a couple of times, then wiped a palm across her eyes. It left a smudge of mascara on her cheek. 'I don't want to go without Jessica…'

Alice reached across the coffee table, over the piles of gossip and car magazines, and took her hand. 'You don't have to go if you don't want to. What would Jessica want you to do?'

A small, brittle smile. 'Stuff myself with poppadums, lamb Jalfrezi, and sauvignon blanc till it's coming out my ears. "You don't turn thirty every day, Liz," she'd say, "might as well enjoy it."'

'Then that's what you should do.'

She stood, laughed. 'God, look at me, better fix my face or the taxi-driver will freak.'

I levered myself out of the couch. 'Before you go, give me Jimmy's name and address. Call it a birthday present from Police Scotland.'

32

The corridor wall was cold against my back, leaching through the damp jacket to the chilled flesh within. 'No, Mackay. M.A.C.K.A.Y. Jimmy Mackay, last known address: Flat 50 Willcox Towers, Cowskillin.'

Rhona repeated it back to me, slowly, as if she was writing it down at the same time. *'OK, got that. Don't worry, by the time we've finished with him, Jimmy's not going within a million miles of his ex.'*

'Thanks, Rhona.'

'Ash?' She coughed. *'Look, I'm* really *sorry I told Ness you think the Inside Man might be a cop. I didn't know it was meant to be a secret. Honest.'*

'Well … just make sure Jimmy Mackay gets the fright of his life.'

'Deal.'

The doorway down the hall opened and Alice backed out, talking too quietly to make out more than a couple of words from where I stood. Then she leaned into the flat and hugged whoever it was.

Alice backed away again and the door closed. She stood there for a moment, then slumped in place, took a couple of deep breaths – arching her back – then turned and gave me a weak smile. Waved.

305

I limped over. 'Well?'

She rubbed a hand across her face. 'Claire Young's flatmates are entrenched in stage three of the Kübler-Ross model – the whole place is like a mausoleum.' Alice shook herself. 'I'm sorry you had to leave, it's—'

'It's OK. I understand. They don't need some policeman intruding on their grief.'

'Pfff...' She stepped in close and leaned her forehead against my chest. 'We did some NLP and some talk therapy and I feel like I've run a marathon carrying a washing machine on my back...'

I gave her shoulder a rub. 'That us?'

A nod. 'Can we get something to eat?'

I turned and guided her towards the stairs. 'The hospital canteen's rubbish, but there's usually a chip van parked outside.'

Building A's stairwell was lined in glass, rather than concrete, with views into the dark boughs of Camburn Woods on one side, and the car park on the other. At least there weren't any journos lying in wait at the front door.

Alice drooped along at my side as I limped over and opened it. She paused beneath the portico, struggling with her collapsible umbrella. 'Can we walk? From here to the hospital?'

Outside the wind had dropped. Now it just hammered straight down, bouncing back off the paving slabs and tarmac in a ricochet mist. Battering the trees and bushes into submission.

'You sure?'

'For the last two hours we've done nothing but drink tea and talk to people in pain, every breath tastes of loss and panic and yes I know that sounds melodramatic, but I'm trying to think like he thinks when he looks at nurses, and now I'm tired and I just want to walk in the rain and not have to wallow in fear and grief.'

'OK...'

She held her umbrella up, so I could hobble in underneath it. Slipped her arm through mine so it'd be above us both. Stepped out from beneath the portico and into the downpour. 'A choir of power and pain.'

We followed the path from the front of the building around the back, where it snaked off in three directions – right: back towards the gloomy brick lumps of Buildings B and C, straight ahead: into Camburn Woods, and left: along the fringes of the undergrowth, dead lampposts sticking up like bones towards the granite sky.

A sign stood at the junction, pointing left. '⬅ CASTLE HILL INFIRMARY ~ ALLOW TWENTY MINUTES'.

Alice pulled in closer as we stepped onto the rain-rivered path, the run-off from the buildings making tiny breakwaters against her red All Stars. 'No one trusts the on-site security, they never seem to do anything unless you force them. I said they should make some sort of formal complaint, I mean what's the point of having security if it doesn't make you feel secure?'

'Anyone hanging around asking about Claire?'

'No one specific. Well, there are peepers all the time, especially if you've got one of the rooms that backs onto the woods. You know what men are like.' She sniffed. 'No offence.'

The nurses' halls disappeared into the rain behind us. Up ahead, high walls hid the back gardens of a block of sandstone tenements. The spires of St Stephen's, St Jasper's, and the cathedral reared above their slate roofs. And just visible in the distance, the twin chimneys of the hospital incinerator, their white trails of smoke and steam making parallel scars across the sky.

The only sounds were the hissing leaves and the drumming raindrops on the umbrella's black skin.

'They say anything about someone taking photos? Going through their rubbish?'

She shook her head.

Two hours of visiting flat, after flat, after flat of scared and worried nurses and the only lead we had depended on Detective Sergeant Sabir Akhtar being the technical genius he always told everyone he was.

Alice peered past me, into the woods. 'It's like something out of the Brothers Grimm.'

'Funny you should say that. Once upon a time, there was a young woman called Deborah Hill, and she—'

'Please.' Alice turned her head away. 'Not this time. Let's just … walk.'

The nurse sniffed, then scrubbed a crumpled tissue across her nostrils, squidging her pudgy nose from side to side. 'No. Well, you know…' A shrug and a sigh. She was short, with thick purple bags lurking under her eyes, her face round in the shadow of her Puffa jacket's hood. The zip was open, despite the rain, showing an expanse of blue scrubs and a name badge with 'Bethany Gillespie' printed on it.

Jessica's flatmate. The one with the stalker ex-husband.

She popped another chip in her mouth, chewed, then leaned in closer and dropped her voice. 'You always get nutters, don't you? I don't mean people with learning difficulties or mental health issues, I mean the kind of nutters who want to sniff your fingers when you come out of the Ladies. Once had a bloke in here who'd scream about abdominal pain, then soon as you got the bed sheets pulled back he'd pee on you.' Another sniff. 'You know: nutters.'

The queue for chips had dwindled to just one more nurse and then it was Alice's turn, the four of us sheltering beneath the van's awning. The air heady with the scents of fried batter, hot potatoes, and vinegar.

Most of the hospital was hidden from this corner of the car park, blocked out by the tomb of Victorian sandstone where they kept people like Marie Jordan. Drugged up to the ears and locked in a room with bars on the windows. The tower

308

rose behind it, but only the top two floors were visible, lights glinting in the windows – grey and thin below, warm and gold on the penthouse level. Where the private patients went.

Bethany broke off a chunk of fish and crunched through the batter.

I nodded towards the hospital. 'What about patients, anyone make any complaints?'

She swallowed. 'About Jessica? God, no. She was completely brilliant with the mums and the dads. A *total* professional in every respect.'

There was a rustle of paper and the other nurse wandered over, face lined and creased as she stuffed in a couple of chips. Thin, with whippet-grey hair pulled back from her face. A small, puckered mouth full of sharp little teeth – chewing with her mouth open. She eyed me up and down, then turned to Bethany. 'Who's your boyfriend?'

Bethany grimaced for a moment, then replaced it with a smile. 'I was just telling this nice policeman how professional Jessica is.'

'Jessica? Professional?' A snort. She bit the end off a battered sausage, chewing and talking at the same time. 'You remember Mrs Gisbourne?'

'Jean MacGruther, that is *no* way to talk of—'

'That's dead people. You're not supposed to speak ill of the dead. Jessica's not dead.' Nurse MacGruther turned to me. 'Is she?'

I opened my mouth, but Bethany got there first. 'You saw what they said in the paper this morning, it's—'

'Rubbish. Police are trying to do their job. You think that's any easier if we all stand about like mealie puddings, telling them everybody loved her?' Another wodge of chips disappeared. 'Have you spoken to Jessica's boyfriend yet?'

'Any reason I should?'

Bethany brought her chin up. 'That was all a misunderstanding.'

309

'Darren Wilkinson.' Nurse MacGruther's eyes glittered as she chewed. 'First shift after Valentine's Day, Jessica turns up with a shiner the size of a dinner plate. Proper beetroot and jaundice job. Course, they couldn't let her deal with expectant mothers looking like that, could they? Had to spend the week doing filing and national statistics and things.'

A big theatrical sigh. 'She *explained* that. They were playing tennis on Darren's Wii, and they were a bit drunk, and it was a complete accident.'

'And the cracked ribs? Were they an accident too?'

'You know she—'

'How about the time he knocked out one of her teeth? A molar, right at the back. *That* takes some doing – lucky he didn't break her jaw.'

Bethany crunched through another bit of fish. 'She was abducted by the Inside Man, *not* her boyfriend. He isn't a serial killer, he works in Human Resources!'

'Any bloke that beats up his girlfriend—'

'She didn't want to make a fuss, it—'

'—ginger bastard. How can that—'

'All right!' I held my hands up and turned on the police-issue inspector's voice that had terrified the two idiots in the patrol car yesterday. 'I get it. He was assaulting her. She didn't report it.'

They both backed away. Eyed me.

Bethany sniffed. 'There's no need to be like that, we're only trying to help.'

Alice leaned back against the two-tone wall – institution green on the bottom half, scuffed magnolia above. 'I shouldn't have eaten all of those chips.' She puffed out a breath, let her shoulders droop. 'An hour of talking to midwives, with rampant indigestion… Well, not the midwives, I mean *I* was the one with indigestion, though I suppose they might have had as well, only no one mentioned it. How about you?'

310

Shouts and swearing echoed down the corridor, punctuated with the occasional scream. The miracle of birth.

'I wasn't there when Rebecca was born. A wee boy got savaged by a drug dealer's dog, I spent the whole day tracking the bastard down. But I made Katie's. She was ... tiny. And all purple and screaming and covered in snot and blood.' A small laugh tried to break free, but died before it could breathe on its own. 'God, it was like an X-rated version of *Alien*.' Back when anything was possible and nobody had to die.

A little rip appeared in the middle of my chest, making every breath sting. I cleared my throat. 'So, did your hour of indigestion get you anything?'

'Everyone I talked to is scared of the Inside Man. They don't walk back to the halls unless there's three or four of them. They don't use the car park here any more, because there's still no CCTV.' She wrapped an arm around herself. 'He's turning into a mythological monster – a sort of cross between Freddy Krueger, Jimmy Savile, and Peter Mandelson...' She checked her watch. 'Are we going to speak to Jessica McFee's boyfriend, because maybe we should, I mean if he's been beating her up then he's obviously got anger-management and—'

'What time is it?'

She checked again. 'Twenty to four.'

'OK, we finish up with Jessica's colleagues, then give the boyfriend a grilling. But I want to be out of here by quarter past at the latest, so we're not late for our mob accountant friend.'

Alice's head dropped, till she was staring at the tips of her little red shoes. 'Can we not call him our "friend", it's—'

'We've been over this. Him or Shifty, remember?' I put a hand on her shoulder. 'I know it's hard, but— Crap.' My phone trilled in my pocket. Still, it was about time Sabir got back to me with that ID. I hauled my mobile out and hit the button. 'What kept you?'

311

'*That you, Henderson?*' Whoever it was, it wasn't Sabir. Instead of the treacle-thick Liverpudlian accent, they had an Oldcastle burr.

I pulled the phone from my ear and checked the screen: 'NUMBER WITHHELD'.

'Who is this?'

'*Some detective: it's Micky Slosser. You were in my office this morning, remember?*' A pause. Some rustling. Then he was back. '*Something's just come in that you might find interesting.*'

Silence.

'Really not in the mood to play, Micky.'

'*One letter. Yellow legal paper. Signed, "the Inside Man".*'

33

The sky was a smear of charcoal-grey. Blood seeped from the horizon as the sun gave up on the day, making glistening spatter-patterns on the wet roads.

'What?' I stuck a finger in the other ear and turned my back on the hospital entrance while an ambulance Dopplered past, its wail lowering as it faded into the distance.

On the other end of the phone, Jacobson tried again. *'Ness got everyone to drop the charges. Mr McFee's a free man again.'*

'Good for him. What about Cooper – did Bad Bill remember Claire Young or Jessica McFee?'

'This letter: you sure your journalist is on the up?'

'He's a journalist.'

'Fair point. I'll get it picked up anyway.' The volume dropped, as if Jacobson had turned away from the phone. *'Cooper, tell him what you told me.'*

There was a scrunching noise, then PC Cooper cleared his throat at me. *'Hello? Yes, OK, so, Bad Bill, AKA: William Moore. I showed him both photos and he thinks he's seen Jessica McFee with a tall, red-haired, IC-One male. Says he can't be certain about Claire Young. She looks familiar, but that might just be cos she's been in all the papers and on the telly.'*

So much for that. 'Don't suppose he's got a security camera or anything?'

'*Said he's never really bothered. Said, who's going to risk a cleaver in the head just to nick a bag of burger buns and some fried onions? Professor Huntly thinks it's unlikely Tim would have taken Claire Young with him when he bought her last meal anyway. He abducted her on the Thursday night, she turned up in the wee hours of the Saturday morning, Huntly says Tim's not going to rape her, hold her hostage, then take her out for Friday lunch.*'

Another ambulance roared past – this one heading the other way.

I checked my watch: ten to four. Have to get moving soon. 'Did you—'

'*So I asked how many, erm...*' Pause. '"*Double Bastard Bacon Murder Burgers*" *he sold between eleven a.m. and three p.m. on the Friday, and he became pretty abusive.*'

Moron.

'It's a burger van, not a three-star restaurant. Cash-in-hand – no receipts. Where was he parked on Friday?'

Silence.

'Cooper?'

'*Actually...*'

I gave my head a little dunt off the wall. 'You forgot to ask, didn't you?'

'*Well, you said he'd be at the B&Q and he was, so I thought ... you know, it would be his pitch.*' A cough. '*Or something.*'

'The whole *point* of a burger van is that the damn thing's got wheels. *Go back* and find out where he was Friday lunchtime.'

'*Sorry, Guv...*'

So I was 'Guv' now? Well, at least that was something. 'You did OK. Just got to keep your eye on the details.'

'*Yes, Guv.*'

'And get on to Control: I want a PNC check on one Darren Wilkinson, works in Human Resources at Castle Hill Infirmary.'

'Yes, Guv.'

'Off you go.'

Someone tapped me on the shoulder, and when I turned around, there was Noel Maxwell. He'd thrown an orange Parka on over his scrubs, bright white Nikes shuffling on the damp pavement. He grinned, making the little soul-patch thing twitch. 'How'd that Prednisolone work out for you, OK?'

Jacobson's voice came back on the phone. *'Come on then: you're the one who insisted shoe-leather was the way to making connections. What did you find out?'*

'Hold on.' I pulled the phone from my ear and pressed mute. 'Did you get it?'

Noel glanced back over his shoulder. Then dropped his voice till it was barely audible. 'This is, like, *industrial* grade, OK? I mean it's not—'

'Did you get it or not?'

Another glance. As if he wasn't acting shiftily enough already. He slipped his hand into his pocket and tugged out the corner of a brown envelope. 'You got the cash?'

I counted out sixty quid from what was left of the hundred Jacobson had subbed me, and handed it over. One five-pound note and a handful of change left.

He had another glance about, then slipped me the envelope. Didn't weigh much. I ripped open the flap.

His eyes went wide. 'Don't do that here!'

'Yeah. Trust isn't exactly high on my agenda today.' Two syringes sat in the bottom of the envelope: clear, with orange caps on the needles. A folded sheet of paper lay with it, covered with small print.

'Just make sure you read the instructions, OK? Stuff's dangerous...'

That was the point.

'How long?'

A shrug. Another glance. 'Depends on body mass. Big fat bloke: three to four hours. Give a whole dose to a wee kid

315

and they're *never* waking up.' A blush. 'You know. If you were that way inclined.'

I popped the envelope into my pocket. Then stopped. Frowned. 'Who else have you been flogging medical supplies to?'

Noel's mouth flapped open and closed a couple of times. 'I … don't know what you're talking about, selling medical supplies, why would I do that? I'm only doing you a favour cos I know you from the old days.'

'Anaesthetics, antihypertensives, disinfectants, sutures, that surgical glue stuff?' The kind of things needed to hack someone open and stitch a plastic baby doll inside them.

He shook his head. 'Nah, you're thinking of someone else, I don't *sell* hospital gear, I'm not some sort of dealer, I'm just a good guy helping out an old mate.'

'Noel, I swear to God I will drag your twitchy arse from here to Dundee by the balls.'

He backed up, stuffed his hands in his pockets, pulled his shoulders forward, making himself smaller. 'I don't do that no more, *honestly*. I did, maybe, a few years ago, but you had that word with me and I straightened up my act. Straight as a bullet me. Dead, dead straight.'

I just stared at him.

He shuffled a bit. Hunched his back a little more. 'OK, so I might have, you know, given someone a hand with their pain management. Couple things of morphine and a few packs of Amitriptyline, maybe some Temazepam, but they had multiple sclerosis and that. Honest.'

Silence.

'Just trying to be a good citizen, you know? Help my fellow man?'

'What about antihypertensives?'

He licked his teeth, making bulges behind his lips. 'Don't get much call for them. Opioids and barbiturates are the drugs *du jour* amongst Oldcastle's bright young things… Not that I would ever, you know: good citizen, fellow man…'

I stepped in close enough to smell the fug of cigarette smoke and bitter aftershave wafting off of him. 'You like us being friends, don't you, Noel?'

He rocked from side to side, hunching up even more, looking up at me like a nervous orange crow. 'We're friends, course we are… Why wouldn't we be friends?'

'If you want it to stay that way, here's what you're going to do: you're going to speak to all your fellow good citizens and you're going to find out who's been filching surgical supplies from the stores. And then you're going to tell me.' I gave him a smile, keeping it nice and cold. 'And you're going to do it by this time tomorrow.'

He got smaller still. 'What if I can't? I mean, you know, obviously I'll try my best, but what if I try and try, but no one's saying anything?'

When my hand landed on his shoulder he flinched. Blinked at me.

I gave the shoulder a squeeze. 'Let's not find out, eh?'

The woman from Human Resources gave us a smile that didn't make it any further than her cheeks. She towered over Alice as she ushered us into a pair of fake-leather seats. Her skin was pale as milk, dark hair long at the sides and hacked into a severe fringe at the front. 'Darren will be joining us shortly, he's on a call at the moment.' She clasped her hands in front of her. 'Now, what's this all about?'

The clock on the wall behind her read twenty past four. Should still be OK if we did this quickly.

I settled into the chair, stretched my right leg out. 'I'm afraid that's between us and Mr Wilkinson.'

A sign, screwed to the middle of the open door, marked this as 'Soft Meeting Room 3'. Lemon-yellow walls, a couple of framed prints, a whiteboard on one wall, and a flipchart on a stand by the door. Six, low, fake-leather chairs and a coffee table scarred with cup-ring acne. It smelled of sweat and desperation.

317

'Ah...' Her smile thinned out a bit and wrinkles appeared around her eyes. 'It's out of the question I'm afraid. Hospital policy states that all members of staff must be supported by a representative from Human Resources during interviews with the media, bereaved families, or police, if conducted on CHI property.' She swept a hand towards the door. 'Of course, if you wish to detain him and remove him from Castle Hill Infirmary, that's your prerogative. *Do* you want to detain him?'

'I haven't decided yet.'

The eyes above the thin smile grew colder. 'I can assure you that Darren is a valued member of my team, Detective Constable Henderson. The day after his accident, he was in here at nine. That shows dedication.' She folded her arms. 'What's he supposed to have done?'

I gave her the stare.

She shook her head. 'He's been employee-of-the-month three times. And that's hospital-wide, not just my department. He's conscientious, hardworking, and really *invested* in our processes and procedures.'

Alice tugged the sleeves of her stripy top down over her fingertips. 'He was in an accident?'

'Hit and run, on a zebra crossing, no less. But he was *still* here, Friday morning, bang on time.' She clapped her hands together, once. Hard and sharp. 'Now, would anyone like a cup of tea?'

As soon as she was gone, Alice leaned over to me, voice low. 'Do we really think Darren Wilkinson is the Inside Man?'

'Why are you whispering?'

A pink bloom appeared on her cheeks. 'I mean I know he works at the hospital, so he might have access to drugs, and he'd be able to find out about surgical procedures – he can probably watch them doing operations if he likes – and all the victims were nurses, and if he's working in the HR Department he's got access to their personnel records not to

318

mention who Jessica McFee was being a midwife for, but…'
Creases appeared between Alice's eyebrows. 'Oh, I see. When you lay it out like that…'

'And he just *happens* to be going out with one of the victims? Bit of a coincidence.'

'Well, maybe—'

'According to the Police National Computer, he's twenty-seven. That makes him nineteen the first time Tim was around. Doesn't exactly fit the profile, does it?'

The hands on the clock crept around to twenty-five past.

Alice wrapped one arm around herself, twiddled with her hair. 'If he's been assaulting Jessica McFee, that means he's got control issues – both internal and external – Jessica's his property, when she doesn't do what she's told that hurts him, it's disrespectful… He has no choice, he's got to punish her, I mean it's not his fault is it, he's *helping* her be a better person, does she *really* want to keep screwing up like that, she should be *thanking* him. She's lucky to have him.'

Alice stuck her knees together, heels angled out on the scuffed carpet tiles. 'It's always the same though, isn't it, women just don't get it, they need a firm hand to lead them in the right direction. They like that: they like a man who can take charge, they *need* to be shown who's boss, like his dad showed his mum…' Alice blinked a couple of times, then stared up at the ceiling tiles. The frown was back. 'But the abduction, the cutting, the dolls – impregnating them – yes, that's a control thing, but Tim does it because he's impotent, powerless in his day-to-day relationships.'

I took out my phone and read the text from Cooper again:

```
PNC on Darren Wilkinson (27) — 14 Fyne
Lane, no convictions, warning for
vandalism when 11, just applied for
combined shotgun/firearms licence.
```

He could sing for his gun licence. No way that was going through now.

'Ash?' Alice brought her heels together, squeaking the rubbery soles against one another. 'We didn't check with Claire Young's flatmates: what if Darren's her boyfriend too? What if he romantically targets his victims, before abducting them?'

Shrug. 'Possible.'

She slumped back in her seat and let her arms hang over the edge, stripy sleeves swinging back and forth. 'But by physically dominating Jessica, by beating her, he's actively *demonstrating* his power...'

I shut down Cooper's text and called Sabir.

'Oh, Christ, what now? I'm working on it, OK? Keep your knickers on, this stuff takes time!'

'Does the name Darren Wilkinson ring any bells?'

Pause. *'Who the hell is Darren Wilkinson?'*

'I need to know if he comes up in the HOLMES data for the original Inside Man enquiry.'

'OK...' There was a long, wet sigh. *'Pick one.'*

'One what?'

'All the stuff you've thrown at me – pick something, and that's the thing that gets dumped to do this instead.'

'Sabir, I—'

'No. Youse lot seem to think I'm sitting on a fifty-man team down here, but there's just me, get it? Me, on me tod, getting buried under all your Jock shite.' What sounded like static boomed from the earpiece, then settled down into crunching – a mouthful of crisps? *'So pick one.'*

'Don't be such a drama queen. It's—'

The door opened and the HR manager was back, a plastic beverage carrier in one hand with three plastic cups steaming away in the holes.

'Sabir, just do it. I'll call you back.' I hung up as she placed the carrier on the little coffee table.

Alice pulled on a smile, eyes wide and bright. 'How does Darren get on with his female team mates? Is he popular?'

The HR manager frowned for a moment. 'I'd say yes: he is. He's personable, well groomed, always brings cakes when it's someone's birthday.'

'So not … you know: making off-colour jokes, invading personal space, maybe even a bit intimidating?'

'Darren?' Her cheeks twitched, then a little laugh slipped out. Followed by a cough. 'He joined my team six years ago. He was only twenty-one. I have *personally* trained him. He's not some sort of misogynistic neanderthal.'

'Hmm…' Alice went back to twiddling with her hair, one heel tapping against the carpet.

The plastic cup was scalding hot as I picked it out of the holder. 'What about attendance? Any absences over the last three weeks?'

'Not even after his accident – which, by the way, your colleagues have done *nothing* about. Darren is a model employee. And—'

There was a knock and a battered face appeared at the door. One eye was swollen shut, the skin dark and mottled with bruising that reached from the tip of his chin all the way up to his forehead on one side. A line of pink Elastoplast crossed the bridge of his nose. He was on crutches, using one of them to ease the door open. Crumpled white shirt, pale-blue tie. His right trouser leg was cut short, showing off a fibreglass cast covered in marker-pen signatures.

Whatever hit him, it must have been a damn sight bigger than a Mini.

His voice was soft and hissing, as if he was missing a few teeth, but the Dundee accent still came through like a foghorn. 'You wanted to see me, Sarah?'

She turned in her seat and nodded. 'Ah, Darren, perfect timing. I was just telling these officers what a valued member of… Darren, are you OK?'

321

His one good eye had gone wide at the word 'officers', mouth hanging open, exposing four or five ragged scarlet holes where teeth should have been. He backed away.

'Darren?'

He glanced up and down the corridor, as if planning on hobbling for it. Then sagged against his crutches. Closed his eyes and swore.

34

Darren blinked across the table at me. 'I...' He picked at the lining of the cast on his left arm. 'It's not like that.' A sniff. *'Wasn't* like that.'

Twenty to five, and we were still stuck here, the clock's minute hand sweeping ever closer to Paul Manson's appointment.

Alice leaned forwards, elbows on her knees. 'It's perfectly understandable. You're only looking out for her, aren't you? She does all these stupid things and you're the one who has to clean up the mess. She needs to learn, doesn't she? Needs to do what she's told, *when* she's told.'

He kept his head down.

The HR Manager, Sarah, narrowed her eyes. 'I'm not comfortable with this line of questioning. Darren has already told you that he didn't assault Jessica McFee. I don't see why you're fixating on this.' Playing the lawyer.

Alice placed both hands, palm up, on the table. 'And if she steps out of line, it's only understandable you should give her a slap every now and then. For her own good? It works with dogs, doesn't it? Why should women be any different?'

'I can *assure* you that not only did Darren excel in our gender-parity training, he's one of the hospital's Equality Champions. This is completely inappropriate and—'

'Come on then, Darren,' I picked up my walking stick and poked him in the chest with the rubber end, 'tell me about this hit-and-run.'

He shrank back into his seat. 'It was dark. I was crossing the road and a car came out of nowhere and hit me. Didn't see it.'

Another poke. 'Where?'

Pick. Pick. Pick. 'Just down from the chipper on Oxford Street.'

'When?'

Nothing.

So I poked him again. 'When – did – it – happen?'

'Ow! ... I don't know.'

'Please stop poking him.'

No chance. 'I checked the Police National Computer – there's no record of you being run over on Oxford Street, or anywhere else. What, you decided it wasn't worth reporting? Accidents will happen?'

He kept his eyes down. 'Didn't think there was any point. You know. Cos I didn't see the car or anything...'

'Right.' One more poke for luck. 'You got flattened by a car. Your leg's broken, arm too. You look like you've spent an hour being a trampoline for skinheads, and you didn't think it was worth reporting?'

'Detective Constable Henderson, if Darren says—'

'You see, Darren, you told your boss here you were hit on a zebra crossing, but there's no zebra crossing on Oxford, is there?' This time I aimed the rubber tip at his ribs and he winced. Recoiled in his seat. Wrapped a hand around the impact spot. So I did it again, going for the other side instead. Same result. 'The only person in a hit-and-run who *doesn't* go to the police is the driver. Take off your shirt.'

Sarah stiffened. 'All right, I think we've been patient enough. That's completely—'

'There wasn't any car, was there? Take off the damn shirt.'

She stood. 'I'm going to have to ask you to leave. If you want to conduct some sort of strip-search, you can do it under caution at the station. Until then— What are you doing?'

I lunged across the coffee table, grabbed two handfuls of his shirt and yanked. The buttons pinged off like tiny bullets, the tails wrenched out of his trousers. His tie dangled over the purple, scarlet, and yellow mess of his chest. Bruises covered both sides – not in a hard line like you'd get from a car bonnet, or a bumper but haphazard and patchwork. And right in the middle of his stomach was the perfect negative image of a bootprint.

'Strange tyres on that car. Looks more like a size nine than a Dunlop radial.'

Sarah jabbed a finger at me. 'I'll be making a *formal* complaint to your superiors. How dare you subject a member of my staff to this humiliating—'

'Oh, grow up. He wasn't in a hit-and-run, someone beat the living hell out of him.' I put my stick down. 'Why did you lie, Darren? Who's got you so scared they can do *that* to you and you don't even report it?'

He bit his bottom lip, the one good eye glistening in the light. 'Nothing happened…'

'Really?' I rapped my cane on the coffee table and he flinched. 'Is that why you're after a shotgun licence? Bit of revenge?'

She pulled out her phone. 'I'm calling security. You're both—'

'No!' Darren grabbed her arm. 'Please. No. I… I don't want to make a fuss. Please?'

She stared at him for a moment. 'Are you certain this is what you want?'

He lowered his eyes and went back to picking at his cast. 'Can I get a glass of water, or something?'

Sarah placed a hand on his shoulder. 'Of course you can.' She scowled at me. 'And *no* more questions.'

* * *

325

Darren Wilkinson licked his lips and blinked as the door clicked shut behind her. Then gave a little shuddering sigh. 'I ... never meant to hurt her.'

Alice patted him on the arm. 'You need to—'

'It was...' He cleared his throat. Stared at the coffee table again. 'Sorry, you first.'

'No: what were you going to say?'

'Jessica... She wasn't like...' Another sigh. 'She *wanted* me to hit her.' He dug his thumbnail into the lining of the cast, gouging out a tuft of white. 'I don't mean "she was asking for it" in a misogynistic way, I mean literally. She *literally* asked me to hit her. I just wanted to be like normal couples, holding hands, walks in the park, but...' He puffed out his cheeks. Hacked out another tuft.

I stared at him. 'Aye, *right.*'

Silence.

'It's OK, Darren. What happened?'

'The first time, I thought she wanted me to spank her. You know, just a bit of fun? And I know it enforces gender stereotyping and patriarchal dominance, but she told me not to be so bloody wet. She didn't want spanked, she wanted me to *hit* her.'

'And did you?'

His eye came up, wide. 'No! Of course I didn't. I don't believe in the physical subjugation of women or any of that outmoded sexist crap... But she wouldn't let up, she kept badgering me and then she was hitting me and screaming in my face...' Darren turned away. 'And I did it. I slapped her, I didn't mean to, it just... And that was it – she was...' A cough. 'You know.'

Alice tapped her fingertips on the coffee table. 'She became sexually aroused.'

'Sometimes I think she ... confused violence with love. Like they were the same thing. And that's how it went. She ... *needed* it to feel wanted and valued and I...' He bared his gap-filled teeth. 'I *hated* myself.'

There were thousands of excuses – things abusers told themselves to justify pounding the crap out of their other halves – but that was a new one.

While he was scrubbing the tears from his bruised face, I pulled out my phone and flicked through to the photo that Jessica's flatmate, Liz Thornton, had sent me. Held it out to Darren. 'Do you recognize this man?'

He blinked at it a couple of times, then sniffed. 'He's the pervert who went through their bins, isn't he? I chased him once. Jessica and me were going down to the car park – it was someone's leaving do that night – and he was fiddling with the mailboxes. You know, like he was picking the locks or something? So I shouted and he ran and I chased him.'

'Did you see his face?'

Darren shook his head. 'It was dark. He ran off into the woods and there was *no* way I was going to follow him in there and end up getting knifed or something.'

I put the phone away again. 'So who beat you up?'

'I can't...' Deep breath. 'I fell down the stairs.'

'And somehow managed to stamp on your own stomach on the way down?' I leaned back. Stared at him until he dropped his gaze and went back to digging the lining out of his cast. 'You get beaten up on Thursday night. And on Friday you text Jessica McFee and tell her you never want to see her again.'

Pretty obvious really.

He kept his head down.

'It was her dad, wasn't it? Wee Free McFee didn't like some godless Dundonian rutting away on top of his daughter.'

Darren's head snapped up, one good eye wide open. 'No! It was nothing like that he never touched me it was an accident. *I'm not pressing charges!*'

'I'm sorry...' Alice fiddled with her keys in the darkness between our stolen Jag and the scabby Renault parked next

327

to it. Tried the button on the fob again. 'It was working earlier...'

'Give.' I held out my hand and she passed the keys over.

The multi-storey smelled of rotting weeds, laced with a dirty ammonia tang. A puddle stretched most of the way across the concrete floor – ankle-deep by the lifts – empty plastic bottles and crisp packets marking high tide with a dirty flotsam line. At least it was reasonably dry over here by the far wall. Even if the stairs had been used as a urinal.

Alice wrinkled her nose. 'Maybe it needs a new battery, or we could—'

'Or we could just do this.' I stuck the key in the lock.

'Ooh, I forgot about that...'

Kids today.

The boot creaked as I opened it. Nothing in there but a tartan blanket and a dog-eared 'Collins Road Atlas of Scotland' twenty years out of date. I pulled out the blanket and dumped it on the back seat.

'Ash, I'm sorry, I didn't think it'd take that long and—'

'Nothing we can do about it now.'

The stuff we'd bought at B&Q clanged and thumped as I dumped it into the boot, leaving the tarpaulin till last, spreading it out over everything else. Making a little waterproof pouch.

'Maybe, if we hurry, the traffic won't be too bad? Ash?'

I clunked the boot shut.

'Ash?'

'Maybe.' I limped around to the passenger side and eased myself into the seat. According to the dashboard clock it was nearly quarter past five. Should have got out of there when we had the chance.

The Jaguar's windscreen wipers squealed back across the glass, smearing the rain into scarlet arcs, catching the tail-light glow of the queue of traffic crawling across Dundas Bridge. Streetlights made orbs of sickly yellow. The sky tumour-dark.

On the other end of the phone, Chief Superintendent Ness went silent for a bit. Then, *'I see… And are we supposed to prosecute him for domestic abuse?'*

The car crept forward another couple of feet.

'Jacobson said it was up to you. Darren's got an alibi for when Claire Young went missing, and Alice says he doesn't fit the profile. So, probably not the Inside Man.'

Alice's voice was barely audible over the engine's rumble. 'Ask her about the letter.'

'What about the letter? What did you tell Wee Free?'

A sooking hiss came from the earpiece. *'Mr McFee has been informed that we've received another letter from someone purporting to be the Inside Man. I wanted to persuade the* News *and* Post *not to run it, but Dr Docherty thinks if Tim doesn't see his letter in print he's going to think we're not taking him seriously. Jessica McFee's in enough danger as it is.'*

'You giving Wee Free an advance copy?'

'Might as well: he's going to find out tomorrow morning anyway.'

Alice waved at me.

Right. 'We'll need one too.'

'Come into Division Headquarters and you can pick up a press pack.'

'Email it through. I'm following something up.'

There was a pause. *'What?'*

'Ask Jacobson. My organ-grinding days are over, remember?'

Another trundle forward. More silence, punctuated by the groan of rubber on smeared glass.

'I see.'

We crept forward another couple of feet.

'Mr Henderson, let's get something sparklingly clear: as you so eloquently pointed out earlier, you're not a police officer any more. Do you seriously believe that you merit a personal briefing from the head of a major investigation? If you want to know what's going on, you can get off your backside and turn up to the team meetings.'

All one big happy family.

Up ahead, the traffic was thinning out, escaping the bottle-neck of the bridge and the roundabouts on either end.

'*I don't care how big a wheel you were in Oldcastle CID – that means nothing to me. You want something? You earn it.*'

A clunk, and the line went dead.

I blew out a breath. 'Think she likes me.'

Rain drummed on the Jaguar's roof. Bounced off the bonnet.

Alice's knuckles stood out pale around the steering wheel. 'What if we can't get there in time?'

'We go to plan B.'

35

She looked at me. 'We've got a plan B?'

I popped the back off the handset I bought, fiddled the sim card out and replaced it with one of the spare ones. Then dialled the mobile number biroed on the back of Paul Manson's photo. Got my notebook out.

'What's plan B?'

'Shhh...' I pointed at the phone.

A prim voice came on the other end. *'Paul Manson, can I help you?'*

Time to drag out the Glaswegian accent Michelle always hated. 'Aye, hello. Greg here from Sparanet Vehicle Security. I'm sorry, Mr Manson, but the system's thrown an automatic alert about your Porsche Nine-Eleven. Nothing to worry about, just routine.'

'I beg your pardon?'

'Can you just confirm the car's location? We're showing it on Leith Walk in Edinburgh.'

'What?' Some scrunching noises. What sounded like a car door thunking shut. Then he was back. *'It's right here outside my office, you idiot. Not Edinburgh: Oldcastle.'*

'Are you sure?'

'Of course I'm bloody sure, I'm sitting in it.'

'Oh dear… Well, sorry to have bothered you, Mr Manson. Drive safely.' I hung up. Dropped the accent. 'He's just leaving now.'

Alice crawled the Jag forward, until we were a couple of car lengths from the Barnett roundabout. 'What if he gets away?'

I held up a finger. 'Plan C: we turn up at the meeting empty-handed, pretend we've killed him, then kill everyone else before they kill Shifty.'

She looked as if she'd just swallowed something bitter. 'I don't—'

'OK.' Another finger. 'Plan D: we track down Mrs Kerrigan and we kill *her* before she can kill us. Rescue Shifty. Then disappear off into the night before anyone comes looking for us. Get that house in Australia with a dog and a pool.'

Alice shifted in her seat, craning her neck to see past the people-carrier turning right at the roundabout. She put her foot down, swinging the Jaguar out into the flow. 'Why do all your plans have killing in them?'

'Because I doubt baking Mrs Kerrigan a cake is really going to cut it. You saw what she did to Shifty.'

She took the second exit, onto Darwin Street. 'There has to be a way that nobody has to die… How about plan E: we get in touch with all of David's friends in Oldcastle Division and we turn up mob-handed, I mean there's no way Mrs Kerrigan would hurt him with all those police officers there, would she, we could arrest her, and we wouldn't have to kill Paul Manson, and it'd be like…' Alice frowned at me. 'What?'

I tried not to laugh, I really did. 'You heard her: who knows how much of CID is in Mrs Kerrigan's pocket? Two years ago I could've spotted them. Now?'

'But—'

'The only person we can trust for *sure* is Shifty.'

Alice drove the stolen Jag right up behind the Volvo in front. 'But… Manson's a mob accountant, OK? What if we got him to give Queen's evidence and he went into a witness protection programme or something like that?'

'And rat out Andy Inglis? He'd be dead before the end of the week. Now back off a bit before we end up in their boot.'

Down Darwin and onto Fitzroy Road. Past the Polish delicatessen, the Tesco Metro, and the Italian where Marco Mancini got his throat cut in the walk-in chiller. Right onto Sullivan Street, the rain getting heavier with every turn.

Alice took one hand off the steering wheel and reached over to grab my hand. Squeezed. 'He's going to be OK, isn't he?'

Bob the Builder grinned at me from the back seat.

Probably not.

I squeezed back. 'Of course he is.'

Time for another call. I hit redial.

This time, when Manson picked up, the dark growl of the Porsche's engine rumbled in the background. *'Paul Manson, can I help you?'*

Back on with the accent. 'Aye, Greg from Sparanet Vehicle Security again, Mr Manson. Erm... Sorry to bother you, but we're still showing your Nine-Eleven in Edinburgh, just turning onto Easter Road, near the cemetery? Are you sure—'

'As far as I'm aware, Porsche didn't fit my car with a bloody teleporter, so no, it's not in bloody Edinburgh.'

'Ah. Right. So where is it, *exactly*?'

'Begby Street.'

I hit mute. Pointed at the junction coming up. 'Right there. Then first left.' Back to the phone as Alice did as she was told. 'Are you positive? The GPS has *definitely* got you in Edinburgh, and—'

'I know the difference between Oldcastle and bloody Edinburgh, you moron. Your system's wrong!'

'Oh...' A little pause – look at me being contrite and incompetent. 'So you've not just taken a right onto Albion Road?'

'*Albion… Are you mentally deficient? I told you: I'm on Begby, about to turn onto Larbert Avenue. There. I'm on Larbert now.*'

Mute.

'Take a left, past the off-licence.'

Alice did, and the Jag swung onto Larbert Avenue.

'I'm sorry about this, Mr Manson, we take your vehicle's security *very* seriously. Can you bear with me while I try to sort out the problem? You're still on Larbert?'

'*Of course I bloody am.*'

'Heading north or south?'

'*South. I'm at the traffic lights with … Blackford Street?*'

I sat up in my seat. Coming the other way was a silver Porsche, stopped at the lights so someone could hobble across the road: an old man bent almost double by the curve of his spine. The street was deserted except for that solitary hunched figure, and the rain hammered against his back and shoulders, dripped from the brim of his tweed bunnet. Punishing him for venturing out while everyone else stayed indoors.

From here it was impossible to tell who was behind the Porsche's wheel – the windscreen was washed in the neon glow of a kebab shop, blocking out the interior – but the number plate matched. 'Ah, right, excellent. I've got you. Thank you, Mr Manson. Drive safely.'

'*Moron.*' He hung up.

The lights changed and the Porsche accelerated towards us.

Alice swore, head swinging left and right. 'We'll have to turn round…'

Closer.

Now or never.

I reached across and grabbed the steering wheel – forced it right. The Jaguar swung across the dotted lines, then the off-side corner of the bonnet battered into the driver's door of Manson's Porsche. Metal screeched as the Jag gouged its way along the bodywork. Then lurched to a stop – the engine stalled.

'Oh God…' Alice turned in her seat and stared at me, her

eyes wide and pink. 'What did you do *that* for? You made me crash, how could you make—'

'Not your car, remember?'

In the Porsche, Manson had his hands wrapped around his wheel, teeth bared, lips twitching around something bitter. Face going a shocking shade of pink.

Behind us, someone leaned on their horn.

'Wind your window down and apologize to the nice man.'

She stared at me for another beat. 'But I didn't—'

'Soon as you like.'

She screwed her face up, then buzzed down her window. The drowning hiss of the rain collapsed into the car, bringing a cold mist with it. Alice pressed a fist against her chest. 'Oh God, I'm so sorry, I don't know what got into me, are you OK?'

Another horn howled in the night. Then another...

Manson glared back at her. 'WHAT THE BUGGERING WANK DO YOU THINK YOU'RE DOING?' Spittle popped from his lips, gleaming in the headlights of the other vehicles.

Alice held up her hands. 'I'm sorry, I'm really, really sorry, I didn't—'

'MORON!' He stabbed a finger at her. 'BLOODY WOMEN DRIVERS, YOU'RE A MENACE!'

More horns joined the chorus.

'I'm sorry, I didn't mean it, it was—'

'DON'T JUST SIT THERE IN THE MIDDLE OF THE BLOODY ROAD! PULL IN – OVER THERE, NOW!'

I laid a hand on her arm. 'Do what the nice man says.'

'Oh God, oh God...' It took three goes to start the Jag again, then she wrenched the wheel to the left. The car inched forward, tearing another tortured squeal of metal-on-metal from the Porsche's flank.

'YOU'RE MAKING IT WORSE, YOU BLOODY IDIOT!'

A ping, then a clang, and the Jaguar lurched free. Alice pulled into the kerb, outside a closed furniture shop. Turned

335

off the engine. Slumped over the wheel. 'Why would you *do* that?'

Headlights glittered in the dark shop windows as the traffic got moving again.

I undid her seatbelt. 'You need to get out of the car.'

'Ash, he's... Oh dear.'

Manson marched across the road, both hands curled into fists, teeth bared in the downpour. Black overcoat sweeping out behind him like a cloak. He stopped by Alice's door, twisted himself back a pace, then a dull metallic thunk sounded as he slammed his foot into it.

Alice squealed.

'It's OK, he's not going to hurt you. All mouth and no trousers.' I pulled a pair of blue nitrile gloves out of my investigation kit and snapped them on. 'Out you go.'

'Oh God...' She fumbled with the door handle, took a deep breath, then stepped into the rain, hands out as she blinked up at him. 'Look, I know you're angry, but—'

'ANGRY?' Manson towered over her. Threw a hand back towards his Porsche. 'THAT'S A BRAND NEW NINE-ELEVEN! DO YOU HAVE ANY IDEA HOW MUCH I PAID FOR IT?'

'It was an accident, I really didn't—'

'YOU'RE A MORON!'

I undid my seatbelt and climbed out. It was like getting into a cold shower – plastering my hair to my head, soaking right through my jacket.

On the plus side, there was no one on the pavement.

Traffic slowed as it passed, everyone having a good rubberneck at the battered sports car. A massive dent cratered the driver's door, the paintwork gouged down to the buckled metal all the way along to the spoiler.

No one seemed interested in the old Jag's crumpled bonnet.

'WHAT ARE YOU? YOU'RE A MORON!'

'Please, I didn't—'

'A MORON!'

A Transit van crawled past, then a little Fiat.

I stepped off the kerb. Skirted the Jaguar's boot.

'PEOPLE LIKE YOU SHOULDN'T BE ALLOWED TO DRIVE!'

The brown envelope rustled as I fished one of the syringes out.

Alice backed away, onto the pavement. 'I really think it'd be better if we could all just calm—'

'DON'T YOU TELL ME TO CALM DOWN, YOU STUPID BITCH!' He followed her, screaming in her face, waving his arms about. Water dripped from the hem of his overcoat, made his face shine. 'YOU RUINED MY CAR!'

The orange-plastic tip popped off between my teeth.

'YOU'LL BLOODY PAY FOR THAT, DO YOU HEAR ME?'

A quick squeeze and a tiny jet of clear liquid arced into the night.

'Please, it was an accident, I didn't—'

'BRAND NEW PORSCHE NINE-ELEVEN AND YOU— ulk...'

I wrapped an arm around his throat and rammed the needle into the side of his neck, just below the ear. Squeezed the plunger down. Jammed my right knee into the small of his back and pulled him towards me – leaning against the Jag. Holding him up as his hands flapped, fingers scrabbling at the syringe.

Getting weaker.

And weaker.

And then his arms went limp, his knees sagged, head fell forwards.

'Open the back door.'

Alice wrapped her arms around herself. 'Ash, this isn't—'

'All you've got to do is get the door, no one's going to see.' Not with the car between us and them.

She scurried forward and pulled the Jaguar's back door open.

I turned and tipped Manson in, so he was slumped in the footwell behind the seats. Shoved his knees up so his feet didn't stick out. Took the tartan blanket from the back seat and draped it over him. Clunked the door shut.

'Snug as a bug.' Even standing right next to the car and staring down between the front and back seats, you'd never know he was there.

I waited for a break in the traffic, then limped across the road to the Porsche, pulled out the sticker I'd liberated from the traffic office and plastered it across the windscreen: 'POLICE AWARE'. The thing could stay there for weeks now and all anyone would do is moan about what a lazy bunch of sods Oldcastle plod were.

Plan A was back on track again.

36

Alice shifted from foot to foot, peering back towards the Jaguar. Her voice was little more than a hiss. 'Is he dead?'

I clicked the bolt cutters through another wire diamond in the chain-link fence. 'Drink your tea.'

Rain drummed on the skin of her umbrella. The droplets caught the streetlight's glow and sparked like fireworks. On the other side of the car park, Parson's Bargain Cash-and-Carry squatted in all its corrugated steel glory – two of the neon letters in the sign flickered on the brink of death, three more already there. A couple of oversized shopping-trolleys lay abandoned on the wet tarmac, next to the catering van where we'd got two teas, a Kit Kat and a caramel wafer.

Debris clung to the chain-link in patches. Escaped carrier bags. Crisp packets. Ruptured newspapers, spewing their stories on damp grey wings.

She took a sip from the polystyrene cup and grimaced. 'Are you sure this is a—'

'Positive.' *Click*. 'And he's not dead, he's just resting. According to Noel, our friend Mr Manson's going to be unconscious for about another three hours.' And even if he did wake up before that, he wasn't going anywhere.

Click.

And finished.

Had to admit, it was a pretty decent job – an escape hatch snipped into the chain-link, just big enough for a small person to squeeze through. A little shoogling and the gap was barely visible.

A rectangular building lurked on the other side of the fence, the signage visible through the barbed wire looped around the top: 'LUMLEY & SON – CHANDLERS EST. 1946'. The yard was empty, the building streaked with rust, all the windows on the ground floor boarded up with plywood. No lights, just silhouettes and shadows.

Alice stood on her tiptoes and peered. 'I don't like it. It looks creepy.'

'That'll be why Mrs Kerrigan picked it. Somewhere nice and atmospheric to hand over a dead mob accountant.' I took out a couple of carrier-bags and tied them to the chain-link in the middle of the hatch. Marking it.

I straightened up, popped the Jaguar's boot open.

Paul Manson lay on his side, in a little nest of blue tarpaulin. I'd invested a whole roll of silver duct-tape in securing his ankles together, then his knees, and then both wrists behind his back. The length of washing line was looped around his throat, the other end tied to his bound ankles – struggle and he'd garrotte himself.

OK, so the gag was a bit of a risk. If he reacted badly to the anaesthetic he'd choke on his own vomit, but … tough. If he didn't want to end up like this he shouldn't have gone into business laundering money for gangsters.

The tarpaulin scrunched and rustled as I folded one edge back and slipped the bolt cutters in with the rest of the stuff we'd bought at B&Q – well, it wasn't as if Manson could get to it – then grabbed the lump hammer. Short wooden handle. Heavy head. Nice and sturdy.

Just right for caving someone's skull in.

The boot lid clunked shut again.

I opened Alice's satchel and slipped the hammer inside. 'Right, here's the rules. One: If someone's chasing you, you twat them one. But *only* if they catch you, OK? No standing your ground or going on the offensive. If they're chasing you: keep running.'

'But—'

'No buts. Rule two: you don't stop.' I pointed at the hatch in the fence. 'You slip through here and you keep going. Because soon as you're one hundred yards away, our ankle monitors go off and Jacobson's SWAT team come steaming in with all guns blazing. That's our security blanket.'

She pulled a face, jerked forwards, as if a ghost had just slapped her backside. Then pulled her phone out of her back pocket. It buzzed in her hand.

Mine did the same thing in my pocket. When I took it out, the words 'DOWNLOADING UPDATE ~ 20% COMPLETE' flashed on the screen. Thirty percent. Forty percent...

'Rule three: Mrs Kerrigan is dangerous. She'll kill Shifty, she'll kill you, she'll kill me, and she won't even flinch. I don't care what she says, what she promises. You don't trust her. You run.'

When it hit a hundred percent my phone bleeped – a text message.

> 1 app for ankl monitors, 1 filtered photo (x3). Still lookin fr pic match in systm.
>
> No sign of Ur new m8 in HOMLES DB.

Yeah, he might whinge, but Sabir always came through.

'Rule four: Paul Manson is scum. He's got rich off the back of drugs, prostitution, violence, robbery, and murder. You don't worry about him, you don't feel guilty. Mrs Kerrigan is

341

going to kill him whether we hand him over or not. He's already dead.'

I checked the attached photographs. They were all versions of the picture Liz Thornton had texted when we went to see her this morning – the Camburn Creeper, caught in the car park outside the nurses' halls. Sabir had cropped out the Fiat the man was standing next to, zooming in on the face.

In the first photo the features were slightly plastic, the skin tone rendered by algorithms and educated guesswork rather than nature. Wide forehead, round nose, bags under the eyes, long chin bisected by shadow. Photo number two took a different approach. The shadows under the woolly hat had turned into a pair of thick-rimmed hipster glasses, the nose thinner with a bend to one side, as if it'd been broken a couple of times. Photo three ditched the glasses, but swapped the shadow running from the bottom of the nose to the tip of the chin for a weird vertical soul-patch thing...

Back to number two. Then three. Then two again. Put them all together and... A smile broke across my face.

Alice shuffled over and stared at my phone. 'What?'

The smile turned into a grin and I thumbed out a reply:

> Sabir, no matter what anyone says, you are a sodding STAR!

'What? What's funny?'

I stabbed up the contacts menu and dialled Jacobson.

He answered with a sigh. *'If you're calling looking to weasel out of the team meeting, you can—'*

'Fancy arresting someone?'

Alice tugged at my sleeve. 'Who are we arresting?'

'Jessica McFee was being targeted by a stalker, and I know who he is.'

'Oh aye...?'

'So, we can all sit about on our thumbs, *talking* about the

342

investigation, or we can get off our backsides and *do* something about it.' I limped back towards the stolen Jag. 'Interested?'

Dr Docherty's voice oozed out of the car radio. '*... an excellent question, Kirsty. You see, the man who's committing these acts doesn't see himself as an avenging angel, or the hand of God, he's acting out of rage and loneliness...*'

Patterson Drive curled around the base of the cliff. Up above, the old battlements were visible against the heavy sky, crumbling stonework lit by coloured spotlights. The Victorian buildings of Castle Hill clung to the edge, like wide-eyed children, too scared to jump, staring down at the dirty sandstone tenements below.

Wet cobbles burred beneath the Jaguar's wheels. Windscreen wipers moaning and groaning their greasy arcs through the rain, passing commentary on Docherty's interview.

'*... of course. But you see, Kirsty, a psychopathology like this is a lot more common than you might think...*'

'OK.' I poked my mobile's screen, closing the dialogue box with the instructions on it. 'Here's how it works: Sabir's app uses our phones' GPS to tell how far apart we are. Green is less than thirty-three yards; yellow covers from there to sixty-six; then it's red; and if it turns blue and flashes, Jacobson's goons are probably on their way. There's a sort of optional Geiger counter ping as well.' Would have been nice to have something that stopped the bloody things going off in the first place, but it was better than nothing.

'*... have to admit that I do have a certain degree of experience in this field, and that's why I can say for certain...*'

I pointed, through the windshield and over to an alleyway that snaked off towards Kings Park. 'Pull in there.'

'*... deeply damaged individual. But if you're listening, I want you to know that we can get you the help you need...*'

Alice bit her bottom lip and did as she was told, slotting the car in behind a row of municipal wheely-bins.

'... *professionals. I'm even prepared to offer my own considerable expertise to facilitate your*—'

She killed the engine, cutting Docherty off mid-boast. 'Maybe we should've swapped vehicles, what if someone—'

'No one's going to see it.' And with Paul Manson bound and drugged in the boot, there was nothing incriminating on show. Well, except for the dent-buckled bonnet. I climbed out into the rain and waited for her to do the same.

Alice locked the car, then huddled in next to me, slipping her arm through mine, keeping the umbrella above us. Stood there, staring down at the boot. 'Are you sure it's OK to leave him in there, I mean what if he—'

'He's not going anywhere. Three hours, remember?' Plenty of time to get everything in place. 'Soon as we're done here, we pick up the Suzuki, drive both cars out to Moncuir woods, and dump yours there. All set for a quick getaway when we burn the Jag.'

The cane's rubber tip thunked against the concrete slabs as we made our way along Patterson Drive. Streetlights cast stepping stones of sodium yellow on the wet pavement.

Dark ginnels led off to the right, cutting through the terrace to the next street. A smell of rotting garbage and old nappies. The sound of someone's telly, up too loud, blaring out the news. Water gurgling from the mouth of a broken downpipe.

She cleared her throat. 'What if Mrs Kerrigan decides she's not going to give David back? What if she keeps him and tortures him and we have to keep doing horrible things for her?'

'I'm not going to let that happen.'

With a little help from my friend, Bob.

We passed by a window with the curtains open. A pair of middle-aged men slow-danced in candlelight, wrapped up in each other and the music. Next door boomed with country-and-western. The house after that...

I stopped. Pointed. 'Up there.'

A big black Range Rover sat by the kerb, exhaust trailing grey wisps into the gloom. As soon as we drew level, the driver's door swung open and PC Cooper climbed out. He'd put a stabproof vest on over his usual outfit, complete with baton, handcuffs, and airwave handset. Peaked cap in place, rain pattering off the plastic cover he'd put over the top.

He pulled on a fluorescent yellow jacket. Nodded. 'Guv.'

'What did Bad Bill say?'

'Friday lunchtime he was parked outside the castle. There was this big protest about the council trying to close Midmarch Library. Crowds, TV crews, the lot. Says he made a fortune.'

I patted Cooper on the shoulder. 'Good work.'

Given the smile that burst across his thin face, you'd think I'd just offered his dying mum one of my kidneys. 'Thanks, Guv.'

'Soon as we're done here, I want you on to the TV companies. We need all the footage they've got of the protest – not just the broadcast stuff, the bits they edited out too.' I hooked a thumb towards the building we were standing outside. 'If we're lucky, Laughing Boy here's been caught on film buying Claire Young's last meal.'

The smile got bigger. 'Right, Guv.'

A *thunk* sounded on the other side of the car, and Jacobson appeared, bringing a friend with him. Officer Babs towered at his shoulder, shoulders back, wearing a big grin.

She hauled on a pair of gloves, working the leather down into the gaps between her fingers. 'We ready?'

'Thought you'd gone home.'

'And miss all the fun? Nah.' She slapped Jacobson on the back and he nearly fell over. 'Bear decided to extend my contract.'

He recovered, brushed some imaginary lint off the front of his leather jacket. 'When I reviewed Mr Robertson's record, I decided it would be best to proceed with caution.'

345

I turned in place, giving the street a good once-over. Obviously 'proceeding with caution' didn't extend to asking Ness for some backup.

Alice tugged at my sleeve again, keeping her voice to a whisper. 'Who's Mr Robertson?'

Cooper led the way into the building's hallway. A bulkhead light was fixed to the ceiling, the glass dome peppered with the bodies of dead insects. Its pale greasy light oozed across the scuffed walls and concrete steps. A pair of broken wooden chairs lay tangled in the remains of a wheel-less pram. Cooper straightened his cap and headed up the stairs, Jacobson stomping up behind him.

I jerked my head at Babs. 'You want the front or the back garden?'

'Front.' She rubbed her gloved fingertips together. Frowned. 'No: back. People do runners out the back.' Babs turned and lumbered down the hallway, disappeared into the gloom.

The thump of a door closing, and Alice and I were on our own again.

She twisted round, bending backwards to stare up the gap between the stairs. 'So ... Mr Robertson?'

'Alistair to his friends.' I steered her back out onto the street. 'Rock-Hammer Robertson to everyone else.'

'Is he...?'

'Very.'

She put her brolly up and we huddled beneath it. I propped the front door open with the tip of my cane, keeping it ajar.

Alice closed her eyes. Blew out a breath.

'It's OK. Soon be over.' One way or another.

She squeezed my arm tighter. 'I don't want to die. What if Mrs Kerrigan—'

'It won't come to that. Rule number one, remember? You run away.'

'I don't want you to die either.'

'Then that makes two of us.'

346

Banging echoed down the stairwell and out through the open door, followed by Cooper's voice. *'MR ROBERTSON – THIS IS THE POLICE! OPEN UP!'*

Alice had a little shiver. Then a deep breath. 'So, "Rock-Hammer Robertson"... Sounds nice.'

'COME ON, MR ROBERTSON, WE ONLY WANT TO TALK.'

'Once upon a time, there was a wee boy called Alistair Robertson, whose mummy and daddy loved him very much. They also loved to rob Post Offices. And one day—'

'Does this story end with him battering someone to death with a rock hammer?'

'Oh, you've heard it?'

'MR ROBERTSON? I'M EMPOWERED TO FORCE ENTRY, MR ROBERTSON. DON'T MAKE THIS ANY HARDER THAN IT HAS TO BE.'

'Why can't any of your stories have teddy bears and fluffy bunnies in them?'

I nodded. 'OK. Once upon a time, there was a fluffy bunny called Alistair, and when Mummy Rabbit and Daddy Rabbit got sent down for eighteen years to life, he and his wee sister got put into care. There was a very nasty teddy bear working in the care home who liked to interfere with little girl bunnies...'

A crash sounded upstairs. Followed by a thump. Followed by swearing, and then a high-pitched scream. More swearing.

It didn't sound as if Rock-Hammer Robertson was assisting Cooper with his enquiries.

'OK.' I put a hand on Alice's back and gave her a gentle push towards the road. 'I think you should go stand behind the car, don't you?'

She wrapped her hands around the brolly's handle. 'But—'

Someone bellowed, and then there was a splintering crack. A crash. And chunks of baluster pinged and clunked down from the staircase above.

'Now would be good.'

347

Footsteps on the stairs. Thumping down. Getting closer.

Alice backed away towards Jacobson's Range Rover.

The front door yanked open and there he was: Rock-Hammer Robertson. He froze on the threshold. His white shirt was torn at the collar. Little flecks of red stippled the fabric across his chest. He'd lost a lot of hair since last time – what was left was greying and shorn short. Sabir's algorithms hadn't done that bad a job, but they'd screwed up with the vertical soul-patch thing. It wasn't facial hair, it was a deep scar that ran in a straight line from just below his nostrils, slashed through his lips, bisected his chin, and kept going four inches down his throat. A pair of Eric Morecambe glasses sat squint on his face.

My hands ached themselves into fists as I gave him a smile. 'Evening, Alistair. Remember me?'

'Aw … *shite*.' He slammed the door – or at least he tried to. It hit the tip of my cane and bounced, battering open again as he turned and legged it for the back door. He disappeared out into the wet night.

I gave it a count of ten. Then another ten for luck.

Alice shuffled up next to me. 'Aren't you going after him?'

'No need. But we can if you like.' I hobbled down the hallway, past the nest of broken chairs and the scattering of shattered balusters before pushing through into the back garden.

Patchy grass filled the narrow gap between this row of tenements and the one behind, jaundiced in the light seeping out through curtained windows. A wooden fence enclosed an area not much bigger than three parking spaces, a crumbling shed slouched in the corner, a couple of washing poles standing sentry – their lines drooping under the weight of sodden towels, dripping in the rain.

Rock-Hammer Robertson lay face down on the grass, right arm twisted up behind his back, kicking and swearing. Officer Babs had her knee between his shoulder blades and, as he struggled, she leaned forwards until he grunted and stopped.

She grinned up at us. 'Oh, I do *like* Oldcastle.'

Jacobson sat in the armchair, a packet of frozen peas pressed against his right cheek. Cooper perched on the arm of the sofa, a box of fish fingers clutched to the side of his head and a wodge of toilet paper poking out of each nostril.

Rock-Hammer Robertson stood in front of the two-bar fire, working his right shoulder around in small circles. Both hands cuffed behind his back. He nodded towards the hall. 'You're going to pay for that.'

Jacobson glowered at him. 'That a *threat*, Mr Robertson?'

'Statement of fact. You owe me one door.'

'You were given ample warning before we kicked it in.'

'I was on the bloody bog! You'd have heard me shouting if it wasn't for your idiot sidekick making all that racket.'

The living room had striped wallpaper, a swirly rug, and arty black-and-white prints of people on bicycles either side of the fireplace. An old-fashioned roll-top writing desk sat in the corner, next to a bookcase laden with tatty paperbacks.

The desk's wooden top rattled up when I pulled it, revealing sets of small drawers on either side and a magazine-rack-style bit in the middle.

Robertson bared his teeth at me. 'Let's see a search warrant.'

'Don't need one.' I took a handful of paperwork from the centre section. Flipped through it: telephone bills, gas bills, council tax, electricity. Several of each, and all for different names and addresses.

'I know my rights, and—'

'Tough, because I'm not a police officer.' I dumped the bills and tried one of the little drawers instead. 'Members of the public don't need a warrant to be nosey bastards.'

The top one was a jumble of paperclips, elastic bands, a box of staples, and a stapler.

He scowled at Jacobson. 'You going to let him invade my privacy like that?'

Jacobson peeled the packet of peas from his cheek and scowled back. 'Where were you on Sunday evening, when Jessica McFee was abducted?'

'Who's Jessica McFee? Never heard of her.'

I pointed at the wastepaper basket sitting beside the desk A copy of the *Castle News and Post* stuck out of the top. 'That's funny, because she's all over the papers. And...' I picked a bill from the pile on his desk and waved it at him. 'And you just *happen* to have Jessica McFee's mobile phone statement in your desk. Isn't that a fun coincidence?'

He pursed his lips, frowned. Then stuck his scarred chin in the air. 'I'm saying sod-all else till you get me my lawyer.'

37

The downstream monitoring suite was getting crowded. Ness and Dr Docherty sat at the desk, staring at the flatscreen TV mounted on the wall. Both of them had headsets on – the kind with a little microphone, as if they worked in a call centre – the cables snaking away into the console. Behind them, Superintendent Knight and Jacobson sat with their arms crossed, leaving just enough space for Alice and me to squeeze against the back wall.

Twenty minutes in, and the smell of garlic, vinegar, and past-its-sell-by-date meat tainted the air, oozing out of someone who needed a stronger deodorant.

On the screen, a line of numbers flickered away in the corner, marking time as Rock-Hammer Robinson no-commented his way through the interview.

The camera lens was wide enough to get him, his solicitor, and the two interview-trained officers – one male, one female – onscreen.

A hard Aberdonian accent crackled out of the TV's speakers. DI Smith: *'You're not helping yourself, you know that, don't you? We've got your—'*

'Stop right there.' The solicitor held up a podgy hand that sparkled with sovereign rings. A gold chain disappeared into

the sleeve of his shirt. He pulled his wide face into a frown. *'My client has already told you that he didn't abduct Jessica McFee. Move on.'*

Dr Docherty leaned forward in his seat, hands clasped in front of his chest, as if he was praying. 'Millie: ask him about his relationship with his mother.'

The detective on the left knocked on the table. She'd rolled her shirt sleeves up to the elbow, showing off forearms thick with muscle, a tattoo of Buzz Lightyear just visible on the right one. Brown hair cut into a sensible bob, tucked behind her ears. *'So, Alistair, did you see your mum much, after she got sent down?'*

'I hardly see what my client's mother has to do with—'

'Mr Bellamy, if you wouldn't mind keeping your obstruction of our investigation to every other question this will go a lot quicker.'

'Detective Sergeant Stephen, do I really need to remind you how the law works in Scotland now? To wit: Cadder versus HM Advocate – 2010. Look it up.'

Alice tugged at my shoulder. 'We need to search for any outbuildings, or maybe he's got access to some property we don't know about, somewhere he could set up an operating theatre and—'

'Believe it or not,' Detective Superintendent Ness turned in her seat, 'we *have* already thought of that. There are teams scouring the land register and contacting letting agencies as we speak. Now, if you don't mind...?'

Alice clicked her mouth shut.

'Must've been pretty terrible, growing up with your mother in prison though.'

'Sergeant Stephen, I don't want to have to tell you again: move on.'

'Especially after what she did to that poor woman.' On screen, DS Stephen reached below the table and returned with a manila folder. *'They ever show you what Gina Ashton looked like when your dear old mum had finished with her?'* She pulled a

photo from the folder – the surface caught the light, obscuring the detail as she laid it on the table. *'Must be hard, knowing that your mum was capable of something like that…'*˙

Robertson glanced down at the photo, then folded his arms. Sat there, not saying a word.

'Detective Sergeant Stephen, I have warned you. If you continue in this vein I'm going to make an official complaint and make sure the court knows of your inappropriate behaviour during this interview. Move – on.'

Alice tugged my shoulder again, then stood on her tiptoes so her lips brushed my ear. 'He's not going to respond to this. If he's the Inside Man, he's been preparing for this moment for years. He'll sit there and say nothing until Jessica McFee dies of dehydration or hunger. They'll have to release him and he won't go anywhere near where he's got her hidden. Dr Docherty will never get him to talk. If we can't find her on our own, she's dead.'

Rhona pointed at the double doors. 'He's through there.'

Division Headquarters thrummed with the sound of the back shift getting on with the day's paperwork, drinking cups of tea, and complaining about the lazy sods on the day shift. I paused with one hand on the door, the other wrapped around a manila folder from the media office. 'How long?'

A shrug. Then she sooked at her teeth. 'Hour and a bit? Brigstock and me went over to the junkyard and gave him a copy of that new Inside Man letter. Next thing we know, bam. There he is. Sitting in reception.'

'And he's not moved?'

'Think he's been for a pee, but that's it.'

I checked my phone – Sabir's app glowed a solid orange at me. As long as we both stayed on this floor it should be fine. Provided Alice didn't go for a wander…

Rhona pushed the door open and I stepped through to the reception area. Plastic seats lined the walls, bolted to the floor and facing the reception desk so no one could get up to anything. The place was plastered with posters: Crimestoppers; rape hotlines; how to spot cannabis farms, terrorists, and abused kids.

Wee Free McFee sat beneath a big corkboard covered with clippings from the *Castle News and Post*, all featuring photos of seized drugs and officers battering their way into scumbags' homes.

There were at least another dozen people in the room – drunks, junkies, a couple of old biddies looking murderous – sitting cheek by jowl. Packed in. But no one sat anywhere near Wee Free. The three seats to his left, and the three seats to his right, were empty.

Rhona coughed, keeping her eyes on the corridor behind us. 'You, erm … want a hand? Only I've got a stack of paper-work…'

I stepped out onto the grey terrazzo floor. 'William?'

He turned his head and a small smile twitched into life beneath his grey moustache. 'You again.'

'Fancy a cuppa?'

He unfolded himself from his chair and the people closest to him shifted as far away as they could without abandoning their seats. 'Why haven't you found her yet?'

I nodded towards the blank door to the side of the reception desk. 'Come on.'

Took me three goes to remember the keycode, but eventually the door swung open on a small room: four chairs; a grey table; a filing cabinet with a kettle on top; and a bin overflowing with Pot Noodle cartons, crisp packets, and takeaway containers.

I placed the folder on the table and headed for the kettle. 'You've seen the letter he sent to the *News and Post*.'

Wee Free lowered himself into one of the seats, legs spread wide, one arm over the back of the chair next to him. 'Stinks in here.'

'They're running it tomorrow morning. Front page.' I clicked the kettle on to boil. Opened the top drawer of the filing cabinet. 'We're still running tests, but a graphologist says the handwriting's a match for the ones sent eight years ago.' A jar of coffee sat next to a box of teabags, a handful of mugs, a bag of sugar, and a pint of blue-top. Two of the mugs went next to the grumbling kettle. 'Did you know someone was stalking Jessica?'

The milk smelled OK, so I slopped a glug into each.

When I turned, Wee Free hadn't moved. The folder lay untouched on the table in front of him, but his face was flushed. Eyes like granite chips. 'Who?'

'We made an arrest this evening. They're interviewing him now.'

'Was she...?'

'No. We're still looking.' Steam billowed from the kettle.

He leaned forward, forearms on the table, hands curled into claws. 'I want a name.'

'He's got form for violence, extortion, and trafficking.' Hot water into both mugs.

'I said—'

'Ever have a run-in with Rock-Hammer Robertson? Used to run with Jimmy the Axe Oldman.' I tapped a forefinger against my chin, drawing in an invisible scar. 'Well, till they had their falling out.'

Wee Free turned his head, staring up at the ceiling in the general direction of the interview rooms. And when he looked back at me, his shoulders slumped. His head drooped. 'You bunch of tits...'

The mugs clunked down on the table top. 'Did you know we found a foot floating in the water at Kettle Docks? DNA matched it to Jimmy Oldman. Pathologist said it was probably hacked off with a hand-axe.'

Wee Free reached for the mug and wrapped his fingers around it. 'How could you be so thick?'

'Some think Jimmy did it to himself. Made it look as if he was dead and dismembered. Figured it was the only way he could disappear and not have Robertson come after him. No point chasing a corpse, is there?' I settled into my seat. 'Me? I think Rock-Hammer got out of hospital, tracked Jimmy Oldman down, and hacked him into little bits with his own axe.'

'Alistair Robertson is … *was* working for me. He didn't abduct Jessica. You morons caught the wrong man.'

'This better be bloody important.' Jacobson stomped into the corridor, thumped the observation suite door shut behind him, and scowled up at me. It looked as if the frozen peas hadn't helped much: the scrape on his cheek had turned into a thick scab riding on a paisley-pattern of red and blue and purple.

I raised my walking stick and thunked the tip against the wall at shoulder height, blocking him in at the end of the corridor. 'He's not our man.'

'He was seen at the nurses' halls and he had—'

'It's not him. Rock-Hammer Robertson's a private investigator now – works for Johnston and Gench in Shortstaine. Wee Free hired him to keep tabs on his daughter.' One quick call to the senior partner's mobile and that was it: we didn't have a suspect any more.

Jacobson closed his eyes, then banged the back of his head off the wall a couple of times. 'Shite…'

'That's why he was hanging around. Going through their bins. Getting receipts and phone bills.'

A frown, then Jacobson peeled open one eye. 'Don't suppose Mr McFee's just playing you? Telling us this guy's legit so we'll release him, and the next thing we know he's being hung up by his thumbs and tortured with a Dremel multitool?'

'I just spoke to the guy who runs the firm. He says Robertson's been on their books for eighteen months. Spent the last six weeks trailing Jessica McFee for her father. They have case reports, a contract, everything.'

'So why's he sitting in there like Lumpy the Garden Gnome saying "No comment" to everything?'

Good question. 'Robertson isn't exactly a boy scout, but Wee Free's a psychotic nut-job. You don't clype on someone like that, unless you're suicidal.'

'Arseholes…' Jacobson turned and paced the two steps to the end of the corridor, then back again. 'Thought you said he was our man?'

'No, I said he was stalking Jessica. Which he was. It just happened to be on her dad's behalf.'

Following her. Finding out where she'd been, who she'd been with. And next thing you know: her boyfriend gets the crap kicked out of him and suddenly decides he's never going to see Jessica McFee ever again. What a coincidence.

Jacobson gave the wall another couple of dunts with his head. 'So we're back to square sodding one.'

I lowered the cane. 'Not necessarily.'

'… complete bloody waste of time.' DI Smith glared at me for a beat, then turned and stormed off down the corridor, hands knotted into fists.

Detective Sergeant Stephen watched him go, then sighed. 'He's going to be a bundle of laughs to work for tomorrow.' She ran a hand across her forehead. Then nodded back towards the interview room. 'Shall we?'

Inside, it smelled exactly the same as it had two years ago – a dirty mix of cheesy feet and stale breath, over a layer of rust and sweat.

DS Stephen slumped back into her chair and reached for the unit built into the wall. Ejected the tapes and dumped them on the tabletop.

Robertson's lawyer puckered his lips, then frowned up at the camera in the corner. The little red light was off. 'Is this intended to intimidate my client? We're not being recorded so you can threaten him?'

Jacobson settled in next to DS Stephen. 'You do know that wasting police time is an offence, don't you, Mr Robertson?'

The lawyer put a hand on his arm. 'Don't answer that.'

I took up position behind Jacobson. Leaned back against the wall. Crossed my arms. 'You have *got* to be the crappest private investigator ever.'

Rock-Hammer Robertson glared at me. The scar that ran from his nose to his throat deepened as he clenched his jaw. 'No comment.'

'Don't be thick – we've got Wee Free McFee downstairs and he's told us all about it. You've been spying on his daughter and reporting back to him.' I pulled on a big smile. 'Only, a *decent* PI wouldn't have been spotted by half the world and chased off not once, but twice.'

The lawyer stiffened. 'Unless you turn that tape recorder back on, my client won't be answering any more questions. This is a gross breach of—'

'You got pelted with empty bottles by a nurse. Not exactly *Magnum PI*, is it? Seriously, how thick can you—'

'I am not a crap private investigator!' Robertson was half out of his seat, face darkening. 'Stakeout like that should've had a three-man team on it – the whole place is hoaching with potential witnesses, people coming and going all hours of the day and night. I was on my own. For six weeks!' He took a couple of deep breaths then lowered himself back into his seat. 'I mean: no comment.'

'Don't be daft – we've got your client downstairs. We've spoken to your boss. We *know*.'

'My client said, "no comment".'

Jacobson leaned forward. 'You see, Alistair – I can call you Alistair, can't I? "Rock-Hammer" makes you sound like an American wrestler – we know you had Jessica McFee under surveillance. I'm assuming you took photographs?'

He didn't move.

'Because if you've got surveillance photos, it's possible the *real* Inside Man's on one of them.'

I nodded. 'Mr McFee wants you to hand over everything you've got. And he says to tell you that if you sod us about, he's going to come looking for you. Either way, we're getting those photographs. It just depends if you want a trip to A&E or not.'

Rock-Hammer chewed on the inside of his cheek for a bit, twisting his scar out of shape. Then looked at his lawyer.

'Or...' Jacobson held up a finger, 'we can talk about your resisting arrest and assaulting two police officers.'

Jacobson's smile turned into a grin as we marched down the corridor. 'You, Mr Henderson, may now call me Bear.' He rubbed his paws together. 'Right. We get the photos, we give them to Cooper and Bernard to troll through, and the rest of us head off for a slap-up Chinese banquet.'

'Can't.' I backed away, hands up. 'Alice has a thing, and if I don't go with her, the ankle bracelets go off and your goon squad gets called in.'

'Oh.' Jacobson sagged. 'You sure?'

'I'd love to, but you know what women are like. Maybe tomorrow?'

Assuming Mrs Kerrigan didn't kill us first.

The Jag pinged and rattled as the engine cooled beneath the dented bonnet. I reached into the back seat and grabbed Bob the Builder by his grinning squishy head.

Outside, the industrial estate was abandoned. Just the cold glow of the streetlights and the drifting rain to keep us company.

Alice skimmed the steering wheel with her fingertips. 'Maybe it's not too late to call—'

'This isn't a Ghostbusters situation. This is "God helps those who help themselves".' The Velcro around Bob's crotch parted with a loud rip.

I pulled out the semiautomatic, checked the safety was on, ejected the magazine – still full – and clacked it back into place. Then leaned forward in my seat and tucked the gun into the waistband at the back of my trousers. 'And what happens if it all goes horribly wrong?'

'Are you sure I can't—'

'Positive.'

A sigh, then she tightened her grip on the wheel. 'Rule number one: run.'

'Good. You don't hang around, you don't do anything heroic, you get your little red shoes on the ground and you *run*.'

'But you—'

I pointed through the driver's window at the passageway that disappeared into the darkness between the chandlery warehouse and a line of decaying offshore containers. Where the shadows were thick and deep. 'And I want you over there. Where they can't see you.'

'But if I—'

'No. You run.' I put a hand on her knee. 'Promise me.'

She gazed up at me for a minute, then lowered her eyes to the steering wheel. 'Promise.'

'Go for the hole in the fence we made. No heroics. No stopping. No looking back.' I gave her knee a squeeze. 'And if someone grabs you, you batter their head in with the lump hammer.'

'No looking back.' She let go of the wheel and took my hand. 'And you: no getting stabbed, shot, beaten, or killed. *Promise*.'

'Promise.' I popped open my door, leaned over and kissed her on the cheek. She smelled of mandarins and mangoes. 'Now: get your backside over there where it's safe.'

She got out of the car, popped her umbrella up and loped away into the gloom. Her dark jacket and black jeans were swallowed by the darkness, leaving nothing but the flash of white around the bottom of her trainers. And then even that was gone.

I stepped out onto the weed-cracked tarmac.

Rain thrummed against the shoulders of my jacket, soaked through my hair as I hobbled around to the boot of the car and popped it open.

Paul Manson blinked up at me, his eyes wide, wet, and bloodshot. The washing line dug into his neck, making the skin around it swollen and red. 'Mmmmmnnnffff, mmmnnnnphnnnn!'

Manson's cheeks glistened above the gag.

Poor baby.

Still, got to love duct-tape. Both arms were stuck behind his back, and so were his ankles and knees. The tarpaulin crackled in the boot beneath him as he wriggled.

According to my watch it was ten to nine – just over three hours since he got the full dose of Noel's drug cocktail. Well done Noel.

I leaned in and patted Manson on the tear-streaked cheek. 'This is what happens when you steal from Andy Inglis. What the hell were you *thinking*?'

'Nnnffff! Nmmmnnnnph mmmffff!'

Yeah, that's what they all say.

'Should've thought about that before you went into business laundering money for organized crime. Murder, extortion, drugs, prostitution. You got *any* idea how much misery and suffering you helped create? How many ruined lives? Ever think about that while you toddle off home in your fancy sports car to your fancy wife and private-school brat?'

'Nnnfff! Nnnnnggggnnn nffffffp!'

'You deserve everything you're going to get.'

'Nnnnnnnnnnnngh…' He screwed his eyes shut, squeezing out the tears.

I patted him down, then pulled his jacket open and fished the bulging wallet out of the left hand side. Couple of credit cards, three supermarket loyalty cards, frequent flier programmes. Photo of him and the wife and kid grinning it up on a beach somewhere exotic with palm trees. A wad of receipts. And about two hundred and fifty quid in cash.

I fined him two hundred for being a scumbag, then stuck the wallet back where I'd got it.

'Nnnngghnnnphhhnn…'

'Let me guess, you're sorry? You don't want to die?'

'Nnngh…'

'So if I *save* your miserable arse you'll rat on Andy Inglis's operation, won't you? You'll detail every arms deal and drug operation; every bank account, offshore tax-haven. Everything. And you'll do it in court too.'

The eyes flickered open, eyebrows pinched together. 'Nnn, nnnmmmph nnnghh!'

I leaned in nice and close. 'I know what you're thinking. You're thinking she'll have you killed if you talk to the police. Too late – why the hell do you think you're here? She *already* wants you dead. Either you talk to me and end up in witness protection, or you don't and end up in a shallow grave. No skin off my nose.'

Manson's eyes scrunched shut again, his shoulders shook, tears rolling down his cheeks. Probably spent years thinking he was untouchable. Accountancy's not exactly hands-on, is it? Not like robbing a bank or breaking someone's knees. It's all computers and numbers. Not like *real* crime.

Bastards like Paul Manson were all the same.

I pulled the envelope from my pocket and took out the last syringe. Popped the cap off. Gave the plunger a wee squeeze to get rid of any air bubbles, then reached in and pinned his head to the plastic sheet with my left hand.

'Nnnn! Nnnnnn! Nnnngghnnmmmmnnt!'

'Oh, shut up. If you don't look dead she's not going to buy it.'

The needle slipped into his neck. I pressed the plunger. He screamed behind the gag. Twitched… And went limp.

Lay there like a big, ugly parcel wrapped up in duct tape with a washing-line bow.

No way I'd be able to get him out of the boot all trussed up like that.

I cut through the plastic line, untied the ends from his throat and ankles.

Much better.

Behind me: a rattle of metal on metal.

Over at the front gate, a man in a suit worked the chain out of the gap between the two sides, then let it fall to the ground. A big black BMW 4x4 rumbled behind him. Rain turned its headlights into two shimmering knives, reflected in the wet tarmac.

It was time.

38

The guy in the suit waited until the 4x4 drove into the ware-house car park, then shut and chained the gate behind it.

The car's headlights swept across the chandler's walls.

It pulled up in front of me.

Joseph got out of the driver's seat. That left eye of his looked even worse than it had this morning – puffed up like a purple grapefruit. Blue and yellow bruises spread across his chin, and his bottom lip was swollen and cracked. He reached back into the car and when he straightened up again, there was a pick-axe handle in his hand. Not risking another kicking. His voice still had the gravelly edge only sixty-a-day or a kick in the throat gets you. 'Mr Henderson, I trust we're not going to have to revisit this morning's … unpleasantness?'

'Depends, doesn't it?'

The guy who'd got the gate marched over, through the rain. He was just a silhouette against the lights from the cash-and-carry next door until he reached the car: Francis. A strip of pale pink sticking plaster stretched across the bridge of his flattened nose, both eyes racoon black. A swathe of bandages covered the top of his head; that tin of beans must've cost him a *lot* of stitches.

Good.

Water dripped from the end of his ginger ponytail, turned the grey of his suit to funeral black. He nodded in my direction. ''Spector.' The word was wet, misshapen around the edge.

'Francis.'

He produced a black umbrella from the BMW's passenger side. Popped it, then opened the car's back door. Held the brolly up as Mrs Kerrigan stepped down into the warehouse car park.

She stood there, beneath the brolly, smiling at me. 'Mr Henderson, yez are here. Good for you.' She pointed at the stolen Jaguar. 'Do ye have a present for me?'

I didn't move. 'Where's Shifty?'

'Oh, yez are so *masterful*!' She tilted her head at Francis. 'Go get Mr Henderson's little friend.'

A grunt, then Francis handed her the umbrella and disappeared around the back of the 4x4. Something clunked. There was some rustling. And when Francis returned he was bent over, dragging a body by the armpits. It was partially wrapped in clear plastic sheeting, streaks of burgundy and scarlet clearly visible against the surface. Naked.

Francis stopped, right in front of the 4x4's bonnet, where the headlights glowed through the plastic. It was definitely Shifty. His face and body were covered in bruises and scabs, pale skin stained with his own blood. A patch of gauze was taped over the place where his right eye used to be.

'He alive?'

Francis dumped the body, then squatted down and felt at Shifty's throat. Stayed there for a bit. Then stood and nodded. 'Still ticking over.' At least three teeth were missing from the grin that followed. 'Just.'

'There ye go, Mr Henderson, one hostage. Your turn.'

Fair enough.

The Jag's boot popped up. I leaned my cane against the bumper, reached in and grabbed Manson's limp body by the

365

lapels. Hauled him up, twisted him sideways till his torso was hanging over the lip. Took a handful of collar and belt, and tipped him out of the boot and onto the tarmac. Left him lying face down in the rain.

'One mob accountant.'

She rose up on her toes, peered at Manson. 'He dead?'

'What do *you* think?'

'Maybe he's faking it.'

'He's a great actor if he is.' I took hold of the duct tape holding his wrists together and stood, pulling both arms with it, raising his chest off the ground. Wrapped my other hand around his index finger and bent it back, hard. When I let go it pointed at ninety-degrees to the natural. So I did the same with the next finger. And the one after that. Finished off with his pinky. He didn't so much as twitch, but it was going to hurt like hell when woke up in four hours. 'Want me to do the other hand?'

Mrs Kerrigan picked her way between the puddles, rain sparking off the umbrella. 'Paul Manson...' She stopped, six foot away. Licked her cherry-red lips. 'Turn him over. I want to see his face.'

I pulled him onto his side, then let him roll the rest of the way. He flopped back to the wet ground. Rain spattered against his face and the gag.

'Well, well, well, Paul Manson.' A laugh broke free. 'That's what ye get for being a boring arrogant wee caffler. Not so feckin' gobby now, are yez?'

I thumped my toe against his leg. 'Got a shallow grave all ready and waiting for him.'

'Ye know, it's a shame. I thought ye'd bottle it, turn up with the fecker still kicking so I could do the honours.' She reached into her coat and came out with a small black semi-automatic. 'But it's the thought that counts. Right?'

Shite... I reached for the small of my back—

The gun kicked in her hand, a blare of white light seared

across my eyes, and Paul Manson's head jerked up off the tarmac. Then thudded down again.

The gun's roar echoed off the metal warehouse.

A dark hole sat in the middle of his forehead, the ground beneath him was spattered with glistening lumps and flecks of white. One eye open, the pupil pointing off to the left.

Sodding hell.

She lowered the gun. 'Now, will ye look at that? Must've been nice and fresh to still be all wet inside.'

A knot formed beneath my ribs, then spread up into my throat. Cutting off the air for a couple of deafening heartbeats. Then faded.

So much for getting him to testify against Andy Inglis. Still, if you run with wolves you're going to get bitten sooner or later. Really, it served the bastard right.

Still...

I leaned against the car, fingers wrapped around the pistol's handgrip.

Mrs Kerrigan took a step to the side, avoiding the puddle spreading out from what was left of Manson's head. 'What's up, Mr Henderson? Yez are looking all shocked.'

'Nothing. Why should I give a toss about some mob accountant scumbag?'

She laughed, a proper full-on belly laugh, rocking backwards and forwards beneath her funeral-black umbrella. 'Ahh...' A sigh. A smile. Then she wiped her eyes on the back of her sleeve, gun still in hand. 'Don't be thick – do ye really think I'd let yez anywhere near Mr Inglis's accountant? Feck that. You'd try to get him to squeal.' She waved the semiautomatic at Manson. 'Had to sit next to this gobshite at some charity boxing dinner last night. Banging on about how lovely his wife is, and how great his kid is, and how much they love each other. And would I like to see photos of their feckin' holiday in Spain?'

Not Andy Inglis's accountant?

367

Oh shite.

Just an innocent bystander.

Oh *buggering* shite.

The knot was back, and it'd brought friends, curdling my lungs.

The gun kicked in her hand again, punching a hole in Manson's chest, leaving another scar on my retina. Then another. And one more, the body twitching with every bullet. 'Does it look like I want to see yer manky holiday snaps?'

'You said he was a bloody mob accountant!'

She brought the semiautomatic up to point at my chest. Pouted. 'Did ye really think I'd stop feckin' with ye just because ye got out of prison?'

'You...'

'Don't blame me: ye're the one who grabbed him. Ye killed him. Ye brought him here. Ye left his poor wife a widow and his precious wee boy without an old man.' She stepped back a couple of paces. 'And now ye can clean him up. Dig the bullets out though, eh? Don't want anything left lying about now, do we?'

Used me. Played me for a moron.

And I did it.

Didn't matter who pulled the trigger, she was right: I gagged and tied him, injected him with a cocktail of surgery-grade anaesthetics, and dragged him out to a disused chandler's warehouse to be shot in the head. All on me.

Mrs Kerrigan gave one last laugh, then turned and started towards the car.

I dragged the gun out from my back. 'You think that's *funny*?'

She didn't stop. 'Oh grow up, Mr Henderson. It's feckin' hilarious.'

My semiautomatic barked, digging a chunk out of the tarmac at her feet.

She froze. 'Seriously?'

'He bored you at dinner, and that's *it*?'

'Mr Henderson,' she shook her head, gun arm hanging slack at her side, 'do ye really think I'm after being that thick? That I'm just messing here, with no insurance like a Muppet?' She glanced over her shoulder. 'Joseph?'

Silence.

'Joseph, I'm all for yer dramatic moment, but it's time for show-and-tell. Give Mr Henderson one of his little girlfriend's ears. No need to gift wrap it.'

I pointed the gun at the back of her head. 'He touches her: the next bullet takes your face with it.'

She sighed. Turned. Frowned. 'Joseph?'

Somewhere in the distance a motorbike revved its engine, then faded away into the night, leaving nothing but the hiss of the rain behind.

'Where the feckin' hell...' She shook her head. Closed her eyes and pressed the flat of the barrel against the skin between her eyebrows. 'But would I listen? No: give the bastard another chance, I said. Let him prove himself. Too bloody soft, that's my problem.' She lowered the gun and raised her voice. 'Francis! Get the bitch out the car and cut her feckin' ear off.'

Lying flat on his back, half-wrapped in clear plastic sheeting, Shifty groaned.

Rain thrummed against Mrs Kerrigan's umbrella.

'Francis?' A sigh. 'For feck's sake, turn yer back for two seconds... Fine.' The gun came up again, pointing right in the middle of my chest. 'Can't get the feckin' staff.'

A dark shape emerged from behind the 4x4. Cleared its throat.

Mrs Kerrigan nodded. 'About time. Now get yer arse in gear, before I change my mind about your career prospects.'

The figure stepped forwards, into the headlights. Tall and thin, blue jumper on over a white shirt turned see-through by the rain, hair plastered to his head. Wee Free McFee.

369

'Francis, I'm not going to tell ye again.'

Wee Free raised his right hand. What looked like a lump hammer glistened in his fist. 'He's busy.'

Mrs Kerrigan spun around. Wee Free's arm crashed down, battering the hammer off the side of her head. Blood glittered in the air, caught in the 4x4's headlights like burning fireflies. She kept turning, spinning as she crumpled to the tarmac, hitting it like a bag of wet laundry.

She lay there, groaning, right arm twitching, the gun still clasped in her hand.

Clunk – the lump hammer hit the ground.

Not so big now, was she?

I stepped forwards. 'OK, that's—'

'"Thus saith the LORD: Execute ye judgment and righteousness, and deliver the spoiled out of the hand of the oppressor."' He stepped on her gun-hand, grinding the heel of his shoe from side to side, until the semiautomatic clattered out onto the tarmac, then bent and picked it up. Turned it over in his hands. Ran his fingers along the barrel. Sighed. 'You know, I never really saw the appeal. It's impersonal. Weak. Give a three-year-old a gun and they can kill someone. How can that be right?'

She coughed, retched, then struggled over onto her side. Blood dripped from the tip of her nose. 'Gnnnghh...'

I limped closer, gun up. 'OK, nobody move.'

Wee Free grabbed a handful of Mrs Kerrigan's hair and dragged her to her knees. Forced her head back, so she was looking up at him. 'Listen carefully, sweetheart, because this is your only telling.'

She spat at him, a frothy gobbet of phlegm tainted with red. 'I... I will ... feckin' *end* ye!'

'Ash Henderson is looking for my daughter. While he's doing that, he's under my protection.'

'I'll kill ye and everyone yez've ever loved!' Getting louder with every word.

I circled her with the gun. 'You and me have unfinished business.'

'I'LL TRACK THEM DOWN AND I'LL—'

Wee Free smashed a fist into her face.

Her head snapped back, rolled from side to side. Then she shook it, and glared up at him, blood dribbling down her chin. 'You better feckin' kill me right now, cos if you don't...'

He smiled. 'I know how it works. You see, you and me, we're the same. We just fight on different sides.' A wink. 'What do you think, Mr Henderson?'

'She has to die. Right here. Right now. And I'm going to do it.'

Wee Free glanced over to where Shifty lay, flat on his back in the rain. 'What happened to the fat naked guy?'

'*She* did. Tortured him, gouged out his eye.'

'And you want to kill her for it?'

I threw my arms out. 'Do you *think*? She's a vicious, nasty, murdering piece of filth. Leave her alive and she's not kidding: she'll come after both of us. She *needs* to die.'

Wee Free sighed. 'That's not very Christian of you, Mr Henderson. Leviticus 24:19, "And if a man cause a blemish in his neighbour; as he hath done, so shall it be done to him – breach for breach, eye for eye, tooth for tooth. As he hath caused a blemish in a man, so shall it be done to him again."'

Mrs Kerrigan's face was candlewax-pale. 'Matthew 5:38, "Ye have heard that it hath been said, an eye for an eye, and a tooth for a tooth, but I say unto yez, that ye resist not evil, but whosoever shall *smite* thee on thy right cheek, turn to him the other also."'

I jabbed the barrel of the gun against her forehead. 'Bible study's over. It's—'

Wee Free's fist hit me like a car crash. Yellow and black blobs burst across the inside of my eyes, followed by a deafening hiss and thump as I hit the wet tarmac. Dear Jesus...

'We're talking, Mr Henderson. Don't interrupt.'

Pressure on my right wrist. My fingers were peeled back, one-by-one, from the handle of the gun. Then the pressure was gone and I was left with the grinding feel of rusty metal working itself loose beneath the skin of my cheek. He didn't need a lump hammer – his fist was hard enough on its own.

I blinked away the spinning dots, lying on my side in the rain.

Wee Free slipped my gun into his pocket. Then grabbed Mrs Kerrigan's hair again. 'I'm disappointed: quoting scripture for forgiveness? That's beneath you.' He gave her head a little shake. 'See, I've been doing my research, I know what you've done. And it's time to atone for your sins.'

She bared her teeth. 'I'll see you in *Hell*.'

'Probably.' He glanced at Shifty. 'But you'll have to squint.' Her gun barked in his hand. 'Let us pray.'

39

There was a moment's silence, then the screaming started. Mrs Kerrigan's eyes bugged, mouth twisted around bared teeth, sitting on the wet tarmac rocking back and forth, both hands wrapped around her right ankle. Blood dripped from the hole in her shoe.

'AAAAGGGHHH!'

'Told you I'd done my research.' Wee Free tossed the gun away into the darkness. '"Burning for burning, wound for wound, stripe for stripe." You had someone shoot Mr Henderson in the foot, and now you're reaping what you've sown.'

'CHRIST AND FECKING… AAGGHH!'

Rain pounded against the tarmac, sparking in the 4x4's headlights, battering me down with it.

He bent and picked up the lump hammer again. Twitched it towards me, then the stolen Jaguar. 'I think it'd be best if you got back to work, don't you?'

'JESUS! AAAGGHH BASTARD!'

I grabbed my walking stick and levered myself to my feet. Stared down at the wailing figure curled up at his feet. 'We have to kill her.'

'Eye for an eye.' Wee Free nudged Mrs Kerrigan with his boot. 'That's next.'

'She'll come after you, and she'll come after me. She'll go for our families...' Oh God – Alice.

I turned, hobbling as fast as I could, straight through puddles, past the Jag. Making for the passageway between the warehouse and the shipping containers.

If she'd done what she was meant to – ran for it – we were all screwed. Soon as she crossed the hundred-yard mark, the alarm would go up and Jacobson's firearms team would hot-foot it over here. Where all the blood and bodies were.

Shite.

I yanked out my phone and powered up Sabir's app. The thing took a moment to load, then pinged, slow and steady, the screen amber. Wherever she'd got to, it was no more than sixty-six yards away.

I stopped. Cupped my hands into a loudhailer. 'ALICE!' Took another couple of steps towards the containers. Towards the hole we'd made in the fence. 'ALICE!'

The screen went from orange to yellow, the pinging slowed.

Further, into the darkness. 'ALICE!'

Green.

A shape lay in the gap between two of the containers.

Joseph.

He was on his back, one arm up above his head, legs bent. The pickaxe handle lay beside him, the thick end smeared with thumb-sized blots of red, just visible in the gloom.

I checked my phone. The screen was green. She was near.

'Alice?'

Two steps further into the darkness between the containers, the rusting metal walls not much more than shoulder-width apart. The smell of burnt plastic and mould. Another two steps. Then two more.

'Oh no...'

She was on her side, curled, knees up to her chest, little red shoes sticking out at twenty to nine. One arm draped across herself. A line of blood ran sideways across her forehead. Her satchel lay open beside her, the lump hammer notable by its absence.

Bastard.

I knelt beside her, brushed the damp hair from her face. 'Alice? Can you hear me?'

Two fingers in the dip behind her jawline... There – a pulse.

Breath hissed out of me. My head curled forwards until it rested on her shoulder. Thank God.

Then something dark burrowed into my chest.

I stood, marched back to where Joseph lay and slammed my good foot into his stomach a couple of times. Nothing. Grabbed the pickaxe handle. 'You rancid little shite.'

Pick a leg, any leg.

The impact shuddered up the wood and into my hands. Once. Twice. Three times. He didn't even grunt, just lay there as I shattered the bones.

One more kick for luck, then I dumped the pickaxe handle, scooped Alice up in my arms and hobbled back to the car park, right heel thumping against the ground with every step, knives of dirty ice shredding through the bone and tissue.

By the time I'd made it to the car, there was no sign of Shifty, or Mrs Kerrigan. But Paul Manson was still stretched out on the ground, face up, the bullet holes in his chest and forehead glistening like mini black holes.

Wee Free stood where I'd left him, holding the lump hammer in one hand and my gun in the other. He jerked his chin up. 'She all right?'

I lowered Alice into the Jaguar, laying her along the back seat. 'She's alive.'

'Good.' He walked over and nudged Manson with the toe of his shoe. 'Take this with you. I've got enough bodies.'

The door clunked shut. I pulled my shoulders back. 'Where's Shifty?'

375

'The fat naked guy? I'm keeping him. *You* get to keep the dead accountant, and the girl. And then you get out there and you find my daughter.'

My mouth was full of sandpaper. 'I'm not leaving without him.'

'Jessica's fifth birthday. We had the party in the hospital so her mother could be there. Smiling away with tubes in her arms and nose, barely able to lift her head off the pillow. And Jessica kisses her on the cheek and tells her she's going to be an angel soon.'

'He needs help.'

'Asks if she'll come back and be her guardian angel and turn pumpkins into carriages and mice into horses.'

'Wee… William, he *needs* a doctor.'

Wee Free raised the gun. 'When she was six she asked for another slice of wedding cake at the reception, and when her stepmother asked why, she said her mum always loved cake, and that next time we visited her grave we could give it to her.'

I turned my back on him, searched the ground around the car. Where the hell was Mrs Kerrigan's gun?

Everything was darkness and clumps of weeds and rain-filled potholes.

'When she was seven, Jessica's rabbit died. She cried for a week, because rabbits can't get into heaven, because they haven't got souls. Took me that long to convince her they don't go to hell either.'

Where was the sodding gun?

'She grew up. Got rebellious. Turned her back on the Lord. But she's still my little girl.'

It wasn't as if I had another three hundred quid to buy a new one.

'So this is what's going to happen. I'm going to keep your friend until you find her. And every day she stays missing, I'm going to send you a bit of him. And if…' Wee Free's voice crackled for a moment. He cleared his throat. 'If she dies—'

'Let me guess: "Burning for burning, wound for wound, stripe for stripe"?'

Where the hell was the *bloody* gun?

Wee Free bent down and picked something up from the ground at his feet. 'This what you're looking for?' Mrs Kerrigan's semiautomatic. He ejected the clip, dropped it, then tossed the gun over. It clattered against the wet tarmac, two feet from me.

'Did you kill her?'

'An eye for an eye. Now find my daughter.'

He climbed behind the wheel of the big 4x4. The engine roared into life. Then the BMW backed away, turned, and headed out through the open gates.

Rain seeped through my jacket, stuck my trousers to my legs, dripped from my face as the car's tail-light glow faded into the night.

Bastard.

Now there was nothing left but the lights from the closed cash-and-carry next door.

Don't just stand there. Get the scene tidied and get the hell out of it before someone calls 999 to report the gunshots.

I snapped on a pair of gloves from my investigation kit. Picked up the gun. Then limped over to where Wee Free had been standing and collected the magazine. Four bullets left.

It clacked back into the handgrip, then the whole thing went in an evidence bag. Just in case. No way in hell I was getting my fingerprints on the murder weapon.

I popped the Jag's boot, pulled out a couple of the rubble sacks and worked them over Paul Manson's head and shoulders, covering the mess where the back of his head used to be. Dragged and shoved him into the boot. Stood, staring down at his body, still bound with duct tape.

Killed because he'd boasted about his family at a charity dinner.

'I know it doesn't help, but I'm sorry.'

I clunked the lid shut.

The firelighters stank of paraffin as I clicked them into chunks and scattered them across the driest bits of wood I could find – sticks and twigs and newspaper at the bottom, bigger branches on top. All arranged in a ditch beside a drystane dyke in the depths of Moncuir Wood. It'd probably been a farm at some point in the distant past, slowly smothered beneath the boughs of beech and pine. Now it was just a few lines of stone drawn through the dead nettles and mourning brambles. Secluded and forgotten.

Only the darkness and the rain for company.

Paul Manson seemed to have got a lot heavier since death. Who would have thought four little bullets would weigh so much? I dragged him over and tipped him in on top of the sticks.

His top half was still covered with the rubble sack, what was left of his head pressing against the black plastic, making it bulge.

At least I couldn't see his face.

I stood. Rubbed at the small of my back.

Picked up the five litre container of methylated spirits.

'Like I said, I'm sorry...' I poured half of it over him, let it seep around his body and into the wood beneath him. Then tossed in a couple of lit matches. Stepped back and watched it take hold.

Branches popped and crackled, tendrils of smoke joining the blue flicker of burning spirit. Then the kindling caught and gold joined the blue.

OK, so there wasn't nearly enough wood to cremate the body, but that wasn't the point. It just needed to burn long enough and hot enough to get rid of any DNA and trace evidence Alice and I had left.

Half an hour later, I shovelled dirt over what was left, and limped back to the lay-by.

The Jaguar sat on one side, Alice's Suzuki on the other.

The methylated spirit nipped my eyes, catching my throat as I drenched the Jag's upholstery with the last two-and-a-bit litres. I chucked the shovel into the back, along with the tarpaulin, then wound down the windows and closed the doors.

There was one chunk of firelighter left in the bottom of the box. I dropped a lit match on it and waited for it to catch...

A voice behind me: 'Ash?'

I turned.

Alice wobbled on unsteady legs, one arm out, holding onto the Suzuki's roof.

'You're awake.'

She blinked at the Jaguar. Pointed. 'What...?'

'It's OK, get back in the car. I'll only be a minute.' Smoke oozed out from the cardboard box in my hand. I tossed it in through the driver's window and the methylated spirit went up with a *whump*. Gouts of flame belched from the open windows, curling up into the rainy night as the first wash of volatiles burned themselves out.

The lay-by was thrown into sharp relief for a moment, then the light faded, leaving everything wrapped in gloom again.

I snapped off my SOC gloves and lobbed them in after the box. 'I've lost count of the times we've turned up to one of these only to find the silly sod who stole it lying on the other side of the road with second-degree burns and a face full of safety glass. They don't wind the windows down, so the whole thing's just one big bomb.'

It was a fiddle, but I dug the sim card I'd used to call Manson out of my unofficial phone and chucked it into the burning Jag. Replaced it with the original one.

Leaving nothing to connect us.

379

Alice's face rippled and swam in the light of the blazing car. A massive lump sat on her left temple, it's crown cracked and oozing blood. 'Where's Paul Manson?'

OK.

It took a bit, but I managed a smile for her. 'I got Witness Protection to pick him up. He's going to turn Queen's Evidence.'

Her mouth twisted. 'Don't *lie* to me!'

'I'm not. He's—'

'Ash, I saw you carrying his body off into the woods. You said you were going to get him to testify!'

Brilliant. Exactly what I needed to round the day off. As if things weren't bad enough...

'It was Mrs Kerrigan, she—'

'You said no one had to die, I *trusted* you.'

'I did my best, OK?' I waved a hand at the burning car. 'He was lying there on the ground and she shot him. Four times. Grinning while she did it.' Sentenced to death because he was boring at dinner. 'There wasn't anything I could do.' My shoulders dipped. 'I'm sorry. I really, *really* am.'

Alice leaned back against the tree, covered her eyes with her hands. 'Oh God...'

I cleared my throat. Looked away so she couldn't see my face. 'Rule number four: he was a mob accountant. Soon as he started stealing from Andy Inglis he was dead. It's nobody's fault but his. His and the people he worked for.'

Liar. It was all mine. Just like everything else. Just like it always was.

40

'Feeling any better?'

Alice squinted up at me. The tea towel had darkened, beads of water ran down her hand and dripped off her palm onto the sticky table top. 'No.'

Over at the far end of Buffalo Bob's, the only other couple in the place were having a low-volume argument. Throwing their arms and hands about, baring teeth and hissing at each other over barbecue chicken, beans, and chips.

Dark wood panelling covered the walls, just visible between the tsunami of framed photos and vintage memorabilia. A long bar with hand pumps and neon 'BUD LIGHT' and 'COKE' signs. A ceiling fan creaking round and round. Bruce Springsteen grunting out of the speakers.

'We should get you checked out. It's—'

'I'm not going to the hospital.'

'—got a concussion, and—'

'Please. It's…' She shuddered. Prodded at the spare ribs on her plate. 'So, is Mrs Kerrigan dead too?'

The woman jumped to her feet, snatched up her milkshake, and threw the contents in her partner's face. 'BASTARD!' Then stormed out into the car park, slamming the door behind her.

Two beats, then the man was on his feet, dripping with pink, hurrying after her. He paused at the door to throw us a pained smile. 'Sorry...' And then he was gone.

I dipped a chip in blue cheese sauce, scowled at my reflection in the window. 'I don't know. Maybe.' Maybe Wee Free McFee was hacking her up on his butcher's block, feeding strips to his dogs. Eating some himself. His chest smeared with blood and scars.

She should have been *mine*.

A nod. Then Alice picked up a rib. The meat dark and sagging against the charred bone. 'I'm sorry.'

I reached over and squeezed her hand. 'Hey: you've got nothing to be sorry for.'

'He was just ... there, and I tried to get away, but he hit me and...' The bone clattered back onto the plate. 'I'm sorry.'

'It's going to be all right. All we have to do is rescue Jessica McFee, get Shifty back, and that's us.' One more squeeze. 'You did everything you could.'

'But—'

'Wee Free's got Mrs Kerrigan, so she can't come after us. He's not going to hurt Shifty because he needs us to find his daughter. The only thing that happened tonight is a mob accountant died.'

She nodded.

I took another bite of burger, forcing it down like a greasy slab of cardboard.

Just a mob accountant. Not an innocent man who bragged about his family to the wrong person.

Alice tried the rib again, getting it as far as her mouth this time. 'Wonder what his wife and son will think. That he's run away with another woman? Been grabbed by a rival gang?'

I kept my eyes on my chips. 'Probably best not to think about it.'

Alice sighed. Plopped the rib back on the plate and pushed

it away. 'I know this kind of thing probably happens all the time when you make your living laundering cash for crime lords.' She lowered her eyes, fidgeted with her napkin. 'But I can't help feeling sorry for him.'

And now the burger tasted like burnt flesh marinated in methylated spirits. I shoved my plate to the side. It clinked against hers.

'OK.' My fingers spread across the table top. 'How do we catch the Inside Man?'

She reached into her leather satchel and pulled out a folder. Placed it on the table. Pulled out a sheaf of papers.

'Excuse me?' The young bloke who'd taken our order appeared at the end of the table. Denim shirt going grey around the collar, American-flag waistcoat spattered with stains, a name badge with 'HI Y'ALL, I'M BRAD ~ YOU WANT IT? WE GOT IT!!!' His baseball hat was squint on top of his greasy curls. 'You need any more ice? It's not a problem, we've got loads?'

Alice took the tea towel from her head and handed it over. 'Thanks.'

The egg on her forehead had settled down. Now it was little more than a bump, crowned with a pink-and-yellow scrape. Joseph was bloody lucky to get off with a shattered leg. If I'd had more time...

Brad pointed. 'You want another round of drinks?'

She nodded. 'Can I have a large Jack Daniel's with ice please? And a pint of lager. And a pot of tea?'

'Perfect: Jack on the rocks with a beer back, and a tea.' Brad scurried off with the dripping dishtowel, and Alice spread her papers out on the table.

Each one had two photos of an Inside Man victim on it: the head-and-shoulders photo of them alive above the deposition site where their body turned up. She put all nine of them in date order. Doreen Appleton – the oldest – on the left, then Tara McNab, Holly Drummond, Natalie May, Laura

Strachan, Marie Jordan, Ruth Laughlin, and Claire Young, finishing off with Jessica McFee on the right.

Alice went back into the folder for post-mortem photos. And followed those up with the copies of the letters she'd charmed out of Micky Slosser.

And last, but not least, the letter that had arrived today.

She rocked backwards and forwards in her seat, one arm wrapped around herself, the other hand twiddling its way through a strand of brown curls. 'Well, the handwriting's clearly very similar. Not identical – the angle of the letters is a bit more pronounced, the loops messier, which is a good sign.'

'It is?'

'Is your handwriting *exactly* the same today as it was eight years ago? Mine isn't, it gets worse every year, I think it's because we all spend too much time on computers and not enough with a pen and paper, no one writes letters any more, well, unless they're serial offenders...' She picked up the newest one and squinted at it, eyes disappearing under the furrow of her brow. Then she went back into the satchel and came out with a pair of glasses. 'That's better. Right. Ahem... "Have you missed me? Because I know I've missed you. All of you. My victims, my pursuers, my public. I've missed you like a drowning man misses the cold hard earth beneath his feet."' Alice blew out a breath. 'Not exactly subtle, is it?'

'Maybe he's a literature student, you know what they're like.'

'"The first one wasn't right. She wasn't strong enough for my dark purpose. Didn't make my heart sing. But Jessica is different. Her cries and curses are the finest wine to my jaded palate. Her flesh, my feast."'

The tea was cold, but I drank it anyway. 'I take it back, not even literature students are that pretentious.'

'It gets worse. "She's worthy of the love that burns within...", "The pale skin of her breast rises and falls as she

384

breathes me in, her heart quickening like a startled hare…",
"And soon I will plunge my knife deep into her quivering
flesh, laid out naked before me. A sacrificial offering to climb
inside…"' Alice put the letter down, tapped her fingers against
the Formica. 'Is it just me, or is he writing torture porn? I
mean, there's nothing like that in any of the other letters.
Yes, they're just as pretentious, but now he's going out of his
way to push the sex angle.'

'Sex sells.'

Her fingertip danced across a line of handwritten text. '"The
pale swell of her hidden pleasures call to me. Oh how she
begs for me to enjoy their warm, dark embrace…" If serial
killers sent letters in to *Playboy*, this is what it'd sound like.'

I picked the very first letter from the set. Dated the day
after we found Tara McNab's body in the lay-by. No mention
of sex, or breasts, or warm dark embraces. Lots of stuff about
power and control and how disrespectful it was of the papers
to call him the Caledonian Ripper, but no sex.

The next one was dated the day before Holly Drummond
turned up. The content was much the same as the first letter.
And so was the next one. And the one after that. 'Maybe his
handwriting's not the only thing that's changed? Perhaps he's
just being more honest about what's driving him?'

'But he's impotent. He has to be, what he's doing doesn't
make any sense otherwise. He can't get a woman pregnant
the normal way, so he's got to cut her open to impregnate
her. The power feeds the sexual fantasy, he's potent and
rampant, and gets women pregnant…' She stole one of my
chips. 'Why isn't he on Viagra or something? Why not go to
see an erectile dysfunction specialist?'

I picked the plate up and placed it in front of her. On top
of the letter about Laura Strachan. 'If he's impotent, how
come he managed to rape Ruth Laughlin?'

Alice chewed for a bit, frowning her way through it. Then
picked another chip from the pile. 'Maybe attaining an

erection's not the problem, it's the motility of his sperm?' She arranged seven chips in a straight line on the plate, side by side like the posts of a fence. Then another two below that. Picked up the squeezy bottle of tomato sauce and dripped a blob onto each of the first four chips. Then one more on the first chip on the second row.

'So, what: you want we should start with the fertility clinics? See if they've got anyone who matches the profile? We'd never get a warrant for that.'

Brad was back, holding a tray. If he was bothered by the post-mortem photographs and pictures of dead women, he hid it well. He handed out the drinks. Passed Alice a fresh tea-towel bulging with ice. Smiled. 'Anything else, you just let me know, OK?'

Alice held up a finger, then knocked her Jack Daniel's back in one go. ''Nother of those, thanks.'

Soon as he was back behind the bar, she stuck her tongue out between her teeth and frowned at the paperwork. 'Dear Boss, or From Hell?'

'Not this again.'

'One has details that weren't released to the public, the other arrives with half a human kidney... When did Dr Docherty come up with the profile?'

'Not sure. Henry didn't get called in till we'd found Tara McNab in the lay-by. So, after Holly Drummond?'

Alice stacked the victim sheets, PM photos, and letters for all the other victims into a pile and put it to one side, leaving the info for Doreen Appleton, Tara, and Holly in the middle of the table. 'So the profile was based on these three victims.' She placed one letter beside Holly's photo. One beside Tara's. 'And Doreen didn't get a letter...' Frown, fiddle, twiddle. 'Dr Docherty thinks it's because she was just a dress rehearsal, but what if he just didn't write one because he didn't need to, I mean it's not till the papers start calling him a sicko and the Caledonian Ripper that he has to defend his honour, before that he's happy to just chunter along doing his thing in private.'

Brad was back with her drink. 'Here you go.'

She necked it and asked for another.

His smile drifted a bit. 'You sure?'

'Positive.'

And he was gone again.

She gulped down a mouthful of lager. 'What if *none* of the letters are Jack the Ripper? What if they're two separate people claiming responsibility for something they didn't do?'

'You think the Inside Man letters are fake? They can't be – they're all postmarked the day before the victims are found.'

'The letters are about power and control and look at me, I'm so special. The *bodies* are about trying to create life...' She picked up the two letters and added them to the pile at the end of the table. 'Remove the letters from the scene and he's painting a very different picture.'

I poured a fresh cup of tea. 'You can't – they arrived, they're there, and they've got info only the killer could know.'

'Or anyone on the investigation.'

'So, what: it's a wannabe with a time machine? Hops back a couple of days and mails them off before we've found the body?'

She tapped her fingers against the post-mortem photos. 'But the bodies tell a different story to the letters... What if...' The frown deepened. 'What if the letters are real, but at the same time they're fake too? The Inside Man doesn't write them because he wants to explain himself, he writes them to confuse the issue, I mean he knows we're going to use them to try to catch him, so he writes *fake* letters that have nothing to do with what's really going on, they're there to make us look in the wrong place.' Alice sat back and grinned at me. Then took a big gulp from her pint. Stifled a belch. 'It's *him*, but he's lying to us.'

'Pfff... Sounds a bit advanced, doesn't it? Thought most serial nut-jobs weren't meant to be all that bright.'

Brad was back with Alice's drink in one hand and the bottle of Jack Daniel's in the other. 'How about I just leave this with you?' Wink. 'Staff discount.' Obviously angling for a nice fat tip.

Alice downed her drink, topped up her glass, then went back into her satchel for a pad and a pen as Brad wandered off to clean something.

'We need to rework the profile from scratch, ignore the letters, focus on the victims, the bodies, and the act.' She drew nine boxes on the pad, filled each of them in with one of the victims' names, then connected them with arrows. More lines with jobs and ages on them. More lines, keywords this time: SEX, PROCREATION, RAPE, LOVE, ANGER, PREGNANT, BABY, LOVE ME!!!...

She started adding dotted lines and circles. 'Statistically, he's going to be Caucasian – plus all the baby dolls are pink, not black or Asian and it's not like you can't buy ethnic dolls, I've seen them in the shops. And he's at *least* mid-to-late twenties when he starts, because that gives him enough time to realize he's sterile and work on his fantasy. He's controlling, measured, narcissistic, very centred and sure of himself in public, but in private, or at home with people who know him, he'll be shy and have trouble engaging socially.' Alice doodled a baby's dummy in the corner of the page. 'I know that sounds counter-intuitive, but an inverted social anxiety disorder goes with the idea that he's wearing a mask the whole time, he can be in control, because he's someone else.'

Alice topped her Jack Daniel's up again. 'It won't have been instant, he'll have had to work at it, getting more controlled as he grows, more adept at burying the real him, hiding what he really is when other people are there.'

A shy, nervous young man, turning into a controlling tosspot who's full of himself. Someone close to the police who knew how to manipulate the investigation. Someone who could send us all off on a wild bloody goose chase and make it look as if it was all our idea in the first place.

I sat back in my seat, drummed my fingers on the table top.

Someone who could write misleading letters, then make sure they were given centre stage. Someone who could side-line Alice's input, because he had the ear of the King...

The Wizard's Apprentice.

'He's even got his own narrative arc, hasn't he? From bumbling curly-haired sidekick to this slick TV personality in a suit, right? And we all know what Nietzsche says about staring into the abyss...'

Someone like Dr Frederic Docherty.

41

Carriage lamps cast discreet golden blooms on either side of the front door. A little sign was screwed to the wall above the bell, telling residents to ring after eleven p.m. if they wanted in. So that's what I did.

The Pinemantle Hotel sat two-thirds of the way down Porter Lane – less than five minutes from Division Headquarters – its concrete-and-granite bulk nestling amongst the crumbling grandeur of sandstone townhouses. A front garden, thick with rhododendron bushes and denuded beech trees, lurked in shadow behind Alice's Suzuki.

She peered out at me from the passenger seat, one eye closed, swaying from side to side. Blinking in slow motion. She fumbled with her seatbelt and creaked the door open. Puffed out her cheeks. Slapped a hand over her mouth.

Perfect. Just what we needed at check-in – her blowing ribs and chips all over their gravel driveway.

A pause. Then she shuddered and picked herself out of the car. Lurched over, stiff-legged, to the portico. Slumped against me. 'Mmmsleepy.' The words slithered out in a fog of Jack Daniel's and barbecue sauce.

A shadow moved across the rippled glass panel in the door.

'Try not to look like you're about to puke everywhere or they won't give us a room.'

'Sleeeepy...'

Great.

The shadow filled the pane, then *clunk* – the door opened.

A man in slippers and a black cardigan blinked up at me, his face lined and sagging. Wafts of Ralgex and peppermint rolled out of him. 'Can I help you?'

'I need two rooms.'

He did a bit more blinking, going back and forth between me and Alice. 'I see.' He flexed his shoulders beneath his baggy cardigan then glanced down at Alice's suitcase and my holdall. 'Would you like some help with your bags?'

'We're fine, thanks.'

Alice tugged at my sleeve. 'Twin room. I don't want ... want to ... alone?'

'Two rooms. Have you got anything adjoining?'

A handkerchief appeared in his hand, followed by a long snottery honk on his nose. 'I think we might be able to accommodate you.' Then he turned and doddered back into the hotel.

Tartan carpet surrounded a wooden reception desk with a stag's head mounted above it. Hunting scenes and portraits of men and women in olde-worlde uniforms and dresses punctuated the walls – surrounded by heavy golden frames.

The man took our names, car registration, an imprint of Alice's credit card, then held out a pair of room keys. 'Breakfast is from half six till nine thirty in the Balmoral Room. I'd suggest you leave it until after seven though – we have a large party of police officers staying with us and they tend to hog the buffet.' He pointed off to the left. 'And if you'd like to put your car in the car park around the side, I'll give you a token to get in.'

'Thanks.'

He rummaged under the desk for a bit. Then emerged with a frown. 'Could've sworn they were here... Just be a tick.' And he was off, slippers scuffing at the tartan carpet.

Soon as he was out of sight I reached over and plucked the register from the reception desk. Flicked back through it a couple of days.

The page was covered in cops. Rhona was right: the whole team from the Specialist Crime Division had checked in, along with Jacobson and his Lateral Investigative and Review Unit.

And last, but not least: Dr F. Docherty, room 314.

'... was Love Amongst Ruin and "Home". Five to midnight and you're listening to the Witching Hour, with me, Lucy Robotham.'

The token I'd got from the night porter opened a barrier that led into a car park built beneath what looked like conference facilities. I took the Suzuki between the thick concrete pillars and dumped it in the first available space. Sat there for a minute with my head back as my right foot throbbed.

'... take a look at tomorrow's papers and the Daily Record leads with "Gotcha!" Scandal rocks Number Ten as the Business Secretary Alex Dance is arrested for perjury and attempting to pervert the course of justice...'

Another couple of breaths and it had settled down a bit.

'... Press and Journal has "Parents' fear for missing Charlie", going with the hunt for missing five-year-old Charlie Pearce...'

God what a day...

'... The Independent and the Scotsman both go with the ongoing manhunt in Oldcastle for the Inside Man. While the Castle News and Post devotes its front page to a letter supposedly sent in by the killer to—'

I clicked the radio off. Levered myself out of the car. Leaned heavily on my cane, and hobbled back towards the exit.

Couldn't get a mobile signal in the car park, but as soon as I stepped outside it was up to four bars. My thumb picked out the numbers, the hotel concrete scraping against my jacket as I leaned back and listened to it ring.

A porridge-thick Easterhouse accent brayed out of the earpiece. 'Police Scotland, Oldcastle Division.'

'That you Daphne? It's Ash Henderson. I need to know if you've still got Rock-Hammer Robertson kicking about.'

'*Ash, you auld bugger, how's the foot?*' The sound of fingers attacking a keyboard rattled down the line.

'Like I've got a hedgehog in my shoe. Joe well?'

'*Silly bugger fell down the stairs and broke his collar bone... No – according to this Mr Robertson has been released without charge.*'

After what he'd done to Cooper and Jacobson? Lucky Mr Robertson.

'Got a number for him?'

'*Give us a minute...*'

Wednesday

42

'… *Are you serious? It's gone midnight!*'

'How much?'

There was silence from the other end of the phone as I hobbled into reception. Then Rock-Hammer Robertson was back. *'Hundred and twenty a day. Plus expenses.'*

'And I want a full background check by seven a.m. Parents, childhood, police, the lot.'

'Tomorrow morning? You're off your—'

'Thought you said you were good.'

There was no sign of the night porter as I popped behind the reception desk and searched through the keys on their hooks. Three-one-four was missing. Which meant Dr Fred Docherty probably had it on him. One key, right at the bottom of the rack, had a red leather fob with the word 'Master' on it.

'Not exactly giving me a lot of time, are you?' A sigh. *'I'll see what I can do. No promises though.'*

I grabbed the master key, limped to the elevators and thumbed the button.

'When I checked with your employers they said you weren't as gormless as the nurses' halls made you look. I'm trusting you not to screw this up. Because if you do, we're going to be having words, understand?'

'*I told you, it wasn't my fault. A job like that should've had—*'

'And this is strictly between us. Nothing goes through the company books. You report to me, and if anyone asks you're just taking a couple of days off for personal reasons. Tell them you've got the norovirus or something; there's a lot of it going around.'

Ping – the lift doors slid open, bringing a wash of Vivaldi's 'Four Seasons' with them.

'*Done.*'

I pressed the button for the third floor. The lift whirred and clunked its way up the building as I pinned the phone between my shoulder and my ear and snapped on a pair of blue nitrile gloves. 'I want to know where he goes, who he talks to, if he's got a lock-up, or a house somewhere.'

'*I'll be all over him like plukes on a teenager.*'

Ping – the doors opened on a tartan-floored corridor. A sign on the wall: '← Rooms 301–312 ~ Rooms 313–336 →'

The corridor to the right took a dogleg, then up a couple of steps.

'You see anything dodgy, you call me. You don't touch anything, you don't go charging in, you call me.'

'*Yeah, yeah, I know the—*'

'Say it.'

A sigh. '*I call you.*'

'Good.' I took out the master key. No sign of light seeping out under the door of 314, so either Dr Docherty was already asleep, or he was out. 'Now shut up for a minute.'

The key slid into the lock. Turned delicate and slow. Then *click*. I eased the door open.

The curtains hadn't been closed properly, letting in a thin wash of yellow light that leached the colour out of the room, turning the tartan carpet monochrome.

Bed was still made, the blanket tucked in tight, a room-service menu on one of the pillows. Nice room. Big enough for a small couch and a coffee table by the window. Spotless.

Back to the phone. 'I want you outside the Pinemantle Hotel on Porter Lane from half five at the latest.'

'*And you want a full background tonight as well? You have heard of sleep, haven't you?*'

'Time for that when you're dead.' I hung up and slipped the phone back in my pocket.

One bedside cabinet had nothing but a Gideon Bible and a hairdryer in it, the other was neatly layered with socks and pants. The narrow drawer under the desk was stuffed with all the usual hotel information bumph – folders, binders, and leaflets. Nothing under the bed. Bathroom: a stick deodorant, pink toilet bag, toothbrush in a plastic holder, toothpaste, floss, two tubs of hair gel, bottle of aftershave.

The wardrobe hid a red wheelie suitcase. I hauled it out and had a rummage inside. A Tesco carrier-bag full of dirty underwear sat in one corner, a couple of books in the netting pouches built into the lid. There was a solid, zipped compartment above them. I eased it open.

Well, well… I reached in and pulled out three pairs of black lacy thongs. A scarlet lipstick was next, then a pair of dangly silver earrings with blue stones in them, and right at the bottom: a push-up bra.

I sat back on my haunches. So, maybe he liked to dress up and become Susan at the weekends? Didn't prove anything. They all went back where they came from.

The two suits, three shirts, and the overcoat hanging in the wardrobe got a quick search, then I was back out in the corridor, as if nothing had ever happened.

Locked the door again.

Stood there, frowning at the wood.

Docherty wasn't likely to leave anything incriminating lying about in his hotel room, was he? Housekeeping would find it. He wasn't thick, after all…

*   *   *

399

Retching echoed out from the open bathroom door of the adjoining room. Alice's feet stuck out at right angles to each other, white socks twitching as she heaved.

She'd only been in it twenty minutes and her hotel room already looked like a teenager's bedroom. Clothes all over the floor, more on the chair, the bed rumpled, papers spread all over the little desk.

Her socks twitched again.

'You're a disaster...' I picked up the jeans, folded them and draped them over the back of the chair. Hung the jacket up in the wardrobe, and the stripy tops. Picked up the scattered socks and underwear. Put them back in the suitcase. Stuck it in the corner.

Alice groaned, then appeared in the doorway. Pink pyjamas buttoned up wrong. Her hair hung in a lank curtain, covering her face. 'Urrgh...'

'Well, whose fault is that?'

'Where were you? I ... I needed ... someone ... hold my hair.'

I pulled back one side of the blankets. 'Did you drink a pint of water?'

'Bounced.' She shuffled over and collapsed, face-down onto the bed. 'Where were you?'

'Had to hand some keys in at reception. You want to be sick again?'

'Urgh...'

Her legs were like lead as I rolled her round the right way. Folded the blankets back over her. Then fetched the hotel bin and put it beside the bed.

'You're going to end up with liver failure, that what you want?'

'Urrrrrrgh...'

'Thought so.' I paced to the window and pulled the curtain back a couple of inches. A car drifted by on Porter Lane, headlights picking out the bones of trees. 'What would you say if someone suggested Dr Docherty might be the Inside Man?'

'I'd … I'd say … leave me alone … I want … to die.'

The branches trembled, and a fistful of rain beat itself to death against the window. 'He's the right age, he ticks all the boxes you were talking about, and he's on the inside, isn't he? Can't *get* more inside than he is.'

'It's a bit… He can't be the … Inside Man … he's … he's a knob.'

The curtains fell back into place. 'What, serial nut-jobs can't be knobs?'

'He… He…' She squinted at the ceiling. 'What do we … do we know about his … background? Does… Does he have a mother? Well, of course he's got a mother, but is she alive and did she beat him when he was little, and why's the room going round like that, make it stop!'

I brushed the hair from her damp face, leaned in and kissed her on the forehead. 'Your breath's minging, by the way.'

'What if … what if it's not him? What if we go chasing … chasing after … and Dave…'

'He fits your profile, that's all. We're not abandoning everything else.'

She wobbled a hand at the adjoining door. 'Leave … leave it open?'

'Promise.' I turned out the bedside lamp. Now the only light was what filtered through from my room. 'No booze tomorrow, OK?'

'Ash?'

'What?'

'If I hadn't seen you … seen you carrying Paul Manson's body … off into the … the woods… Why … why did you lie to me?'

'When Rebecca's guinea pig died, we hid the body and told her it'd gone away to live on a farm. Didn't want its death to darken her.' I picked at the handle of my cane, scraping

401

back a patina of varnish with my thumbnail. 'Suppose it was a bit like that...'

Silence.

'Alice?'

'Thank you for trying...' Her voice was little more than a fuzzy mumble in the darkness. 'Ash? If ... Dr Docherty is ... is the Inside Man, then ... then ... why start again, after all this time? Eight ... eight years, nothing, just like that.'

'Go to sleep.'

'Maybe ... maybe he... Maybe he misses the screaming?'

43

A permatanned guy in a suit waved his hand across the map of Scotland. *'Unfortunately, that area of high pressure means the rain's going to be with us till at least the end of the week, and—'* I killed the sound and moved to the window. Pulled back the curtains, phone pressed against my ear.

A battered Audi was just visible through the bare beech trees.

'That you in the blue estate?'

Rock-Hammer Robertson grunted. *'Since half five. You want this background check or not?'*

'Go on then.'

'Dr Frederic Joshua Docherty, thirty-five, graduated from Edinburgh University with an MA in psychology—'

'What about his childhood?'

'Born to Steven and Isabella Docherty in Stirling. Middle child of three. Elder sister killed in a car crash when he was six. Younger brother did two years for possession with intent. Fred was referred to Social Services twice – once for a broken arm, and once for setting fire to a derelict house. He was eight.'

Through in the other room, the sounds of groaning and moaning were interspersed with the occasional swearword and promise never to drink again.

'Don't suppose he tortured any animals, did he? Family pets – something like that?'

'*Not that I could find. Married Sylvia Burns six years ago, been divorced for eighteen months. Can't find out why till the solicitors' open at nine, but going by his ex-wife's blog it's got something to do with sex.*'

Not bad, considering he'd only got the job in the wee small hours.

I tapped a finger against the glass. 'Got to admit I'm impressed, Rock-Hammer.'

'*Alistair. Not Rock-Hammer. I left him behind last time I got out.*'

Sure he did.

'... drug raids in Kingsmeath, so stay out of their way till noon.' The duty sergeant checked his clipboard, voice droning out through the crowded room. 'Next up – Charlie Pearce. We've got one dog unit going into Moncuir Wood this morning, and another searching the Swinney.' He turned to Detective Superintendent Ness. 'Super?'

She stood, shrugged off the black suit jacket and picked up a stack of paper. The purple bags under her eyes were clearly visible through the makeup. 'Charlie Pearce has now been missing for over twenty-four hours, statistically that means we're probably now looking at a murder enquiry. I – do – not – want – this – getting – out. Are we clear? The family has enough to worry about. I catch *anyone* talking to the media and I'll make the Spanish Inquisition look like a Chuckle Brothers tribute act. DS Massie, DCs Clark, Webster, and Tarbert – you'll report to me for assignments after we're finished.'

Alice slumped further down against my shoulder. 'I think I'm dying...'

'Don't be such a baby.'

Sitting in the back row, Professor Huntly had his mobile phone out, poking away at the screen with his thumbs. Dr

Constantine was knitting what looked like a Shetland sweater. While Jacobson scribbled notes in a black A4 pad.

'Why did you let me drink so much?'

'You're a grown woman, and I'm not your mum.'

The duty sergeant pointed a remote at the ceiling projector and the screen behind him filled with a familiar face. Hooked nose, high forehead, hair swept back from his head.

Something tightened in my stomach.

'Paul Manson: reported missing by his wife last night. Probably holed up somewhere with a mistress, but just in case – keep an eye out, OK?' The sergeant poked the remote again and CCTV footage replaced Manson's face.

Oh God, they had us on film abducting him…

The duty sergeant grinned. 'I think you might enjoy this.'

But it wasn't Larbert Avenue on the footage, it was a section of pavement and road beneath some sort of canopy. No sound, picture only – the camera high up, looking down on a bald bloke in a dressing gown smoking a cigarette and talking on his mobile phone.

A nurse walked past.

'Wait for it…'

A black 4x4 lurched to a halt beneath the camera. The passenger door swung open and a figure was shoved out: Mrs Kerrigan. She tumbled to the ground and lay there, sprawled on her back, her right arm stretched towards the smoker.

Mr Dressing Gown dropped his cigarette and backed away.

Wee Free should've killed her when he had the chance.

Nurses burst into view. Bustled around. Shouted in silence. Then someone turned up with a wheelie porter's chair and they bundled her inside.

The duty sergeant pressed another button and the screen went blank. 'At quarter to ten last night, one Mrs Maeve Kerrigan was unceremoniously dumped outside Castle Hill Infirmary A-and-E. Some kind soul shot her in the foot, then gouged one of her eyes out.'

A ripple of laughter was punctuated with a couple of gasps and the occasional, 'Bloody hell. Someone's not feart.'

He held up a hand. 'Because it's a gunshot wound, the hospital had to inform us. We will, of course, be treating this as a serious assault and pursuing the culprits to the fullest extent of the law. I don't want to hear any talk about giving the guy a medal or buying him drinks, OK? Bad enough as it is.'

A couple of people turned in their seats to stare at me.

Brilliant. As if things weren't bad enough.

Why the hell did Wee Free have to shoot her in the foot? Now Andy Inglis would think I had something to do with it. Or he would as soon as the briefing was over and his pet police officers got on the phone.

Ness was on her feet again. 'All right, that's enough. Settle down.'

She waited till there was silence. 'The Inside Man, slash, Unsub-Fifteen. We got a nine-nine-nine call at three seventeen this morning.' She held out her hand and the Duty Sergeant passed her the remote.

It hurt, but I crossed my fingers as crackling hissed out of the speakers. *Please* let it not be Jessica McFee. Not another pre-recorded message by a victim with her stomach slit open. Don't make it too late to save her.

Because if she was dead then so was Shifty.

A woman's voice: '*Emergency Services, which service do you require?*'

The man who answered could barely catch his breath, the words broken and jagged. '*She's gone! She's missing. I … it was … and I went through … and she was* gone *and you've got to help me find her!*'

'*Who's missing, sir, is—*'

'*My wife. She's gone… Oh God, what if he's got her?*'

'*All right, sir, calm down, give me your address and we'll get officers right to you.*'

'*It's Thirteen Camburn View Crescent, in Shortstaine. Strachan. Laura Strachan. She's pregnant!*'

'*I'm going to put you on hold for a second while I get a car dispatched. Stay on the line for me—*'

Ness lowered the remote. 'Three patrol cars are going street to street in Shortstaine broadcasting Laura's description. Scenes Examination Branch are sweeping the house. Do I really need to tell anyone how much of a cocking disaster this is?'

Alice scrubbed her face with her hands. Voice low. 'Focus. Come on, you can do this.'

Ness pointed. 'Dr Docherty?'

Dr Frederic Docherty stood, smoothed two hands down the front of his suit jacket. 'Thank you, Detective Superintendent.' He turned a smile on the crowd. 'Clearly we have to assume that the Inside Man has begun abducting his former victims. We have three possibilities here. One: he feels his ownership of these individuals has been threatened by the actions of Unsub-Fifteen. By copying the Inside Man's MO, Unsub-Fifteen is stealing his thunder, threatening his legacy.'

Alice shifted in her chair, face scrunched up in a frown, head tilted to one side.

'Two: Unsub-Fifteen has decided to lay claim to that legacy, not just by adopting the Inside Man's MO, but by taking his victims as well.'

She snorted. Gave her head a little shake.

'Three: Unsub-Fifteen has been the Inside Man the whole time, and he's taking the opportunity to wipe the slate clean. Dispose of the survivors and start again from scratch. This plays into his narcissistic belief in his own power and authority.' Docherty gave the duty sergeant a cue, and the screen filled with scrawled handwriting on a yellow legal pad. 'Given the letter published in the *Castle News and Post* this morning, this is the preferred scenario. You'll notice the reference in here to a "sacrificial offering", and—'

'Oh for goodness' sake...'

407

Up at the front, Dr Docherty scowled. 'You have something to contribute, Doctor?'

Alice wobbled to her feet, holding onto the chair in front. 'Why would he do that? Why would he want to dispose of Laura Strachan, she's his only success.'

Docherty looked at the ceiling for a second, before staring back at her, one eyebrow raised. 'Because, Doctor, she's *isn't*. Laura Strachan, Marie Jordan, and Ruth Laughlin all survived the procedure, so it's clear his success rate is—'

'Laura's the only one who achieved pregnancy. Impregnating them with the dolls is all about that, about putting a baby in their tummies, Laura Strachan is—'

'Nonsense, the Strachan pregnancy is nothing to do with the Inside Man.' Docherty's smile was back, his voice like someone talking to a small child. 'It's been eight years since he,' Docherty made inverted quotes with his fingers, '"impregnated" her. Rather a long gestation period, don't you think?'

Alice pinched the bridge of her nose. Spoke slowly and clearly. 'Yes, for a normal *rational* adult, but would you call the Inside Man normal and rational? This is all about laying claim to Laura Strachan's—'

'Well, *Doctor* McDonald, you'll excuse me if I don't share your complacency.' He stuck his nose in the air. 'The Inside Man is targeting his previous victims. We need to place a guard on both Marie Jordan and Ruth Laughlin, assuming it's not already too late.'

'Yes, fine, get a guard on them, but you're missing the point. He—'

'*I'm* missing the point? Sit down, Doctor, you're embarrassing yourself.'

Alice glared back. 'Why don't you—'

'All right, that's enough.' Ness was on her feet again. 'Dr McDonald, you'll have your chance to register any concerns after the meeting. Dr Docherty, continue.'

Alice stayed where she was.

Ness sighed. 'Sit *down*, Doctor.'

She glanced at me, then thumped into her seat. Arms crossed, legs too. Bottom lip pulled in by her teeth.

Up front, Docherty grinned, then wiped it from his face. 'The Inside Man is on the path of escalation from serial to spree killer. Given the timings between Claire Young and Jessica McFee's abductions, it's clear we're going to see another victim go missing either today or tomorrow. Which means we need to get a warning out to every nurse in the city.'

I put a hand on Alice's arm, but she shook it off. Glowered at the floor tiles. Her eyes glittered in the strip-lights' lifeless glow.

Ness nodded. 'Agreed. DS Stephen – liaise with media, I want a press release ready to go by nine. Next.' She held up a tabloid red-top.

Half the front page was taken up with photos of Claire Young and Jessica McFee, beneath the headline 'Is "INSIDE MAN" POLICE SICKO?'

A groan went up.

Someone near the front: 'God's sake, not this *again*.'

Ness hurled the paper out into the room. It broke apart, mid-air, and fluttered down as individual sheets. 'How did the bloody *Scottish Sun* get hold of it? It's all in there – the missing evidence, the letters, the screwed up HOLMES data. EVERYTHING!'

No one volunteered.

She jabbed a finger towards the back of the room. '*Mr* Henderson.'

I levered myself out of my chair. 'Before you ask: no I sodding didn't.'

'You said the HOLMES data from the original investigation was a mess.'

'According to our computer guy, there was no way it was ever going to come up with a sensible action – everything's misfiled and referenced incorrectly. It's a not a mess, it's a total sodding farce.'

'Well, *my*-computer guy tracked down the user ID for the entries, and guess who's responsible.'

Oh no... It would be my user ID, wouldn't it? Whoever it was, they'd hacked my ID and used it to screw up every entry in the HOLMES database to make sure, when it came out, I was the one who got the blame.

Son of a bitch.

My chin came up. 'Now you wait a sodding—'

'Sergeant Thomas Greenwood.' Ness raised her hands, as if she was about to bless the congregation.

Another groan from CID.

Knight and the guys from the Specialist Crime Division just shrugged at each other.

Who the hell was Thomas Greenwood?

DS Brigstock turned a grimace in my direction. 'AKA: Thom Dumb, Thicky Greenwood, and Sergeant Tommy Two-Planks.'

Tommy Two-Planks – a scrawny halfwit, devoid of common sense and blessed with the ability to turn a minor irritation into a catastrophic disaster. How he managed to pass his sergeant's exam was anyone's guess. 'Who the hell put him in charge of the HOLMES suite?'

Ness nodded. 'And do you know where Sergeant Greenwood is now? He's not out there cutting nurses open, he's in a hospice in Dundee with early-onset Alzheimer's.' She turned her back on the room. 'So you can remove that from your list of conspiracy theories, Mr Henderson. Now sit down.'

No chance. 'That doesn't explain the missing productions. Someone's—'

'SIT – DOWN!'

Pretty much the whole room flinched, but I stayed where I was.

Alice reached up and tugged at my sleeve. Her chin trembled as she mouthed the word, 'Please...'

410

I stared at the back of Ness's head.

OK. For Alice.

The seat creaked under me as I settled back into it.

Ness rolled her shoulders, then stared up at the projector screen. 'This division leaks like a punctured lung, and every time it does, it takes oxygen from the investigation. It *suffocates* our efforts to get Jessica McFee back. Whoever's talking to the press will stop. Now. Or you can consider yourself person-ally responsible for her death.'

Silence.

'It – stops – now.'

'... deeply disappointed by your behaviour.' Detective Superintendent Knight leaned in, looming over Alice as the assembled troops shuffled out of Morning Prayers. Narrowed his eyes. 'Are you hungover? Is this how you think forensic psychologists are supposed to behave? Is it?'

She pulled a manila folder from her satchel and held it out. 'If you'll just *look* at the behavioural evidence analysis, you can—'

'Clearly, you have no grasp of the case and no business criticizing Dr Docherty who *does*. I was perfectly prepared to support Detective Superintendent Jacobson's LIRU initiative, but it's becoming obvious my trust has been misplaced.'

'The Inside Man letters aren't—'

'That,' he pointed at Dr Docherty, standing in the corner with Ness, both on their mobile phones, 'is what a *professional* forensic psychologist looks like. I don't know what amateur outfits you're used to dealing with, but Police Scotland will not tolerate incompetence.'

'All right, that's enough.' I put a hand in the middle of his chest and pushed him back. Getting him out of Alice's face. 'If you've got a problem with people challenging your precious little team, you can pack up your toys and sod off back to Strathclyde. But you *never* speak to Alice like that again.'

411

He glared. 'Get – your – hand – off – me.'

A voice came from the other side of the room. 'Carl?' Docherty strode across the room, a beaming smile on his face, Ness following right behind him.

Knight brushed a hand down his dress jacket, as if I'd left dirty fingerprints on it. 'Yes, Frederic?'

Docherty's smile cranked up another inch. 'Ah, *Dr* McDonald, so glad you're here to hear this. Detective Superintendent Ness sent cars to check on Ruth Laughlin and Marie Jordan. Guess what they found.'

Ness nodded. 'Marie Jordan is still in the secure facility, but the team who went round to Ruth Laughlin's flat found the front door open and the place ransacked. She's missing.'

'Well…' Alice licked her lips. 'Maybe she's—'

'They say they found a small plastic key ring in the middle of the bedroom floor. Little plastic baby. Yale key. He's taken her back.'

Alice's head fell. 'I see.'

'Oh, I don't doubt you mean well, Dr McDonald, but sometimes it's best to leave these things to those with older, wiser heads, don't you think?'

'Excuse me.' She squeezed past, and shuffled out the door.

Docherty clapped his hands together. 'It's not her fault. She's young. Dealing with this kind of case takes experience.'

Ness sniffed, then pulled out her phone and marched off. 'No, I do not want to talk to the husband, give me the search team leader…'

A pause. Docherty shot his cuffs. Straightened his tie. 'Well, if you'll excuse me, I have to record a piece to camera for Sky News.'

He swaggered away, leaving Knight and me alone.

Knight stuck his chest out. 'I think you'll find your position becoming rapidly untenable here, Mr Henderson. Both you and your amateur psychologist friend.'

I stepped in close. 'The only reason you and Dr Dick aren't slumped in the corner right now, picking up your teeth, is that I've got a killer to catch.' His cheek was smooth and shiny as I patted it. 'But as soon as I've done that...'

44

A couple of the strip-lights clicked and pinged, flickering in the dusty gloom. From somewhere deep inside the archives, hidden behind the metal shelves packed with boxes, came the sound of a murmured conversation.

I limped deeper into the maze.

Left. Right. Left again – PC Simpson appeared around the corner, flinched and staggered to a halt, eyes wide.

He leaned on one of the shelves, puffing. Belly wobbling with each breath. 'You trying to give me a heart attack?'

'She here?'

He hooked a thumb over his shoulder. 'Next right, keep going past the poll tax riots, and right again. And be nice to her, OK?'

Then he squeezed past and disappeared into the darkness.

She was exactly where he said she'd be.

Alice sat, cross-legged on the floor, surrounded by open file boxes, leafing through a stack of forms, shoulders trembling. A sniff. Then she ground the palm of her hand into her eye socket. 'I'm sorry.'

'Don't be, he's a—'

'Detective Superintendent Knight's right.'

'He's a dick. And so's Docherty.'

Another sniff. 'I don't have a grasp on the case. Dr Docherty said the Inside Man was after his old victims and I said no. But he was, wasn't he? Dr Docherty was right and I was wrong.'

I hooked my cane on a shelf and squatted down in front of her. 'What if he got it right because he did it? Because *he* abducted them?'

She looked up at me, eyes all pink and puffy. 'What am I doing here, Ash? I'm out of my depth. I'm useless and horrible and I shouldn't be on the case, and if Henry and Dr Docherty couldn't catch the Inside Man what...' Her shoulders trembled. 'What chance did ... did I ... ever have?'

'Come on, don't do this.' I leaned forward and pulled her against me. Her hair smelled of hotel shampoo and stale Jack Daniel's. Her forehead hot against my neck. I gave her a squeeze. 'Shhh... It's just the PTSD talking, like you said. Maybe you should have some of that MDMA? Go play a violent video game, or something?'

'I shouldn't be—'

'You're the cleverest person I know; you shouldn't be doing yourself down like this.' I pulled away, brushed the hair from her face. 'Docherty's a prick, that's all there is to it.'

She sniffed and nodded. Heeled the tears from her eyes again. Managed a little smile. 'Being hungover doesn't help...'

I sat on the ground, stretched my legs out. Pointed at all the files and paperwork. 'So where do we go from here?'

Simpson lumbered out of the shadows, with a mug in one hand and a green paper towel in the other. 'Here.' He handed them both to Alice. 'Tea. And some gingersnaps.'

She held the mug against her chest. 'Thank you, Allan.'

I raised an eyebrow. 'Where's mine?'

'You're not upset. And I'm not a bloody teaboy.' He nudged the archive box next to me with his boot. 'I hope you're going to put all this back where you found it, Henderson. Place is bad enough as it is.'

'Like it'd make any difference. Your domain's a disaster area, Simpson, you should be ashamed of yourself.'

He leaned his elbow against a shelf. 'And don't get me started on them tossers from Operation Tiger-Sodding-Balm.' Both hands came up, elbows jammed into his sides, fingers wiggling as his voice jumped up half an octave. '"Oh, we're the Specialist Crime Division, we don't need to sign things in and out, we're so sexy!" Tossers. Come on, is it really that hard to check the damn box out, then check it back in again? What's the point of having procedures if no bugger pays any attention to them?'

I leaned back, drummed my fingers on the lid of a file box. 'Who's been messing with the boxes? All of Knight's team? Just some of them?'

Simpson puffed his cheeks out. 'Let's see... I've caught that DI Foot down here rummaging through stuff more than once, and DS Grohl...'

'What about Dr Docherty?'

'Pffff... He's the worst of the lot. Soon as the MIT got called in he was down here digging about like a kid in a sandbox. No respect, any of them.' Simpson straightened up. 'Anyway, some of us have work to do.' He turned and stamped off into the maze. 'And make sure you put everything back where you got it.'

I swung the Suzuki around the roundabout and into Shortstaine. Into the rows of identical cookie-cutter houses in pale brick and pantiles. Cul-de-sacs and twee road names. Labradors and 4x4s.

Alice slapped a hand down on the papers in her lap, holding them in place. 'I know he's in a position to skew the profile away from himself, but—'

'And he's always talking up the letters. He had unsupervised access to the archives. Every time you disagree with him, he tries to make it look as if you don't know what you're talking about, or he buries your opinion.'

'That doesn't mean he's the Inside Man.' She smiled at me,

squeezed my arm. 'It's sweet, but you don't have to make him a suspect, just because he was mean to me.'

'I paid his room a visit last night, while you were bringing up your dinner. No sign of him. Bed was still made.'

She turned over another sheet, 'Well … maybe he's got a lover in town?'

'He's got panties and a bra in his suitcase. Lipstick and earrings too.'

Left onto Camburn View Avenue – the woods loomed between the houses, their tips catching the sun as it struggled through the dove-grey clouds.

'That doesn't mean he can't have a lover.'

I glanced across and she shifted in her seat.

She shrugged. 'What? Transvestites need love too.'

Right into Camburn View Crescent. A pair of patrol cars sat a third of the way down the road, the SEB's dented Transit van parked between them.

'Thought you'd be banging on about him having identity disorder issues and putting on a fake face.'

She frowned as I pulled in behind the second patrol car. 'Well, the need to adopt a different personality would fit in with the revised profile. And the persona he displays professionally fits the power-obsessed narcissist exposed in the letters…' A hand drifted up to fiddle with her hair. 'Are we really considering him as a viable suspect?'

'Thinking about it.'

More twiddling. 'What do we know about his childhood?'

'Social Services got called in twice. Once for wilful fire-raising, and once because they thought his parents were beating him. Wife divorced him for something sexual, don't know what yet.' But him wearing women's underwear probably featured in there somewhere.

The frown deepened, pulling wrinkles around her eyes. 'Arson's a typical indicator of psychological problems, and if his parents were abusive… Can we see the reports?'

I opened the door and climbed out. My breath fogged in the shadow of the homes. 'Someone's working on it.'

She stuffed all the papers back into her satchel and followed me down the pavement to the cordon of blue-and-white 'POLICE' tape. The same plukey officer from Monday was guarding the line. His eyes goldfished, and he snapped to attention. 'Guv.'

'No sausage roll today, Constable Hill?'

His hand flinched up and wiped imaginary crumbs from his fluorescent yellow waistcoat. 'Sorry, sir.' He licked his lips. Then pulled up the tape so Alice could duck underneath.

I nodded towards the house. 'They find anything yet?'

He leaned in and dropped his voice to a whisper. 'One of those little plastic baby key rings. It was in the back door.'

Another constable made us sign in before she'd let us into the house.

Inside, almost every surface was covered by a thin patina of silver or black dust, clear rectangles marking where prints had been lifted with tape. The lock was intact, no splintered wood.

Raised voices came from upstairs – '*You should be out there finding her!*'

'*We're doing everything we can, sir, please, you need to calm down, OK? Deep breaths.*'

No sign of anything broken in the lounge, or the kitchen. A stack of mugs and plates were lined up on the draining board, all covered with fingerprint powder. In the daylight, the window overlooked a postage-stamp garden with a bird table in one corner and a whirly washing drier.

An SEB tech was just outside, on his knees at the open back door, dusting the white UPVC with amido black, earbuds in – nodding in time to whatever the music was.

I tapped him on the shoulder and he nearly fell off the step. 'Gah! Don't *do* that!'

'Where's the key fob?'

He pointed at the stainless-steel flight case in the middle of the floor. 'Doesn't fit the lock though. Well, you know, it goes in, but it won't turn.'

'You try it in the front?'

'Doesn't fit there either.' He sat back on his haunches. 'You here to talk to the husband?'

'Any sign of a struggle? Break-in?'

'No so much as a squint picture on the walls.'

'Don't forget to check the flowerbeds for footprints.' I headed back through into the hall. Stopped. Lowered my voice as the argument continued upstairs. 'She knew him. She came downstairs, she opened the door, and she went with him. Didn't put up a fight.'

Alice looked up the stairs. 'Would she know Dr Docherty?'

'You don't understand: she's pregnant. Pregnant!' The voice got louder. *'What if he hurts our baby?'*

'He was her therapist for a while, after the attacks.'

Laura's husband – what was it, Christopher? – appeared at the top of the stairs. Both hands were linked over the back of his head, as if he was trying to pull it into his chest. 'He can't hurt our baby. You've got no idea how *hard* it was to get this far!'

A uniformed officer emerged behind him. She'd ditched the fluorescent waistcoat and the stabproof vest, her black fleece hanging open – showing off the black T-shirt under-neath. 'We're only trying to help. Maybe there's someone you could call? A friend, or relative?'

Christopher turned all the way around, mouth pinched tight shut... Then he stopped and stared at me. 'You.'

I nodded. 'Any chance we can have a word?'

I let the curtain fall back into place. 'That's Sky TV arrived.' Making it four TV crews, half a dozen photographers, and a handful of journalists.

Christopher sat on the edge of the bed, folded forward so

his chest rested on his knees, still pulling his head down. 'Why can't they just go out and *look* for her?'

Alice sat down next to him and placed a hand on his shoulder. 'It's not your fault.'

'Of course it is. I'm supposed to look after her. I *promised.*' A shudder. 'Especially after last time…'

I leaned back against the windowsill. 'Who else knew you were living here?'

His head came up. 'No one. Not even my mum knows where we are. We run this place like something out of a spy movie. Laura…' His head went down again, voice wobbling. 'She doesn't want anyone to find us.'

Alice gave the shoulder a little rub. 'Has she been seeing anyone for her anxiety? A doctor? Or maybe a therapist?'

'She did all that years ago. She's not paranoid, she's just… She wants us to be careful, that's all.'

Not careful enough.

I took out my notepad. 'When did you notice she was missing?'

A sigh rippled through him. 'We've been sleeping in different rooms for a couple of weeks. She's too hot, with the baby, and she needs to spread out. When I got up to pee at three, her light was on. Sometimes she falls asleep with a book, so I went in to switch it off, and she wasn't there.' He rocked forwards and backwards, making the bed creak. 'I checked everywhere. Going room to room, switching on all the lights. Ran up and down the streets, shouting for her. Oh God…'

'So you last saw her…?'

'I took her up a cup of camomile tea at eleven before I went to bed.' He picked at the duvet, wrapping the cover around his fingers.

Alice looked at me, face pinched, then back to him. 'Christopher, I know this is going to be difficult, but if you keep focusing on what happened last time, it's going to eat you.'

420

'What if you can't find her?'

'We'll find her. But I need you to understand that just because she was raped and cut open last time, there's no reason to... What's wrong?'

He stiffened. Sat up. 'Raped?'

Alice pulled her chin in. 'When she was abducted?'

'She wasn't raped! Who said she was raped?'

Alice nodded, kept her hand on his shoulder. 'A lot of rape victims don't tell their partners. Sometimes they feel guilty – even though there's nothing to feel guilty about – it's not their fault, it's—'

'She would've *told* me.' He folded back over again. 'We don't keep secrets from each other. Ever.'

The media scrum faded in the rear-view mirror, then disappeared as we turned back onto Camburn View Avenue. On the radio, an old Foo Fighters song clattered to a halt, and the pips filled the car. *'It's nine o'clock and you're listening to Castlewave FM. News now, and we're joined in the studio by Dr Frederic Docherty. Dr Docherty—'*

I turned off the radio.

Alice ran her hands around the wheel. 'Maybe he *didn't* rape her eight years ago?'

'Why wouldn't he rape her? He raped Ruth Laughlin.'

She took us out onto the main road, heading for Cowskillin. 'Or maybe he didn't rape her till after she was drugged?'

'Perhaps he couldn't get it up? Or there wasn't time? Or perhaps she just didn't tell Christopher? Misplaced guilt, like you said. Or—' The phone in my pocket rang – not the official one, the burner. I dug the thing out. Pressed the button. 'What?'

Wee Free McFee's voice snarled out of the earpiece. *'You found my little girl yet?'*

'We're looking.'

'Tick-tock, Henderson. Tick-tock. Your fat friend's not looking so good.'

421

'He needs a doctor.'

'And I need my daughter. You remember how that feels, don't you? Knowing she's out there and some bastard's got her?'

Houses and shops swept by as Alice took the turning marked 'CITY STADIUM'. The First National Celtic Church spire rose above the houses. A drop of rain spattered against the windscreen.

'You still there, Henderson?'

'We're going as fast as we can, OK? As soon as we've got something I'll call you.'

'Your fat friend's only got one eye, doesn't need two ears as well, does he? Why don't I stick one in the post for you?'

'We're...' I closed my eyes and dunked my head off the window. Held it there. The road vibrations burred into my skull. 'I remember what it feels like. We're doing everything we can. We're *going* as fast as we can. We'll find her.'

'You better.'

45

Down on the street below, a single patrol car sat outside Ruth Laughlin's building, its blue-and-whites spinning, catching the falling rain and turning it into sapphires and diamonds.

There might have been a media scrum outside Laura Strachan's place, but, so far, not so much as a photographer from the local rag had turned up here.

But then Laura had always been the popular one. Most people couldn't even name the other two survivors, let alone the four women who died eight years ago.

I backed away from the bedroom window.

The mattress was half off the double bed. All the drawers were pulled out of the chest by the door. The wardrobe lay open and emptied. Skirts and jackets and trousers littered the floor, mixed in with socks and pants. The photos on the walls sat in crooked frames, the glass cracked.

Alice settled onto the edge of the bed frame, her purple nitrile gloves squeaking as she wrung her hands together. 'He's going to kill David, isn't he?'

'Looks as if someone went through the place with a base-ball bat.' I bent and picked a teddy bear from the floor. He was ancient and grey, almost no fur left, the chest patched together like Frankenstein's monster. I put him on top of the chest of drawers, back to the wall so he wouldn't fall over.

A uniformed constable stuck his head around the door: big ears and a squint nose, hair cut so short it was barely there. 'Just checked with the downstairs neighbour. Old fart's deaf as a post – didn't hear anything suspicious.'

'Why haven't they dusted for prints?'

He pulled his shoulders up around his ears. 'SEB are all round Laura Strachan's place. Got to wait till they're done there. Cutbacks and that.'

Alice stood. 'The Inside Man turns up at Laura Strachan's house and she goes with him without so much as a whimper. What's different here? Why the struggle?'

The hall was littered with coats. I picked my way between them and into the lounge. Both of the armchairs lay on their backs. Whoever took Ruth had ripped the cushions out of the couch – stuffing prolapsed through slashes in the brown corduroy. The three-bar electric fire was dead, the TV face-down in front of the window.

'What if Ruth recognized him for who he really was?' I scuffed a toe through the broken glass of a clip-frame. 'She wouldn't go without a fight. Not after last time.'

The sound of heavy metal music thrummed through the floor beneath my feet. No wonder the guy downstairs was deaf.

I did a slow three-sixty. Frowned at the opened sideboard, the broken dishes and paperbacks lying crumpled on the floor. 'He was looking for something. He ransacked the place, then smashed everything.'

The kitchen was the same, and the bathroom too – the contents of the medicine cupboard strewn across the floor.

Alice squatted down by the bath and poked through the bottles and jars. Then frowned up at me. 'Her antidepressants are missing. She told me she'd just got her prescription for Nortriptyline refilled. Should be at least three or four boxes here.'

'Why would he want her antidepressants?'

'Well … mix Nortriptyline with alcohol and it's a pretty good sedative?'

'He's got access to surgical anaesthetics, why would he— God's sake. What now?' I pulled my mobile out and pressed the button. 'Henderson.'

The voice on the other end was low, twitchy, as if she was trying not to be overheard. *'We're screwed. We're all* totally *screwed!'*

I pulled back and stared at the screen. Wasn't a number I knew. 'Who is this?'

'You need to get over to Carrick Gardens, now. Virginia Cunningham's house. He's dead: we need to get our stories straight. Oh, we are so screwed...' And then she was gone.

I stuck the phone back in my pocket.

Virginia Cunningham – your friendly neighbourhood pregnant child abuser.

Alice stared at me. 'What?'

'No idea. Get in the car.'

DC Nenova was waiting for us at the front door, huddling out of the rain. It hurtled down from a heavy grey sky, pummelling the garden flat.

She shifted her feet, glanced back over her shoulder. 'It's not our fault, it wasn't as if anyone knew, how could we? It's...' Nenova licked her lips. 'We just need to all calm down and work out what we're going to do. Right?'

Alice peered past her, into the house. Holding the umbrella in both hands as it trembled in the downpour. 'Is everything all right?'

'Of course it's not all right: we're screwed.' Nenova turned and marched off down the hall, got to the end and started back again. 'We didn't know, OK? How could we know?'

I stepped inside. The lounge door was open – her partner, McKevitt, sat in the middle of the couch, knees together, shoulders hunched, one leg twitching like it was marking time to a death-metal beat. The bitter-sharp smell of sick rolled out of the room. He looked up as we passed. 'It's not our fault...'

Alice thumped the front door shut and propped her dripping umbrella in the corner. 'Ash, what's going on?'

'No idea.'

Nenova turned the corner and paused between the bathroom and the bedroom door, pacing the corridor's width, one hand up to her mouth, biting at the skin around her nails. 'We just need to get our stories straight, that's all. It'll be fine. We just—'

I grabbed her. 'What the hell is this?'

She shook my hand free. 'We...' A glance at the bedroom door. 'We came to search the place for more video tapes, or laptops, or photographs of kids. Should've done it yesterday, but they've cut the unit and we've got three officers off on the stress, and we've got a massive load to monitor and it's not our fault!'

God's sake. 'What – did – you – find?'

She reached out and turned the bedroom door handle. Pushed. A familiar cloying smell slumped into the hall. Like meat left a little too long in the fridge.

Nenova pointed at the wardrobe.

The floor creaked beneath my feet as I picked my way past the bed to the open wardrobe. Shirts and jackets hung in the top part, a couple of long summer dresses to one side. Shoe boxes on the shelf above the rail. A knee-high pile of shoes and boots in the bottom... A little pale hand stuck out from underneath it, the fingers waxy and curled.

A knot tied itself in my chest.

She killed someone. Planked the body in here. All the time we were in the house, she had a dead child in the sodding wardrobe.

Bitch...

My hands curled into fists, the knuckles aching.

'Call the SEB: I want a full team down here. Seal the street off. Get the kid photographed and canvas the neighbours, see if anyone's missing, and... What?'

Nenova stood by the bedside cabinet, shaking her head. Then pulled on a pair of blue-nitrile gloves and picked up a mobile phone. The thing was mounted on a little stand-tripod thing. She cleared her throat. 'It was set up pointing at the bed, so I checked it.' A glance at the wardrobe. 'That was before we found...' She powered the phone up and poked the screen a couple of times, then turned it around and held it out towards me.

A video clip played on the screen.

Virginia Cunningham is in her bra and pants, pregnant bulge pressing against the figure she's got pinned to the bed. A young boy – can't be more than four or five – struggles beneath her.

Her voice crackled out of the phone's speaker, slightly distorted as she sang.

'*When things seem dark and scary, there's no need to be afraid. Just think of lots of lovely things, like crisps and lemonade...*'

She wraps her hands around the little boy's throat and squeezes, hunching over him, bringing her full weight down on his neck.

'*And you can sing the "Bravery Song", whenever you get a fright. And, before you know it, everything will be all right...*'

The kid's hands slap at her bare arms, one leg jerking in time as she rocks forwards, choking him.

'*So forget the ghosts and goblins – no they can't scare us today...*'

He gets a hand up to her face, but she pulls her head back, out of reach and thumps her weight down on him again.

'*Cos we can sing the "Bravery Song", and* make *them go away...*'

The kid's arms go rubbery, no longer able to support their own weight. Then fall at his sides.

'*The "Bravery Song", the "Bravery Song", sing it and you'll feel big and strong.*'

I swallowed. 'When was this? Is there a timestamp on the camera? We need to know when the kid went missing.'

'And you can sing it all night long, till good things come along.'

She lets go of his throat and sits up, a grin stretching her face wide. Pants a couple of times.

Then faint banging comes from the tiny speaker, followed by a muffled, 'SHUT THE FUCK UP!'

My voice.

That was *me* banging on the wall. Didn't need a timestamp, it was filmed when we were in the house.

Right there in the next room waiting for her to get dressed...

Cunningham rolls off the bed, grabs the little boy by the legs and drags him off screen.

Some thumps and bumps, then she's back, looming large as she reaches for the phone.

A clunk, and the door behind her opens. Officer Babs stamps in. *'All right, that's enough. Get your bloody clothes on already!'*

The screen went blank, then reverted to a load of stills arranged like tiles.

Alice had her hand over her mouth. 'Oh no...'

All the breath in my body leaked out, pulling my shoulders down. We were right *there*.

Nenova put the phone back on the bedside cabinet.

I sank down onto the end of the bed, stared at the wardrobe – that pale hand sticking out from the pile of shoes. 'We could've saved him...'

She paced up and down beside the bed. 'We have to get our stories straight. We couldn't know, right? We couldn't search the house, we didn't have time.'

I should've *made* Babs stay with her. Made sure she wasn't left unsupervised. I was in charge.

What was it Cunningham said, sitting on the couch in her maternity dress, flexing her hands, spitting venom and defiance? *'It's all your fault. That's what I'll tell them. All – your – fault.'*

I pulled on a pair of gloves from my kit and got down on

428

my knees in front of the wardrobe. Lifted shoes and boots out one by one and lined them up on the carpet until I could see the kid's face.

Blond hair. Ears he'd never grow into. Freckles standing out like ink spattered on milkbottle skin. Familiar, but not quite right. I screwed up my eyes. Why did he look...?

'Oh, *shite*...'

Nenova shuffled up close. 'We are so screwed.'

It was the blond hair that was wrong. The bathroom stank of ammonia the first time we were here – a box of dye sitting beside the bath. She'd dyed his hair.

It took two goes to get the words out. 'Call Control. Tell them we've found Charlie Pearce.'

'... deepest regret I have to announce that the body of Charlie Pearce was discovered by officers today at a home in the Blackwall Hill area of the city. The parents have been informed, and have asked for their privacy at this terrible time to be respected.'

Rain lashed the windscreen, sounding like a thousand hammers on the Suzuki's roof.

'Detective Superintendent Elizabeth Ness there, speaking at the press conference a few minutes ago. Sport now, and there's troubling times ahead for Partick Thistle—'

I switched off the radio.

Wind buffeted the car, rocking it on its springs.

On the other side of the chain barrier, Kings River was thick and dark, swollen against the harbour walls. A lone seagull swooped past, going sideways, wings bent with the strain of holding onto the air.

Alice curled forwards around Bob the Builder, and rested her head on the steering wheel.

When my phone rang, we both flinched.

I pulled it out. '~ THE BOSS!' flashed on the screen.

Yeah, that could go to voicemail.

You'd think, after two hours, Jacobson would take the hint.

Silence.

Alice shifted in her seat. 'He was right there, all the time.'

Yes. Yes he was.

My neck popped and cracked as I stretched. 'We need to find Jessica McFee.'

'Ash, he was only *five*.'

'We didn't know. How could we?'

She blinked a couple of times. Then sniffed. 'He was right, wasn't he? Detective Superintendent Knight? I'm an embarrassment—'

'You're not an—'

'—amateur. Unprofessional. She had a terrified little boy trapped in the house, *while we were there*. I should have known.' Alice scrubbed a hand across her eyes. 'I've got no right to call myself a psychologist.'

'Alice, don't, OK?'

'Can't get anything right. Should just go into private practice. Marriage guidance, or something, where screwing up doesn't kill people...'

Sigh. 'Are you finished?'

No reply.

'*You* didn't kill Charlie Pearce, Virginia Cunningham did. You didn't screw up. You're not psychic.' My other phone went, playing the default ringtone I hadn't bothered to change.

God's sake. As if things weren't bad enough.

I dug it out and hit the button. 'I know, I know – tick-tock.'

'*Eh?*' A pause. '*This Ash Henderson?*'

Not Wee Free after all. 'Rock-Hammer. You got something for me?'

'*I told you: it's Alistair, and yes. You got an email address I can send these reports from the Social to?*'

What, and let Jacobson and his team find out what we...? You know what? Sod it. Too late to worry about that. I gave him my LIRU email.

430

'And I spoke to his divorce lawyer. Turns out officially *Docherty versus Docherty was about irreconcilable differences brought on by pressures of work. She got half of everything and a regular stipend as well.'*

'And unofficially?'

'Mrs Docherty wasn't down with the role-playing or the pornography. And I don't mean roll-a-dice-and-pretend-you're-an-elf role-playing: he liked her to pose like the dead women in his crime-scene photographs before doing it. Even covered her in fake blood.'

'Yeah, I can see why that'd be kind of a turn-off.'

Alice rose from the steering wheel, Bob pressed tight against her chest. 'What?'

'Dr Frederic Docherty has a thing for dead women.' Back to the phone. 'Anything else?'

'Right now he's at Division HQ. Patrol car picked him up from the hotel at six forty-five. Not been out since.'

The seagull was back, a pale streak against the dark sky.

'Does he have a car, or did he come up by train?'

'Got the number plate from the register this morning. Hold on...' Some rustling.

My official mobile bleeped. That'd be the reports from Social Services. I dug it out, called up the email, then handed the phone to Alice. 'Read.'

'Sorry, the DVLA's slow this morning... Right: it's a dark-blue Volvo V-Seventy. You want the reg number?'

I scribbled it down in my notepad. 'Thanks, Alistair. Let me know if Docherty goes anywhere, OK?'

'Will do.' And he was gone.

I tapped the phone against my chin. A thing for dead women...

Time to give Noel Maxwell a shout – see what info he'd got from his fellow hospital drug dealers. His mobile rang nearly a dozen times, before,

'Yeah?'

'Noel? It's me.'

A pause. *'Ah, right, Mr Henderson, great. Erm … what a co-incidence, I was just about to call you.'*

Sure he was. 'Well?'

'Still a couple of guys on nights I've not spoke to yet, but I did hear rumours about someone flogging on a couple vials of Thiopental Sodium. Kinda like the stuff … you acquired, only a bit more risky for breathing and heart problems and that.'

I got the pen back out. 'Who to?'

'Like I said, I've not spoken to everyone yet, so could just be locker-room bollocks. You know what these guys are like.'

'Who, Noel, before I come up there and divine it from your entrails.'

'OK, so word is Boxer's been flogging stuff to that psychiatrist bloke off the telly. You know: the one who caught the serial guy butchering those wee boys in Dundee?'

Dr Frederic Docherty.

'This "Boxer" – I want a real name, and an address, and a contact number.'

'How do I know his address? I'm not his—'

'Find out and text me.' I hung up. Looked across the car to Alice. Grinned. 'Better and better.'

The wind tried to rip my door off when I clambered out into the slanting rain. It battered icy nails into my face and neck as I limped around to the driver's side and shooed Alice across into the passenger seat.

She scrambled over the handbrake and gearstick, taking Bob the Builder and my phone with her. 'This is … *interesting*.'

'Thought it might be.' The engine growled into life, drowning out the rain for a moment until the diesel warmed up. 'Put your seatbelt on.'

She did what she was told. 'Where are we going?'

'Breaking and entering.'

46

Overhead lights made pools of grey on the concrete floor, the bulbs not quite strong enough to banish the gloom.

I checked the number plate against the note again, just to be sure. Not that the hotel car park was stuffed with blue Volvo estates, but better safe than sorry. Docherty's car sat in the corner furthest away from the entrance, passenger-side tight into the wall, leaving plenty of space between it and the next bay. Trying to make sure no one would dent or scratch the bodywork.

Nice try.

My crowbar squealed along the driver's door, curling off twin strips of paint, exposing the metal beneath. Oops.

The place was nearly empty – most of the guests would be away at work or attending conferences, or doing whatever it was tourists did on a rainy Wednesday lunchtime in Oldcastle – leaving just a handful of hatchbacks and one Range Rover Sport, all parked near the door that led back into the hotel.

Alice shuffled her little red shoes, glancing back through the grid of pillars towards the entrance. 'I'm really not sure we should be doing this, I mean I know the whole "making his wife pretend to be a murder victim" thing is creepy, but—'

'You read the reports from Social Services.'

'Yes, I know, I just...' She wrapped her arms around herself. 'What if we're wrong? What if it's *not* him?'

I took hold of her shoulders and gave them a squeeze. 'He's got to keep his abduction kit somewhere. He can't leave it in his room, or housekeeping will find it. He can't leave it at the station, not even Docherty is that egotistical. So it's either wherever he takes the girls, or it's in the car.' The motorcycle gloves I'd liberated from the traffic office were a bit bulky, but they'd do. The crowbar slapped into the leather-clad palm of my other hand. 'Anyone coming?'

'No.'

'Good.' The crowbar crunched through the driver's window, spattering the front seats with glittering cubes of glass. All four hazard lights burst into life, the horn honking, alarm screeching. I ran the crowbar around the edge of the window, clearing the remnants away, before reaching in and pulling the lever to release the bonnet.

Limped around to the front and hauled the thing open, then jammed the crowbar's forks in under the battery cover and shoved. The red terminal snapped away from the battery and everything was silence again. Five seconds. Not exactly a record, but not bad either. Helps when you don't have to worry about driving the thing away afterwards. 'Anyone?'

'Ash, what if he's not the Inside Man, we—'

'Is anyone coming?'

A sigh. 'No.'

I pulled open the car door and leaned across the seats. Popped open the glove compartment. Maps, half bag of Fox's Glacier Mints, and the vehicle's service book. Nothing in the passenger footwell, or under the seat. Nothing in the door pocket either.

The storage compartment between the seats was empty, too. 'If he's not the Inside Man, we sod off out of it and no one's the wiser. He gets back tonight and thinks someone's vandalized his car. Look on it as payback for him being a dick.'

Driver's side: a neoprene folder full of CDs – a mix of country-and-western and Phil Collins – sweet wrappers, sunglasses. My gloved fingers brushed through cubes of safety glass under the seat. Found a hard edge. Something there... 'Hold on.' I got grip on it and pulled.

A blue folder stamped 'PROPERTY OF GREATER MANCHESTER POLICE'.

It was full of crime-scene photographs. All women. All lying where they'd been discovered. And not one of them had an easy death. Shootings, stabbings, stranglings, beatings, throats cut, bodies ripped open. Blood and bone and suffering. The last eight in the pile were Inside Man victims.

I handed them to Alice. 'Still think it's not him?' Then opened the back door.

An orange carrier-bag sat behind the driver's seat, full of something. I peered inside. Tissues – all scrunched up, and a suspiciously bleachy smell.

Alice looked up from the photos. 'What is it?'

The carrier-bag went back where it came from. 'Think the technical term is "wankerchiefs".'

A frown. Then her top lip curled. 'Ew... He's been sitting in his car masturbating to photos of murdered women?'

'Told you.'

I searched the Volvo from nose to tail. Even had the rubber floor-mats up and the spare wheel out. Nothing.

'Ash?'

Had to be here *somewhere*.

Somewhere accessible from inside the car. Somewhere he could get to it easily. But where? I knelt on the concrete floor and went back under the seats, inching my fingers along the glass-strewn carpet.

Couldn't feel a damn thing in the motorcycle gloves. I stripped the right one off replacing it with the last of my blue nitriles.

Alice's voice was a hissing whisper: 'Ash!'

There – a little cylinder. Pen top? I teased it out and sat back.

You wee *beauty*. It was an orange syringe cap. The same kind I'd... Yes. Well, far too late to do anything about that now.

It wasn't exactly an abduction kit, but it was a start.

Put it back, call Jacobson, tell him to get a search warrant, and—

She grabbed my sleeve and yanked. 'Someone's coming!'

Sodding hell.

I grabbed the crowbar. 'Knew we should've worn ski-masks.'

No point trying to hide – if the place had been packed with cars, we could have slipped away between the vehicles. But it wasn't.

Dr Docherty marched across the concrete, overcoat billowing out behind him. 'WHAT THE BLOODY HELL DO YOU THINK YOU'RE DOING?'

The hotel manager was at his heels, all wringing hands and shiny bald spot. And behind *him*: Rhona. She scuffed along at the back, mouth pulled down at the edges, hands in her pockets.

He'd brought reinforcements. Of course he had. Little sod must've got a lift to the station this morning, how else was he going to get back here?

'GET AWAY FROM MY BLOODY CAR!' Face flushed, eyes wide.

I let the crowbar's tip clank against the floor and leaned on it. 'Where are they?'

He stopped four feet away, arm raised, finger pointed at the middle of my chest. 'Detective Sergeant Massie, I want that man arrested! He's broken into my car, and... WHAT DID YOU DO TO THE PAINTWORK?'

A little squeal from the manager as he surveyed the damage, and the hand-wringing intensified. 'While the Pinemantle Hotel carries out every reasonable safety precaution I have to remind you that we're, unfortunately, unable to accept any liability for damage—'

'THAT WAS BRAND NEW!'

Rhona held her hands out. 'All right, let's all calm down.' She looked from the crowbar, to the scrape along the car, to the snowfall of broken glass, then up to me. Bared a line of thick teeth. 'Guv?'

'It was like this when we got here, wasn't it, Alice?'

'Like...?' The veins in Docherty's neck looked as if they were about to pop. 'I WANT HIM ARRESTED, RIGHT NOW!'

'Yeah.' I reached in and grabbed a handful of the photographs. 'Then we can all go down to the station and chat about why you've got a collection of murdered women to masturbate over.'

'I have no idea what you're—'

'These.' The photos thumped against his chest and fluttered down around his feet. 'Care to explain?'

He didn't even flinch. 'I'm a forensic psychologist. Those are *research*.'

'And the carrier-bag full of wankerchiefs – that research too?'

'What I do in the privacy of my own vehicle is of no business of yours.' The nose went up. 'Frankly, Dr McDonald, I expected slightly better of you. Though I'm not sure why, given what you let happen at Victoria Cunningham's house.'

Alice nodded, then put a hand on his arm. 'I'm sorry about your parents. It can't have been easy growing up in that kind of environment.'

His mouth tightened. Then he brushed past me and slammed the Volvo's back door shut. Leaned against it. Folded his arms. 'I'm going to make damn sure neither of you are allowed to consult on any investigation *ever* again. You,' his finger jabbed at me, 'are going back to the dank cell you came from.' Round to Alice. 'And *you* have no business calling yourself a psychologist. You should be ashamed of yourself.'

'Nothing you ever did was good enough for them, was it? You tried and you tried, but they just kept on hitting you. It wasn't your fault.'

'WHO HAVE YOU BEEN TALKING TO?' Spittle arced from his lips. He reached out, as if he was going to grab her. Then stopped. Curled his hand in to a fist and settled back against the car door. Sniffed. 'Detective Sergeant Massie, I want to press charges against both of these individuals for breaking into my car and vandalizing it. If you're not prepared to arrest them, I'll be making a formal complaint about your conduct as well.'

Something wasn't right.

Why the car's back door? The front door was lying wide open, photographs of dead women all over the seat, but he hadn't slammed that one shut and stood in front of it. What was in the back? What had I missed?

Rhona grimaced for a beat. 'Let's just take some deep breaths and—'

'I should've known it! This is why you insisted on coming with me, isn't it? Your deeply unprofessional behaviour is clearly motivated by some twisted sense of loyalty. Well, I will *not* put up with it!'

Glass crunched under my feet as I went back to the Volvo.

'I want him arrested *now*, DS Massie.'

Rhona pinched the bridge of her nose. 'I know you do, Doctor, but I'm sure if we all calm down we can sort this out.'

But there was nothing *in* the back. I'd been through it twice already.

Why would he guard it if there was nothing there?

Alice tilted her head to one side. 'Is that why you set fire to the old house? Taking your frustration out on a world that never cared about you? I mean, it must have been wonderful to feel in control like that. To have power over something for a change, after all those years of being powerless.'

438

Had to be something incriminating...

Docherty brushed his hands down the front of his overcoat. 'Spare me your attempts at analysis, Dr McDonald. It's not amateur hour.' He pulled out his phone. 'Well, Detective Sergeant, if you won't do your job, you leave me no choice.'

'Oh shut up.' I pushed him out of the way and wrenched the door open.

'Get away from my car!'

He clutched at my jacket. I put my hand in the middle of his chest and shoved. Hard. He landed on his backside by the rear wheels, spluttering. 'He assaulted me! You saw that!'

What had I missed?

Under the seats. In the seat pockets. In the door pockets. Under the mats...

Where the hell was it?

He's sitting in the back seat, with his collection of dead women spread out on the seat next to him, carrier-bag of tissues at his feet.

Had to be the centre arm rest.

Docherty scrabbled to his feet again.

I pulled it down. Just a couple of cup holders. Sodding hell.

Hands grabbed my back.

I threw an elbow. The impact jarred. Someone grunted.

It *had* to be here...

Hold on: the recess the armrest fitted into had a fabric backing. It looked cheap. Rough around the edges. As if it hadn't come with the original car.

A little loop of black poked out from the top left corner.

'GET OUT OF MY CAR! YOU HAVE NO RIGHT!'

I took hold of it and pulled.

The sound of Velcro tearing filled the back seat as the lining came away, revealing a leather folio about the size of an A4 envelope. Tan leather, tied with scarlet ribbon.

Bingo.

'I DEMAND YOU GET OUT OF MY CAR!'

I stood. 'Rhona: get a pair of gloves on and come open this.'

Blood oozed from the corner of Docherty's mouth. He grabbed me again, shoving me back against the bodywork. 'YOU PLANTED THAT, IT'S NOT MINE!'

'Get off me, you moron.'

He swung a fist at my head.

Might as well have stuck his knuckles in the post, they would've got here quicker. A quick bob right and they went singing past my left ear. I grabbed the arm and twisted. Then slammed my elbow into his face again.

He went skittering back and landed sprawled on the concrete, scarlet bubbles popping from his nostrils. Lay there, moaning.

'Any time today would be good, Rhona.'

She squeezed past me, snapping on a pair of blue nitrile gloves. Pulled the folio from its hiding place and laid it on the seat.

Docherty's arms and legs flailed as he struggled over onto his side.

Behind me, Rhona whistled. 'Guv? You *really* need to see this.'

Docherty made it to his knees. Stopped there, one hand leaning on a support pillar.

I took a step towards him. 'Come at me again and I'm going to break your arm. Clear? You stay where you are.'

Alice shuffled over, peering past Rhona into the Volvo.

And then she was off, making for Docherty. Three paces away she sped up and slammed a little red shoe right between his legs.

He folded over, both hands clutching his groin, a silent scream pulling his bloody mouth wide. Backside in the air, knees clamped firmly together.

'Guv?'

I turned.

Rhona pointed at the folio.

A scalpel sat on top of a stack of yellow paper, along with a baby-doll key ring, a little plastic container with what looked like dead spiders in it, a heart-shaped locket, an engagement ring... Everything missing from the archives was here.

No wonder Alice had kicked him in the balls.

She turned her back on him and launched herself at me. Wrapped her arms around my chest and hugged, her face buried in my shoulder. 'We got him!'

Rain hammered the driveway that led into the hotel car park. It made little rivers between the thick dark rhododendrons, hissed against their leaves. The concrete entrance smelled of mould and dank earth. I leaned against it and listened to the phone ring.

The pool car Dr Docherty had arrived in purred past – Rhona in the driving seat, wearing a grin full of thick grey teeth. The psychologist sat in the back with his hands cuffed. Blood caked the lower half of his face, spreading out from his battered nose. He glowered out at me. Turning so he could glare through the back window as well.

I gave him a smile and a little wave.

Then Wee Free McFee's voice rasped in my ear. *'What?'*

'We've just arrested someone.'

A small pause, then: *'Who.'*

'We're not allowed to say, yet. But he had trophies from the victims in his car. I just wanted you to know before it was on the news.'

'Where's Jessica?'

'That's what we're trying to find out.'

Clunks and rattles came down the line, as if Wee Free was grabbing something. *'You get that bastard and you take him some-where nice and quiet. And I will—'*

'We can't. It's not the wild west, Mr McFee. There's not going to be a lynching party. We've got him, and we'll break him.' Deep breath. 'But it might take a bit of time.'

Rain rattled the naked beech trees.

I shifted my feet. 'Hello? You still there?'

'You thought I'd be so grateful you'd caught him that I'd just let you have your fat mate back, didn't you? Just like that? OK, which bit would you like – how about that ear I promised you?'

'I just need more time.'

'Tick-tock, tick-tock. You find my daughter, or I start slicing.'

47

'… completely unacceptable.' Superintendent Knight jabbed a finger into the boardroom table. 'That poor little lad's mother, is *devastated*.'

I stared at him.

He tugged at the tails of his dress uniform jacket, stretching the gap between the buttons. 'Clearly the Lateral Investigative and Review Unit is unfit for purpose, and—'

'Oh *really*?' Jacobson was on his feet, fists pressed against the polished wood. 'I don't know if you noticed, but LIRU just delivered the Inside Man into custody! If that's not fit for purpose, what is?'

Alice sat at the far end of the table, hunched over a sheaf of paper, twiddling with her hair. Ignoring everyone.

Knight puffed out his chest. 'That doesn't excuse the revolting lack of common sense displayed in leaving a known paedophile alone with a small child! For God's sake, Simon, what were you thinking leaving someone like him,' the finger jabbed at me this time, 'in charge of a team?'

'He's—'

'At the very least they should have had a police officer with them. Someone who could follow bloody operational procedures!'

Jacobson bared his teeth. 'Charlie Pearce's death—'

'Was *entirely* preventable!'

Silence.

Alice looked up from her papers. 'I can understand your need to lash out, Superintendent Knight, it's a perfectly normal psychological defence, but counter projective identification isn't healthy.'

He blinked at her. 'What?' Then threw his hands in the air. 'You see, this is exactly what I was talking about!'

'Your anger over what happened to Charlie Pearce helps reduce the anxiety you feel about hiring Dr Docherty to consult on murders and abductions he was actually responsible for. Going on the offensive, instead of accepting the blame for your actions.'

Knight opened his mouth a couple of times. Pink rushed up his neck and into his cheeks. Burned at the tips of his ears. 'I hardly think that's the same thing.'

Jacobson grinned. 'Oh, I think the high heedjins will think it is. Actually, they'll probably think it's a lot worse.'

'That's not—'

'Alice was standing up to Docherty, questioning his judgement, and there you were: backing him up and shouting her down.'

'That's a gross misrepresentation of—'

'Hold on.' I dunked the head of my cane off the tabletop a couple of times. 'What was it you said about Frederic Docherty being what a *professional* forensic psychologist looked like? Then something about amateur outfits and Police Scotland not tolerating incompetence?'

Knight shut his mouth. Licked his lips. Took a deep breath. Then marched to the end of the table and stuck his hand out for shaking. 'I owe you an apology, Dr McDonald ... Alice. Obviously Docherty had everyone fooled. I would never have involved him if there'd been the *slightest* hint of malfeasance.'

Alice put down her highlighter pen and took his hand.

Which was big of her. I'd have snapped the thing off and rammed it down his throat. She nodded as they shook. 'Thank you.'

'He's been manipulating the investigation ever since the beginning. Even Henry Forrester was taken in by him. Really, no one could've known.'

My unofficial phone chimed in my pocket. Text message.

    Boxer — reel name Angus Boyle

    Flat 812, Millbank West, Kingsmeath

And a mobile number. Noel Maxwell wasn't quite as big a waste of skin as he looked.

Ness stepped back into the room and slipped her mobile into her pocket. 'That was Manchester. The lipstick, earrings, and underwear in Docherty's suitcase are from a series of rape-murders they've had on their books for six years.' She perched on the edge of the meeting table, next to the triangular conference-call unit, and looked me up and down. 'Seems you and Dr McDonald were right about him.'

'Has he said where Jessica McFee is?'

'Docherty's still in with his solicitor, being schooled in the art of "no comment".'

I printed the details from Noel's text in clear biro letters on one of the conference pads. Tore the sheet off and handed it to her. 'Angus Boyle, AKA: Boxer, works as a nurse up at CHI. We think he's the one who sold Docherty the drugs.'

Ness took a deep breath, head on one side as she read the address and phone number. 'Will he say that in court?'

'Might if you cut him a deal.'

She narrowed her eyes and squinted at me for a couple of beats. 'Thank you, Mr Henderson. Looks like the stories about you might actually have been true.'

Alice stood up straight. 'I'd like to advise on the interview.'

That got her a thin smile. 'Ah, yes...' Ness glanced at Jacobson. 'It's not that we don't think you'd do a terrific job, but you're too close. And his defence will use the fact you kicked him in the balls to question your judgement and our impartiality.'

'But he's manipulative, he knows what you're going to ask him, he can make it sound like—'

'Thank you, Doctor, but we have to be *beyond reproach* on this. I'm not letting some slimy weasel lawyer get him off on a technicality.'

'Oh...' Her shoulders drooped.

I limped over to the window. The blockade of lenses and microphones was growing thicker. 'OLDCASTLE DIVISION CATCH THE INSIDE MAN' would be all over the news tonight, and in every paper tomorrow.

Assuming Docherty was capable of doing the decent thing and putting his hand up to it.

I turned my back on the press. 'What about DNA?'

Knight grimaced. 'He's had access to every crime scene since the third victim, and every bit of evidence we've ever gathered. He's even attended the post mortems. Finding his DNA's not worth the spit it's in.'

'Then you stick him in a room with nice thick soundproof walls, and you give me twenty minutes with an extension lead.'

Ness pinched the bridge of her nose. 'Mr Henderson, which part of "by the book" are you having trouble with?'

'The part that ends up with Jessica McFee dead.'

And with her, Shifty.

A knock at the door, then Rhona stuck her head into the room and waved at Ness. 'Boss? Docherty's solicitor says he's ready to make a statement. You want me to put it on the thing?' She pointed at the flatscreen TV mounted on the side wall.

'I want to hear this in person. Superintendent Knight?'

Knight rolled his shoulders. 'I don't trust myself to be in the same room with the little bastard right now.'

'Bear?'

Jacobson grinned. 'Wouldn't miss it for the world.'

'Then Superintendent Knight can keep Mr Henderson and Dr McDonald company. Rhona – as soon as you've got the link set up, get back to the team. He's got Jessica McFee hidden away somewhere: I want her found.'

Ness marched out, back straight, chin up. Jacobson sauntered along behind her, hands in his pockets, whistling.

Rhona picked a remote control from the cabinet in the corner and fiddled with it until the big screen filled with a view of Interview Room Two. She placed the remote on the table. Grinned. 'Great job, Guv. Knew you'd do it.'

I looked up at the empty room that filled the screen. 'We've not burst him yet.'

'Yeah, but we will.' She backed towards the exit. Held up both thumbs. 'Anyway, got to go chase up those—'

'Rhona? Do me a favour – get onto the secure psychiatric ward at CHI and see if they've got any record of Docherty visiting either Ruth Laughlin or Marie Jordan, OK?'

'Err... Yeah, sure, no problem.' She slipped out and closed the door behind her.

Knight pulled out a chair, almost settled into it, then stood again. Cleared his throat. 'Would anyone like a tea, or a coffee?'

Talk about overcompensating.

Alice wrapped an arm around herself, the other hand working its way through the curls of her hair. 'If he's giving a statement it's so he can mitigate our finding the trophies. He's not going to admit to abducting Jessica, Laura, and Ruth, killing Claire or any of the others. This will all be a big misunderstanding and he's desperately sorry about that, but he's not the man we're looking for, that man is still out there and that's why he's doing the decent thing and coming forward at this time.'

I sank into one of the conference chairs. 'Where does he take them?'

'If it's a house, it's a place he's known for years, it takes a lot of effort to set up an operating room, time and money, and you've got to know your investment's secure, I mean what if someone breaks in? They'll see everything, and it's not as if he's in Oldcastle *all* the time, he's off around the country, helping the police with their enquiries, so what makes this place safer than anywhere else...?'

A PC appeared on the big flat screen, followed by Dr Frederic Docherty – hands cuffed in front of him. A thin woman in a dark suit followed them in: short grey hair, pinched face, nails pointed and scarlet. Docherty waited for her to sit, then squeezed himself into the chair next to her. Bit awkward, what with it being bolted to the floor, but he managed.

Bruises spread across the skin beneath his eyes. A plaster sat across the bridge of his nose. Another bruise at the corner of his mouth.

Poor baby.

The PC took up position behind Docherty and stood there, picking his nails, killing time. Probably done this hundreds of times before. Knew the routine off by heart. Lead the suspect in, sit him down, and let him sweat for a bit.

One minute.

Two.

Five.

Fifteen.

And all the time Docherty just sat there, still and calm, a little smile pulling one side of his face out of line. Of course, he knew the routine too...

Finally, Ness walked in, put her phone in her pocket, and took the seat closest to the door, with her back to the camera. Jacobson took the last slot, rubbed his hands together, then went through the usual date, time, and caution bits.

I turned the volume up.

448

Docherty's lawyer pulled out a sheet of paper and pursed her lips at it. *'My client has authorized me to read the following statement. He's aware that there will be certain factions within the investigation who will put a very negative interpretation on the alleged discoveries this afternoon, but—'*

'Negative interpretation?' Ness leaned forward, head tilted to one side. *'He was found with a collection of trophies from the—'*

'Please, Detective Superintendent, we'll get through this much quicker if you can contain your outbursts until I've finished.' She flicked the paper out. *'My client deeply regrets any confusion he has inadvertently caused by removing the items from evidence. These were used to facilitate his understanding of the unknown suspect you are pursuing. He felt that keeping these so called "trophies" close by would help him get into the mindset of your killer. The photographs and evidence of masturbation were part of that attempt, and something he found deeply distasteful, but felt necessary. Far from being censured, Dr Docherty deserves your praise for going above and beyond the call of duty to rescue Jessica McFee and bring Claire Young's killer to justice.'*

Sitting next to her, Docherty nodded, then spread his hands wide. *'Detective Superintendent, I understand that my actions might look suspect to those unfamiliar with my methodology.'* He gave a little shrug, combined with a little smile. *'It was my responsibility to make sure that you and the other senior officers were aware of my processes, and it was an error of judgement on my part to have kept that from you. I apologize for that. Unreservedly.'* He clasped his cuffed hands together. *'But I'm sure you can see now that this is all just a misunderstanding. A case of someone trying a bit too hard to get the right result.'* His eyebrows pinched above that self-deprecating smile. *'For the victims.'*

Staring up at the TV screen, Knight wriggled in his seat. 'Dr McDonald, is that ... standard practice for forensic psychologists?'

'Well, everyone works in their own way, but certainly I've never heard of anyone doing it, then again why would I, I

449

mean it's not like they're going to say, "Hey, you'll never guess what I was up to last night with a box of tissues and some photos of dead women..."' Pink rushed up her cheeks. 'I mean, no, it's not normal. Is it getting warm in here?'

On screen, Ness drummed her fingers on the table. Thumping out a little tattoo while Dr Docherty sat in perfect stillness opposite. *'And you really expect us to believe that, do you?'*

He leaned in, cranked the sincerity up a notch. *'I'm coming forward at this time to prevent the investigation from stalling. To stop you from diverting your attention from the real issue. The Inside Man is still out there. We need to re-examine the evidence and move on.'*

Jacobson shook his head. *'There is no "we" any more, Dr Docherty.'* He produced a small evidence bag and placed it on the table, a sliver of orange just visible through the clear plastic. That would be the syringe cap. *'Care to explain why you purchased Thiopental Sodium from a Mr Angus Boyle, also known as "Boxer", a nurse at Castle Hill Infirmary? It's a surgical anaesthetic.'* Jacobson leaned forwards in his seat. *'Have you been performing surgery?'*

Docherty wrinkled his nose and dipped his head. Silly me, how could I forget to mention that?

He gave Ness a smile. *'That's part of the process I should have told you about. At low doses it can act as a mild consciousness suppressant. Dr Henry Forrester would suppress his with whisky before beginning a profile. Dr McDonald does the same. After much experimentation, I've found Thiopental Sodium works best for me.'* Another shrug, hands spread palm-upward. *'But I can understand why you'd be confused about that.'*

Alice wandered over to the screen, staring up at the interview. 'Can we talk to her?'

I pulled the conference phone over. 'What's Ness's mobile number?'

Knight reached into his pocket and came out with a BlackBerry. 'She did say Dr McDonald wasn't to consult.'

More hair twiddling. 'But she's not asking the right questions.'

He fidgeted with the phone. 'We have to maintain evidential *integrity*.'

I leaned in close. 'Docherty's going to keep his mouth shut, and Jessica McFee, Ruth Laughlin, and Laura Strachan are going to die. They're going to starve and dehydrate till their organs pack in. And you're just going to sit here and let it happen?'

Not to mention what Wee Free was going to do to Shifty.

'It's not that simple, it—'

'You called Docherty in on the investigation. He's here because of you.'

Knight chewed on the inside of his cheek for a moment. 'Fine.' He reached across and punched a number into the conference phone. Sat back.

The speaker burred, then what sounded like a hard-rock version of 'Scotland the Brave' came from the TV. Ness sagged a little, swore, then pulled out her phone. *'I'm busy.'*

Tough. I tapped the microphone. 'You're asking the wrong questions.'

On screen, her back stiffened, she turned her back on the table, voice dropping to a whisper. *'Do you have any idea how unprofessional you're—'*

'Hey, I'm not the one who left my phone on during a major interview, OK?' I pointed. 'Go on then.'

Alice leaned over the table, her voice raised. 'I know you said you didn't want my help, but whoever's advising you isn't doing it right. He's rehearsed for all this, every bit of evidence you bring up, he's going to have an explanation for.'

'And you think you can change that, do you?'

'He's laid down a challenge for you – if he's been doing all this to get into the Inside Man's head, what insights has he got?'

'I really don't—'

'Docherty's egotistical and narcissistic in public, shy and uncertain in private. The persona you're dealing with right now wants to show off. Let him. If we can get him caught up in the fantasy that this is all just an innocent misunderstanding he can talk about what he's done as if it's someone else and we can use that to find his victims.'

'*Thank you.*' She held the phone against her chest. '*So, Dr Docherty, if you did all this to understand the Inside Man better, what did you come up with?*'

He turned and smiled up at the camera. '*Well, well, well. If it isn't Dr McDonald. What an excellent question.*'

'*All that "distasteful" masturbating over photos of murdered women, what did it get you?*'

He kept his gaze where it was. '*I want you to know that I won't be pressing charges for assault, Doctor. I know it was just a misunderstanding. Heat of the moment. Anyone without all the facts would have done the same.*'

Jacobson knocked on the table top. '*Come on then, Dr Docherty: what did you learn?*'

He pulled his gaze away from the camera. '*The Inside Man is a very complicated animal. His hatred of women stems from his abusive relationship with his mother…*'

The CID room was packed – everyone on the phone to some agency or other, chasing things down. A blown-up photo of Dr Docherty sat in the middle of the whiteboard, surrounded by boxes and lines and question marks.

I perched on the edge of Rhona's desk. 'Anything?'

She pulled the biro from her mouth. 'He's got a handful of elderly relatives with property in Castleview, Blackwall Hill, Dundee, and Stonehaven. The Mire and Tayside are running theirs down. Waste of time – no way he's butchering them in Dundee then wheeching them up the A90 to dump them here – but you know what it's like. We've got cars out to the others.' Rhona swivelled her chair left and right, arms hanging limp at her side. She nodded at Docherty's photograph. 'Always knew he was a slimy tosser… The Super still not burst him yet?'

452

'Says he was only taking trophies from evidence so he could think like the Inside Man.'

'You should have a crack at him, Guv.'

'It's not a movie. They don't let civilians interview serial killers in real life.'

'Hmmm...' A nod. Then she pulled out her notebook and flipped it open at the marker. 'I spoke to the guy in charge of the psychiatric wards at Castle Hill Infirmary, a Professor Bartlett. Seems Dr Frederic Docherty was a regular visitor when Ruth Laughlin and Marie Jordan were admitted. Spent about six months doing follow-up therapy, *pro bono*.'

Poor sods. What the hell did he say to them? Sitting there, once a week, all alone in a room with the women he'd violated. Did he mock them? Relive the fantasy, playing with himself while they sat there, doped up to the eyeballs?

I thunked my cane off the floor a couple of times. Stared out of the window at the carrion-crow clouds draping their dark wings over the city.

Where the hell did he take them...

'Get onto the CCTV monkeys – I want them going through all the ANPR tapes for the last four days looking for Docherty's Volvo. If we're lucky, we might get a clue what part of town to look at.'

'Might take a couple of days to run everything through the Automatic Number Plate Recognition System – you know what they're like.'

'So threaten them.'

'Sold.' Rhona grinned. 'Tell you something: there's *definitely* going to be a party tonight.' The smile slipped. 'You're still coming, right?'

'Wouldn't miss it for the... Sodding hell.' I dug out my unofficial phone. 'Henderson.'

Wee Free McFee: '*Where's my bloody daughter?*'

I put a hand over the mouthpiece and stood. 'Sorry, got to take this.' Then limped out of CID and down the corridor.

'We're running down every address he's had access to in the city. We'll find her.'

'"*After the number of the days in which ye searched the land, even forty days, each day for a year, shall ye bear your iniquities. Even forty years, and ye shall know my breach of promise.*"'

'God's sake – we're doing it, OK? Now sod off and let me do my job!'

Silence.

'You still there?'

Nothing.

'Hello?'

Pfff...

I settled back against the wall, took the weight off my right foot. Let the hot glass settle between the bones. 'I know how it feels. When Rebecca went missing, we thought she'd run away. Thought we'd done something wrong. Been bad parents.' I closed my eyes, allowed the darkness in. 'Then twelve months later, I got the homemade birthday card with a photo of her tied to a chair on it. And soon as I opened it, I knew. I knew it was him, and she wasn't missing – she was dead.' The floor was hard against my right foot, setting the glass moving again, driving the shards through the skin. I leaned in to set it burning. Got the fire good and stoked. 'And I knew that it wasn't quick. That every year, from then on, I'd get another card showing how he tortured her.'

Wee Free's voice was a cold hard rasp. '*And what would you have done if you knew they had him in a cell, all safe and cosy? Three square meals a day and a nice cup of tea.*'

I'd have torn the bastard's throat out, and done the same to anyone who'd got in my way.

48

Docherty's lawyer sighed on the TV screen. *'We're not really going over this again, are we? My client has made his statement and offered his insight, that's as far as we're prepared to be drawn on the matter. My client needs a break.'*

Ness didn't move. *'He's just* had *a break.'*

Jacobson pulled a sheet of paper from a folder. *'Well, why don't we have a bash at something else, then. Dr Frederic Docherty: where were you between the hours of ten last night and three this morning?'*

Here we go.

'In my hotel room. I ran a bath and read through the case notes on a rape-murder in Birmingham I'm consulting on. Watched a little TV to unwind, then went to bed about … eleven thirty?'

Jacobson sat back. *'So, when Laura Strachan and Ruth Laughlin were abducted, you were in your room, alone, in bed.'* He put a finger on the sheet of paper and shoogled it from side to side. *'Really? Don't want to think about that a little more?'*

Detective Superintendent Knight was on the phone, hunched over a notepad, doodling gothic skulls-and-cross-bones across the paper. 'Uh-huh… Yes… No, sir, I understand, but it wasn't my… Yes… No, I suppose it wasn't…' A red tidemark throbbed above his collar, stretching up his neck and into his cheeks. He stopped doodling and ran a hand across his bald head. 'Well, with hindsight... Yes, sir.'

Alice stopped scrawling boxes and lines on the whiteboard to take a sip of the twelve-year-old Glenfiddich I'd confiscated from the CID office. Then went back to her marker pens.

I leaned on the conference table, stared up at the screen. 'Stop sodding about and burst him.'

Jacobson made a big show of writing something down. *'Half eleven... And you're sure?'*

'That's where I was, Detective Inspector, right through till my alarm went off at six this morning.'

'Because we've got a witness who says you weren't in your room at midnight. In fact, your bed was still made and there was no sign of you.'

Docherty pursed his lips.

His lawyer placed a hand on his arm. *'I really must insist on that break.'*

Ness stared at the ceiling for a moment, then looked at Jacobson.

'Why not.' He reached for the recording equipment. *'Interview suspended at sixteen-o-five.'*

Ness slumped into the chair behind her desk, scrubbed her face with her hands. Sighed. 'Docherty's not going to pop. He's been on our side of the fence too often – he knows how it works.'

The walls were lined with faces – head-and-shoulder shots of people smiling at weddings and parties, on the beach, birthdays, holiday snaps... Never the same person twice.

Alice peered at one of a man standing behind a BBQ, 'Snog The Chef' on his apron, tongs in one hand, a beer in the other raised in salute. 'Isn't this Tony Hudson? Dismembered body washed ashore at Cullen?'

Jacobson slouched in one of the visitor's chairs, hands clasped over his belly. 'We'll find out where he's got them sooner or later. Going to be much worse for Docherty if it's later and they're dead.'

I settled into the chair opposite. Stretched my leg. 'In the old days—'

'These aren't the old days, Ash.' He sighed and shook his head. 'The eyes of the world are watching. If renowned psychologist and TV personality, Dr Frederic Docherty, starts falling down the stairs, people are going to notice. We'll *all* be out of a job.'

'I'd rather be out of a job than let Ruth Laughlin, Laura Strachan, and Jessica McFee die because we let the bastard wait us out. Ten minutes, in a room. I won't leave a mark on him.'

Ness gave a snort. 'And then what – watch the case collapse and him walk free because we violated his human rights? No thanks.' She blinked a couple of times, then stuck her hand over her mouth, covering a cavernous yawn.

Alice moved on to a woman in a trench coat: blonde, big all over, mouth wide as if she was singing. 'And that's Rose McGowan. Abducted, raped, and strangled.' Alice pointed at a framed picture of three kids in swimsuits grinning in a paddling pool. 'Liz, Janet, and Graeme Boyle. Stabbed by their mother... They're all victims, aren't they?'

Ness let her head fall back, arms limp at her sides. 'Did you get anything from Docherty's "insights" into the Inside Man?'

Alice did the hair-twiddling thing; leaned back against a filing cabinet, frowning at the walls of the dead. 'Many points correlate with his own childhood: the abusive mother, the distant father, the trips to hospital; lashing out by burning things, a major arson event in the pre-teen years... He deviates when he talks about Tim having an unskilled job, but then he says he's got low self-esteem, which would tie into the private persona, not the "Dr Docherty" he presents to the world.'

'Anything that'll help us find where he's keeping them?'

'I'm sorry.'

Ness covered her face and groaned.

'I mean, if the teams can come up with some viable addresses we can run them through what he's told us, but it's not enough right now to point at somewhere...' Alice cleared her throat. 'Sorry.'

Jacobson dunted the toe of his shoe against the desk's modesty panel. 'Any reason our illustrious colleague Knight's not here?'

I didn't bother hiding the smile. 'Detective Superintendent Knight has been summoned to a telecom with the SCD and the top brass. *Apparently* hiring serial killers as consultants is against official policy.'

Jacobson's lips pinched, cheek muscles twitching. But at least he didn't laugh. 'What a shame.'

'Yes, well,' Ness let her arms fall limp again, 'we're in no position to gloat. The Chief Constable has taken an interest in Virginia Cunningham and Charlie Pearce.' She blew out a sigh, then sat forwards. 'Mr Henderson, did you do "A Song for the Dying" in school? No? It's a poem: William Denner, I think it is. "The raven folds his blood-black wings, and struts before what darkness brings, to feast upon the dying breath, and murder sacred things..." Why does that make me think of you?'

'We didn't know Charlie was there. We *couldn't* know.'

She reached into a drawer and pulled out an evidence bag, snapped on a single blue nitrile glove, and tipped the mobile phone into her palm. Thumbed the screen a couple of times, then held it out so Jacobson could see.

The sound of Virginia Cunningham singing the 'Bravery Song' came from the little speaker.

When it was over, Ness slipped the phone back into the bag and sealed it.

Jacobson blew out a breath. 'That's ... bad.'

I poked the desk. 'What else could we do? We didn't have powers to search the place, and—'

'I know, I know.' Ness shook her head, snapped off her glove and dumped it in the bin beside her desk. 'It's going to kill Charlie's parents when that gets played in court. Not to mention the lawsuits. And someone's *bound* to call for a public enquiry.'

Alice tucked her hands in her pockets. 'Maybe I could speak to Virginia Cunningham? I mean it's obvious she did it – she filmed herself killing him – but perhaps we can find out why she did it and maybe give Charlie's mum and dad some closure?'

'Well ... I suppose it couldn't hurt.'

As soon as the door closed behind Alice, Ness sagged back in her chair again. Let another yawn ripple through her. Blinked at the piles of paperwork on her desk. 'We've got nothing: no witnesses, no victims, the forensics are compromised, and unless he confesses, all we can do him for is theft and attempting to pervert the course of justice. He'll be out in four years. And we're back where we started.'

Jacobson slapped his hands against his knees. 'No, we're not. We've got the bugger in custody – that's something. We keep at him, we apply for a detainment extension, and we find his operating theatre. In the meantime,' Jacobson stood, 'I think the team needs to blow off a little steam. We caught him.'

'I'm sorry, Bear, but I don't think that's really appropriate. We've got three women out there who're going to die if we don't find them.'

I levered myself out of the chair. 'Nobody gets to celebrate till we've got Ruth, Laura, and Jessica back.'

He lowered his voice. 'I understand, but—'

'They've got what, thirty-six hours? Maybe forty-eight? We don't have time to sod about with—'

'First off, it takes between three and ten days to die of dehydration. Secondly, look at the pair of you.' He pointed. 'Elizabeth, how long were you on for yesterday? Fourteen hours? Sixteen? And the day before? And the day before that?'

She waved a hand in his direction. 'That's not the point. We have to—'

'It's *exactly* the point. You're dead on your feet, and Limpy the Boy Wonder here has bags under his eyes only a panda could love. The rest of the team's the same. Won't be long before they start making mistakes.'

I banged my cane against the filing cabinet, setting it ringing. 'We need to *find* them.'

Ness looked from the pile in her in-tray to the one in pending, to the stacks of forms littering her desk. 'It's a lovely idea, Bear, but we can't.'

'I'm not saying we should all troop off to the pub for beer and karaoke, I'm saying give the team a little space. Send half of them home on time for a change. We'll draw up a big list of actions and make the nightshift chase them down. Then you can head off.'

'But—'

'Jessica, Ruth, and Laura aren't going to die just because you went home to get some sleep. If nightshift get something, they'll call. Tomorrow morning everyone's going to be recharged and ready to nail the son of a bitch.'

And Wee Free would start carving bits off Shifty.

Nenova squeaked her chair closer, squinted at the TV in the downstream monitoring suite. Her partner, McKevitt, tore open another packet of cheese-and-onion, ferrying them from bag to mouth like a factory robot, crunching as the screen filled with Virginia Cunningham.

She settled into her seat, then her solicitor shuffled into view and sat next to her. He was a rumpled man in a corduroy jacket with leather patches on the elbows. A single horn of hair stuck out above his left ear. He took a sheaf of papers from his brief-case and ruffled through them. Didn't look at his client once.

Alice leaned her head against my shoulder, let out a low shivery breath.

460

I rubbed her back. 'You OK?'

She didn't look up. 'Long day.'

On screen, Detective Superintendent Ness got a PC to do the date and time thing, then nodded. *'I believe you want to make a statement.'*

Cunningham smeared her fingers across the tabletop. Her maternity frock was rumpled, the white cardigan missing a button. *'I...'* She licked her lips. *'I want to plead guilty to the abduction and murder of Charlie Pearce. I've been thinking about it, and I want to...'* A frown, as if she was trying to remember something. When she started again, the words sounded dead and flat. Rehearsed. *'I want to spare his parents the grief of a trial. They have suffered enough.'*

'I see.' Ness looked at the solicitor. *'And...?'*

He slid the top sheet from his stack across the table top. *'Full confession and admission of guilt, signed, witnessed, and dated. We want this taken into account during sentencing.'*

Cunningham kept her eyes down. *'I just... I kinda want to apologize for what I did and, you know, so they can put me somewhere I can get the help I need. So I can get better.'* One hand reached down to stroke the pregnant bulge. *'For my baby.'*

Nenova folded forward, until her head rested on the worktop. 'Thank Christ for that...'

McKevitt blew out a crispy breath. 'Yup. Knows she can't win, wants a plea bargain.' A shrug. 'Still, at least it saves the parents having to watch her strangling the poor wee sod. Christ knows I'll be seeing that in the dark for weeks...'

I put a hand around Alice's shoulders and gave her a squeeze. Kept my voice low. 'Proud of you.'

She squeezed back. 'I wish *I* was...'

Alice dumped her satchel on the bar of the Postman's Head. A photo of TV's Dr Frederic Docherty now graced the dartboard – a single arrow stuck between his eyes.

Huntly sat at a table in the corner, slumped in front of a laptop connected to an external hard drive the size of a hotel bible. Chin resting in his hand, head nodding up and down as he popped in a handful of dry-roasted and chewed.

He looked up from the screen, voice deadpan: 'Well, well, the conquering heroes return. I suppose you're expecting cakes and balloons?'

Cooper had taken up position on the other side of the pub, frowning at a laptop of his own, scribbling things down in a notebook. Put his pen down. A smile ripped across his face. 'Guv, Dr McDonald – great result!'

Alice blushed, shrugged one shoulder. 'It was really all Ash, I just—'

'Gah…' Huntly rolled his eyes. 'Yes, yes, false modesty, blah, blah, blah.' He sagged till his forehead rested against the laptop. 'It's all very well for you, but I'm the one stuck in here with hours and hours and *hours* of CCTV footage. And I wouldn't have to wade through the bloody stuff if *you'd* done a decent job and got a confession out of the odious creature in the first place.' A pout. 'I've been sitting here, watching grainy little people whizzing about on a computer screen, for so long I'm at risk of developing *haemorrhoidae*. And there's *still* twenty hours' worth to go.'

Cooper folded his arms and scowled across the room. 'Don't hear me moaning about having to go through the TV footage from that demo, do you?'

'Television footage? I should be so lucky.' Huntly slapped a hand to his chest. 'I've done *all* the CCTV from Claire Young, and all the cameras where Jessica McFee went missing, *and* the surrounding streets.' He slumped forwards again. 'And that's just the modern coverage; Bear wants me to go over the historic stuff too.'

Alice opened her satchel and produced the deposition-site photographs for each of the Inside Man victims. Spread them out in front of the beer taps.

'And you would not *believe* the state of the old CCTV tapes. Some of it's rotted, some's been eaten by mice, a big pile looks as if it's been underwater for the last eight years...'

I limped over. 'Any sign of Docherty?'

The laptop's screen was broken into three windows, each showing alternative views of the same scene. The timestamps clicked over to midnight. Tiny people moved in stop-motion lurches through the darkened streets, heading home after being turfed out of pubs and lovers' embraces, preserved for a moment in the lonely glow of a streetlight.

Huntly pursed his lips and stroked his chin. 'You know what? Now I think of it, I believe I *did* just see him on the clip I was watching a minute ago. He was outside a betting shop on Donovan Lane, with a dead woman thrown over one shoulder and Jessica McFee tucked under the other arm. I wasn't going to mention it – seemed rather trivial at the time – but as you've asked—'

'Don't be a dick.'

Huntly raised an eyebrow. 'I am not, as you so *crudely* put it, "a dick". I'm refreshingly challenging.'

'You keep telling yourself that.'

Alice unfolded a map of Oldcastle and started marking the dump sites in red pen.

I took the barstool next to her. 'So, how did you get Cunningham to confess?'

She frowned at the map, forehead furrowed. 'There has to be something significant about the distribution of deposition sites. *Not* just that they're within quick emergency response time of the hospital and a working phone box, I mean they have to be close to the operating site as well, don't they? There's no point going to all that effort, making sure an ambulance can attend in under fifteen minutes, if it takes you an hour to get your victim there in the first place.'

'What did you say to Cunningham?'

The blush was back. 'So we have to work back from where

he left their bodies. What's within ten, fifteen minutes of all of them?'

'Other than the hospital?'

She rocked backwards and forwards in her seat a couple of times. Sighed. 'I told her it wasn't fair to make Charlie's parents go through the mobile-phone video in open court, in front of everyone. That it'd make things much worse for them. That every time they thought of him, every time a song came on the radio he liked, they'd see her strangling him.'

Wow. 'And that was it: she decided to plead guilty?'

'Of course not.' Alice picked up her pen again. 'So I told her about all the people I'd helped in prisons all over the country – all those people with mental health problems and violent tendencies – and how it'd only take one word from me and they'd be falling over themselves to make her life a living hell. Well, not one word, obviously, it'd probably take at least a dozen, but the point's the same.'

She drew a circle on the map around the spot where Claire Young's body had been discovered, covering Blackwall Hill and part of Kingsmeath. 'I thought, if Mrs Kerrigan could do it, why couldn't I?' Another circle went around the lay-by where we'd found Tara McNab. Eyes fixed on the map. 'And before you ask: no, I'm not proud of myself.'

'Well, I am.' I poked a finger at Castle Hill Infirmary. 'What about the hospital?'

She chewed on the inside of her cheek for a bit. 'A disused operating theatre?'

'Or mortuary? Been a hospital there since the seventeenth century. Every hundred years or so, they'd build new bits on top of the old structure. *God* knows what's down there. There's even supposed to be secret tunnels heading out to the docks.'

'I don't know… It's all a bit, Dan Brown, isn't it?'

'Probably.' I pulled out my phone. 'Worth a call anyway.' I dialled Rhona's number and made for the pub door, pushed through into the little airlock.

Rain bounced off the pavement, battered against the chip-board barrier on the other side of the road. Soaked into the abandoned breezeblock.

'*DS Massie.*'

'Rhona, I need you to take a look at Castle Hill Infirmary. Any old operating theatres or mortuaries in the place? Anything that's not been in use for years?'

'*Yeah, let me guess – someone's just figured out that the hospital's the only thing definitely within emergency response times: there and back?*'

'Ah...'

'*I looked into it last week. The original mortuary got turned into a museum as part of that Oldcastle Millennium bollocks, so that's a nonstarter. There's an old surgical wing that's not been used since the seventies, but it's been completely stripped for a refurb. Not so much as a kidney dish or a bed pan left in the place.*' A yawn ripped free, followed by a long sigh. '*And there's been architects and builders and councillors in and out of there on a regular basis for months.*'

So much for that. 'Should you not have gone home by now?'

'*We're hitting the Monk and Casket after work.*'

'All right for some.'

A pause. '*Are you not coming?*'

Jacobson's big black Range Rover growled out of the rain, headlights glowing back from the wet road. Dr Constantine grinned at me from the driver's seat. Waved.

I waved back. 'What about the addresses Docherty had access to?'

'*Hold on... Right, everything's been searched top to bottom. We've had a dog team up to the Castleview place, and Moray-and-Shire have done the one in Stonehaven. Nothing. Now we're waiting for the dogs to get to the properties in Dundee and Blackwall Hill so we can get them ticked off too.*'

'You don't sound hopeful.'

A sucking sound came through the earpiece, as if she was breathing in through her teeth. '*He's not daft, is he, Guv? He's*

465

a slimy turdhole, but he's not stupid. He knows we'd connect him to those houses. He's got them somewhere no one knows about, but him. Maybe renting under an assumed name?'

The Range Rover's lights went out, and Jacobson climbed down from the passenger side, turned his collar up, reached back into the car for half-a-dozen carrier-bags and hurried for the pub entrance.

Renting…

I stood to one side and let him squeeze past. He held up one of the bags. 'Lots and lots of wine.' Then he grimaced. 'But Docherty's still not owning up.' And he was through into the pub.

Renting a house? A flat wouldn't work, you couldn't drag victims up and down the stairs without someone noticing.

Dr Constantine lumbered her way around from the boot, laden down with boxes of Grolsch and fruity cider. She paused as I held the door open for her, stood on her tiptoes and kissed my cheek. 'Not bad for a copper.' Then she was gone.

You'd need something secluded. Out of the way…

'What about that static caravan park, south of Shortstaine? You're what, two minutes from the dual carriageway there – could be anywhere in the city in ten, if traffic was light.'

'Like it: they're big enough to set up a wee operating room, no one's going to bother you, and the older ones probably cost peanuts. Bet they don't ask for ID if you pay cash either… Nice one, Guv, I'll get someone out there.'

'And when you're done, forget the Monk and Casket: Postman's Head on Millen Road, opposite where they were going to put that care home. Looks like we might be having some sort of shindig tonight – consider yourself invited. Might be an idea to bring a bottle.'

With any luck, we'd be celebrating more than just catching the bastard.

49

Rain crackled against the window. Outside, on the street below, a man slogged past, baseball cap pulled low, shoulders hunched against the onslaught. He didn't stop. Didn't look across the road at the Postman's Head.

But that didn't mean he wasn't watching it.

The sound of a TV news bulletin oozed up from the bar downstairs.

If anything, it made the silence in the manager's flat even thicker. Nearly all the furniture was gone, leaving a small table, two wooden chairs – that looked as if they'd been liberated from the pub – and a cracked mirror above the bathroom sink. A broken chest of drawers in the bedroom. An ancient fitted kitchen with no cooker or fridge, just grey tidelines of dust and grease to mark their passing.

I went back to my phone. 'And?'

On the other end, Noel Maxwell huffed out a breath. *'Still off her face on morphine and sedatives.'*

The guy in the baseball cap kept going, until the night swallowed him.

'She had any visitors?'

'Couple of heavies been in since nine this morning. Scary, scary

467

blokes all covered in bruises. One of them's got his head bandaged up like a mummy, the other's on crutches.'

That would be Joseph and Francis.

Noel cleared his throat. *'Listen, about Boxer, you didn't tell anyone I clyped on him, did you? Cause if the guys find out—'*

'When they releasing her?'

'—reputation and they'll kick the crap out of me too.'

God's sake. 'I didn't tell anyone, OK? Now when are they letting Mrs Kerrigan out of hospital?'

'Not today. Probably not tomorrow either. You know what it's like up there on the private floor – place is a sodding hotel. Fine dining, wine, and all the drugs you want, who'd leave?'

So twenty-four hours, maybe forty-eight before she came looking for us... Of course, she'd want to be there in person to rip out our teeth with pliers, but there was nothing to stop her getting a few of her dogs to grab Alice and me off the street any time she wanted. Keep us somewhere cold, dark, and painful until she was ready to play.

Outside, there was no sign of the guy in the hat making another pass.

'Hello?'

I blinked. Looked down at the phone. 'Thanks, Noel.'

'Hey, no probs. What are friends—'

I hung up.

'Ash?' Alice stood in the doorway to the living room, tumbler in one hand, pint glass in the other. She scuffed her way across the floorboards and held the pint out. 'I got you a Coke.'

'Thanks.' Cold and brown and sweet and fizzy. And somehow it still managed to taste of death.

'So... We're ordering pizza, do you want something specific, or do you just want one of those mixed jobs, and what are you doing up here?'

I turned my back on the window. 'Nothing. Just getting some air. Thinking about Shifty.'

She peered at the case files spread out on the rickety table. Victims and deposition sites. Post-mortem results and statements.

'You should come down for a bit. Try to switch off for ten minutes.'

A sliver of varnish peeled away beneath my fingernail, leaving a streak of pale wood on the head of my cane. 'He's my friend. And he's only in trouble because... The only reason she did that to him, is because of me. I screwed up, Alice. I should've killed her when I had the chance.'

'You can't—'

'If I had, Parker would still be alive. Shifty would be safe.' And I wouldn't have spent two years in prison. I could have gone to my little girls' funeral. I wouldn't be stood at the window, waiting for the dogs to come.

Well, I wouldn't be making that mistake again.

Alice put a hand on my arm. 'You think she's going to come after us, don't you? Mrs Kerrigan.'

Force a smile. Lie. 'No. Don't be daft: she'll be after Wee Free. We didn't lay a finger on her, did we? It was all him.'

Alice blinked at me. Tried to hide a sigh. Then nodded. 'You need to take a break. Prolonged periods of concentration deplete the mind's ability to process new information and make connections. Take fifteen minutes. Come downstairs and argue with Professor Huntly, or tease Constable Cooper. Or just hang about watching TV till the pizza gets here.' She reached up and tapped a finger against my forehead. 'Let the little grey cells percolate away on their own for a bit, and maybe they'll have something for you when you come back.'

Well, it wasn't as if I was getting anywhere here.

I followed her down the crooked wooden stairs to the pub kitchen – all dusty stainless steel and the ghost of chip fat – then through the door and into the bar. The wall-mounted TV was playing News 24: a fat bald bloke in a suit refusing to answer whatever question the woman in the studio had asked. '… *if you'll let me finish, I think you'll find that under the* last *government, the financial—*'

I picked the remote off the bar and killed the sound.

Jacobson stood in front of the whiteboard, glass of red in one hand, pen in the other, drawing boxes and lines, filling them with dense blocks of tiny letters.

Dr Constantine sat at the bar, with a bottle of cider and a packet of Monster Munch, leafing her way through a stack of post-mortem photographs. She glanced up at me, then grimaced. 'They did rape kits on the dead victims, but there's no sign of semen or alien pubic hair in the combings. No sign of vaginal bruising either. Nothing we can use to nail Docherty.'

Huntly and Cooper were in their separate corners, still hunched over their respective laptops. Huntly looking almost suicidal with a tin of pre-mixed gin-and-tonic.

He took a sip. 'Can we please not discuss vaginal bruising? Some of us are trying to concentrate…'

While Alice sorted out the pizza order, I joined Jacobson at the whiteboard. It was covered in case names and reference numbers, all linked to a box in the middle, with 'DR FREDERIC DOCHERTY' printed inside it.

Jacobson gave a small grunt. 'He's been working as a police adviser for eight years. Eight years of rapes and murders and abductions and missing persons… How many of them was he responsible for?'

'Waterboarding doesn't leave any marks.'

A little smile tugged at his lips. 'We've been over this.'

'Just saying. We'd know where they were in fifteen minutes, half an hour, tops. No one would ever find out.'

'Ah, the good old days…'

I skimmed the board again. 'Got to be something we can do.'

Jacobson's smile died. 'Tell me about it.'

My phone vibrated – a new email. I opened it up.

Hoy, Jock-cop Tartan Boy.

Don't say I'm never good to you: audio files from the pre-recorded 999 calls (attached). I've isolated all the girls' voices and removed them, everything left is the background noise you asked for.

Got what sounds like a mobile phone on H-Drummond.wav @ 92sec and @ 46sec on M-Jordan.wav Really faint though. Don't think it's from the control room, so might be where the phonebox was, or where he recorded it in the first place.

Tried running the electronic buzz through the database, but nothing came back — probably cos it's a recording of a phonecall of a recording. You got three layers of buzz all mooshed together.

L8R haggis-munchers,

Sabir Lord Of Teh Tech

p.s. your mam says Hi.

Alice stared at me. 'Well?'

'Sabir.'

A frown. 'No: pizza. What do you want?'

'Anything that doesn't have pineapple. Or anchovies.' I poked the icon for the attachments and nothing happened. Tried again. 'Mushrooms are good.' Still nothing. 'Huntly, we got any more of those laptops?'

He sat back and rubbed at his eyes. 'Nnnngh... You can have this one if you like. I'm beginning to suffer from ocular cuboidism. Complete waste of time, anyway. Docherty isn't going to march about in plain sight, is he? No, he'll be wearing a hoodie and a baseball cap. Hiding his identity. Avoiding the streets controlled by CCTV. He might be a vile serial scumbag, but he knows how the system works.' Huntly clunked the laptop shut, then stuck one hand above his head and snapped his fingers. 'Dr McDonald, be a pet and make sure mine has extra peperoni on it. And some jalapeños, I'm feeling spicy.'

Lucky us.

I disconnected the external hard drive and tucked the laptop under my arm. Warmth oozed through my sleeve and into my chest as I headed back through to the kitchen. Making for the stairs.

Huntly's voice echoed out behind me, 'You're not exactly great company yourself!'

I called up Sabir's email and played the audio files again.

Most of them were nothing but hiss, crackle and the occasional buzz. All but those two files – the ones Marie Jordan and Holly Drummond had been forced to record before Docherty slit them open.

Even with the laptop's speakers turned up full pelt, it was barely discernible. Five or six seconds of a faint tune on M-Jordan.wav, nine on H-Drummond.wav. Too vague and fuzzy to be recognizable.

I logged in to the laptop's video conferencing software, scrolled through the list of contacts and clicked on Sabir4TehPool.

Thirty seconds later a round face peered out of the screen at me over the top of a pair of little round specs. His skin was the colour of ancient tarmac, the jowls rough with stubble. Bags under his eyes. Bald, with a tiny mouth for such a big head. He curled his lip. *'You look like something out of a George Romero movie.'*

472

'Well, you look like the Teletubby they kept locked in the attic, in case it scared the kids.'

He leaned back – letting a little of the room leak onto the screen. *'Flattery's not your main strength, mate. What you after this time?'*

'That ringtone: did you try matching it to manufacturers?'

'These days you can get anything your greasy little heart desires on your phone. Download it from iTunes, or your provider, or get some software off the net and rip it yourself.'

'Yes, but it sounds pretty basic. Probably one of the default ones on an older handset.'

'Pffff… It was eight years ago. They were all *older handsets then. Hold on.'* He hunched forwards again, the clatter of fingers on keyboard crackling out of the laptop's speakers. *'Got something you'll properly love, by the way. There.'*

My phone vibrated – another email. I opened it up. Looked like a web address. 'What's this?'

'Been off a-hacking in your local radio station's servers, haven't I? And guess what I found?'

'What?'

'Click on the link, you scone-head.'

I tried. Nothing.

'It's not working. How do I get it up on the laptop?'

'God save us…'

Two minutes later and there was a window on the screen full of little video previews with nonsense filenames. People in white T-shirts and big grins.

'It's the fund raiser they had at that train station. Where you landed on your arse and the Inside Man legged it? They posted highlights on the website and that, but I had a geg and snooped out all the raw footage for youse.'

I hovered the mouse across the first file. 'Did they get me on film?'

'Nah. It's all people dancing in their trainies, and having a pie-eating competition, and doing one of them stupid static-bike rides.

473

Couple of fit judies in there though. You know: if you like them sweaty...' A frown. *'How come I can't hear a party or anything?'*

'Because we—'

'You caught the bastard, and you're sitting there on your tod in the dark? You should be off filling your boots, mate. Then I could get back to climbing on top of your ma. She's feeling frisky tonight.'

'We can't find Ruth, Jessica, or Laura.' I tried a smile. 'Don't suppose you fancy doing a bit of digging and see if you can find any properties Docherty's paying rent for, or bought under a false name or something? Go through his credit cards like you did Laura Strachan's boyfriend? We've been looking for somewhere he could set up an operating theatre, but the guys up here don't have your ... unique talents.'

Sabir chewed on his bottom lip for a bit. *'Give it a go, I suppose. Take a while though.'* More clicks from the keyboard.

I shrunk the window with him in it, selected the first video clip and set it playing. Laughter boomed from the speakers, tinny and distorted by the train station roof. I turned the volume down till it was almost non-existent.

A group of young men in Oldcastle Warriors tracksuits are cheering on an older man in a suit and tie as he rides the static bike. Poor sod looks ready to peg out. Didn't he used to be the manager? The timestamp ticks over in the corner – 11:10:15, 11:10:16, 11:10:17...

'Here, you thought about a van or something? Big Transit van. Strip out the load bay and you'd get a decent operating theatre in there. You could shift it about, park it up and do the business, then just drive off to the dump site. No sodding about.' Sabir nodded, giving himself another three chins. *'Better yet, want to make sure they're still alive when the ambulance gets there? Do the surgery on site, drop the vic out the back, then drive away. Did youse lot check for tyreprints at the scenes?'*

'Nothing conclusive...'

Next clip. A group of little school kids dance to a Britney Spears number. All elbows and knees and cheesy grins for

474

the camera. It keeps zooming in on one wee girl with dark pigtails and a smile that's missing two front teeth. Lingering. As if the cameraman is auditioning for a role on the sex offenders' register. 10:31:01, 10:31:02, 10:31:03...

'Yeah, well, I'm getting the same from that ringtone. Just been running it through a dozen different filters and some military-grade algorithms I'm really not supposed to have. And it's definitely poly-phonic, but it's that generic, it's useless. Can download it from anywhere. Got hits from Nokia, Motorola, Sony, Siemens...'

The next clip is an interview with one of those local celebrities who's famous for being on reality TV, and then completely forgotten about. Pretty certain he got done for soliciting and possession-with-intent a couple of years later. 15:18:42, 15:18:43, 15:18:44...

'Case you're interested, it's called "Cambridge Quarters".'

'OK.' I scribbled it down in my notebook, underlined it twice and stuck a couple of question marks on the end.

Next clip. A group of three young women grin for the camera, bouncing up and down in time to the music... They're all nurses – that's why they look familiar – Laura Strachan's flatmates. Down to raise money in her name, while she's in intensive care wired up to half a ton of machinery. 12:41:58, 12:41:59, 13:00:00...

'You want anything else, or can I go back to giving your ma a good time? She's pretty demanding. You know, sexually?'

'Your own fault for digging her up. Should've left her where we buried her.'

The noise from the bar downstairs grew louder, as music replaced the drone of the TV.

Then creaking on the stairs, and Alice thumped in through the door. An extra-large whisky sloshed in one hand. 'Ash? Pizza's going to be here soon, you should... Oh, is that Sabir?'

She scuffed over to the laptop and hunched down in front of the screen. 'Sabir!' Took a sip of whisky, waving at the camera while she drank. 'We're having pizza. Are you having pizza? You should have pizza, I've not seen you *forever*, would you like a drink?'

He raised a can of something caffeinated to the monitor. *'Alice. How's me favourite Looney Tunes character then?'*

She pouted. 'You have to do the voice.'

'Nyeaaaaaaah, what's up, Doc?'

Next clip. More nurses cluster around the bicycle, cheering on a short woman who's sweated through her T-shirt. Is that Jessica McFee's flatmate? It is. A young Bethany Gillespie. Presumably before she married Jimmy the control-freak. 12:25:03, 12:25:04, 12:25:05...

I moved on to the next one while Alice and Sabir gossiped like a pair of auld wifies.

Another bicycle shot. This time there was no problem recognizing the rider. Ruth Laughlin hammered away at the pedals, surrounded by Jessica's friends and colleagues. Sweat darkened her T-shirt, bare knees pumping, face glowing and dripping with sweat. 14:12:35, 14:12:36, 14:12:37...

Poor old Ruth. Hollowed out in a crummy flat in Cowskillin, flinching at her own shadow, terrorized by a bunch of snotty wee kids. Taking antidepressants and being spat at. Wishing the doctors had let her die.

And all because I turned up at the train station, covered in blood, and put her on Dr Frederic Docherty's radar.

How did he get away? Did he hop the train, slip off at the first stop, and get a taxi back to town? Or just nip out of a side entrance to the station. Scurry away through the streets.

Did he go back to work afterwards or take the rest of the day off?

On screen they do a countdown. Ruth throws her hands in the air, grinning as they reach zero, the 'Turn Miles Into Smiles!!!' banner fluttering behind her.

It was the same image Ness had put up at the briefing.

Did Docherty go to bed with a smile on his face that night?

Outwitted the cops again. Made us look like morons. Scott free, with a new victim to target, just because she'd helped me.

And now he had her again, locked away somewhere, waiting to die. Her, and Jessica, and Laura. And it all came back to that one day, in the train station, when I let the bastard get away.

50

Alice put a hand on my shoulder. 'Ash, are you OK? Only you look like you're about to strangle someone...'

Right.

I let go of the mouse. Flexed my hand a couple of times. Deep breath. 'I'm fine.'

Next clip. Four rugby types in Oldcastle University sweatshirts, wolfing their way through a pile of macaroni pies, with a big digital counter in the background. The one with the biggest forehead wins, pumping his fists above his head and lording it over the other three with a big greasy grin.

'*OK, I'm bailing. Got things to see, people to do.*' On the chat screen, Sabir pointed a sausage finger at the lens. '*Alice, get your arse down to London and I'll show you how we do murder cases in the civilized world. And Ash – lighten up, eh? Take the night off. Bleeding crusade will still be there tomorrow.*' He gave a small salute. '*Sabir, Lord of the Tech, signing off.*' And the window went black.

I logged off. Closed it down.

Alice wrapped her arms around my shoulders and squeezed. Kissed the top of my head. 'He's right. You need to relax.'

'How?' I took my mobile out. Placed it on the table. Picked

it up again. 'I want to phone Wee Free – find out if Shifty's OK. But if I do, it's just going to rub it in, isn't it? That I haven't found his daughter yet.'

'You're doing everything you can.'

'Am I?'

'… *five, four, three, two, one, zero!*' The cordon of nurses whoop and cheer, jumping up and down as Ruth throws her arms in the air. Grinning. The 'TURN MILES INTO SMILES!!!' flutters behind her.

And cut.

Downstairs, the music was getting louder.

I hit play again.

Leaned forward and peered at the screen, scanning the faces in the crowd behind the nurses. None of them looked familiar. Well, other than Ruth and her friends. But there was *something…*

What?

Just a woman on a static bicycle, raising money to honour her friend. Blissfully unaware that her own life's about to be ruined.

Footsteps thumped up the stairs, then the flat's door clattered open and Rhona staggered to a halt, face stretched in a wide grin, breathing hard. Bottle of champagne clutched in her hand. 'Guv? We've got him. We've got the bastard!'

Onscreen, Ruth pedals, knees pumping, sweat colouring the fabric of her T-shirt. Faces in the background cheer, smile, chat to one another. Music from the main stage, just audible under the countdown…

I sat up. 'What, Docherty?'

Rhona thumped the champagne down on the table, beside the laptop. 'You were right, Guv!'

'… *four, three, two, one, zero!*' Ruth throws her hands in the air. Turning miles into smiles.

Thank Christ. 'They were at the caravan park?'

479

A frown. 'What? No... We ran the ANPR tapes against his number plate like you said, and guess what? One dark-blue Volvo estate registered to Dr Frederic Docherty leaving the city limits heading north out of the city at ten-o-three p.m.'

'Did he—'

'So I got onto Aberdeen City and Dundee, told them to dig out Friday's tapes and ANPR them from twenty-past ten onwards.' Rhona paced up and down the floorboards, fingers digging through her lank hair. 'He hits Aberdeen at half ten. And guess what: I got them to send me every reported crime in the city that night. Bunch of fights, couple of break-ins, two indecent assaults, one indecent exposure, and...' Rhona pulled a sheet of paper from her pocket and held it out. 'Ta-da.'

It was an incident report from half four in the morning. Someone had found a half-naked woman, dead and covered in blood, just off Midstocket Road. Only when the patrol car got there she wasn't dead after all, just sedated. It wasn't even her blood – it was some sort of artificial theatrical stuff. So they called an ambulance and got her wheeched off to the local A&E.

Alice appeared at the top of the stairs, holding her whisky against her chest. 'Ash? What's going on?'

Rhona licked her lips, raised her eyebrows. 'Want to know the best bit?' She pulled out something else – a print-out of a blurry photograph. 'The guy who reported it took a photo on his mobile phone. Look familiar?'

A young woman lay on her back, in a hollow. Pale skin gleamed between the strips of black underwear. Dark-red theatrical blood covered her belly – making tracks down either side of her abdomen. Both arms up above her head, one leg twisted out to the side. Exactly the same as Holly Drummond.

I handed it to Alice. 'He's recreating the kills.'

She took the photo, frowned at it. 'Why would he—'

'And the coup de grâce?' A grin burned across Rhona's face.

480

'They did a tox screen on the victim's blood. Special rush job, because we told them what to look for.'

'Thiopental Sodium?'

'Thiopental Sodium.'

Alice passed the photo back. 'Why would he recreate his own kills? He's not trying to kill them, he's—'

'Isn't it great?' Rhona threw her arms wide. 'We got him. And I *bet* she isn't the only one either. I've got a call out to the rest of the country looking for any other women he's attacked.'

I sat back in my chair. It was as if something had been sitting on my chest for a week and now it was... 'No.' I folded forward, scrubbed my hands across my face. 'Bastard!'

'Guv?'

'Arrgh...'

'Ash, are you OK?'

I dropped my hands. 'He left Oldcastle just after ten. When did he get back?'

A frown, then Rhona checked her notebook. 'Ten to four. Guv, I don't—'

'Laura Strachan went missing between eleven last night and three this morning. If he was up in Aberdeen drugging and stripping someone, he wasn't down here abducting Laura Strachan and Ruth Laughlin.' My palms clattered against the tabletop, making the laptop jitter. 'DAMN IT!'

Rhona's face scrunched, fists curled. 'He didn't take them.' She kicked the other chair, sending it clattering over backwards. 'We *had* him!'

There was a pause, then Alice twiddled with her hair. 'He's got an accomplice, that's how he can be up molesting women in Aberdeen and abducting Ruth and Laura at the same time, someone working with him...' Wrinkles formed in the gap between her eyebrows. 'Someone he can control and manipulate, someone who thinks they're connected and special and in love, when it's really all about power... Someone local.'

Alice slipped out of the room, then the sound of feet thumped down the stairs. She was back two minutes later with her satchel. She tipped the contents out next to the laptop, grabbed the map and unfolded it. It was the one she'd been marking up – covered in red circles, each one covering a deposition site. 'Think of it as a Venn diagram, the circles represent fifteen minutes' travelling time, and where the areas intersect we've—'

'These are all wrong.' Rhona poked a finger just below Cowskillin and traced it along the dual carriageway. 'He dumps them all at night, or the wee small hours, when the roads are quiet. You can get right across town in five minutes at two in the morning.'

Alice's shoulders dipped. 'Oh.'

Rhona pulled a pen from an inside pocket and drew an 'X' over Castle Hill Infirmary. Then another one up on Blackwall Hill. 'Private hospital. And there's that old World War Two sanatorium here...' An 'X' marked the Bellows. 'And a Victorian loony bin on Albert Road.' She clicked her fingers at me, showing off bitten fingernails. 'Guv, where else? Anywhere there's likely to be surgical facilities.'

'Some of the bigger GP practices will do small procedures.'

'Right.' She made more marks.

Probably useless, but what else did we have? That and a pair of barely audible audio files.

The door thunked open again and Huntly paused on the threshold. Straightened his tie. Gin and tonic in one hand. The words were slightly soft at the edges, but not enough to count as slurred. 'So this is where you're all squirreling away, is it?'

I played the first audio file again, volume cranked up full. There was the ringtone again: distorted, crackly, and – according to Sabir – available on millions of mobiles. It was repetitious, going up and down, but the quality was too poor to make out the actual tune.

Huntly loomed over Rhona and Alice at the map. 'His Royal Highness the Great Bear has sent me to fetch everyone. For lo, *la pizza è arrivata*.' He looked at me. 'Or for those of you with a less classical bent, "grub's up".'

Surgical facilities and a ringtone.

I clicked on M-Jordan.wav and set it playing again. The audio file hissed and crackled in its window, next to the video file I'd been watching. Frozen at the final frame: Ruth Laughlin, arms in the air. Turning miles into smiles.

Why that file? Why keep going back to it? What was wrong with it?

Huntly moved to the other side of the laptop. Made shooing gestures. 'Well, come on then, don't want the pizzas getting cold, do we?'

I set the audio playing again. Hiss. Crackle. A short smear of music, so faint it was barely there.

Huntly sniffed. Then picked up my notebook. It was open at the last page, where I'd been scribbling down points while talking to Sabir. 'I wasn't aware you were into campanology, Mr Henderson.'

I snatched it back. 'What did I say about being a dick?'

'Refreshingly challenging, remember?' He pointed at the notebook. '"Cambridge Quarters".'

'Don't you have someone else you could be annoying?'

'Here's a little fact for you. Did you know that Big Ben plays a variation called "Westminster Quarters"? Four bars of four notes to denote each quarter hour. Hence the name.'

Ruth Laughlin frozen for all time. Arms up in triumph. The timestamp for the last frame unblinking in the corner, '14:13:42'. A cordon of nurses cheering her on. Happy faces arrayed behind her...

Oh. Shit.

Huntly crossed his arms and smiled at the damp-stained ceiling. 'I remember I once had to test two hundred mini Big Bens. An enterprising group of Manchester businessmen had mixed heroin and plaster of Paris, with a handful of coffee grounds thrown in to mask the smell.'

Four bars of four notes.

It wasn't a ringtone.

I pushed back my chair and stood. Grabbed my cane. 'Get Jacobson, *now*.'

Alice tugged at my sleeve. 'What's wrong?'

'I know where they are.'

51

Jacobson peered at the map, leaning on the bar with one hand while he traced a finger around a red-biro circle. 'And this source of yours is sure?'

I shook my head. 'A hundred percent? No. But he's come through in the past. If he says he's seen Docherty going in and out of there, it's got to be worth a try, isn't it?' My finger poked at the map, just south of Shortstaine. 'Think about it. Secluded, easy access to the dual carriageway, all paid in cash, no ID needed.'

Rhona's forehead creased. 'But, Guv, we—'

'I know: you think you should tell Detective Superintendent Ness first, but it's Jacobson's call. He's senior officer on the ground.' I gave him a nod. 'Boss?'

He looked around the room. 'Everyone, get the car. We're going on a field trip.'

Huntly groaned. 'But it's all just *hearsay*. He hasn't got any evidence and my pizza's getting cold and—'

'Then take it with you.' Jacobson pointed at the door. 'If there's any chance of rescuing Docherty's victims, we're doing it. Car. *Now*.'

Another groan, then Huntly slipped two tins of ready-mixed gin and tonic into his pockets.

'But…' Rhona stared at me. 'We—'

'You're right.' I patted her on the shoulder. 'I'll only slow them down.' Then waggled my cane at Jacobson. 'You lot go ahead. Alice, Rhona, and I can get started on the debriefing strategy.'

Jacobson beamed at me. 'I knew you'd be a great addition to the team, Ash.' And then they piled out through the pub doors, leaving the three of us behind.

Pause.

Two.

Three.

Rhona scrunched up her face. 'But we *checked* the caravan park. Other than a couple of disused lots, they're all accounted for. Docherty didn't rent any of them.'

Four.

Five.

Six.

I pointed Alice towards the door. 'Go make sure they've gone.'

She was back ten seconds later. 'Jessica, Ruth, and Laura aren't at the caravan park, are they?'

'Get the car.'

Rhona pulled the Suzuki in to the kerb, hands skittering back and forth on the wheel, as if it was red-hot and she was scared of getting her fingers burned. 'Err… Guv, I *really* think we should've told the boss about this…'

Lights shone in the windows of the houses – happy families and venetian blinds all shut up for the night. Only a week after Bonfire Night and some silly sod had a Christmas tree up already.

The shops on the other side of the road sulked beneath the streetlights: a butcher's, a grocer's, and a vet's. Their boarded-up windows still plastered with posters for the ghost of circus past. Every bit as abandoned as they had been when we'd driven past on Monday.

I undid my seatbelt. 'I'd love to call it in, but I can't get a mobile signal. Can you, Alice?'

She pulled out her phone. Frowned at it. 'I'm getting four bars, maybe your...' And then her face opened up. 'Ah, *right*. No, I'm not getting anything. Must be one of those black spots.'

'Exactly.' I popped the door handle. 'Besides, if we go in mob-handed someone's going to end up dead.' And God knows there'd been enough of that.

Rhona sat forward, rested her head against the steering wheel. 'This is, *way* above my pay grade. What if something happens?'

I climbed out into the rain. 'Then you'll be a hero, won't you?' Water seeped through my hair as I limped around the car and got the crowbar from the boot. Then used it as a cane to hobble across the road.

'Ash, wait, wait, wait...' Alice clambered out of the back seat and scurried up beside me, clutching my other arm, umbrella thrumming above our heads. 'Don't we need that little battering-ram thingie, I mean he's not just going to leave them there with the door unlocked, is he, that would be reckless, they might get out...' A frown. 'Or someone might get in, which I suppose would be us, are we going in?'

It wasn't just the shop windows that were boarded over with chipboard, the doors were too. 'You stay behind me, understand?'

Rhona caught up.

She stared up at the building, water dripping from the ends of her hair, darkening the grey of her suit. 'Do we try to kick it in, or go round the back?'

I hobbled onwards. 'We go round the back.'

An alley led down the rear of the shops, the entrance sealed off with a length of chain bolted to the wall on one side and padlocked on the other. I ducked under it, waited for Alice, then stopped.

A small van sat behind the vet's – dented and rusted. Reversed in so the back doors faced the building, the lettering for a carpet fitters still visible where the vinyl lettering had been peeled away. I pointed. 'Rhona? Number plate.'

'Guv.' She pulled an Airwave handset from her jacket. 'Sierra Oscar Four-Forty to Control, I need a vehicle check on a grey Ford Escort van...'

I stuck out my hand. 'Alice, got any gloves? Used all mine.'

She passed me a pair of purple nitrile gloves and I snapped them on. Tried the van's back doors. Locked. The rear windows were painted over from the inside.

The back door to the vet's was locked too.

Rhona was back. 'Your van was officially scrapped three years ago. Last registered to a Kenny James, deceased.'

Figured.

I wedged the crowbar's hook into the gap between the wooden door and the frame.

Rhona shifted her feet. 'Guv, don't we need a warrant?'

One hard shove and the wood cracked and splintered around the lock. One more and it gave way with a *pop*. 'It was like this when we found it. Wasn't it, Alice?'

A nod. 'Must've been vandals.'

That's my girl.

Inside was a bare room with a raised area off to one side. Dark.

Music coiled out through the opened door – something upbeat and poppy, with lots of snare drums – followed by a sharp whiff of pine disinfectant and bleach, underpinned with dirty mildew.

The crowbar's tip crunched against the painted floor as I limped over the threshold.

Light seeped under a door ahead, but this one wasn't locked. The handle clicked in my hands. I pushed it open and the music got louder.

It was a wide corridor, with a wall of cages on one side – some small enough for a cat, others big enough for a deer hound. One was occupied.

Alice wrapped her hands around my arm and squeezed. 'Is she dead?'

Laura Strachan lay on her side in the biggest cage, curled up in a ball, elbows resting against the swell of her pregnant stomach. Fiery red hair hung limp across her face. Her wrists were held together by a thick band of silver duct-tape, ankles too. A strip across her mouth for a gag.

Rhona groaned. 'Sodding hell...'

Alice knelt in front of the cage, reached a finger through the wire grille and poked her on the forehead.

Laura's eyes snapped open. 'Mmmmmmmnnnnghghnnnph!'

Alice scrabbled backwards, landed on her backside and kept going till she hit the wall, eyes wide. Then a trembling breath, and she was back in front of the cage again. 'Oh God, I'm so sorry, are you OK, I mean obviously you're not OK, but it's all right we're here and you're safe and don't worry we'll get you out of here.' She reached for the hasp holding the door shut.

I grabbed her hand. 'No.'

'But—'

'And keep your voice down.'

Rhona squeezed forwards. 'Are you *mad*, we need to get this woman to—'

'Shhh...' I pointed at Alice, kept my voice low. 'Stay with her. Wait five minutes, then get her out the back. *Quietly.*' I peered into the cage.

Laura Strachan glowered back at me, mouth working behind the gag. 'Nnnnngh mnnnf gnnn, ynnnnn ffgggnnnnr!'

'I'm sorry, but you're safe. Now stop making a bloody racket, before the whole world hears you.'

'Bloody hell...' Rhona fumbled her Airwave handset out again. 'I'll call it in.'

'Do it outside, and tell them if I hear sirens I'm going to ram my crowbar down their throats. Understand? Silent running.'

Four doors led off the corridor ahead. I tried the first one: empty store cupboard.

'Guv?' Rhona grabbed me, her voice a harsh whisper. 'Maybe we should wait for them to get here. What if Docherty's accomplice turns violent? What if they kill Jessica McFee?'

'It's got nothing to do with Docherty. He's a dirty raping bastard, but he's not the Inside Man.' Door number two: a bare room with a work surface and floor units down one wall.

Now it was Alice's turn. 'What do you mean, he's not...' Her eyes widened. 'Oh... Right.'

The next door opened onto a small reception area. With the windows boarded up, the only light in the room came from the corridor behind me. A chair lurked in the gloom behind the desk, a twirly display stand rusted in one corner, a crumpled pile of plastic sheeting slumped in the middle of the floor.

That left door number four.

I gave Alice a poke. 'I told you to stay with Laura, remember?'

She blinked at me. 'But I want to stay with you.'

Of course she did.

I glanced back down the corridor, towards the cages. Laura had managed to wriggle onto her hands and knees, still duct-taped together. I put a finger to my lips.

She glared back.

Right: door number four.

The music got louder as I eased the door open a crack. Then reached a happy-clappy finale and stopped.

'Isn't that great? I love that. Anyway, you're listening to Castlewave FM, I'm Mhairi Rimmington, this is the Evening Show. *Remember, the lines are open and we're talking about the shocking news that*

TV's Dr Frederic Docherty has been arrested for sexual assault. But first, it's Colin with the weather...'

I pushed, and the door swung open.

A wheeled table, like a porter's trolley, sat in the middle of the room, beneath an array of blinding lights.

'... bit of sunshine for a change?'

Took a couple of blinks to get the room into focus.

'Sorry to disappoint you, Mhairi, but it looks as if this area of high pressure's with us till the weekend.'

A woman lay on top of the trolley – the breathing mask over her nose and mouth hooked up to a canister on the floor. She was flat on her back with one towel draped over her thighs and upper legs, and another over her breasts. The stomach in between was distended. Lumpen. Smeared with orange iodine. A line of puckered skin ran across her torso, just below the ribs, another straight down the middle. Both were held together with black stitches, the knots like tiny bugs, frozen on her skin.

Too late.

'But that's all set to change on Saturday – we've got freezing arctic air on the way, that'll ramp the temperatures right *down and we might even see a touch of snow on the hills...'*

The only other person in the room stood with their back to the door, washing their hands in a stainless-steel sink. Green hospital scrubs, white clogs, surgical cap covering their dirty blonde hair.

'Urgh, that sounds horrid, Colin. So, let's cheer ourselves up a bit with REM and "Shiny Happy People"...'

I stepped into the room. Reached out and clicked the radio off.

The person standing by the sink stiffened. Then finished up. Dried their hands and turned. Stared at me.

'Hello, Ruth.'

Silence.

Then the bells of the First National Celtic Church rang out the quarter hour. One bar of four notes, peeling out from the jagged blood-coloured spire. Just like on the audio files. God's ringtone.

She licked her lips. 'You can't come in here, it's a sterile environment.'

I limped forward anyway, circling the operating table. 'Is she…?'

Ruth's hand crept out – the fingers wrapped themselves around a scalpel's handle. She frowned. 'I…' Bit her bottom lip. 'I told you they should've let me die.'

'I finally figured out what was bugging me about the footage of you on the bike. The timestamp on the clip said twelve-past-two. Over an hour *after* I staggered in covered in blood. You were dripping with sweat, but you hadn't even been on the bike by then, had you? You were sweaty from running away. You lied to me.'

'I *saved* you.'

Alice inched in through the doorway. 'It's all right, Ruth. You're safe, remember?' Her voice dropped in tone and volume. 'Warm and safe, and everything's all right and you're comfortable and safe…'

I waved her back. 'What did you do, dump the tracksuit in the bin? Stuff it in someone's backpack? Hide it in the toilets?' Another step. Getting closer. 'And who else knew where Laura Strachan lived? You did – we *took* you there. And she wouldn't see you as threatening, would she? Just an old friend, another one of the Inside Man's victims.'

'I *told* you…' The scalpel came up, gleaming in the bright lights.

'You worked at the hospital, had access to drugs, knew all the victims, and when they locked you up in the psychiatric wing the Inside Man stopped doing his thing.'

'They should've let me die.'

'There's us, looking all over the city for home-made oper-ating theatres when you had a perfectly good one, right here, all along. Volunteering at the vet's. That's why you always dumped the bodies in the wee small hours – you had to wait till everyone else went home before you could operate.'

Clattering sounded in the corridor, then Rhona lurched into the room. 'Backup's on the way.'

Ruth pressed the tip of the scalpel against her own throat. Tears shone in her eyes, bright as the blade. 'Don't!'

A pause, then Rhona put the Airwave handset away. 'OK, let's not do anything stupid here...'

'All I ever wanted was to be a mother. To have something of my *own* to love.'

My crowbar-walking-stick boomed down on the stainless-steel work surface, setting it ringing, leaving a dent in the metal. 'THEN YOU SHOULD'VE GOT A BLOODY CAT!'

She flinched back, and a little bead of blood formed on the tip of the scalpel.

'Ruth?' Alice appeared on the other side of the operating table, hands out – palm up. 'It's OK, you don't have to do this. Laura's safe, and so are you, and there's still time to get Jessica to hospital.'

'I didn't mean...' She bit her bottom lip.

'It's OK. I understand. Shhh...' Alice's voice got lower and quieter again. 'Warm and comfortable and safe.'

'I just wanted a baby of my own.'

'I need you to put the scalpel down. Can you do that for me, Ruth?'

Her other hand pressed against her stomach, following the line of hidden scar tissue. 'A baby in my tummy...'

'You put the scalpel down and we can sit and have a nice cup of tea – all warm and comfortable and safe – and you can tell me all about it.'

The hand holding the knife jerked out, blade stabbing at the operating room door. 'Why did it work for *her*? Why didn't it work for me? I *practised*. It should've worked...'

'Wouldn't you like that, Ruth? To finally tell someone everything? So it's not just you any more?'

493

'By rights, that's *my* baby. Mine. I made it. I put it in her tummy. It belongs to me.' Her chest swelled as she dragged in a huge breath. 'THAT'S MY BABY, YOU BITCH!'

'Shhh... Just put the scalpel down. Everything will be OK, you'll see.'

Ruth's hand trembled. She let it fall to her side. 'It's my baby...'

'I know.' Alice nodded. Smiled. 'But it's over now. You're safe. No one's going to hurt you.'

She put the scalpel down on the work surface. 'Mine.'

I gave the nod and Rhona pulled out a pair of cuffs. 'Ruth Laughlin, I'm arresting you for the abduction of Laura Strachan and Jessica McFee...'

Thursday

52

'… *because it was my fault.*' On the screen, Ruth reached up and scratched her nose. Tilted her head to the side until her ear touched her shoulder. '*I was a … difficult birth. If I hadn't broken her inside she could've had more babies. Better babies than me.*'

Alice nodded. She was sitting with her back to the camera, a line of paperwork laid out in a neat row in front of her. Making notes in a pad. Whatever she was writing, it wasn't visible from the downstream monitoring suite. '*They weren't very nice to you, were they?*'

'*I deserved it. I broke her. I was always clumsy. Walking into doors and cupboards. Falling down stairs…*'

Sitting next to me, Detective Superintendent Ness sighed. 'We pulled her medical records. Had to dig a bit, but she's got more X-rays in her file than any kid under nine should ever have. Arms, legs, ribs, collar bone, dislocated fingers.'

'And no one bothered to call Social Services?'

'*But you were going to be a better mummy, weren't you?*'

Ruth sat forward. '*I was going to be a* great *mummy. I was going to love my baby all the time and cuddle them and never make them sit in baths of ice-water because they cried at night. It was going to be so lovely…*' Her face fell. '*Then he came.*'

Ness took a sip of tea. 'You never said how you found her.'

'She used to volunteer at a vet's. There was an abandoned one five minutes from her house. Operating facilities.'

'*Was that the man you told us about? The man who raped you in the alley by St Jasper's?*'

'*I should've kept the baby, why didn't I keep the baby?*' Her hands came up to her face, shoulders trembling. '*I should've ... should've...*'

Ness leaned forward in her seat, closer to the screen. 'Consultant botched the abortion. Got struck-off eight months later for attacking a patient. Cocaine.'

'*Shh... It's OK, Ruth.*'

'*I should've kept him. He would've been my little angel...*'

'So, what are you going to do after this?'

I shrugged. 'No idea.'

'Jacobson tells me you're a free man. Well, as long as you see your parole officer every week.'

'*Ruth, I want to ask you about the letters you sent to the newspapers.*'

A frown. '*Letters?*'

Alice pulled one from the ordered stacks of paper. '"*Tell them to stop calling me the Caledonian Ripper, it's disrespectful, they don't understand how important my work is.*"'

A small shake of the head. '*No. That's... I didn't write any letters.*' She reached across the table and took Alice's hand. '*Why would I write letters? I just wanted to be left alone so I could have my baby.*'

'*Oh...*' Alice leaned forward and checked her notes. '*Ruth, was someone helping you at the hospital?*'

'*Hospital?*'

'*Where did you get the drugs from? The antihypertensives and the anaesthetics and the wound glue? How did you get the contact details for Jessica McFee's patients?*'

Ruth shrugged. '*I just walked right in and used my old ID card. I thought they would've changed the locks, but... Do you think they'll let me die now?*'

Ness stared at me for a bit.

'What?'

'You bear watching, Mr Henderson.'

Alice sagged in the passenger seat, hands in her lap, arms hanging limp. 'Pffff...'

I took a left onto Thornwood. The windscreen wipers made lazy arcs across the glass. 'I think Detective Superintendent Ness was trying to chat me up back there.'

'Good.' Another sigh. 'You know, it's not her fault.'

'Didn't think I was so irresistible.'

That got me a scowl. 'Not her, *Ruth*. When she was four, her father explained to her where babies came from by sticking a plastic doll up her mum's jumper. Told her that's how it works.'

The traffic was thickening, like a blood clot. A long queue stretched back from the roadworks outside the Shell garage, the rain turning the car tail-lights into angry red eyes.

Alice let her head tilt sideways until it was resting against the passenger window. 'Three weeks later, her mother was sleeping in the lounge. Ruth took her plastic baby doll and slipped it in under her mum's cardigan. Said she wanted mummy to have another baby so she could be happy.'

I took a shortcut down the side of the baker's and out onto Patterdale Row. 'Well, that's—'

'She broke three of Ruth's fingers and dislocated her shoulder.'

Maybe Sarah Creegan had the right idea – some people didn't deserve to be parents. And some parents deserved to die.

Alice's head fell back against the headrest. 'Her mental state's probably been pretty precarious from the start, but maybe she could've coped – could've struggled on – if it wasn't for the rape. After that there was no going back.' A shrug. 'The other women were just practice. She wanted to make sure she could do the operation properly before she tried it on herself. Got started, then found out it wasn't as easy to cut open your *own* stomach…' Alice turned in her seat. 'I thought we were going to the hospital, this isn't the way to the hospital…'

'Got a quick stop to make.'

Half the newsroom's desks were empty – their occupants either off chasing stories, or, more likely, out grabbing lunch. Putting the business of filling the *Castle News and Post* with lies on hold for an hour.

Micky Slosser sat frowning at his screen, pecking away at the keyboard with one finger, a filled baguette in the other hand. Chewing.

He looked up as I knocked on his desk. The frown got even deeper. 'We had a deal. You gave your sodding word I'd get first crack at—'

'Remember these?' I slammed the printouts he'd given Alice down on his keyboard.

Micky sat back in his chair. 'I remember being nice enough to give you copies, and I remember you promising—'

'The Inside Man never wrote these. Because the Inside Man was never the bloody "Inside Man" in the first place. Was he?'

A couple of Micky's colleagues poked their heads over their cubicles. Scenting a fight, or a bit of gossip on the air.

He looked away, put his sandwich down. 'I've got no idea what you're on about. Now, if you don't mind, I've got a deadline, and you can— ulk…'

I grabbed his tie and hobbled past, dragging the wheelie office chair with me. His hands scrabbled at the noose around his neck, eyes wide, face purpling.

Good.

'Do you have any idea how much time we wasted on those bloody letters? How much time we could've spent finding the killer instead of chasing after someone who didn't even exist? How much *damage* you did?'

More heads appeared above the grey parapets.

'Ack… Get off! Security! SECURIT—'

I slapped a hand over his mouth. 'Alice?'

Nearly everyone was on their feet now. The nosier ones moved in to get a better view.

Alice squatted down, until she was eye-to-eye with him. 'Of course, it was really clever the way you managed to get the letters to look like they were posted before each of the victims were found. Clever, but *really* simple, right? All you had to do was post an envelope to yourself every day. If a body got discovered, you wrote a letter claiming to be the Inside Man, dated it the day before, and told everyone it came in the envelope delivered that morning. If there's no body, the envelope goes in the bin, and no one's the wiser.' She smiled. 'Very clever.'

I removed my hand. He shrank back in his chair. Looked at her. Looked at me. Then back to her again. 'I told you: I've got no idea what you're talking about.'

Alice stood. 'And it was your ticket, wasn't it? They were ignoring you here, making you cover stupid kids' projects, and livestock marts, and jumble sales, and am-dram shows. Didn't realize you were a proper journalist. But they sat up and took notice when you got those letters, didn't they? Saw what you were really worth. That you deserved *better*.'

'I don't—'

I smiled. 'We spoke to the guy in the mail room, Micky.'

He blinked. Licked his lips. 'Look, it… I didn't think it would really matter. It was just a bit of creative licence, OK? They—'

His head snapped back, blood sparkling in the air like tiny rubies caught in the overhead light. Then thump, he was lying on his back in the tipped-over chair, legs in the air, both hands clutched over his broken nose, while his colleagues clapped and cheered.

I shook my hand – the knuckles ached like burning gravel, but it was worth it.

* * *

501

Wee Free McFee stood. Looked down at his daughter for a moment, then slipped away from her bedside.

Silence smothered the High-Dependency Unit – its eight beds filled with women wired up to machines, or hidden behind drawn screens.

Jessica was pale as ice, hooked up to a drip. Her mouth hung open as she slept.

I tilted my head towards the bed. 'How is she?'

'Better.' He ran a finger across his grey moustache, putting it into line. 'You got her back.' Wee Free stuck out a hand. I took it and he nodded, those hooded eyes staring at me, like they were trying to peel the skin from my face and see what was underneath. 'I owe you.'

'Do me a favour then: Leave Ruth Laughlin alone. She'll end up in a secure facility for the rest of her life. She's not responsible for what she did.'

His mouth tightened.

'No eye for an eye, or tooth for a tooth, or anything else.'

Wee Free turned, walked back to the bed. 'I'll pray on it.'

Better than nothing...

Alice was waiting for me outside the ward. 'Well?'

'He'll pray on it.'

'Oh...' She fell into step beside me. 'It's really not Ruth's fault. She's a severely damaged individual, it's going to take years of therapy to get anywhere near the real her.'

Down the corridor to the lifts. I pressed the up button. 'As long as Wee Free doesn't get anywhere near the real her, we should be OK.'

Ping. A woman in a dressing gown and slippers stood in the corner, face to the wall, crying.

Alice's hand reached out towards her, then curled back into itself. She looked away. Pressed the button for the next floor.

The doors slid shut.

The lift hummed and clanked its way up, to a soundtrack of stifled sobs.

I leaned on the rail around the inside. 'Did she say why she'd trashed her own flat?'

'She didn't. Probably forgot to lock the door, and the local kids did the rest.'

Which explained where the antidepressants went. Little sods were probably trying to get high on them right now.

Ping. We stepped out, the woman stayed where she was, then the lift took her away again.

I pointed down the corridor. 'Ward at the end.'

Flowers and mylar balloons surrounded the bed next to Shifty's. All *he* had was a bottle of Lucozade and a copy of the *Scottish Sun* – 'TV PSYCHOLOGIST SEX BEAST CHARGED WITH SIX RAPES' above a grinning publicity shot of Dr Docherty.

A pad of gauze was bandaged over Shifty's right eye, and his face was a little more slack and hollow than usual, swathed in bruises and scabs.

He was wearing the 'nightwear' set we'd bought him at the supermarket last night – a grey T-shirt with a picture of a cat's face done up like the Obama 'Hope' poster on it.

Shifty blinked at me a couple of times with his good eye. Scowled. 'Not so much as a bloody get-well-soon card, and this bastard,' he pointed at the unconscious old man in the next bed, 'has a whole bloody Clinton's.'

I settled onto the edge of the bed.

Alice leaned over and gave Shifty a hug – tight enough to make him wince – then a kiss on the cheek. 'I'm so glad you're OK! You look … *terrible.*'

'Thanks.'

'No, seriously, you do. You look like someone's run you over with a lawnmower. Are you feeling OK?'

He hunched his shoulders up around his ears. 'No.'

A striped dressing gown was draped across the end of next door's bed. We'd probably be back before the old bloke woke up, and if not: tough. I grabbed it and threw it to Shifty. 'Come on, Billy no mates, we're going visiting.'

503

'Oh, bugger off.'

I pulled a little leather case out of my pocket and tossed it onto the bed. 'You'll need that too.'

He reached for it. Flipped it open, and squinted at the warrant card inside with his one good eye. 'Why have you got my—'

'Because – that's why. Now, up!'

We helped him out of bed, wrangled his arms into the dressing gown. It was about three sizes too small, gaping open across his belly, but it'd have to do. I liberated the old guy's tartan slippers too. 'Put those on.'

The tartan shorts that came with the T-shirt stopped just above Shifty's knees. His legs were crisscrossed with purple welts and sticking plasters.

He clutched the warrant card to his chest. 'Where are we going?'

'You'll see.'

The crying woman was gone from the lift as we rode up to the top floor.

Shifty picked at the stitching of the borrowed dressing gown. 'I... Thanks.'

'You'd do the same for me.'

Alice nodded. 'All for one.'

The lift mechanism whirred and clanged.

He curled his top lip. 'They're releasing me later. Here's a pack of antibiotics and some painkillers. Don't let the door hit your arse on the way out.'

'Do you want to stay at the flat? It's paid up till the end of the month and Alice doesn't want to go back there.'

A shudder rippled its way through Shifty's body. 'If I never set foot in Kingsmeath again it'll be too soon.'

The number ten lit up on the board, the lift doors slid open and we stepped out onto the penthouse floor.

No cracked linoleum held together with duct tape here. Instead, there were carpet tiles, flowers in vases, and decent paintings on the walls. Quiet and exclusive. The scent of garlic and butter wafted down the corridor.

Shifty sniffed. 'Bloody hell, it's all right for some, isn't it?'

'That's what you get for not having health insurance.'

The young bloke behind the teak reception desk, smiled at us, eyebrows raised, head on one side. 'I'm sorry, but this floor is reserved for private—'

'Police.' I flashed my expired ID. 'You have a patient here: one Mrs Maeve Kerrigan. Gunshot wound and her eye gouged out.'

'Ah...' He reached for the phone. 'Perhaps I should just—'

'Perhaps you shouldn't.' I leaned in close and he shrank back. 'Where?'

He pointed over his shoulder. 'Room twenty.'

I limped down to the end of the corridor with Shifty and Alice in tow.

The rooms on either side were more like hotel suites – each had a little seating area with a couch and a coffee table, a large flatscreen TV, iPod dock, floor-to-ceiling windows, patio doors and a narrow balcony. Most of the occupants sat at their own little dining tables, eating whatever lunch was, with a view out over the city.

Fifteen. Sixteen. Seventeen.

Left at the end.

Eighteen.

Two men stood in the corridor. One tall with a ginger ponytail poking out from beneath a crown of white bandages, two big black eyes. The other was short and stocky, his scalp covered in tiny scars beneath the stubble. Just the one black eye for him, but he was on crutches – his shattered left leg encased in plaster from hip to toe.

Joseph and Francis.

Francis nodded. ''Spector.'

'Francis.'

Joseph gave us a little smile. 'Ah, Mr Henderson. I'm sorry

to announce that our acquaintance must come to an end. Francis and I shall be taking our leave of Oldcastle and setting off for pastures new. What you might call the Costa del Far, Far Away.'

His partner nodded. 'Spain, and that.'

I rolled my shoulders. 'Worried about what'll happen when I come after you?'

'Oh, bless you, no. Let us just say that Mr Inglis is somewhat *less* than pleased with the result of our recent assignments for Mrs Kerrigan. He feels we should have been more rigorous in our protection of the organization as a whole.' A shrug. A wince. 'And so away we must go, before he decides an example needs to be made.'

I stepped in close. 'Run far, and run fast. Because if you're still here in five minutes I'm going to make good on my promise. Remember?'

The smile became a grin. 'You're going to break every one of my fingers and make me eat them?'

'I told you not to touch her.'

'Ah, Mr Henderson, I'm going to miss our little chats. They've been the highlight of my days.' He held up a finger. 'Francis, I believe it's time for us to exit stage right. Say goodbye to Mr Henderson.'

A nod. ''Spector.'

And they were gone, the sound of Joseph's crutches thunking against the carpet fading away down the corridor.

Shifty curled his hands into fists. 'Did you *see* that? Like I wasn't even bloody here. Should go after the bastards and rip their arms off.'

I pointed towards the door, two down on the left. 'I've got something better in mind. Trust me.'

The sound of classical music came from the other side of the door. I didn't bother knocking, just pulled it open and limped inside.

Mrs Kerrigan sat at her private dining table, head down,

hands in her lap. A thick wad of gauze covered her right eye. The tape holding it in place looked a hell of a lot tidier than the stuff on Shifty's head. Her right foot was wrapped in bandages from toe to ankle, just visible through the tail of a long silk dressing gown.

A thick fillet steak sat untouched on the plate in front of her.

The man sitting opposite shrugged. A sweep of grey hair lay across his collar, the top of his head freckly and pink where it had receded. Dark-blue pinstripe suit and white shirt, big antique watch on his thick wrist. Not the tallest of men, but broad, powerful. Andy Inglis.

His accent was solid Glaswegian shipyard. 'Nothing personal.'

Mrs Kerrigan's head dipped even further.

He pulled himself up to his full five four. Sighed. 'What the hell were you thinking?'

She raised one shoulder. 'I'm sorry.'

Then he turned. Stared at me with his mouth hanging open. 'Ash? Ash Henderson, you old *bastardo*!' He came forward, much lighter on his feet than he looked. Skipped back a couple of paces, fists up, then forward again. Threw a couple of jabs that would've taken teeth with them if he'd been aiming. 'Good to see you, man, when'd you get out?'

'Sunday.'

'You should've said! Got this great wee restaurant on Cairnbourne now, you should come: my treat.'

I looked past him. Mrs Kerrigan hadn't moved. She reached up and wiped a hand across her good eye.

The smile on his face drooped a little. He nodded at Shifty. 'This the boy?'

Shifty held out his warrant card. 'Detective Inspector David Morrow.'

'Good for you.' Andy Inglis placed a hand in the small of my back and steered me out into the corridor. Lowered his voice. 'Just between you and me—'

'If it's about the money, I haven't got it. OK?'

507

His eyebrows went up. 'Money?'

'The thirty-two thousand. Mrs Kerrigan says I owe—'

'Don't be daft.' He pulled his chin into his neck. 'Ash, we wrote off your debt when your daughter died. You had enough on your plate without that.'

'You…' I closed my eyes. Took a deep breath. Knuckles aching as they snarled into fists. No debt. She stood there and pushed and gouged and lied.

'Did ye really think I'd stop feckin' with ye just because ye got out of prison?'

When I opened my eyes, Andy Inglis was frowning at me. 'You OK?'

'Thank you.'

He shook his head. 'Nah, what are friends for?' A hand like a wrecking ball patted me on the shoulder. Then he looked back towards Mrs Kerrigan's room. 'You here to arrest her, or kill her?'

'She abducted and tortured a police—'

'No skin off my nose either way.' He marched away down the corridor. 'Don't forget: the Shoogly Goose, on Cairnbourne. You'll love it.'

I stepped back into the room.

Shifty stood by the table, glowering down at the plate with its fillet, frites, and asparagus. A large glass of Shiraz on the side. 'You know what I had for lunch? Cauliflower cheese. And it was *beige*.'

Mrs Kerrigan didn't look up. 'Yez've got a feckin' cheek, showing yer faces.'

I swept my cane up, as if I was introducing a magic act. 'Shifty, if you please.'

'Pleasure.' He cricked his thick neck from side to side. 'Maeve Kerrigan, I'm arresting you for the torture and attempted murder of one Detective Inspector David Morrow. You do not have to say anything—'

'Oh, grow the feck up.' She picked up her knife and fork

and carved off a sliver of steak. Inside it was almost raw. 'Who the hell's going to convict me? Yez've got no proof and no witnesses.'

I poked myself in the chest with a thumb. '*I'm* a witness.'

She smiled. 'No yer not, Mr Henderson, because if ye were ye'd be worrying about yer family. Ye'd be worrying about where yer wife and brother had gone and what was going to happen to them. How many bits they'd end up in.'

'Think that scares me?'

'No?'

I gave her a smile back. 'Shifty, there's a missing accountant called Paul Manson buried in Moncuir Wood. She shot him. Twice. You'll find the gun hidden under the floorboards of the old Keenan house just outside Logansferry. It's got her prints on it.' I let the smile grow.

She popped the slice of steak in her mouth and chewed. 'I'll feckin kill everyone yez've ever loved.'

Shifty flexed his hands. 'On your feet.'

'Feck off, fat boy.' She hacked off another slice of bloody flesh. 'Touch me and yer dead. Yer Ma's dead. Yer boyfriend's dead.'

He loomed over her. 'Go on, resist arrest, I'm *begging* you.'

'Ye think being locked up will stop me? Really?' The fork came up, pointed right at Alice. 'First thing I'm going to do is get someone to grab yer little psychologist friend.'

I helped myself to an asparagus spear. 'He's cut you loose, hasn't he?'

Another slice of steak.

'You've become a liability. You're out of control. Abducting and torturing police officers; killing people just because they bored you at dinner?'

Her knuckles whitened around the cutlery.

'Andy Inglis doesn't want that kind of attention, does he? And how long do you think you'll last inside: a day? A week? He's not going to risk you turning Queen's Evidence.'

Mrs Kerrigan's one remaining eye glared up at me. 'Think Andy Inglis is the only game in town? Lot of people owe me. I know some *lovely* Russian gentlemen who'll show yer psychologist bitch a good time.'

'It's over.'

'Is it fuck. They'll pass her around between ten or twelve of them, till she's nothing but screams and blood and agony.'

Alice backed away towards the door. 'Ash?'

'Oh, and yez'll like this. There's a nice man in Perth with a thing for amputation.'

Hot in here.

'How about when the Russians have finished with yer girl, I let him cut bits off her before he screws her?'

I flipped the snib and pulled the patio doors open. Dragged in a breath of cold afternoon air. The hiss of rain slithered into the room.

'Would yez like that? Maybe I'll arrange for ye to be there so ye can watch him hacking away.'

The only sound was the falling rain.

'Yez're dead, and everyone ye've ever loved is—'

I grabbed her by the lapels and yanked her out of the chair. 'Shut. Up.'

'—feckin dead! You hear me? Dead!'

'Ash!'

A hand on my arm. I looked down, and there was Alice, blinking up at me. Her nose was pink, eyes too. Bottom lip pinned between her teeth. She shook her head. 'Don't.'

I let go. Hissed out a long shuddering breath. Stepped back. 'You're right.'

Mrs Kerrigan straightened her dressing gown. 'Now be a good little boy and feck off home. I'll let yez know when I've got another job for ye.' She grinned. 'Did ye *really* think I was ever going to let ye go, Mr Henderson? Yer my bitch. Ye'll jump when I say jump. Ye'll kill who I tell ye to kill. And ye'll fecking like it, cos if ye don't—'

'No!' Alice lunged, both hands out. Took a hold of Mrs Kerrigan's dressing gown and shoved. *Hard*.

Mrs Kerrigan's eye popped wide, teeth bared, fingertips scratching at the frame as she went backwards through the open door, Alice still holding on, *pushing*.

'Leave us alone!'

Out onto the narrow balcony, wet gravel crunching beneath their feet. Then *thunk*, the handrail caught her in the middle of the back.

'Get off us, ye stupid little hoor!' She wrapped her hands around Alice's neck. 'I'll fecking—'

Alice slammed her little red shoe down on Mr's Kerrigan's bandaged right foot.

Silence.

Mrs Kerrigan's eyes bulged, mouth hanging open, a string of saliva darkened the silk dressing gown. Then she hauled in a deep breath.

And Alice shoved again.

Mrs Kerrigan tipped over the edge – hands grasping at nothing but the rain.

She didn't make a single sound all the way down. Not until the final thud, ten stories below.

Shifty whistled, then shuffled out onto the balcony. Peered out at the ground. Water soaked into the shoulders of his borrowed dressing gown.

I joined Alice at the handrail.

A broken rag-doll body lay with its top half on the pavement and its bottom half crumpling the bonnet of a little Ford Fiesta. An expanding pool of scarlet seeped out from Mrs Kerrigan's chest and head, spreading like paint.

Shifty sniffed. 'Well, *she's* fucked.'

I turned away. Limped back inside and picked my walking stick off the carpet. 'We need to get out of here.'

Alice stood at the rail, staring down. Not saying anything. Not moving.

'Hmm...' Shifty drummed his fingers on the metal. Then nodded, talking slowly, as if pulling the words, one by one out of rain. 'Oh dear. We appear to have got here too late. Joseph and Francis must have killed her, *just* before we got here. Oh, for shame... Uh-ho here comes the cavalry.' He ducked back from the edge, then reached out and grabbed Alice's collar and dragged her into the room. 'Come on, you.'

She lurched on brittle legs, still facing the balcony. 'But...'

I took the napkin from the dining table and wiped the patio door handle clean. 'Did anyone touch anything else?'

Shifty steered her out through the door. 'Time to go.'

I stopped on the threshold. Looked up and down the corridor – scanning the ceiling tiles. Then put a hand on Shifty's back and pushed him towards the lifts. 'Get her out of here, I've got something to take care of...'

Six Months Later

53

Haar curled in off the North Sea, hiding the headland on the other side of the bay. Turned everything into a pale facsimile. A photocopy of a photocopy, faded and indistinct.

Two figures picked their way along the sand, just visible through the fog, one large in a leather jacket and eye-patch, one small in a stripy top.

A tiny dot of black scampered away from them, then back again, its high-pitched barks muffled by distance and weather.

On the other end of the phone, Detective Superintendent Ness sighed. *'And don't get me started on the trial – It's like a bloody circus.'*

I leaned on the fencepost outside the cottage, took another sip of tea. 'Let me guess, Docherty's being a dick?'

'And it's not as if I haven't got enough on my plate with this Kerrigan business. Interpol couldn't be more of a pain in the backside if they tried.'

'Ah, no joy with the CCTV then?'

'None. How do two thugs manage to make every bit of security camera footage disappear from a hospital?'

Wasn't that difficult if you knew the right people. 'No idea.'

Down on the beach, Henry the Scottie Dog made a dash

515

for the water's edge, then yipped and yapped his way back, bouncing up and down in front of Alice.

'*And you're* sure *you didn't see anything?*'

'Wish I had. But by the time I got there, it was all over.'

Of course, the receptionist on the private ward could've made life a little difficult, but one mention of Andy Inglis's name and the poor lad came down with amnesia.

'*Gah… You know, I don't even have last names for them? "Francis" and "Joseph", that's all anyone seems to know. How am I supposed to get international arrest warrants based on that?*'

Down on the beach, they must have had enough, because Alice and Shifty started back towards the cottage, Henry running loops around them, barking his wee hairy head off.

A sigh. '*So how's Dr McDonald getting on?*'

Still waking up screaming in the middle of the night. Still sitting in the kitchen at two in the morning, sobbing. Still drinking too much. At least the nightmares were beginning to thin out a bit. But Ness didn't need to know that.

'Alice is good. Enjoying the quiet life for a change.' I swirled the tea dregs around the mug, then flung them out into the haar. 'Listen, I know you're up to your eyeballs, but if you fancy some time off, you should come visit. We'll have a proper Scottish barbecue: sausages, drizzle, and midges.'

There was a pause. '*Is this… Would this be a* date, *Mr Henderson?*'

'I keep telling you: it's Ash.'

A smile crept into her voice. '*I might take you up on that.*'

Henry charged up the grass bank and wriggled under the bottom wire of the fence. Planted all four feet on the tarmac and shook the saltwater off his coat. Alice grinned behind him, one arm linked with Shifty. She raised her other hand and waved.

OK, so it wasn't Australia, and we didn't have a pool, but it was still pretty damn good.